SUGAR

SUGAR

A SADDLEBROOK FALLS ROMANCE

MICHAELA JEAN TAYLOR

SUGAR

Copy Editor: Britt Tayler

Proofreader: Virginia Tesi Carey

Cover Designer: Cindy Ras

Internal Formatting: Michaela Jean Taylor

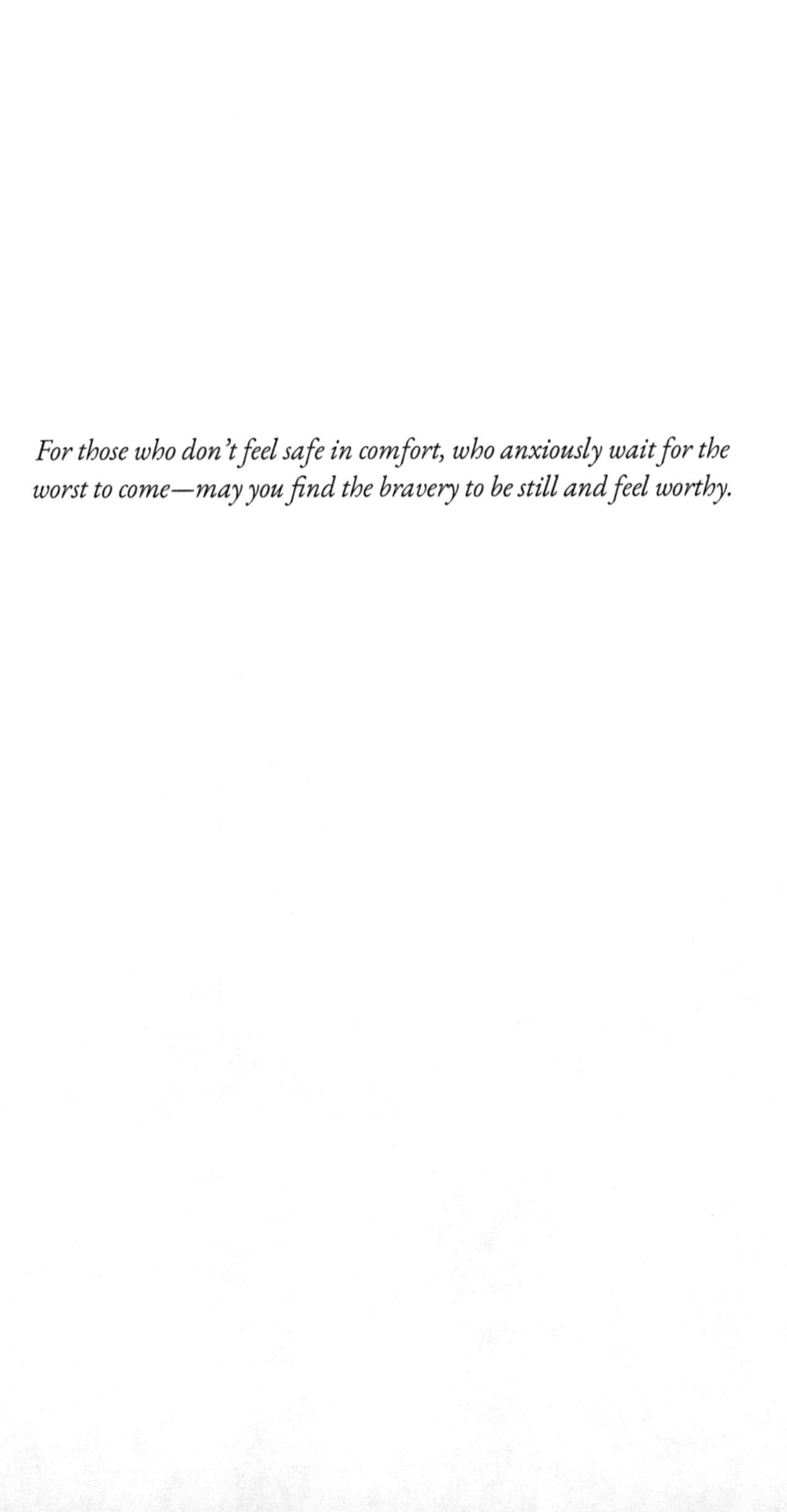

For those who don't feel safe in comfort, who anxiously wait for the worst to come—may you find the bravery to be still and feel worthy.

AUTHOR'S NOTE

This book contains scenes with discussions of mature subject matter including unexpected pregnancy, death, grief, alcoholism, depression, gambling and murder and is intended for mature audiences.

PROLOGUE

KASEY

"Would you like me to drag the arena for you, sir?"

Benny looks at me with warm brown eyes as I hover next to the corral, a grin lifting crookedly from one side of his mouth. "No need," he says, voice gruff. He pats the neck of the horse beneath him with gentle affection. "I'm spendin' a little extra time with my Tormenta this afternoon, so I'll drag it later. But I appreciate the offer. You did well today, Kasey—you've got a natural rhythm in your hips."

Coming from the Benedito Silva, a two-time world champion bronc rider and ProSpur Hall of Fame legend, the praise lights me up from the inside out. "Thank you, sir. I really appreciate you accepting me into your program."

We're only three days into an intensive two-week rodeo camp being held at Benny's ranch just north of Houston, and I've already learned so much from the man in front of me. I spent all of last year mowing lawns and breaking horses for ranchers in neighboring counties to afford the opportunity, knowing damn well there was no way my parents would even agree to let me be here much less pay for it—not after rodeo ruined Dad's life.

They think I'm in Dallas for a football camp.

I almost feel bad for having to carry on such a big lie, but my passion for rodeo has always outweighed any consequences of getting caught. Mom and Dad have no idea that Brooks has been secretly registering us both for small bronc-riding competitions ever since he got his driver's license last summer and could take us without them knowing. He'd gotten pretty good at forging Dad's signature for all the liability waivers and consent forms after doing it so much with his own report cards.

"You've been on horses your whole life?" Benny asks.

I nod. "Yes, sir. My family owns a rescue ranch in Saddlebrook Falls. We get a lot of mustangs and wayward horses throughout the year. I help break 'em and train 'em for wherever they're going next."

His eyes crinkle with a smile. "Don't tell anyone else I said this, but kids like you are exactly why I do this. You've got great instincts. Keep up with your training and I have no doubt you'll enjoy a successful future in rodeo. You could very well be one of the greats."

My eyes burn with an unfamiliar emotion. I'm not sure anyone's ever paid me such a hefty compliment. Taking my hat off my head, I sink my chin to my chest. "Thank you, sir. Sincerely."

A sudden shouting from the other side of the corral snares my attention, and I look up to find Benny's wife, Manuella, attempting to herd a brown-and-white paint horse toward the stables. Its rider frantically waves her hands at the woman, saying something I can't quite hear from this far away.

"Manuella," Benny calls out. Concern ripples along his dark bushy brows. "You okay?"

She turns toward her husband, face pinched in frustration. "Fine, *meu amor*. Just helping Miss Jones back to the barn."

"I'm not ready to put him away," the girl atop the horse shouts. "We need more practice!"

"Yes," Manuella agrees, voice nearly as loud. "You do. But not right now—he needs a break and so do you. We're done for the day,

Miss Jones, and as I've already explained, I'm not going to let you continue training without proper supervision. You're going to hurt yourself."

Benny huffs out a quiet laugh before glancing back my way. "Word of advice: be careful with barrel racers, son." With a dip of his chin, he clicks his tongue and his horse takes off toward the other side of the ring.

I can't help but stay rooted in place, watching as he climbs down from his saddle to speak softly to the pair. The girl eventually huffs out a defeated sigh and steers her gelding to the barn. My eyes stay glued on her, transfixed by the way her face flushes bright red beneath the riding helmet buckled at her chin. Even from yards away, it's obvious she's angrier than a hornet's nest. Emotion bursts from her like sparks of light, and I feel drawn to it.

When she reaches the barn she swings a leg over the horse's back and disappears, tucking herself just inside the doorway. I edge along the corral a few steps until she's back in my frame of view, her long brown hair spilling out as she works to take off the helmet. The ends of it dance along her skin in a way I've definitely seen before, and the realization of who she is hits me: Ava Jones, Sheriff Joe's daughter.

In a town as small as Saddlebrook Falls, it's sort of impossible not to know everyone you go to school with. I might not consider them all friends, but I'd bet money I at least know all of their first names. But somehow it took until sixth grade, when she showed up to football tryouts during our first week of school, for me to notice Ava.

I know of her dad, thanks to my own—something I'd rather not think about—but it evaded me for a long time that Sheriff Joe had a daughter. Coach about had a heart attack when he realized there was a girl on the field running suicides alongside the rest of us. She kept up well enough—she'd gotten through nearly an entire afternoon undetected beneath the cherry-red helmet that covered most of her face, having tucked all that hair inside.

When her cover was blown and Coach demanded she leave the

field, she'd taken off that helmet to let those gorgeous locks flow down her back before opening her mouth to argue against the unfairness of it, for disqualifying her because she was a girl when she'd run faster in every drill than most of the other boys. It was true. She'd been damn fast . . . Faster than even me.

As she stood her ground and made her case, I'd been wholly caught off guard by how pretty she was. She looked so much like she does now in that barn: face tinged pink, arched brows dipped low with that pouty mouth twisted into a frown. And her eyes . . .

Even at eleven, there'd been a fire in them, a desire to burn down the world around her, a hunger for wreckage and ruin. Now, at fourteen, I can see the fire in her sharp gaze is bigger—brighter— and I'm just as hooked as I was before.

We never had a class together, but she was definitely someone you looked at once and remembered forever. Someone you noticed even in the darkest of rooms. After that day on the field it was like a switch flipped and I suddenly saw her in every crowded hallway between classes, like she'd stuffed a location beacon inside my chest and the second she was within range, my eyes were hurrying to find her.

I tried for a long time to work up the courage to walk up to her and say something, but nothing ever felt right. For months, I agonized over what might do the trick. A joke? She'd probably find it lame, especially from a quiet kid like me. I thought maybe I could try my hand at honest flirting, but I'd seen enough fumblings around school to lose any real heart I might have had in putting myself out there like that.

Without a class together or a reason to talk to her, I just didn't think anything I said would be good enough to leave an impression. Plus she hardly ever smiled, at least that I could tell, and I really wanted the first words I said to be worthy of pulling one out of her.

The pressure of it all just became too much, so I resigned to watching her from a distance, waiting for an opportunity that felt right. And now here she is, right in front of me. On a damn horse, no less.

Free of the helmet, her long hair moves lazily with the breeze, but the storm in her blue eyes is mighty as she watches Manuella and Benny walk away, her fists clenching and unclenching in an unsynchronized rhythm at her sides. Then, without warning, she turns to look at me.

I quickly bend over to inspect the ground like an idiot, suddenly interested in the way the grass in the yard gives way to the rich layers of dirt inside the corral, hoping like hell she didn't catch me staring.

"Kasey?"

I cringe. Shit.

There's no pretending now. I stand and turn back to find her looking at me, nose scrunched. There's a rogue strand of hay caught in her hair above her ear. "It is you."

I dip my chin the same way I've seen Brooks do a hundred times to girls in town. "Sure is," I say, a little lamely. "Didn't realize you knew my name."

"What are you doing here?" she asks, ignoring the statement.

I look pointedly at the barn. "Same as you, I think. Rodeo camp."

Her head tilts. "What event are you training for?"

"Bronc riding."

"You've been here this whole time?"

"Since Sunday, yeah." I approach her slowly, eyeing the flush that still stains her cheeks. "You okay?"

"Why wouldn't I be?" she huffs.

A small grin pulls along my cheek. "I dunno. You look pissed."

She crosses her arms over her chest and throws a glance toward Manuella. "I wasn't done working with Duke."

"I didn't know you rode horses."

She looks back at me. Shrugs. "I imagine there's a lot you don't know about me."

"Right." I nod. "That's fair. I just . . . I guess seeing you here is taking me by surprise."

Her eyes narrow. "You think I can't ride?"

I hold my palms up. "Not what I meant," I say. "I actually have a hunch that you're probably pretty damn good."

"Why's that?"

I grin. "I saw you on the football field for tryouts. Something tells me you don't do things you're not already sure you're good at."

She eyes me as the words settle over her. Eventually, she sighs. "That's the thing—I'm here because I'm not that good yet. Duke and I have been training in dressage for three years, but I'm so over the stuffiness of it all. Practicing the piaffe feels so silly when we could be flying across the arena, racing to beat the clock."

"Barrel racing?" I ask, even though Benny already said it. I want Ava to keep talking.

She nods. "For now."

My grin grows at the implication of what might come later. I look at the barn again. "How long have you and Duke been racing?"

There's a beat of silence before she answers. "Three days."

It takes sheer will to hold back my laughter. "You mean you haven't trained for it at all before coming here?"

She shakes her head.

"How the heck did you get accepted into Benny's program?" It's pretty competitive—I asked Brooks to film me breaking six different horses so I could submit the footage with my application.

"I wrote a convincing letter" is all she says.

"I'll say." I chuckle again. "Well, the good news is racing isn't all that different from what you both are used to. I'm sure Duke will pick it up quickly."

Her nose scrunches again, and I have to admit: it's pretty damn cute. "Rodeo and dressage are completely different."

"Eh, the tricks might be different. But it's all about horseman-ship, really. If Duke trusts you, it won't be hard to navigate his training."

She considers it. "You some kind of horse expert or something?"

A muscle in my cheek tics. "Or something."

"Why are you here?"

"I've been on horses all my life, but my parents are strictly against rodeo. My dad had a pretty bad accident . . . Anyway, they don't know I'm here."

She probably already knows everything about my father and his accident. And his drinking. And all his arrests, since her father's always been the one to get him. But if she does know, she's nice enough not to show it. "My dad doesn't know I'm here either," she admits.

I move a little closer—close enough that she's within reach. "Lying to the sheriff." I nod. "Impressive."

She scoffs. And then her expression changes, face relaxing as an honest-to-god giggle bubbles out of her. The sound of it lights me up from the inside out, drawing me nearer. Before I realize what I'm doing, I reach a hand out to pinch the strand of hay in her hair between my fingers, slowly tugging it loose.

All traces of humor leave her face as her lips part, her chest rising with an unsteady breath. Her hair is so goddamn soft I want to bury my fingers deeper into it. "Sorry . . ." I say, showing her the rogue hay. "You had—"

"What the fuck?" someone says with a heavy dose of irritation, piercing through the moment like a popped balloon. We both turn to find a tall boy in a black button-down and jeans staring hard at Ava, his dark boots dusted from a day of riding. I recognize him from breakfast this morning.

"Benji." Ava pulls away from me. My hand drops with a thump against my thigh. "I was just coming to find you."

His mouth twists in a frown. "Sure doesn't look like it."

Ava squares her shoulders as she turns to face him more fully. "This is Kasey, we just ran into each other. I go to school with him." She faces me, but I keep my eyes trained on him. "Kasey, this is Benji. My . . . boyfriend."

He looks like he might be a year or two older—definitely has a couple inches on me. I wonder if he can drive, if one of the old trucks parked in front of Benny's house might be his. The thought annoys me. Still, I take a step toward him and reach a hand out. "Nice to meet you," I mumble, doing my best to overcome the frustration that he interrupted something important between me and Ava. That he even exists in the first place.

Benji looks down at my hand, his frown deepening. Before I even know it's coming, he throws a wild punch, his fist landing with an explosion of pain to the side of my face. "Keep your hands off my girlfriend, asshole."

"Benji!" Ava shouts.

He turns to look at her, pointing away from the barn. "Let's go. Now." I don't like the way he looks at her, like he owns her.

Ava lets out a dramatic sigh. Benji scoffs and turns away from us both, stomping back toward wherever the hell he came from.

"Fuck," I mutter, wrapping my palm around my already-swelling cheekbone. Embarrassment sets its hooks in deep for letting him hit me like that. Brooks would have never let something like that happen. I should have been ready—now I just look like a sucker.

"Come on, Ava!" Benji hollers as he rounds the barn.

Ava gives me a careful look, her eyes locked in on my cheek. "Sorry," she whispers. And then she's following him, disappearing from view behind the barn.

LATER THAT NIGHT, AS I LAY ON MY ASSIGNED BUNK IN a dark room full of other boys—cheek still pulsing uncomfortably with a bruise I know will be nasty by morning—I replay Ava's laugh over and over again, the way her chapped lips parted when my fingers grazed through strands of her hair.

I'd already decided the punch had been well worth it—no question.

If I had any doubts after she showed up at football tryouts, they're long gone now: I'm totally in love with her. What I don't yet know is how this won't be the first time my love for her is going to royally fuck me over. Not even close.

CHAPTER ONE

KASEY

My heart pounds so violently I feel like I can't breathe.

Before I have a chance to register what it means, my feet are already moving, aiming for the burst of light spilling out of the open barn door. I'm only vaguely aware of Wells shadowing behind me, his booted steps just as quiet and careful as mine as we pick up speed. Maybe if I had a little more reason, I'd tell my youngest brother to stay back, to wait in the truck where it's safe. I'd try to keep him away from what I know in my gut is going to be something bad.

But my attention's focused on that gap in the ramshackle building's dilapidated sliding doors, on another brother I know is inside and in danger.

The sound of a loud crash reverberates through the air, and I whisper out a sharp *"Fuck"* before hurling myself faster for the barn. I hear a woman scream.

"What do we do?" Wells asks at my heels. I don't know how to respond because I don't *know* what the fuck to do, so I just keep moving. The Rustler family has always been reckless—even more than ours—but their illegal card games don't typically

"

include screaming, which means whatever's going on in there is much worse than I thought.

Reaching the open doorway, I pause for two full breaths to steel myself before twisting around the outer edge of the door-frame, scanning the god-awful scene inside. Rhett's sprawled out beside an overturned table, Colt Rustler only feet away in a similar position. Both of them are gaping up at a man looming over them on the other side of the table, brandishing a pistol that glints beneath the bald light above.

A gunshot slices through the night, and a man I don't recognize falls to the ground, clutching his neck. There's another scream—Wylie, hiding behind Ellis, is covering her mouth with her hands. My gaze drops again to Rhett, finding him wild-eyed with fear. Playing cards are scattered all around the floor. Another shot cracks, and the man next to Maverick drops.

Maverick shouts, aiming his pistol to shoot the other man again. This time the shot's fatal, and the man goes still. Maverick turns his focus to a second man I don't recognize and shoots him without thought. Then he turns to Ellis. "Was all this worth it?" he asks, voice low and deadly. "Dead cops and all this money gone when I walk out of here with it—was it worth it, Ellis Rustler?"

Holy shit. *Dead cops?* This is *bad* bad.

I know in an instant Maverick won't let anyone out of here alive, not after we've all witnessed him kill two officers. There's enough of us to stop him, but that gun in his hand will no doubt keep firing, and I'm not about to let it anywhere near my fucking brothers.

My mind goes utterly black as I squeeze the shotgun's trigger. The deafening boom nearly knocks me sideways, my eyes closing shut on instinct. I open them to find Maverick's hateful, cold glare changing, growing fearful as a spot of blood swells across the front of his shirt, painting his chest a shade of red so dark it almost looks black.

But Maverick's grip on his gun only tightens. The hole torn

through his chest is somehow not enough to deter him, and the fear in those strange dark eyes dissipates as his mouth curls into a dangerous grin. "You really thought you could stop me?" he asks, voice dripping with venom.

"Rhett, run!" I shout.

But Rhett doesn't have a chance. Maverick aims his gun right at him, and before another sound can leave my throat, he's pulling the trigger. Another loud crack whips through the air, and Rhett is pushed backward from the force of the shot hitting him in the shoulder. Maverick pulls the trigger again and a second shot hits Rhett in the stomach.

Terror floods through my body as I watch my brother, one of the best friends I've ever had, slump forward. His gaze moves to where I stand as Wells screams behind me.

"I'm sorry," Rhett says, blood spilling from his mouth. It runs down his neck. Stains the collar of his shirt dark crimson.

"*NO!*" I yell with everything I have.

My eyes fly open to a white ceiling, darkened by the night. Cold sweat beads along my brow as I gasp for air, my heart slamming against my ribs inside a too-tight chest. Turning to my side, I curl into a ball and heave for a solid breath, but I can't for the life of me catch one. There's a part of my mind still separate from the panic that knows this will eventually pass, just like it does every morning. But it's not enough to ease the bone-deep fear that rockets through me that my brother might actually be dead on the ground of some dirty fucking barn.

I'm home, I tell myself. *I'm home in my bed. I'm not there. Rhett's not there.*

It's been almost three weeks since Wells and I pulled Rhett out of that terrible situation.

Three weeks since I took someone's life.

Mean-Eyed Maverick is not exactly the kind of man the world's gonna miss, but it gnaws at me that he's just . . . *gone.* That his existence was snuffed out of this world because of *me.* I don't regret pulling that trigger—not when I saw the rage in his eyes and knew what he would do to Rhett and the others if given the chance. Still, the anxiety compounds every day as I wait for law enforcement to break down my door and drag me away in handcuffs.

Ellis promised to take the heat should it come to that, but Ellis has been a fucking piss-poor friend for years, far more interested in all the ways he can make a buck than he is in loyalty or human decency. I'd be glad to never see that sad-sack of shit ever again. Maybe this stupid relationship between the Bennetts and the Rustlers can finally die—my brothers have been sucked into their bullshit far too many times.

I hope like hell what happened in that barn was enough to scare Rhett straight. He may have thought he had good reasons to put himself in danger like that, but at the end of the day this ranch and our name isn't worth his life. The possibility of losing everything our family has worked so hard for over generations cuts deep, I get it. I'm going to fight like hell to make sure Uncle Huck has a hard time taking it all from us. But if we fail, if we lose this place, I *know* we'll be okay.

If we were to lose *Rhett* . . .

This family has suffered enough.

It takes several long minutes, but the panic from my nightmare eventually begins to recede. I suck down a deep breath through my nose, filling my lungs with air, and hold it for as long as I can before pushing it out through my mouth. Looking toward the digital clock on my nightstand, the dim red numbers tell me it's a few minutes past three in the morning. I still have an hour before the alarm goes off, but I don't think I'll be going back to sleep anytime soon.

I look back up at the ceiling, rubbing the sleep away from my eyes, and wonder if Brooks is awake in his cabin too. If he's found any semblance of peace lying in his bed alone. I think of Rhett and Wells and the girls they have in their lives—are they happy?

Are they sleeping with the warmth of their partners wrapped around them? Or are they awake too, contemplating every ounce of shit this family has been served in our lifetime.

The grass over Melody's grave hasn't even had a chance to sprout again, and already we have more problems to navigate. When is it enough? When will this family have the opportunity to live an easier life? Isn't that the whole purpose of what we do—to disentangle ourselves from the world outside of these grounds?

Huck is supposed to be one of us. He's a damn Bennett . . . He's supposed to understand the sanctity and beauty of our work; he grew up here, just like we did. But all he seems to care about is what this ranch can do for his wallet, not for his soul.

I groan, sitting up in bed and throwing the covers away. Stepping into my slippers at the foot of the bed, I head for the bathroom and splash a few handfuls of cold water on my face as the weight of the world settles over my shoulders.

This is all on me, I know it is. My dad sure as hell doesn't have the capacity to fight any legal battles with his brother, and Brooks is already going through so much. He just lost his wife, for fuck's sake. That Huck would even think to take advantage of that loss for his own sleazy benefit is disgusting.

Leaning on the edge of the bathroom sink, I look at myself in the mirror. I have to figure something out. I have to find a loophole in the inheritance terms, a way to keep Huck out from what we all know damn well doesn't belong to him. Maybe someone in town knows a good lawyer and would be willing to help us . . .

I heard somebody's in need of a wife?

I squeeze my eyes shut as another wave of anxiety builds. The memory of Ava Jones walking through the doors of Wild Coyote plays on a near constant loop during my waking hours, the sound of her cool and confident voice as she narrowed those sapphire eyes on me.

Turning out of the bathroom, I head down the hall toward the front door, pushing it open so I can get some fresh air. The sky is a blanket of stars twinkling down over the ranch, the moon only a sliver above the distant tree line. Even in the dark I can see an incoming burst of clouds. The humidity in the air is thick, but cool enough that goosebumps swell across my shoulders and chest. I don't mind it one bit, the way it reminds me that I'm of this planet too.

I sit down on the top step of the porch, eyes trailing the worn path below that leads to the main house and other cabins, listening to the song of crickets who have long since awoken. Soon the sun will peek out from over the eastern horizon, and the horses will whinny from their stalls. My brothers will wake if they're not already up, probably brew some strong coffee and pull on their boots for the work ahead.

And we'll spend the day doing what we love: cowboying. Caring for these horses, ensuring they have the opportunity to find good homes with good people. We'll ride the ones who don't want to be ridden and convince them that we're trying to help, and we'll do our best to keep this way of life alive because it's important.

I lean forward, resting my elbows against my knees, and take it all in: our legacy. The purpose of our family name. Breathing in lungfuls of fresh air so crisp it feels like it's right off the Gulf, I find the courage to keep going.

And then I do.

CHAPTER TWO

KASEY

Ice-cold beer floods my throat as I chug from the bottle I've just pulled out of the fridge. It's not even noon yet, but after last night's bullshit medley of nightmares, I fucking need it. The carbonation burns all the way down to my stomach, and I revel in the heat of it, in the discomfort. The reminder that I'm awake, that I'm standing here breathing.

I've been working all morning, my sweat-soaked shirt proof of every stall mucked and horse fed. Rhett got started with breaking the first of three new horses at first light, and after helping me in the main barn, Wells began tinkering under the hood of our old tractor to see if he could get it running again. I almost told him not to waste his time with it, but I know he's eager to help make a difference wherever he can. Plus, if it means we don't have to keep dragging the corrals by hand anymore, I'll be fucking glad for it.

Even Sawyer came out this morning, face still swollen with sleep. He's never enjoyed cowboying like the rest of us, but he's also a damn good brother and knows we need the help. I found myself watching in awe as the most timid and reserved of us all spent the morning hours installing a whole new irrigation system in the pasture. We usually get enough rain to keep things green for the mustangs we have out there, but we've lost a few good trees of late and there are large patches of yellowing grass, so the added water will be a huge help.

It's only lunchtime and the day has been packed with so much forward movement that it's hard not to feel wisps of hope. Like maybe if we just keep working hard and doing our best, the universe will help to balance out some of this crazy.

A knock sounds at the door, and I frown. I was just with my brothers—everyone except Brooks, anyway—and they don't usually make a habit of coming to my cabin during our self-imposed lunch breaks. If my mom needed something she'd just call my cell from the house phone in her kitchen. I glance toward the door, wondering who could be on the other side. Maybe something's wrong, or . . .

Fuck, what if it's the cops?

Anxiety plummets through me, and I feel my stomach nearly fall out my ass. I look around my kitchen at the unwashed dishes in the sink and the crumbs on the counter from the buttered toast I made when I woke up this morning. Should I try to tidy up a little in case they're about to arrest me? It's not like I'd get out any time soon for murdering a man, and I'd hate for someone else to have to clean up after me here.

Relax, some deep part of my mind tugs. *It's probably nothing.*

I sigh, gazing at the front door, hating that I don't know who's on the other side. Maybe it's just Brooks . . . I haven't seen him in a couple of days, not after he asked everyone for space. I don't blame him—the family's been all over him and the boys these last few weeks, and I'm sure it feels like too much sometimes. I know he's okay because I see his truck roll down the long drive in the mornings when he takes Liam and Noah to school, but he hasn't really come out of his cabin otherwise.

I'm trying like hell to respect what he asked for, but it's not easy. I know Mom's checking on him, and the last thing I want to do is overwhelm him and make anything worse. He should be able to grieve the loss of his wife with their children however feels best without all our meddling. Still, it gnaws at me that I can't do anything to help ease the pain of what he's going through. It's not like there's a playbook on any of this shit.

I set my beer down on the counter and head for the door, but instead of finding my older brother on the other side—or the cops—there's a frazzled and very wet Ava framed in the doorway. Looks like the sky finally opened up to let down some rain.

I close my eyes as a small groan escapes me. "What the hell are you doing here?"

She narrows her sharp blue eyes. "You've been avoiding me."

"Oh good, so you already know I'm not interested." I shoot her an artificial smile before stepping back to push the door closed—I don't have the capacity to handle this shit right now. But the door thuds against something, and I look down to find a pointy toe in its path, leading to a sharp heel. "Those things aren't going to help you in this rain," I say.

"No shit—I'm practically a drowned rat out here. Can you let me in, please? We need to talk."

"No," I say firmly.

"Kasey—"

"What is there for us to possibly talk about?"

Her eyes narrow further. "Oh, I don't know. How about the fact that your family is about to lose this place?"

Irritation lances into me. "We're not losing anything."

"Okay, so what's your plan then?"

My silence is deafening.

"Look, I've seen the terms, Kasey. There isn't much wiggle room around any of the parameters. You or one of your brothers needs to be married to legally inherit the land, or your uncle stands to take it."

"Steal it, you mean."

"It's not theft if it's done right."

I scoff. "How the hell have you seen the paperwork?"

She shrugs. "I found some things on my father's desk. I guess Huck's been ripening him up to strike if needed."

A dart of white-hot anger shoots through me. "I fucking dare either of them to step one foot on this ranch."

"Easy tiger." Ava throws her hands up. "My point is you don't have a plan that's going to solve anything. Throwing punches won't stop this from happening, it'll just make matters worse. Let me in. Let me help."

"I don't want your help."

"Dammit, Kasey. Just let me in the goddamn door!" she shouts.

Her raised voice catches me off guard. I give her a long look, trying not to notice the way her hair sticks to her cheek or the flush that blooms beneath it. "I almost forgot how bossy you are," I grumble.

"Thrilled for an opportunity to remind you that I always get what I want."

The words nearly crush me. "Yeah. You sure do."

Her eyes widen. "That's not what I—"

"Just come in so we can get whatever this is over with." I move out of the way to give her room to pass.

She swallows and looks at me. And then she steps inside, carefully moving around me so that no part of her touches any part of me. "Nice place," she says lightly, eyes roaming around the living room.

I try not to let myself feel the weight of what it means to have her inside my cabin. It might be her first time in this living room, but it sure as hell isn't her first time on the ranch. We used to spend hours together in the game barn, drinking stolen beers and smoking stolen cigarettes. I used to peel her clothes off in the dark and fuck her on the old couch by the beer pong table.

I wipe the memory from my mind, anchoring back to the here and now. "Thanks," I say, walking straight for the kitchen. I don't want her to sit down on *this* couch and get comfortable. I don't want her in the same room as me for any longer than necessary. I'll hear whatever she wants to say and then bid her one big fat adieu.

Thankfully, she trails behind me and sidles up to the counter. "Drinking already?" she asks, eyeing the open beer. The tip of her nose is red, matching the flush still lingering in her cheeks. I catch her shoulders shaking with a shiver.

I frown, ignoring her question. "Do you want some coffee? Might warm you up."

"Yeah," she says. "Sure."

Turning to brew a mug, I say, "Let's have it then."

I hear her snort. "I've already told you. Marriage is the quick fix to all your problems."

A wave of heat climbs up the back of my neck where I can feel the weight of her eyes on me. I squeeze my eyes shut as another memory crashes over me: lying with her on a patch of warm sand, a gold band pinched between my fingers and my heart in my throat. It's there and gone in an instant, a mere scrap, but it rips that old wound wide open.

I almost hate myself for it—another slip.

I don't say anything as the coffee drips into the old ceramic mug, trying to force myself to tamp down the effect of her being here, inside my home. Never in a million years did I think I would see her again, let alone be making her a fucking cup of coffee in my kitchen like she didn't utterly destroy me all those years ago.

When the mug is full and the dripping ceases, I pick it up and carry it to the fridge to pull out the creamer. "Sugar?" I ask, the word pistoning through me.

"No thanks," she says softly.

I set the coffee and a carton of creamer down in front of her, reaching in the nearest drawer for a spoon. I drop that down too, and it clangs loudly against the counter. Ava flinches.

"Shit, sorry," I mumble.

Inky black lashes fan across the tops of her cheeks. "It's okay," she says, keeping her gaze on the mug. She wraps both hands around it, pulling it in close. "So . . . Marriage, Kasey."

"Marriage," I repeat.

"I can't think of a better way to handle all of this."

I roll my jaw, watching as she lifts the mug to her lips to blow on the steaming liquid. "I really don't understand why you're here, Ava."

"I'm trying to—"

"Help, yeah, I get that. But why? Why do you care?"

She rears her head back, like I've slapped her. "I know how important the ranch is. Of course I care."

"For fuck's sake, Ava—I don't even know where you've been for the last decade. And now you're just . . . here. Trying to right the wrongs in *my* family."

She eyes me curiously. "I've been in Miami. You never asked around?"

I scoff. "Asked *who*? Your father?"

She winces, her gaze shifting down once more. She sets the mug back on the counter and pulls on a loose thread in the stitching of the cushion beneath her. "I went to Florida," she finally says. "For school . . . and then *more* school. And then a shitty job at a high-profile law firm working for a bunch of really shitty men, which eventually turned into a better job working *with* those shitty men."

Her eyes rise to meet mine, and I nearly fall right into them, so achingly familiar and yet foreign in the way they study me now. They're . . . colder. Almost distant. So unlike the warm burst of sapphire that sparkles in the sunlight. "Why aren't you there then?" I ask.

She frowns. "It's complicated."

I almost laugh. "Right. Well, I'm sure it's not so complicated that you can't just turn around and go back and face whatever it is you're running from. Because you're running from something, right?" There's resentment bleeding through the words, and she knows it.

Ava sighs, lifting the coffee to her lips easing a tentative sip into her mouth. She leaves the creamer untouched, which surprises me. The woman has the biggest sweet tooth I've ever known—I bet if I got a peek inside her purse right now I'd find a handful of candy.

Another vicious reminder.

"Since when do you drink coffee black?"

"Since forever," she retorts.

I shake my head. "Oh no, don't lie to me, Ava. You used to drink vanilla creamer with a splash of coffee."

She shrugs. "I'm not a kid anymore. And I know what you're doing—this conversation is about you, Kasey. I'm giving you a solution. Marry me. Save the ranch and give that uncle of yours a good old fashioned middle finger."

"I think that's the worst idea I've ever heard in my life. I don't know how you think you can just waltz your way back into Saddlebrook Falls and into my life and assume I'm still eager to play these games with you. I'm not a damn kid anymore either. You left me a long time ago. It's ancient history. I've moved on."

Ava snorts. "Oh my *god*, Kasey, I'm not trying to play games with you. I'm well aware of the fact that I walked away." Her words slice into me, but I keep my expression schooled and pretend like they don't. Like nothing about this rattles me to my core. "Me being here has nothing to do with history. I'm just a friend trying to help you out of a situation that looks pretty shitty from the outside. Unless one of your brothers is ready to walk down the aisle with a new bride?"

"A friend?" I almost laugh. "We were never friends, Ava."

"Weren't we?" She lifts the mug to her lips and takes a long pull of the coffee. My gaze trails along her jaw as she swallows it down. "It benefits me too," she says. "If it makes you feel better."

"How?"

"I'd rather not get into it, but it's not just for you is all I'm saying."

I scrub a hand over my mouth in irritation. "Tell me how this benefits you, Ava."

She just shakes her head. "Not your business."

"I think the ways in which you benefit from a *marriage* to me *makes* it my business."

"No, it doesn't," she says firmly. "It has nothing to do with you. It just . . . helps me with a little problem I have. That's all."

I let out a heavy breath. "This is fucking crazy. We can't just get married."

She shrugs. "Says who?"

"Says me."

"Then say goodbye to the ranch, Kasey." She stands, as if to leave. I watch her pull her damp purse over her shoulder and walk back toward the front door.

"How long?" I ask when she reaches for the knob.

She turns to look at me, eyes glinting. The challenge in them is as familiar as the smell of her perfume in the air. She lifts one shoulder in a lazy shrug before crossing her arms over her chest. "Not long. Just until the deed to the ranch is officially in your name. We'd have to be careful not to let anyone think it's fraud—"

"Because it is," I interject.

"Sure. Yeah. But I'm confident we can figure out how to make it all look real." Her lips quirk in a small smile, and another dart of anger pierces through me.

One upon a time, Ava was the single most important thing that mattered to me. My entire life revolved around making her happy and praying like hell I could keep her forever. She was my first love, my first . . . everything. And now she wants to use that history all these years later to get something. And the worst part is she won't even tell me what it is.

"Look, you have to tell me what you get out of this or I won't do it."

The statement throws her off, her chest rising with a deep breath. "Fine. But not now. Like I said, it's complicated and requires some time to explain. But I'll tell you anything you want to know before we seal the deal, okay?"

I nod once. "Fine." We stare at each other, neither of us making any moves. After a while I ask, "So what happens next?"

A small smile returns, that challenge firing back to life. "Now, we tell everyone the good news and make sure they believe it." She winks, and then turns to walk out the door, back into the rain.

CHAPTER THREE

AVA

*E*ven with the heavy downpour, it takes every ounce of self-control I have not to grab my phone from its magnetic mount and chuck it through the window of my Range Rover. A stack of notifications a mile long glares at me from the homescreen, most of them labeled with Tobias's name. Even with the shit emoji I added to his contact before leaving Miami, it's hard to fight the instinct to cower at what I know is his wicked anger shining through—the only explanation for so many texts and missed calls.

He must not have liked the email I sent the partners this morning.

I sigh, turning the volume up on the radio as George Strait sings about exes in Texas. I almost laugh at how on the nose it is as I drive back into town after leaving the Bennett ranch. I *never* thought I'd be back here, on this uneven, rock-filled dirt road that gives access to what was once one of my favorite places in the whole world. It didn't feel like that just now, standing in Kasey's cold cabin while he looked at me like I was a complete stranger.

I guess maybe I am—it's been ten years.

I honestly don't know what I expected. Maybe I'm too

embarrassed to admit that I *need* this place, that I'm home because I ran out of options. But I thought coming back would feel . . . different. Like I could just fall right back into the old song and dance of feeling too good for any of it. Or that maybe there'd still be a Kasey-shaped pocket of this town that would still feel like it was just for me.

But it's been ten long years. Kasey isn't the same boy I left on that beach, and I'm most definitely not the same girl who was convinced he hung the moon that smiled down on us while he held me close.

I guess it's a relief that he doesn't seem to care about me being back in Texas—I know exactly what I did to him back then, and how much it must have hurt. His indifference feels like salt in an old wound, stinging and burning with every stale word and icy glance he throws my way, but I know deep down I deserve it.

The tires roll over a bump as the dirt gives way to asphalt and the first edges of town come into view. I can make out the sun-backed silhouette of the grocery store's curved roof and the water tower with a giant red *SF* painted on the front. I know before even making it to Main Street that there are probably a dozen people out meandering around town square, chit-chatting about weekend plans or whatever juicy piece of gossip they've caught hold of.

From the outside looking in, Saddlebrook Falls is the quintessential southern town, ripe with traditional values and an eagerness to please the good lord above. But what you wouldn't see by just looking at it is all the hypocrisy and judgement that swirls in these streets—especially from the older folks.

It doesn't help that I grew up under the same roof as the town sheriff, or that my father's role in this community undoubtedly contributed to Mom leaving us. I was only nine when she left, and for so long I waited for her to come back for me. I hated her for leaving me behind with him and all these people, but eventually I made peace with it. I still don't forgive her for leaving, but when I was old enough it gave me the courage to do the same, on my own terms.

My phone buzzes from where it's mounted on the dash. There's a chirp in the car's speaker system before a voice says, "New text message from Tobias: *I don't want to fight anymore. I miss you, kitty cat. When are you coming back home to me?*"

I scoff, throwing a sharp look at my phone. Does he really expect me to just go back to him? After *everything* he's done?

He's fucking delusional.

Looking back at the road ahead, I see the bakery quickly approaching and slow down to pull into the lot. There are a few things about Saddlebrook Falls that I've missed dearly, and Luna's walnut brownies are one of them. Nothing in Miami ever compared. Plus, I've been especially queasy today and a little dose of sugar will help ease my stomach.

I park in front of the bakery, eyeing the counter inside through the big front window. Luna stands behind it, talking with an old woman wearing a vibrant floral caftan. Even with her back turned toward me I know it's Maeve Meadows, or *Nosy Maeve* as most of us like to call her.

Sighing, I look at the café next door and see it bustling with patrons, thinking of all the evenings I spent across a worn booth from my father, eating one of June's dinner specials as I avoided having any sort of meaningful conversation with the man in front of me. I remember feeling so trapped, so overwhelmed with a pressure I didn't know how to get away from. If I could go back . . .

I shut the thought down and unbuckle my seat belt, pushing out the car door. The rain's only a low drizzle now, but it's still enough to ruin any chance of saving these shoes. I didn't have the heart to pull out my old boots from the back of my closet this morning—I don't have the right clothes to wear them with and doubt I'd fit in any of my jeans from high school. I think pulling them on would be too harsh of a reminder of everything

I've lost, of everything I might never have actually had to begin with.

There's a rush of warm air that hits me when I open the door. A loud jangle sounds from a windchime attached to the frame, and both women turn around to face me. Luna's eyes grow wide as a big smile spreads across her face. "Ava?" she asks, squinting. "Is that you?"

I smile back, the smell of burnt sugar and lemon wafting from the kitchen behind her. "Hi, Luna," I say affectionately. "Please tell me you have a brownie back there for me?"

Luna claps her hands together before setting into motion, hurling around the counter to wrap her arms around me. I squeeze her back, the sweet smell of her hair a comfort I'd somehow forgotten about. "What are you doing home, sweet girl? And why did it take you so long to come see me—everyone's been talking about you being back!"

We pull apart, but she keeps her hands on my shoulders. Her golden eyes swim with emotion, and it makes me pause. "I have some things to work through," I say. "I've missed you and your baking so much. There's nothing like it in Miami."

"Of course not!" She clicks her tongue. "This bakery is one-of-a-kind, you know that."

"I do," I agree, laughing.

"Are you okay?" she asks, brow furrowing. "I thought we might never see you again, but then Rosie told me she heard from Georgia that you were at the Wild Coyote for Melody Bennett's funeral. Is that why you're back, baby? You come back for . . . him?"

"I—" I start, eyes jumping to Maeve, who watches us with her arms crossed over her chest. The old broad never liked me much, but she's certainly listening in. And Luna's just basically handed me the perfect opening to start some rumors about Kasey and me. "I guess I did. I heard about Melody and reached out to Kasey to see what I could do, and then one thing led to another, and . . . here I am."

To Luna's credit, she tries to hide her frown. "You and Kasey back together?"

I didn't expect to feel so guilty about lying, but as I work up the courage to paint the story of our rekindling, I'm hit with all the flashbacks of my teenage years, sitting at one of these restored wooden tables crying to Luna over a plate of strawberry cheesecake or a chocolate raspberry tart. I think of how, for so long, she was the one person I trusted with everything, the person I told about every crush, every heartbreak.

I don't know what I was thinking coming in here without a plan. I just . . . I'm not ready to go back to my father's house yet, and with all the rain there're only so many options. This bakery is one of the few places I ever felt like I could be *me*.

I look at Maeve again and force a smile. "We're giving it another shot," I explain. "I think, now that we're older, we might have a real chance at getting things right."

Luna's eyes twinkle. "As long as you're happy, baby. That's all that matters." Maeve *harrumphs* and grabs her to-go bag from the counter, excusing herself as she moves around us and out the door. Luna gives her a quick goodbye wave before grabbing my hand and pulling me to the counter. "Now, we have some catching up to do. I have all your favorites—you said you wanted a brownie?"

My stomach swoops with excitement. "Yes, with walnuts if you have them?"

"Of course I do!"

I reach for my wallet in my purse, but Luna balks. "This one's on me, doll."

"I insist," I argue, accidentally pulling out a wad of cash when I'd meant to only grab a single twenty.

"Goodness gracious. Miami has been good to you, hasn't it?"

I feel the burn in my cheeks. "I'm a lawyer now," I say. "It pays well."

"Good for you," she says sincerely. "You deserve success, Ava. Now pick a table and get settled while I warm this up for you."

I SPEND HOURS AT THE BAKERY WITH LUNA.

Even as other customers come in, she's so focused on me, doling out pastries and slices of cake without ever breaking from our conversation. Lots of people look back and forth between us as we talk, lingering longer than necessary as they pretend to grab napkins and wipe down perfectly clean tables.

A long time ago, it would have bothered me: the way they dawdle. The way they take their time to absorb as much as they can before their presence becomes impolite. But today I don't care about any of it—I'm absorbed by how good it feels to catch up with Luna, the way she hangs on every word like my thoughts and feelings and experience outside this town *matters* to her.

It's the way she used to listen to me back when I felt like I didn't have anyone else, when I felt suffocated and caged and under constant scrutiny by my only remaining parent. Luna never judged me or made me feel small for the messes I created—she was always there, willing to listen. Willing to offer advice and support about boys or school or my future.

I tell her about law school, about rooms filled with men who couldn't be bothered to look my way unless it was to ask for my number. I show her pictures of my first apartment, the couch I thrifted and the cheap yellow rug that unraveled and spread pieces of thread everywhere. I tell her about the firm where I eventually got a job, about how I kept my head down and worked *so* fucking hard for every scrap of success, how even after a handful of big wins in court the men in that office still wouldn't spare me an ounce of recognition.

I tell her about eventually getting a seat at the table with the partners after I caught an error that saved one of their asses. How I thought all of the work would eventually help me earn a spot for my own name on the building next to theirs. How, not for the first time in my life, I let men paint me a pretty picture of my place in their world, and I took it in with eager hands.

I don't tell her about Tobias or the real reason why I left Miami—it would demolish any chance Kasey and I have at pulling off a sincere engagement. But I *want* to. I want to tell her everything, to hear her say I didn't deserve it, that everything will be all right. Instead, I tell her Kasey and I reconnected over the holidays. That I don't think I ever stopped wondering what it would have been like if I'd never left.

At least that part is true.

Later, after inhaling a brownie *and* a strawberry cupcake, I feel utterly exhausted. I'm not sure if it's the humidity from the storm or the overcast sky, but all I want is to crawl into bed and close my eyes for a nap. I give Luna another tight squeeze and stuff cash in her cupcake-shaped tip jar before trudging back out to my SUV to finally head home.

It only takes me six minutes to get back to the house I grew up in. I park along the curb in the front and turn off the ignition, looking up at it through my wet windshield. It looks like it always has: pristine and unaltered outside of the fresh paint that looks to be only a few months old. It's the same color green though, like the leaves of the black walnut trees growing in the backyard. The trim is a startling white caught in this gray after-noon, the tips of the gabled roof pointed high in the storm-filled sky. Red rosebushes line the front walkway, pruned and manicured.

I remember being nine or ten and losing control on my roller skates down that walkway, falling so deep in the bushes my dad's new wife had to pull thorns out from my skin and clothes in the bathroom. It looked like I'd been attacked by a feral cat. Dad was more upset I hadn't minded the flowers, that I'd broken half a dozen branches during the tumble.

They were Gloria's pride and joy, after all. And Dad worked *really* hard to keep Gloria happy.

I've only been back a week and I already want to run away again, hightail it out of here in the middle of the night. I used to consider it a work of art, the way I'd silently pop the screen out of my bedroom window and climb out onto the roof before using the trash bins to hold my weight as I carefully shimmied down the gutter's downspout. It's a shame I have nowhere to go—no teenage boys in idling cars with the headlights turned off, waiting for me to jump into the passenger seat so we can jet off to some party, or to a quiet creek in the woods.

Now I'm just a grown woman who ran back home to escape her problems out in the real world, where she swore she'd make it. Where she *swore* she'd create a life for herself that she could be proud of, standing on her own two feet.

My car chimes to signal another text message. I shut off the ignition to cut off announcement, but the words still come: "*New text from Tobias—*"

Fucking car. I pull the phone off the mount and grab my purse, pretending I can't hear the words of Tobias's latest text. I can't wait to get up to my room so I can shove the phone beneath my mattress and forget about it for at least the rest of the day.

Dad's cruiser isn't parked in the driveway, but I know Gloria's home—she's always home. I'm hoping she's too busy organizing her china to notice me coming in. I'm almost thirty years old, and I refuse to explain myself or my whereabouts to anyone ever again.

I hadn't even planned on staying back at this house when I got here, but Abbott from the inn tipped my father off that I was back in town as soon as I checked in to the room I booked, which led to the good sheriff showing up to escort me home after shaking the innkeeper's hand in the lobby.

So fucking embarrassing.

Being treated like a kid again isn't worth the money saved on accommodations, that's for damn sure. But it's not a battle worth fighting right now. The real fight has been getting Kasey on board with this marriage, and based on the way we left things this morning, I think I might finally have him.

I have to admit, this ruse was not something I originally planned. But after overhearing Georgia Moore whispering in the supermarket about Brooks Bennett losing his wife and it being all her husband's *good friend* needed to gain access to the land and finally boot out the Bennetts, I knew it was an opportunity laid at my feet. A means to an end that will hopefully help us both out with the shitty hands we've been dealt.

The front door to the house opens quietly, its hinges likely recently oiled—a big win for me. I can see all the way through the kitchen window at the back of the house thanks to its open floorplan, and there's Gloria's pinned-up curls bobbing in and out of view. She must be covering her plants from the rain—I don't know and certainly don't care. She's always babied the hell out of her garden.

I smile in relief, closing the door behind me before hurrying up the stairs on silent feet into the safety of my room.

CHAPTER FOUR

KASEY

"Whoa, boy . . ." The chestnut stallion beneath me bucks harder, the power in his massive thighs shooting me up into the air. My stomach plummets as we both drop back down.

"Easy!" Rhett calls from outside the corral.

"Trying," I grit out. The horse twists hard to the left and bucks again, and it's enough to shake me loose from the saddle. I fly through the air, tucking my chin into my chest as I try to roll into the fall. I land on my shoulder though, pain exploding from my collarbone to my shoulder blade. "Fuck!" I shout, frustration cutting deep. I haven't been thrown from a horse in years.

"Shit," Rhett mutters.

"You okay?" Wells asks.

I stare up at the sky as my brothers hop over the fence. Rhett jogs toward the horse to catch his lead before he has a chance to finish what he started and trample over me. Wells comes straight to me, his head flooding my field of vision and blocking out the blue of the sky. His eyes scan over me, settling on the shoulder I'm clutching with a death grip.

"Dislocated?" he asks.

I sigh out an irritated breath, squeezing my eyes shut. "I fucking hope not."

"Can you stand?" He scratches at his brow, his dirty ball cap pushed high on his forehead.

"My legs are fine, Wellsy boy."

He frowns. "Let's see you use them then."

I almost chuckle. Rolling toward my uninjured shoulder, I get my legs underneath me and work to stand. As I straighten, I try pushing my chest out to bring my shoulder blades together and my left one screams. "Fuck," I say again, wincing.

"How bad?" he asks.

I give it another experimental roll. My muscles tense as pain radiates. "I don't think it's dislocated, but I definitely pulled a muscle. Maybe bruised some bone."

"Try holding out your arm."

I slowly extend my left hand, raising my arm until it's perpendicular to my torso. It hurts, but not enough to signal anything major. "I'm all right," I say. "Just gonna be sore."

Wells lets out a long breath. He's always been one to worry.

"We shouldn't bring him in yet," Rhett calls from the other side of the corral. His arms are spread wide as he herds the wild horse toward the fence. "He's stubborn. We can't let him think he's won."

"Have at it," I holler back. "All yours."

"Come on," Wells says, nodding his head at the corral's gate. I follow him through it and take Rhett's place on the sidelines, watching as Rhett takes mine on the horse, carefully stepping into the stirrup resting at the animal's belly.

The horse starts bucking before Rhett's even seated, but he manages to get himself into the saddle, determination set in his brow.

"He's got it," Wells mumbles, eyes fastened to Rhett like he's readying for the potential of another brother falling.

"Yeah." I nod. "Rhett's just as stubborn as that horse. They can work each other out."

Wells snorts.

"Hey." We spin to find Sawyer coming our way from the house. He's wearing shorts and a CSU T-shirt. "What are you all up to?"

"Kasey just got dusted by that mustang," Wells says. "Went flying and everything."

I knock him against his shoulder and then grimace, realizing too late I used my bad arm. "Dick," I mutter.

Wells laughs. "When are you leaving?" he asks Sawyer.

Sawyer shrugs. "I was supposed to head out this morning, but . . ." He hesitates. "I'm not sure if it's a good time."

"What do you mean?" I ask.

His eyes flit to the cabin that sits a few hundred yards away, the only one in eyesight of the main house. "I probably should stay, right? Maybe a couple more days?"

"Sawyer," I say. "You've already stayed longer than you were supposed to. Didn't school start back this week?" We'd all been lucky that he could be here during his spring break, but as far as I know that's already ended.

"Yeah, but I've been logging in online. My professors know what's going on."

"We've got him," Wells says quietly.

Sawyer looks at him, unsure.

"We've got him," he repeats. "You need to get back to school."

"For the love of god, *someone's* gotta finish college," I grumble.

Sawyer cuts me a confused look. "I already have a degree."

I smile. "I know, kid. I'm just fucking with you."

His face wipes clean of his bewilderment. "Oh."

Of all of us, Sawyer's definitely gotten the furthest with his education. After Wells dropped out of Texas A&M his senior year, Sawyer's the only Bennett to have gone all the way. And as if that weren't impressive enough, he's now in the middle of a graduate program for wildlife conservation.

He's always been way more book smart than the rest of us. Cowboying never came natural to him and he's struggled to fit into social spaces, but the kid's brain is a powerhouse. He deserves a lot of success.

"Seriously, Sawyer—you need to get back," I say.

"Yeah." Sawyer nods. "I'll look for flights after dinner. Try to catch one in the morning."

I reach for him with my good arm and wrap my hand around his shoulder. "We're all so fucking proud of you. I know there's a lot going on here at home—hell, there's always a lot going on—but none of it takes away from your accomplishments, okay? Keep hustling for your dreams."

"That's not true," Sawyer says, eyes shining. "We all deserve good things."

"Except Rhett," Wells snarks.

"I heard that!" Rhett yells from atop the mustang. The horse neighs and bucks again, trying to shake Rhett off his back.

Sawyer laughs. "Thanks, Kasey. It means a lot."

We all turn back to Rhett. It's obvious the stallion's getting tired, but he's not ready to quit yet.

"Can I ask you guys a question?" Sawyer asks. He sounds nervous.

"Shoot," I say, turning to look at him.

"How do you know when a girl's into you?"

Wells snaps his attention to Sawyer, grinning. Neither of us says anything for a moment as we watch Sawyer's ears grow a bright shade of crimson.

"Actually," he says, "never mind. Forget I said anything—"

"How long have you known her?" Wells asks.

Sawyer shrugs. "Since we had a biology class together last year. We were paired for a group project and argued the whole time.

She was so controlling about everything and I thought she hated me, but now . . . I'm not so sure."

"What makes you say that?"

Sawyer considers that. "I try not to bother her," he explains, "because I don't want to upset her. She always seems to get so flustered when I say anything to her. But lately she gets mad at me for ignoring her too, so I don't understand what I'm supposed to be doing."

I scoff. "That's women for you. They *want* you to want them, but then pretend like you wanting them is a bother."

"I don't know," Wells says. "Sometimes I think they just don't know what they want. It can take time for girls to let their guard down."

"Or," I counter, "they like being chased, but don't like being caught." A certain sun-kissed brunette running down the shore of Scorpion Bay flashes through in my mind, my hands wrapping around her waist to pull her down into the high tide, her screeching laughter echoing in my heart long after the sun goes down. "What's her name?" I ask, distracting myself from the memory.

"Elizabeth," Sawyer mutters.

"Well, that's fuckin' proper," I say. "No Lizzy? Or Beth?"

His cheeks are red now. "She's pretty adamant about being called Elizabeth."

Wells chuckles as he adjusts the dusty ball cap on his head. "Do you like her?" he asks.

Sawyer shrugs. "I don't know whether to like her or be scared of her."

"Oh yeah." I whistle. "He likes her, all right."

"Just forget I asked," Sawyer mumbles, turning back toward the house.

"Sawyer, wait!" Wells bellows, pulling Sawyer back by the arm. "Look, man. If you like her, just ask her out. Something simple, like dinner. If she says no, then you know she's not interested."

"But if she says yes," I chime in, "then it's a good place to start. Just be cool and keep it low pressure, you know?"

"I don't know what 'be cool' means."

"Just be yourself."

"I'm not cool, though."

"Yes you are," Wells says, frowning.

"You're a Bennett," I add. "Of course you're cool."

"The worst thing that could happen is she says no." Wells knocks Sawyer gently on the shoulder. "And it's not a bad thing if she does. You just move on with your life, and at least you'll know."

"Yeah," Sawyer hedges. "All right. I'm gonna go see if Mom's ready to go to the store."

Wells and I watch him disappear back into the house.

"Do you think he's ever been laid?" I ask Wells seriously.

"Honestly? I don't think so."

"Hm," I hum, turning back to Rhett. "We should work on that."

Wells laughs, and I grin back at him. I know Sawyer needs to get back to school, but it's been really nice having him home, even if the circumstances are shitty. There's a rightness to all five of us being here.

I glance over at Brooks's cabin and wonder for the hundredth time what he's doing in there, if there might be something I can do to help him. I wonder how long it'll take for the grief to lessen, if it ever will. I want to protect all of my brothers as best I can, but I don't always know how to go about it.

It definitely starts with protecting this ranch, and unfortunately that's going to take a deep cut into my pride.

"I think he's done for now," Rhett hollers from the center of the ring. The horse is still huffing, but he's not bucking anymore. "We can bring him back out in the morning."

"Good," I say. "I need to talk to you guys anyway. Meet me in the office?"

THE AIR INSIDE THE MAKESHIFT OFFICE IS STILL HEAVY with humidity from yesterday's rain storm. Even the breeze kicking up outside does little to help air out these old wooden walls that once housed the horses previous Bennetts marked as theirs. After the second big barn was built, this smaller one was converted into a bit of a command center for the whole ranch, where we store file cabinets of records and keep the books on all our big transactions. We also store a bunch of old furniture and equipment that've become an eye sore over the years.

I stare back and forth between my brothers from where I sit in my plastic chair. Both of them look like they want to throttle me.

"You're not *really* thinking of marrying her?" Wells asks, eyes wide.

"We may not have a choice."

"We're the ones who *actually* have women in our lives," he says pointedly. I scowl at him, and he winces. "You know what I mean."

"These aren't ideal circumstances for getting married, Wells," I say. "Does Layla even want marriage? Have you guys talked about it before?"

I watch my baby brother look down into his lap, hesitating.

"See," I say gently.

He frowns. "Her mom kind of fucked her up on marriage. I think she might be open to it someday, but . . ."

I lean forward. "I'm not going to ask you to risk your relationship. Layla is good for you. You two are so in love it's gross. Don't let something like this complicate it."

Wells presses his lips together as he glances at Rhett.

Rhett's cheeks burn pink, and I almost laugh. "I'm sure as shit not asking you, Rhett, so wipe that look off your face."

Rhett's brows pinch with a glower. "What, you don't trust me to do what's needed for this family?"

I sigh. "It's not about trust or your commitment to the family. But you already put Olivia through the ringer with your little card game last month, and you two are too new for this. You really think a wedding is a good idea only a few weeks into a relationship? It's not practical."

"Better than a wedding between my *very* single brother and the fucking crazy ex-girlfriend he hasn't seen in ten years."

"She's not crazy." I shoot him a warning look. "And I really don't think it's that bad." I hope they can't hear the lie floating straight through my teeth. "I got over her a long time ago. I honestly have no idea why she's back in Saddlebrook Falls, nor do I really care. But she's a lawyer, she can help us navigate through all the paperwork with the inheritance trust, and she's offered an arrangement that benefits us both. It feels like a win."

"It feels like *fraud*," Wells retorts, voice low. "I think you've done enough bending of the law lately, Kasey."

It's instant, the way the memory rips through me. The dim light of that old barn. The smell of gunpowder wafting as Maverick's eyes flared. I push out a breath, shoving the image down. "It's not fraud if you dipshits don't say anything to anyone."

Wells rolls his eyes. "That doesn't make it not fraud, asshole."

"Who else knows?" Rhett asks.

I turn my focus on him, finding his gray eyes calculating. "Only us three. And Ava."

"You don't think she's going to tell anyone?"

I shake my head. "I don't know why she would. Plus, she could probably be disbarred for it. She's not going to risk her career."

"What about Mom?" Wells asks. "What about Brooks?"

My shoulders slump. This is where things get tricky. "The last thing I want to do is lie to either of them. The family deserves the truth. I just have to navigate telling them carefully. If Sheriff Joe gets a whiff of this thing not being real, he'll have no problem sending the wolves after me."

Rhett snorts. "You think?"

I frown at him. "Despite what he thinks, I wasn't the reason she left." If anything, I tried like hell to be the reason she stayed—but I keep that portion of the thought to myself.

"Hopefully his daughter will handle him" is all he says back.

"Fuck," Wells mutters, shaking his head.

"Look, I know it's not the greatest idea," I admit. "Ava's always been a little—"

"Crazy," Rhett interjects.

"*Unpredictable*," I counter. "And it's going to take some convincing that suddenly getting married after ten years apart isn't for any reason other than wanting to be together—I know it won't be easy. But Huck is coming for us, fast and furious. We don't have time to beat him the right way. If marrying Ava gives us a shot at deterring him until we can get a grip on the rest of it, then it's worth it. I need you guys to support me on this."

Rhett blows out a breath, crossing his arms over his wide chest. "What can we do?"

I shrug. "We want this town to believe it's legitimate? Let 'em think they're the ones uncovering the story."

Wells grins. "You want to leak it."

I nod. "Carefully. It can't be obvious."

"Olivia can let something loose at June's," Rhett offers.

"And Layla can spill it to her mom. Lynette will spread it fast."

"You and Ava need to give people clues too," Rhett says. "Something for people to gnaw on. They're probably already champing at the bit for the reason she's back here after all this time—find a way to make it about you. A date night in town.

Maybe hold her hand out on the street. Get caught behind a closed door." He winks.

"There'll be none of *that*," I say firmly.

His grin is wolfish. "Why not? You two used to be pretty damn good at getting caught in all sorts of places. In fact, I remember you both getting caught beneath the bleachers during a fucking football game that you were *supposed* to be playing in."

God, how could I forget? I'd been out of my damn mind.

"Yeah, well, that's all over," I say. "Died a long time ago."

Rhett's eyes soften and it throws me for a loop, seeing the proof of his calloused edges dulling. The way he's been leaning into his own vulnerability lately—no doubt the effect of new love in his life. "I'm just saying, brother, I'm sure it won't be hard for you and Ava to get the gossip train barreling right through the middle of town. You've done it before. Probably like riding a bike."

Wells huffs a laugh. "Sheriff's gonna wanna kill you all over again."

"As long as he believes the lie." I shrug. "Then I don't care. Let him have at me."

Just like that, Rhett's gaze hardens.

Wells leans forward. "I'll talk to Layla." He stands to walk out of the office, probably heading to get ready for a shift at the bar.

"Thanks. I'll see you in a few hours." I look at Rhett again. "I know it's not ideal . . ."

Rhett shakes his head. "I owe you a lot, Kasey. I'll do whatever I can to help. Just be careful, okay? I remember how hard this was on you last time."

I feign confusion. "What do you mean?"

His mouth presses into a thin line. "She ripped your fucking heart to shreds. It took you a long time to put it back together."

"I'm not sure I ever did," I admit, letting the facade crumble. "Haven't been in love since. But that's what'll make it easier this time, I think."

He frowns.

I force a smile. "I'll be careful. Promise."

His pale eyes watch me for a long moment, like he's sifting through the words to find the trace of bullshit we both know's there. It makes me feel exposed in a way I don't like—especially not with my brothers. I need to keep a clear mind. Lead us all through. "Let me know if her daddy gets too rough," he finally says. "I've been itching for a little chaos."

"Jesus, Rhett," I grind out. "You've had enough trouble to last a lifetime. Be good, for fuck's sake."

His returning smile is dark and wicked.

CHAPTER FIVE

AVA

After spending all of yesterday holed up in my room with my laptop trying to tie up some loose ends in Miami, I'm relieved when Kasey texts me about meeting up.

Ava? the message came through from an unsaved number—but I'd know that number anywhere, even after thinking if I deleted it I'd eventually forget it.

I've been wondering if I'd hear from you, I write back. *Thought you were going to make me chase you down again.*

We need to talk, he says, ignoring my quip. *You free this afternoon?*

When and where?

Ranch. Can you be here in an hour?

I sent him the saluting emoji and leaped out of my bed to take a shower. My hair's still damp when I pull my SUV up the long drive to the main house. I pass by it and head straight for his cabin, wondering briefly who might be watching through the windows, vaguely aware of the fact that I probably look like a lost yuppie from the city. And then I fight a laugh because that's exactly what I am.

Kasey answers the door on the second knock, shirtless with

worn jeans slung low on his hips. He fists a shirt and his cowboy hat in one hand, pulling the front door shut behind him with the other as he steps out onto the porch.

"Let's take a walk," he says as he steps past where I stand, not even deigning to look at me as he pulls the shirt over his head. I watch muscles along his back work with the movement before it all disappears behind white cotton.

I realize my mouth is hanging open and swiftly clamp it shut. "Oh," I say, hiking my purse higher on my shoulder. "Okay, sure." I follow him down the front steps and out onto the worn dirt path that leads either back to the main house or out to the other cabins. The sun is ripe today, and sweat pools along my spine beneath my satin blouse. "Gorgeous day," I say, carefully stepping around a cluster of rocks that he stepped right over.

"Mhm," Kasey hums back, pushing his hat down over his head, casting a shadow around his shoulders. My eyes follow a path down his body until I catch myself staring at his ass and have to look away.

When he veers right toward the big barn, my heart leaps as the possibility of getting to see the horses I know they keep in there up close; I haven't been around a horse in so long. But then a sinking feeling comes over me. "Wait, we're not riding today, are we?"

"No," he says. I swear I hear the hint of a sarcastic laugh in the way he says it, like putting me on a horse would be simultaneously hilarious and terrible.

I glare at the back of his head as I stumble forward, trying to keep up with his long strides. "You don't have to say it like that." I have my own reasons for not wanting to get on a horse right now, but he doesn't know those. As far as he should be concerned, I still know my way around a saddle.

He turns to look back at me. "You're wearing those things again," he grumbles, ignoring what I said, eyes flickering down to my feet.

I drop my gaze to the one of the many pairs of Manolos I've been collecting over the past couple years, evidence of my hard work and success. "As opposed to . . . ?"

"Those aren't the right shoes."

"Well, I didn't realize you'd be taking me on a hike."

"It's not a hike. We're literally walking on flat ground."

"Fine." I smile. "I didn't realize you'd be taking me on a *walk*."

He rolls his eyes. "You're going to sink into the mud."

"I don't plan on stepping into any mud, Kasey."

"And then you're going to get spitting mad and take it out on me."

I narrow my gaze. "I don't take my anger out on you."

He has the audacity to snort. "And *then* you're probably going to cry. You'll try not to because you're stubborn and don't want anyone to see you cry, least of all me. But you will."

I stop walking. "What are you doing?" I ask, feeling the temperature of my blood rising with this charade of a conversation.

He turns to face me, two brown eyes roaming lazily down to my waist before dropping again to my feet. "You know damn well *those* shoes don't belong on *this* ranch."

"Yeah? Well, get used to it, because soon these shoes are going to be all over *this ranch*."

"What do you mean?" A spark in his eyes catches hold in my chest, a warmth that's so familiar it scares me. I haven't seen this man in a decade, and yet my body still responds to him as if nothing's changed. As if all this time and distance hasn't cleaved us in two.

I stare at him. "You think I'm going to keep living at home after we're married?" I ask.

He curses, turning away to look out toward the pasture. And then he's on the move again, steering us back toward the barn. When he walks through the wide double doors and into the shade

I follow suit, eyes tracing down the line of horses who look curiously at us from their stalls.

"There's so many of them," I say out loud, more to myself than to him.

"Twenty-two right now," Kasey says. "Four more come in next week."

I nod. "You guys have gotten bigger."

He shrugs. "We have our ups and downs. It's been slower the last couple years, but lately it's been busier." I watch as he grabs a shaving fork from the rack on the far wall and heads for the first stall. He gives the horse inside a tentative rub on the nose before unlatching the door and disappearing inside.

"Um," I say, "are you working right now?"

"Yep," he calls back.

"I thought you wanted to talk."

He easily pokes his head over the stall's wall—it's gotta be at least six feet high. "I do," he says. "But I also have to work. Thought I might be able to rope you into helping, but . . ." He looks at my feet again before his head drops back down.

I shift my weight from one foot to another, feeling ridiculous just standing here while he mucks. "I'm a lawyer," I tell him. "Not a ranch hand."

"Don't read into it, Ava. Just find a place to sit down and I'll work while we talk."

I look around the barn, but there's definitely no place to sit. I sigh. "Do you want to start or should I?"

"Ladies first," he grumbles.

"Great. Okay. Well, since it already came up, let's get back to the topic of housing. I'm going to have to stay here, Kasey. You know that, right?"

The stall is silent for a long beat. A horse behind me whinnies.

"I have a second bedroom," he finally says. "It's furnished. Should have what you need."

"Works for me," I reply, keeping my voice light.

"And you're going to stay in it," he adds.

I frown, confused. "Yeah, that would be the idea."

"And my room is for me," he continues. "Me only."

I bark out a laugh, understanding where he's going with this. "Damn, Kasey. I get it. No funny business. Won't be a problem."

"What about your job?" he eventually asks over the rhythm of the rake sliding across the ground. "Don't you have, like, court? Or something?"

"Uh . . . I'm taking a bit of a break from work. And even if something comes up, I should be able to handle it remotely from my laptop."

"Fancy," he says flatly.

I look around the barn again, growing uncomfortable on my feet. I find a beautiful golden mare eyeing me intently. I move closer and hold out my hand for her to sniff. "So, I guess to kick this off, we'll need to get engaged. Maybe in the next week or so? A whirlwind romance? I don't want to move too fast, but the clock's ticking. Plus, it's not like we don't already have history. Maybe you could ask me in the gazebo—"

"I already proposed to you once, sugar. That was enough for me."

His use of *sugar* sears through me, as does the memory of a small diamond ring and a flannel blanket on the beach. It leaves me feeling painfully raw. He comes out of the stall and finds me petting the golden horse as she nuzzles her nose into my ear. After watching for a second, expression curious, he turns to unlatch the door of the next stall and disappears from view again. "Okay." I nod. "No public proposal, not a big deal. I'll just start wearing a ring around town when we're ready. People will . . . figure it out."

"Works for me," he says, voice even, betraying no emotion.

"What about the wedding?"

"What about it?" The rhythm of the rake sounds through the barn again.

"We should probably host it here on the ranch. It's what people would expect—"

"No," he interrupts. "We can go to the courthouse."

I sigh. "That's not enough. Anyone who might suspect this is all a sham will find it highly convenient if we marry in a courthouse. It can't look like an item we're checking off a list. We need to make an event out of it, show people it's a cause for celebration."

"Well, we're not getting married here. Find someplace else."

"No one will believe you'd want to get married in the church, Kasey."

The stall door bursts open. He storms out, rake in hand, looking surprisingly murderous. For a moment I catch a glimpse of a seventeen-year-old Kasey who's just found me skinny dipping in some rich kid's pool in the middle of a house party. "You know what this ranch means to me, Ava," he says, eyes wild. "It's the *only* reason I'm agreeing to any of this. But I draw the line at inviting a bunch of strangers here to sit and watch me make *you* my fake bride." His voice goes deathly quiet. "Especially not after everything you've already fucking put me through."

His eyes drop down the length of my body, like he's cataloguing the myriad of changes that serve as proof of my betrayal. Like he just might demand I reconcile all the new details he finds against the ones he knew so well before. And for the first time since marching into his bar with this harebrained scheme and a quiet, desperate need to see him, I realize how scared I am.

Scared of what he might find beneath the surface of my armor.

Scared of what I might find beneath his if I look hard enough.

I always knew coming home would lead to this: me, terrified, with an open, bleeding heart; and Kasey, wearing that guarded mask of indifference to protect himself. It's why I tried like hell to stay away, why it took me so long to come back. I knew when I left all those years ago I'd be walking away from him for good, that he'd never forgive me for breaking his heart. I knew if I ever *did* see him again, he'd keep me at an impossible distance, and I'd never have the emotional access to him like I once did. I knew I'd be losing him forever, and I still chose it.

I thought I was prepared to face it, but I don't think I am.

"Okay," I relent, taking a step back from him. The heel of my shoe clacks against the wooden floorboard, and for the third time today, his gaze drops to my feet.

He takes a deep breath in, squeezing his eyes shut. "Okay."

"We won't do it here," I continue, trying to maintain some semblance of control. Of peace between us. "I'm sure Pastor Brown would love to officiate for us in the church when we're ready."

"Right."

"I mean, we don't have much time, really. But once we get this train going down the tracks, the rest should start happening pretty quickly."

"Great."

"Yeah." I pull my bottom lip between my teeth, relishing the sting. "Should be."

He finally opens his eyes again. They're softer, gentler, like his surge of anger sputtered out somewhere in the space between us. But they still aren't warm like they used to be—they're distant. Tired. When they land on mine, my heart aches. "I told Rhett and Wells today," he says, crossing his arms over his chest. There's a smudge of dirt on his right sleeve, an old tear at the hem. "I told them marrying you is a temporary solution that will give us more time to figure out a permanent one. They're going to help . . . uh . . . spread the word about us. Layla and Olivia will let some things slip in town."

I blow out a breath. "That's a lot of people who know the truth."

"I trust my family with my life," he says. "They want to save this ranch just as much as I do."

There's a quiet force in the way he says it, enough to tell me this isn't something I should argue. As a lawyer, I hate the possibility of any risk . . . especially with something so personal. But the Bennetts are good people, and as someone who used to fantasize about *being* one of them, I know I need to have some faith. "Okay. Then I'll trust them too."

Surprise splashes over his face, and then he's clearing his throat, scratching at the side of his neck. "Look, Ava," he starts, and I brace myself. "I know I agreed to this, and while I'm not exactly thrilled about it, I'm also not going to change my mind. I'd just really like to make sure we don't hurt each other any more than we already have in the process. It's been a long time, since . . . *everything*, and I've long moved on."

"You never hurt me, Kasey," I breathe out. "Not once." His gaze slices to mine again, pinning me in place. "You didn't," I insist. "And I don't plan on hurting you again, either. I'm . . . I'm sorr—"

"You said you were going to tell me what you get out of this."

I cringe. "I was kind of hoping you'd forget about that."

"I don't forget anything." He studies me so hard my face flames.

I look around the barn, trying to come up with anything that might save me. "Got any plans tonight?"

His brow furrows. "Work at the bar, why?"

"Can one of your brothers cover you?"

He shrugs. "I guess so. Probably."

"Okay, let's kill two birds with one stone: take me out on a date in town where people can see, and I'll tell you why I'm here."

His face falls, and I pretend like it doesn't hurt. He scrubs a hand over his jaw. "Where?"

"I don't know. We could share a pizza and a couple of milkshakes? Just an hour, maybe two."

In high school, we spent countless nights at Mustang's Pizza. I'd sit cross-legged in a red vinyl booth while he folded our napkins into triangle footballs. It was one of very few places we ever spent time together in town. Usually we were too busy hiding from my dad or trying to take each other's clothes off.

"Okay," Kasey says. "I'll pick you up around six."

He turns back toward the stall he abandoned, all evidence of his fire gone. I look at the waves of his overgrown hair wisping out from beneath his hat, damp with sweat and sticking to the back of his neck. I think of how I used to run my hand through that very sweat-slicked hair while he moved inside me, hungry and urgent and not at all careful. And then a thought hits me.

"Wait," I say. He turns around to face me and I give him an apologetic smile. "What about . . . physical boundaries?"

His eyes sharpen, and he goes preternaturally still. "What do you mean?"

"Like, affection? In public? We need people to believe that . . . that we're in love, so we should probably talk about what's allowed."

He looks at me like I've asked him to set this barn on fire, and I'm not sure what's worse: that even the mention of touching me is sending him into a tailspin, or that my hands are shaking at the mere idea of it. "Let's"—he clears his throat—"uh . . . let's not push it. At least not yet." He clears his throat again, looking pained. "Maybe we could hold hands, but—"

"Right." I nod. "Okay. That works. See you at six."

"Yep," he says, turning away from me.

I march out of the barn and all the way back to my car. As soon as I'm inside, I lock the doors, bow my head, and force myself not to cry.

CHAPTER SIX

KASEY

It wasn't hard to convince Rhett to take my shift tonight, not after I told him why I needed the night off. I thought he might put up more of a fight, but it seems he's eager to see how all of this plays out. Probably just as eager to watch it blow up in my face, but I get it. Rhett and Brooks saw the worst of the fall out when Ava left. I'm sure I'd have similar feelings if our roles were reversed.

Wells already finished working the horses on the schedule for today, so after I wrap up all the barn chores I decide to use some of my spare time to visit Brooks. Now that this plan with Ava's in motion, I don't feel right moving forward without talking to him about it. He's just as affected by this bullshit with Uncle Huck, and even though it's not the most important thing going on in his life right now, he still should know I'm working on a solution.

I close up the second barn and trail the path that leads to his house. There's a small bike turned over in the front yard, a handful of plastic animal figurines scattered about. I pick up the bike and carry it to the porch, setting it on its wheels off to the side. There's broken pieces of chalk in front of the door, a wiggly drawing of a tree and a sun. I can hear the boys playing inside, and for a moment I stand still and listen to it, thanking the universe for their resilience.

A smile spreads across my face. Those kids are three of the bravest, strongest humans I know, the way they're still able to find reasons to play and laugh despite how hard things have been. I swear, we could learn so much from them.

When I finally knock, their little voices get louder, no doubt excited with having a visitor. It takes a couple minutes, but eventually Brooks opens the door, and I get a good look at my brother for the first time in weeks. His dark hair is disheveled, a beard growing across his face. He's got on a black tee and a pair of pajama pants that have seen better days. But all things considered, he doesn't look as bad as I expected.

"Brooks," I say, my throat thick. I reach out and step into him, wrapping my arms tight around his body. "How you doing, brother?"

Brooks returns the hug. "I'm hanging in there," he says.

I squeeze his shoulder as I pull away. "Is it okay if I come in for a sec? I have some things I want to talk to you about if you're up for it."

He nods, moving back to make space. The house is a disaster: toys are all over the floor, there's dirty dishes on the coffee table—including a cereal bowl with old milk that looks questionable as fuck—and at least half a dozen empty bottles of beer. Brooks starts picking things up. "Sorry it's such a mess."

"You have nothing to apologize for," I assure him, just as all three boys come barreling down the hall. Is it possible that Liam's grown two inches? "Hey, boys," I say, smiling. "Who wants to make twenty bucks?"

The two little ones jump up and down, but Liam's smart. "What do we have to do?" he asks, eyeing me.

I nod to the coffee table. "Dishes. And toys."

Liam considers. And then he looks at his younger brothers. "You guys put all the toys away, and then come meet me in the kitchen." Just like that, all three are in motion, working around the living room with focused expressions.

"I'll throw in another twenty if you guys get your rooms cleaned too. I can only imagine what they look like."

Liam nods. "Deal."

Brooks shakes his head, the ghost of a smile on his lips. "Shoulda known money would talk."

I laugh. "How about we head out back while these boys get busy?"

Brooks heads for the door and leads us out onto the back half of the wraparound porch, where more bikes and scooters lie in disarray. It looks like a tornado came through. "Guess I should bribe them to cover out here next," Brooks mutters.

"Nah," I say, sitting in one of two reclining patio chairs. "Let 'em be wild outside."

Brooks gruffs and sits down in the seat beside me. "So," he says. "What's going on?"

I look at him. "First, I want to see how you're doing. You need anything?"

He shakes his head. "Mom comes over nearly every day. Takes care of groceries and meals. We're doing all right."

"What about mentally?" I ask quietly. "Emotionally?"

"Some days are worse than others. But I think that's just life now."

I nod, blowing out a breath. "You know I'm here, right? Say the word, and I'll drop everything."

Brooks sighs. "I know, Kasey."

We let the words settle over us. Eventually, I say, "So, there's some shit going on with the ranch that I don't want you to worry about. All you need to know is I've got it handled."

Brooks turns toward me. "I know about the inheritance trust," he says. "Mom told me."

Relief spikes through me. I figured he knew about it already, but a part of me worried I'd have to be the one to tell him. That

I'd have to somehow explain how we might lose the ranch because he didn't file some stupid fucking paperwork while his wife was still alive. "I'm going to make sure Uncle Huck doesn't so much as step foot on this ranch."

"How?"

I scratch my jaw. "Ava's back."

This gets his attention. "I saw her at the bar after Melody's funeral. What does she have to do with anything?"

"She's a lawyer now," I explain. "And she's got a plan."

"What plan? A countersuit?"

I shake my head. "Better. She's going to torch Huck's plans to sue us in the first place. One of us needs to be married to gain control of the trust. So she's offered herself up."

"*Jesus*," Brooks chokes out, sputtering around a cough. "You dumbass motherfucker—you cannot just *marry* that girl, Kasey."

I shrug. "It's the only way. We get married, we get to transition ownership of the ranch."

"Yeah, okay, and then what?" He sounds pissed. *Good*, I think. Let him feel something other than his pain.

"And then we end the marriage and move on with our lives like it never happened."

"It's gotta be more than that," he argues. "Does she want ownership too? Her name on the deed? Or does she want money? Not sure if you've looked around lately, but we don't exactly have any. We just emptied the coffers burying my *actual* wife."

"Whoa, Brooks," I say, working to stay calm. "She doesn't want money. It's not like that. She doesn't want anything." But my stomach sours with guilt, because I still don't actually know why she's offered to do this, or what's in it for her. I guess I'll know after our date tonight . . . Maybe I should have waited to tell Brooks about it until I had all the facts.

Still, I can't imagine Ava actually trying to swindle us out of what's ours. She might have been cold-blooded with my heart, but she's a good person. "She's just here to help. It might . . . it might be a way for her to make amends, or something. I don't know. But I'm not going to let her fuck the family over. I promise."

Brooks looks out into the horizon, staying silent. "What about you?" he finally asks. "How are you going to make sure she doesn't fuck *you* over?"

"I'm not going to let that happen," I say, my tone making it clear that I've considered this from all angles. "This is just about paperwork, nothing else. It isn't . . . There're no feelings in it this time. We have to give the gossip mill just enough so people think it's all believable and Huck doesn't come after us for fraud, but we both know it isn't real."

He shoots me a long, hard look. "Sure, Kasey, you say that now. But I know you. I know how much you loved that girl. This sounds like nothing but a surefire way to get you all twisted up again."

"It's not," I say. "And fuck, even *if* I get hurt again, it's worth it to save this ranch." I point my thumb back toward the back door. "If I have to pretend to love my ex-girlfriend to make sure those boys in there get to inherit Bennett Rescue Ranch one day and continue our way of life, I'd do it in a heartbeat. I refuse to let some dickwad like Uncle Huck shove us out so he can build a fucking hundred-room hotel out in that pasture."

Brooks scoffs, shaking his head. "Jesus," he mumbles to himself.

The back door squeaks open, and Noah slinks outside. "Dad?" he asks, his voice a little shy. "I'm hungry."

Brooks looks at him, forcing a smile. "Okay, buddy, I'll be in in a minute."

"I got it," I say, standing. I turn to look at my brother. "I know what I'm doing," I promise.

"You shouldn't have to do this," Brooks says back.

"I know," I agree. "But there's a wolf at the gate, and someone's gotta take him down."

He doesn't respond, his eyes going withdrawn as he looks

back toward the distant tree line. I know he's carrying the weight of so much right now, and I don't want this threat to pile on. Brooks has always been firm and steady in the way he's led this ranch, but right now he's not in a position to take the reins.

I turn back to Noah. "Come on, kid," I say, grabbing his hand. "Let's go find something to eat."

Brooks stays outside while I prepare sandwiches and a pot of macaroni and cheese in the kitchen. Liam scrubs dishes at the sink while his younger brothers clean their shared room. I realize as I stir the yellow pasta that it doesn't actually sound like there's any cleaning being done—there's a loud thumping against the wall that doesn't sound too good.

"What the . . ." I mutter to myself, grabbing the kitchen towel to wipe my hands so I can go investigate.

"They're practicing roping," Liam says, focused on a particularly dirty plate.

"*Roping*?" I frown. "In the house?"

He hums. "They practice on stuffed animals."

I can't help but laugh. It sounds like something my brothers and I would have done as kids. "Is that allowed?" I ask.

Liam shrugs. "Mom wouldn't have let them, but . . . Dad doesn't say much about anything now."

"Right." I let out a long sigh, reaching to turn the sink faucet off. I wait for Liam to look at me, and when he does, I see the pain in his eyes. God, he looks so much like Melody. "Are you okay, kid?"

He looks down, old enough to have enough pride to want to hide his emotion. "I'm fine," he says.

"It's okay if you're not."

He looks through the window at the back of the house. "Is he ever gonna be as happy as he was?"

My heart throbs. "I don't know," I admit. "He loved your mom very much, and I think losing her is something that will change him forever." A deep chasm of sadness spreads on Liam's face, and I hate it. I hate what's happened to them all. "The pain will get easier though," I promise. "It will always be there, in his heart, and in yours. But it won't always feel this heavy and dark. Your mom wouldn't want you guys to hurt forever—she'd want you to remember her with happy feelings."

"I don't know if I can," he says, looking up at me. A tear spills out of his eye and down his cheek. He's quick to wipe it away.

"You will, Liam. It just takes time." I bend down to pull him in for a hug, feeling his heart beat through his shirt, and think what a miracle it is that he exists. That the love my brother shared with his wife led to three new pieces of our family that I can't imagine not having now. Pulling away, I grin at him. "Let's go tell your brothers to knock it off, yeah? Your mom wouldn't want those walls torn to shit."

Liam nods. "Yeah."

I GET TO AVA'S HOUSE FIVE MINUTES BEFORE SIX, frowning at the cruiser parked in the driveway. I leave the truck running and hop out, heading for the front door and trying not to notice all the ways this place looks exactly as it did when we were kids. How I used to help her sneak out at night to go fool around in the rec room at home, or in the back of an empty movie theater.

God, I was so crazy about her back then. Picking her up for a date like this feels like a slip back in time, into another life when there was still so much hope for a future together. I *cannot* let the allure of it get to me—we have a job to do, and that's it. Nothing more. I won't go down this road again.

I rap my knuckles against the cream-painted front door and wait. When it opens, it's not Ava on the other side. Sheriff Joe glowers at me, still in uniform, resting his hands against his utility belt. "Kasey Bennett," he booms nice and loud. He's always been a bit of a showman. "Is there something I can help you with?"

Once upon a time, this man sure scared the shit out of me—but I haven't been scared of him for a long, long time. "I'm here for Ava," I say calmly, giving him my best dose of eye contact.

He frowns. "What business do you have with Ava?"

"Dad!" I hear Ava shout from somewhere deeper into the house. "He's picking me up." The sheriff's frown drops lower just as Ava comes up behind him, squeezing past him through the open door. "Don't wait up," she says, not sparing him a glance.

Because she's smiling up at me.

Beaming, actually.

For a heartbeat, time stops. I think I might fall right into it—that smile. I forgot how much I love it, how hard I used to work for it. She tucks an arm beneath mine, wrapping a hand around my bicep, and presses up onto her toes to kiss me on the cheek. I close my eyes as her lips make contact with my skin, and I think I might pass out.

We definitely did *not* discuss kissing of any sort.

"Ready?" she asks. Her perfume wraps around me, vanilla and something sweet. Sugar cookies, maybe. Or frosting. She's wearing heels again, but at least she smells like the Ava I know. That's a win, right?

Wait, no. *Wrong*.

There's no winning here, and I don't care what she smells like. I don't care that she's wearing expensive-looking heels or a black dress that was made for a woman and not a girl. I don't care that her hand is sliding down my arm, aimed for my hand, because it's not real. She might be Ava, but she's not *my* Ava.

I frown. Dammit, I don't know why I let this shit get under my skin. She's had an entire life out there in the world, and I just keep expecting her to be the same girl who left. I shouldn't even want that—she left to become someone different. And it's not fair to either of us that I'm so stuck in the past.

"You okay?" she asks, her blue eyes reflecting traces of orange from the setting sun. I realize we're still on her porch, and I'm just . . . *staring* at her.

My eyes flick to her father before moving back to her. I force a smile, even a chuckle. "Of course," I say. "Just happy to see you." The words feel like a knife in the chest. I see the way it stabs her too, the lie in them. Her bright eyes go distant, but her smile stays put.

"We should go," she says, tugging me toward my truck.

"Ava, what in the world are you doing?" Sheriff Joe chides from the doorway, still glowering.

She finally turns to look at him. "Going out."

I toss him another glance and feel the weight of his disapproval. "I'll take good care of her, sir," I say, shooting him a wink.

The door slams shut before we reach the truck, and Ava's soft laugh spills between us. "Some things don't change," she teases.

I look down at her face, trace the curve of her nose in the golden glow of the sky. "Guess not," I say back.

CHAPTER SEVEN

AVA

The drive into town is quiet and a little awkward. I've spent the last few hours readying myself for this date, to sit across a booth from Kasey and force a happy conversation that's *just* flirty enough to feed any onlookers. But what I didn't prepare for was sitting shotgun in this truck, for the visceral memories that have been firing off since the moment he opened the door for me and I was hit with the old familiar smell of the inside.

God, this truck has seen some things . . . Like Kasey crouched on the floorboard of the passenger seat, the skirt of my dress pushed up around my waist as his tongue made me see stars. Or the time we camped out on the beach of Scorpion Bay, a mess of blankets and pillows crafted in the bed. It'd been so cold that night, but he'd kept me warm with a bottle of wine stolen from the bar and his arms wrapped tight around me.

I've spent such a long time shoving memories of our relationship away that it's a bit overwhelming to be battered by them all now, especially while buckled into this torn seat. "Still driving this old thing, huh?" I ask as we slow down at a stop sign.

"Yep," he says, his gaze focused on the road. He's got one

hand wrapped around the top of the steering wheel and the other on his knee, his pointer finger rubbing absentmindedly against the seam of his Wranglers. That's all I get from him until we're parked in the lot in front of Mustang's Pizza, when he turns off the ignition and peers into the restaurant through the dusty windshield. "Looks busy," he says.

Indeed, it does. Nearly every table is occupied, mostly with teenagers. I wonder if there's a new version of us curled around each other in a booth somewhere in the back. "Looks the same."

"Mhm."

"Well, busy is good. If we're going to do this we might as well make an impression." I don't mean for the words to sound so clinical. But then again, I guess that's how they're supposed to sound.

"All right," he says. His chest fills and expands with a deep breath before he lets it out with a sigh. "Hang tight." He doesn't look at me, and my stomach knots.

I watch him push out through his door and round the truck to mine, opening it with a wide smile plastered to his face, the expression utterly ridiculous. To anyone who might be looking, they'd think he was happy as a clam. But I can clearly see the lack of light in his eyes, the wariness in the pinch of his jaw. At least his eyes are on me. We just have to make it through a couple hours of pretending.

When he holds a hand out, I smile back. "Thank you," I say, letting him support my weight as I work to step down in my heels. The dress I'm wearing is tighter around my thighs than the ones I used to covet, so it makes getting out of his truck much more difficult.

People are staring before we even make it to the door, heads turning all throughout the restaurant to catch a glimpse at us through the window. Most of the teenagers look away again without much thought, likely not knowing or caring who we are.

But there are a handful of older folks who know plenty, and their stares linger.

Inside, a young hostess directs us to a two-person table against the wall, and Kasey pulls my chair out before I sit down in it. The chair shifts beneath my weight, rocking on a loose leg—everything in here looks as though it were preserved in a time capsule, and none of the furniture has been replaced.

"Careful," Kasey warns, moving to sit in his own seat.

"I'm sure falling on my ass would make your whole night," I say in jest, picking up the large plastic menu.

"No, it wouldn't," he grumbles, looking at his own menu. "What kind of pizza do you want?"

My stomach rumbles on the spot. I haven't eaten anything since a piece of toast this morning and have been fighting back nausea for the last hour. "Something with a lot of meat," I say back, finding the list of options. "Pepperoni, sausage . . . oh, maybe jalapeños and mushrooms too?"

Kasey's brows pinch. "You hate mushrooms."

"Not anymore," I say.

I sense his attention, but I keep my focus on the menu.

When our server comes by to take our order, Kasey asks for a large pepperoni and sausage pizza with jalapeños and mushrooms, and two Cherry Cokes. My heart squeezes that he remembered my favorite soda—I haven't had one in years. Tobias kept our fridge stocked with nothing but bottles of water and two-liters of tonic for his nightly serving of gin.

"Do you still come here often?" I ask Kasey as the server—a boy who looks not one day older than sixteen—walks away with our menus.

He shakes his head. "Hardly ever. I don't spend a lot of time in town anymore. Just the feed store now and then."

"Too busy working?"

He shrugs. "That," he says. "And also, if I want to blow off some steam, I don't want to do it here."

I smile. "How does Kasey Bennett blow off steam these days?"

He gives me a knowing look.

I laugh. "Do any of them ever stick around?"

"Who?"

"The girls you sleep with," I say in a whisper.

He clicks his tongue. "Ava, I'm not answering that. That's not even what I meant."

I laugh again. "Yeah right."

The server comes back with our drinks and drops two straws in the middle of the table. Kasey picks them both up, ripping the paper from everything but the tip, and dunks one in each of our glasses. "We're supposed to be focusing on you tonight," he says blandly, looking around to make sure no one's listening. "You owe me some *specifics*."

I internally groan, dreading this conversation. Not because I'm scared of the truth, but because of how it might change the way Kasey looks at me. I know it shouldn't matter, but . . . it does. He knew a version of me that was so confident, so headstrong. I guess maybe I'm a little ashamed of how far I've drifted away from that girl.

"There's a guy . . ." I say, looking at the wall instead of at him.

Kasey snorts.

I crumple my napkin and throw it at him. "Don't be a dick."

"Let me guess," he says, eyes sparking with challenge. He smiles like he's teasing, but I think it's just for show because he's got that look he used to get when he was frustrated. Sharp gaze, tense jaw. Even his fingers curl halfway to a fist before he releases them again. "You thought you'd mess around with someone who had something you wanted: power, money, maybe a slick new Jaguar—"

"I drive a Range Rover," I interrupt. "Jaguars are ugly."

"—and you thought you could keep control of the relationship, thought you could get what you wanted and get out before things got messy." He lowers his voice as someone walks by our table, headed for the bathroom. "But then you realized you were right smack dab in the middle of a mess you helped make." His grin is lethal. "Am I close?"

I want to smack him, but his read on the situation is annoyingly spot-on. "Guess some things don't change, huh?" I quip as I try to shove away my shame. "I was always pretty shit at dating."

"You weren't shit at dating, Ava. You just liked to play games. Liked to win. But you also had a habit of picking assholes who knew how to outplay you."

"*You* weren't an asshole."

"We weren't a game," he counters roughly.

The words clang like a falling hammer. I pull my soda closer and rip the paper hat off my straw, sucking down a long sip. "Anyway," I say. "Tobias works at the same firm as me. I was in consideration to make partner for months, and I *thought* he was going to be supportive about it. I worked my ass off to prove myself to the other partners." I think that's what hurts the most, how close I got to finally being recognized for my ability. To *earn* something for myself. "Turns out he went behind my back and called a meeting with them to downplay my impact. He convinced them he was better suited for the opportunity, that they needed another *strong man* at the helm.

"And then, when he got it, he tried to gaslight me into believing he was better than me. Tried to convince me I never had what it took. I knew it was bullshit, but what could I do? He'd already won. So I ended things. Packed up my shit from our apartment and left. I crashed with a friend and did my best to ignore him, but . . ." I trail off, trying to find the right words.

Kasey's gaze is sharp enough to cut glass. "What happened, Ava?"

I know I should tell him everything—I need to give him the whole truth. But I can't do it . . . not yet.

"He just . . . he wouldn't leave me alone. He kept showing up, kept trying to talk me into getting back together. It became too much. He showed up at my friend's house one morning and caused a scene in the front yard. I tried talking to one of the partners about his behavior and was essentially told that's what happens when you sleep with coworkers. So I decided to cut my losses and leave."

"This guy was actively harassing you and they didn't do anything about it?"

I shrug. "He's one of them now, right? Having to formally discipline your newest partner wouldn't look good for the firm. It's easier to blame me."

Kasey's jaw tics.

The server comes by holding a large pizza pan with a towel. He smiles as he sets it down on the stand in the middle of the table. "Peppers or cheese?" he asks.

"No thank you," Kasey clips, eyes still fastened to me.

The server's smile slips before he scampers off.

"What does any of that have to do with this?" he asks.

"This?"

"Us."

"Oh." My stomach rumbles at the delicious smell of the pizza, so I start divvying out pieces onto two plates. "He's proven to be persistent," I explain. "He's still trying to get a hold of me. I mean . . . I obviously didn't come back knowing anything about your uncle or your ranch. I only thought of this . . . *marriage* when I realized you guys were dealing with that. But Tobias knows where I'm from—I've talked about Saddlebrook Falls. If he happens to come sniffing around looking for me, it wouldn't hurt for him to find proof that I've moved on." I put a plate with two slices of pizza in front of Kasey. He just keeps looking at me, mouth tight. It's a little unnerving—

"Did he ever physically hurt you, Ava?" He sounds way too calm, considering what he's asking.

"No," I reply quickly, focused on carefully floating a large slice of pizza to my plate. It's not a lie, but I don't have the heart to look at him. I don't want him to see all the things I'm not saying. "Nothing like that."

He exhales through his nose, finally looking away.

"Kasey Bennett!" a man shouts. Kasey turns around in his seat. I look over his shoulder to see Gus Romano marching toward us from the kitchen, a lopsided smile plastered to his face. "Well, I'll be—it is you!"

"Yes, sir," Kasey says, standing to shake the man's hand, his blue jeans stretching around muscled thighs. He towers over him by at least a foot. "Nice to see you again, Gus."

"Been way too long, kid—*way* too long." Gus pushes his glasses up his nose and looks at me. "And Ava! What a blast from the past seeing you two here together. I didn't know you were home, sweetheart."

I find it hard to believe he hasn't heard I'm back in town by now, sure he's just being polite, but his delight seems genuine. I return his smile with my own. "Been back for a couple weeks," I confirm.

"Gosh, it's been years, hasn't it?"

I nod. "Almost ten."

His eyes widen. "Get out! Ten whole years?" He looks to Kasey and then back to me. "Well, it sure is good to have you back. Are you staying for a while?"

"That's the plan," I say, feeling Kasey's gaze shift my way. I look over at him, letting a secret smile play on my lips. "Finding it hard to stay away, you know?"

Kasey shoots me a strange look, but then Gus turns to him again and his face wipes clean. "Yeah, uh," he stumbles, "it's been . . . great . . . having her back." His mouth tips up into a sad attempt at a smile, but it looks so painful and forced I almost laugh. He's *so* not good at this. Like, really bad, actually.

"I bet," Gus says, nodding. "Well, look, you've made my night coming in here. Can I get ya a couple milkshakes or a slice of cake? On the house of course!"

"You don't have to do that, sir, really," Kasey says.

Gus sighs. "You're a man now, Kasey, no need to call me sir. And I insist, please. Let me treat you."

Kasey looks at me, brows raised.

"Milkshakes, please," I say. "Vanilla."

"Extra cherries," Kasey adds. It surprises me that he remembers. *Again*.

Gus smiles wide, slapping Kasey on the shoulder. "Nothing's changed with you two, has it?"

Kasey flushes instantly.

"Guess not," I tease.

"I'll have Derek bring those right out. Please, stay as long as you'd like and let me know if you need anything else, okay? And don't be strangers!"

"Thank you, Gus," Kasey says, sinking down into his seat again.

Gus moseys back to the kitchen. I lift my slice of pizza, hovering it in front of my mouth. "Well, your acting could use some work, but all things considered I think I'd call that a win." I take way too big of a bite and nearly moan with pleasure, closing my eyes as I savor all the rich flavors. The pizza is *damn* good.

When I open my eyes again, Kasey is studying my mouth. He catches me staring and clears his throat. "My acting was fine," he grumbles.

I laugh, taking another bite. He shakes his head and picks up his own slice, eyes tracing over the meat and vegetables before he digs in too. "Good, huh?" I ask.

He nods. "It's good."

A comfortable silence settles between us. I inhale my first slice and far too quickly serve myself a second, eager to put as much food in my belly as I can manage. Halfway through my third piece, I realize Kasey's still watching me.

"What?" I ask, narrowing my eyes on him.

A small smile touches his lips, so tiny I almost don't catch it. "I always liked watching you eat," he says quietly.

"Why?"

He shrugs. "Your whole face changes."

I stare at him. "It does not."

A low laugh spills out of his mouth, and my focus homes in on the sound. "It does," he says. "When you enjoy something—or when you don't—it's written all over your face. It's one of . . . uh . . ." He scratches the back of his head, eyes dipping down to his lap as he hesitates.

"What?" I press.

He looks at me again. "It's one of the few real glimpses I think I ever actually had at your feelings."

The words squeeze uncomfortably, like a vise around my ribs. Kasey was one of very few people in the world I trusted with my feelings. Doesn't he remember? "Kasey—"

"Two vanilla milkshakes," our server announces, eyeing Kasey warily as he sets down a pair of frozen glasses. They're filled to the brim with the frothy dessert, mounds of whipped cream sitting atop each one, covered in rainbow sprinkles and at least half a dozen maraschino cherries.

"Thank you," I tell him before he disappears again.

Kasey pushes one of the milkshakes my way before pulling the other toward him. I find the straw with my lips and take a deep gulp. "We should probably discuss plans for a . . . wedding," he says, frowning.

I laugh, pointing at his face. "Every girl's dream is to see *that* expression when discussing her dream wedding."

He snorts. "Ava, come on. *Dream* wedding?"

My shoulders rise to my ears as I suck down more of my shake. It's . . . delicious. A perfectly sweet pairing to the savory pizza. "We might as well have fun with it."

"I don't find any of this fun," he mutters.

I roll my eyes. "Fine, you grump. We'll go see Pastor Brown and find out what we need to do to get married in the church. And for a reception . . ." I trail off, thinking. "Maybe we can host it at Wild Coyote?"

"Fine," he concedes. "Nothing fancy though. Just the bar and what comes with it."

"Fine," I agree. "Basically the dream, anyway."

He cocks a brow. "A dive bar with sticky floors and mean-as-hell regulars?"

"Literally what I have written in a diary somewhere."

"Liar," he says around a gulp of his milkshake.

"You don't know!"

Dark brown eyes trace over my face. I watch his throat work to swallow down the sip he just took. "You wanted a party on the beach."

I blink as the memory snares me: whispering that exact wish to him as we lay curled around each other in the bed of his parked truck, gazing out into the dark ocean blanketed by stars. I remember thinking marrying him was everything I'd ever want, not knowing how painfully fear would crack through me when it all became real.

I don't like this feeling, that he still knows me so well.

"Maybe in another life" is all I can say now. I don't look at him, keeping my eyes trained on a black-and-white team photo of the Mustangs football team from decades ago hanging on the far wall.

"Hm," he hums. We finish the rest of our slices in silence, and Kasey waves down the nervous server to ask for a to-go box for the rest of the pizza, offering the box to me once it's packed.

"You keep it," I say. "Take it to your nephews."

He pulls it back. "Sure."

Gus Romano appears again, having just dropped plates off at another table. "You kids all set?" he asks.

Kasey smiles up at him, lines around his eyes etching into sun-kissed skin. "Yes, sir. The food was as good as ever. Thank you for the milkshakes."

"Any time." He waves a hand. "Hope to see you back here soon."

We both nod and watch Gus disappear into the kitchen again.

I reach a hand across the table, wrapping my fingers around Kasey's. He goes still, eyes snagging on mine.

I feel it like a current.

"Thanks for a sweet date night," I say.

His smile fades. "Let's go."

CHAPTER EIGHT

KASEY

Pastor Brown blinks at us, utterly unconvinced. Leaning forward to rest his elbows on his wide mahogany desk, he steeples his fingers together in front of the thin line of his mouth. "Two weeks?" he asks, eyes bouncing from me to Ava.

Ava nods, a smile radiating from her lips. Her teeth are stark white against the dark pink lipstick she's wearing today, and I wonder if he finds it as distracting as I do. "Yes, sir," she says, full of confidence. "I've been back in Saddlebrook Falls for just a couple weeks." I always admired that about her, the way she could convince anyone of just about anything when she had her mind set to it. It's also one of the things that drove me out of *my* mind. She's stubborn, and she knows how to get what she wants. I bet it serves her well as a lawyer.

I bet she still brings men to their knees.

It was her idea to come to a church service together today. I guess she thought if we played our cards right, we could convince the man at the helm of this congregation to marry us. I've only stepped foot in this building a handful of times, but the pastor knows me; my family's reputation is probably enough to give him pause. It's going to take more convincing than Ava thought.

"But, if you remember," she continues, "our relationship really began ten years ago."

"Ah, yes." The pastor nods. "I certainly remember. Your father was quite concerned about your . . . *infatuation* with each other."

"Not an infatuation." Ava smiles. "We were in love." She turns to me, her sapphire eyes shining beneath the pendant light that hangs from the ceiling above us. The corner of her mouth rises higher, and my stomach swoops. She looks back toward the pastor, tucking a rogue piece of dark hair behind her ear with painted nails. "And we've realized our love never went anywhere. It's endured, even after all this time, *despite* the opinions of my father."

Pastor Brown clears his throat. "Is he aware of your plans to wed?"

Ava shakes her head. "We'll make a formal announcement once we confirm a date—we'll invite the whole town! Do you have any availability this month? I think March is a perfect time of year for our anniversary—"

"Don't you think your father should know this is happening?" Pastor Brown interjects, his eyes slightly narrowed as they flick to me. "Wouldn't it be tradition to ask for his blessing?"

Ava maintains her composure, but I can see the way she stiffens, the way her hand twitches in her lap like she has to fight the urge to clench it into a fist. "With all due respect, Pastor Brown, I don't think it's necessary to provide you with a signed permission slip. I'm nearly thirty years old and perfectly capable of understanding when and to whom I'd like to marry."

The words send my heart into a tailspin as the echoes of a teenage Ava rattle through me. She was never one to back down from a fight, especially when it came to her own agency. Ten years ago, I would have burned the world down for her, would have probably thrown some choice words at this old pastor in her defense. But we aren't those kids anymore. Plus, it would likely only piss her off.

She doesn't need my help.

"That may be so, but marriage is a sacred covenant, and I don't make a habit of marrying anyone unless I wholeheartedly believe in the sturdiness of their union."

"So what are you saying?" I chime in. Both of them look at me. "You won't marry us?" The skin around my hands feels tight, fingers fidgeting in my lap.

Pastor Brown considers my question for a long moment. "Pre-marital counseling," he finally announces. "Two sessions. The first will cover logistics, and the second is all about heart. I require it of all couples. Convince me that this isn't a flame set to kerosene, that your love won't eventually burn out, and I'll marry you."

"When do we start?" Ava asks, undeterred.

The pastor shuffles around some paperwork on his desk to uncover a leather notebook. He opens it, revealing pages of a calendar with handwritten notes throughout. "The church is rather busy these next few weeks, but it looks like I have a morning open, ten days from now, that would be an ideal timeslot for a ceremony should we decide to proceed. It means our sessions would need to happen soon." He flips another page, peering through square-framed glasses. "I can take an appointment for our first session on Wednesday. Say, noon?"

"I've got the ranch—"

"We'll take it," Ava rushes out. She glances my way, shooting me an expectant look.

I sigh. "Works for me."

"Good." The pastor nods, shutting his notebook with a thud and setting it down on the desk. "I look forward to seeing you both back here." He gives us a final look before rising to his feet, a clear dismissal.

I stand. "Thank you, sir," I say, reaching for his hand. He's hesitant, but takes it. His skin is rough and dry, and I realize how clammy mine is in comparison.

"I want to be clear," he says, "that the successful completion of these counseling sessions does not signify a guarantee of my participation in officiating anything. You can of course choose to marry in any venue with any officiant that so pleases you, but in this church, I take the sanctity of a union like this very seriously."

"We understand," I concede.

"Trust me," Ava chimes in, wrapping her arms around me. "A few hours with us and you'll understand how deep and sacred our love is."

"I certainly hope so." Pastor Brown stuffs his hands into his pockets. He nods toward the closed door of his office. "I'll see you Wednesday."

"THAT WASN'T SO BAD," AVA REMARKS AS WE WALK through the church's double-doors and out into the piercing sunlight. I have to squint my eyes to keep them from watering.

"I don't know if this is gonna work."

She sighs. "I mean, I get that he's not falling over himself to marry us, but he didn't shut us down either. We can get through two more meetings."

I can't help but snort. "*Counseling* sessions, Ava," I say. "I don't even know how to wrap my mind around that."

"Don't worry," she assures me. "We just have to play our parts. It's easier, I think, than if this was actually real."

I look at her. "What do you mean?"

She shrugs. "It's not like we're placing much stock in his judgement. What if we really loved each other and he decided it wasn't good enough? I mean, to hell with him, honestly. But it's not like we're going to get our feelings hurt. We know how to win this. It's you and me."

I swallow, focusing back on my truck across the lot. "If you say so."

I open the car door for her, watching as she folds herself into the passenger seat. She's wearing a dress again. This one's lavender and much more like the ones she used to wear. I'm sure it was a strategic choice for church, but it claws at me all the same.

It's you and me.

I shut the door a little too hard, shooting her an apologetic smile through the window before heading toward the back of my truck. I steal a quick glance at the shape of her head through the window before bending down, pretending to inspect the hitch while I take a few deep breaths. This shit is only just beginning and I already feel like it's too much—being in that church with her, talking about marriage. I mean, hell, her father's the goddamn sheriff. What happens if he learns about that night at Rustler's Ranch, about the lives lost in that barn? This is all *way* too close for comfort.

The blood of those dead cops might not be on my hands, but my hands are bloody all the same. And at this point I'm complicit in a cover-up. Marrying Ava might be the only path I have to protect the ranch, but the risk is greater than she realizes. Whether I like it or not, her father is going to soon learn about our plans. He's going to push back against it, might even try digging for skeletons.

If they come after me, will they come after her now too?

"Everything okay?" I hear her ask from the front of the truck. I stand, finding that she's cracked her door open to peer at me.

"Yep," I answer, rolling my still-sore shoulder before heading for the driver's side. She shuts her door again as I open mine. "Sorry, I thought I saw something."

"No problem," she says, unzipping her purse. She pulls down

the visor and looks at herself through the small mirror, swiping that dark-tinted lip shit across her bottom lip. Is it lipstick or lip gloss? Fuck if I know.

I force myself to look away, to start the engine and release the parking brake. "I gotta get back to the ranch," I say, eager to move on with my day. "Where should I take you? Home?"

"I'll go with you."

Shifting the truck into reverse, I grip the back of her headrest to twist and look out the rear window, slowly pulling out of the parking space. "Why would you do that?" I'm almost hesitant to ask.

"I don't have anything else to do today. I can help."

I look at her before shifting into drive. "Help?"

"Yeah. With the horses? Or . . . whatever you need help with."

"I don't need help."

"Oh, come on, Kasey. You're going to have to get used to me being around. Might as well get started."

My chest deflates. "Right."

I keep my eyes trained on the road as we meander through town. Silence settles between us, and I don't like it. It's not the comfortable silence we used to share in this truck, when I had one hand wrapped around her knee while she gazed out her open window. Now it feels like an unwanted third party.

She must feel it too, because soon she's flipping on the old radio, twisting the knob through the stations until she finds a song she knows. It's fast-paced and belty, some pop song I've never heard before. She turns the volume up, singing along and nodding her head in tandem with the beat.

God, she always had terrible taste in music. Guess that's something that hasn't changed.

Fifteen minutes later, I pull up the narrow dirt road that leads to my cabin. I don't know what Ava's plans are, but I meant it when I said I didn't need her help, and I'm not sure I have the heart to stick around and make her comfortable. She's a big girl, and she asked for this. Plus, maybe she's right—she's going to be staying here soon, so I might as well get used to it.

I park, and we both jump out of the truck. She trails behind me up the handful of steps to the front porch and through the door. "There's stuff for sandwiches in the fridge if you're hungry, and I think there's still a couple of beers. Remote for the TV is on the coffee table." I don't look at her as I set my hat crown down on the kitchen table before heading to my room to change.

"I'm not hungry," she says. I head for my dresser, yanking a fresh T-shirt out of the middle drawer before working to unbutton the dress shirt I put on this morning for church. As soon as I get it off, I let it drop to the floor. "I said I wanted to help."

I turn to find her watching me through the open door to my bedroom, her eyes roaming across my chest. It sends a lick of heat down my spine. "Do you mind?"

Her cheeks pink, and she turns around. "Didn't realize you'd become such a prude."

"I'm not a prude," I grumble, pulling the tee over my head before marching back out into the living room. She's hung her purse on the hook by the door and holds my hat in her hands.

"Let me help," she whines. "I could use an afternoon with horses."

I look pointedly at her dress and her little sparkly sandals as I snatch my hat back. "You're not dressed for ranch work, Ava."

"How about I decide what I'm comfortable working in, *Kasey*."

I shake my head. "Fuck. Stubborn as hell."

She has the audacity to laugh. "Surprised you expected anything different. Let's go, cowboy."

I watch her head toward the door, a hot dose of irritation flooding through my skin. This isn't helping . . . being near her like this. Her smell is all around me and her eyes seem to have become a brighter blue in the last ten years—is that even possible?

And, shit, her *hair*. The way it blows in the breeze, kicking up along her elbows and shoulders. I can't stand it.

I need to figure out how to stay unaffected, how to numb myself to her. As much as I hate to admit it, maybe her sticking around will help—exposure therapy, like when we introduce a new horse to the rest of the herd in the pasture. It takes some time, but usually everyone figures out how to exist together in harmony.

Harmony might be a stretch, but . . .

"You coming?" she calls from the porch. I didn't even realize she'd made it out the door.

I let out a resigned sigh. "Yeah."

Jumping back in the truck, we make the short drive to the main house and my stomach rolls with the thought of my family seeing Ava with me. My brothers know what's going on, but I haven't broached the subject with my mom. Although, knowing Brooks, he probably already told her. I doubt she's happy about it. I bet my dad is losing his mind at the thought of me making the sheriff's daughter a Bennett, but it's not like he'll leave the house to come tell me to my face.

I park in front of the house and cut the ignition, pushing out the door. Ava follows suit, scrambling to keep up with me as I move swiftly toward the main barn. I'll feel better when we aren't in view of the windows, which is ironic considering I'm a full-grown man and should have zero qualms about my parents seeing me with a girl.

We round the house toward the barn and find Wells on a horse in the corral. Layla is perched up on top of the fence, her legs dangling beneath her, a pair of flower-embroidered boots on her feet. A design of Melody's, if I were to guess. She turns to look at us, eyes widening when she notices Ava. "Hey!" she calls out over the distance, waving a hand in the air.

This gets Wells's attention. He turns in the saddle to find us, scratching a knuckle over his brow. There's a streak of dirt smeared across the front of his shirt, like he's been rolling on the ground. "Where do you need me?" I ask him.

"Rhett's finishing up in the barn," he says back. "Check the board—we need to pull three or four more horses out today before we're done."

"Pull them out for what?" Ava asks next to me.

"Training," I say, beelining it for the office. She stays hot on my heels, looking at the piles of old furniture and gear once we get inside.

"Was this here before?" she asks.

"Yep."

"Huh. I don't remember it."

I look at her through slitted eyes. "You were never here to work. You came here to . . ." The words trail off as my neck heats.

She smiles. "I *definitely* remember the rec room."

I'm not sure how to respond. Refocusing on the whiteboard, I see Biscuit, Knight, and Oreo are all scheduled for training today and haven't been marked as being pulled yet. Wells and I should be able to finish up in the next hour or two.

"What does all this mean?" Ava asks, scanning the board with names of horses listed in different colors.

"It's how we keep track of who needs what," I tell her. "Names in red are horses with specific medical needs. Blue means they're new. This," I say and point to the list of days beside each name, "shows when we need to pull them for training."

"What does training entail?"

I shrug. "Basics. Getting them used to being saddled if they aren't already. Making sure they're good with a rider. Some of them will go off for more advanced training to work with kids or veterans, so it's our job to make sure they're capable."

"Wow," Ava breathes out. "Impressive."

I turn to look at her again. "We love what we do. It's hard work, and there always seems to be something going wrong. But this is my family's livelihood."

Her eyes soften. "We're not going to let him take it, Kasey."

I shouldn't be surprised that she knew where my thoughts were taking me. If Uncle Huck takes control of this place, there's no telling all the ways he'd dismantle our mission to save horses, to give them purpose. Breathing in deep, I let out a loud exhale. "Yeah, well. Better get to it."

CHAPTER NINE

AVA

"Oh my god, I love this song," Layla squeals across the table, spinning in her stool to see who requested Trisha Yearwood's "She's in Love With the Boy" at the jukebox on the other side of the bar. Wells meets her gaze where he stands next to it, smirking, holding a hand out to show her a small pile of quarters in his palm. He shoots her a wink.

"Gross," I whine.

Layla laughs, blowing him a kiss. "He's pretty great."

"Exactly my point."

Layla turns back to me, eyes flashing, her dark curls framing her pretty face. "Don't tell me you're one of *those* types," she says, still grinning.

"What types?"

"You know . . . the 'good guys are so boring' and 'I love toxic bad boys' type."

Holding a hand over my heart, I let out a teasing scoff. "You've only known me for like, five minutes, and you're accusing me of being attracted to toxic men?"

She shrugs. "I've known *of* you since middle school. When

you skipped town, everyone lost their shit. I remember Maeve working herself into a tizzy trying to figure out where you went."

I can't help but grimace. "Perks of small-town living, huh? Everyone thinks your business is their business."

Her eyes roll. "Girl, I know all about it."

"Oh yeah?"

"Yeah." She tilts her head. "Do you know how Wells and I got together?"

I shake my head. "No clue. Why?"

Her eyes widen, like this truly surprises her. "I mean, I guess that makes sense. You haven't been here." She leans in closer. "I planned on marrying his best friend."

"No way!" Layla might wear shit kickers around the ranch, but she's got the poise of a prim and proper southern lady. I'd never expect a scandal like that involving her.

Her face grows solemn. "And then he died."

"Oh fuck," I say. "What happened?"

"Car accident. He'd been drinking."

"Shit. I'm so sorry."

"Thanks. But there's more." Layla pauses and gives an exasperated *Where do I even start* sigh. "The Bennetts threw his celebration of life here at the bar, and his *other* girlfriend showed up."

"Oh *hell* no!" I screech. Saddlebrook Falls certainly has its share of drama, but I've never heard of anything like this.

"It was fucking horrible," she mutters, sighing. "But, Wells helped me through it. And we realized there were feelings there between us. Well, *I* realized there were feelings."

Something small cracks open in my chest. "He already knew?"

She smiles. "He had them the whole time. Kept it to himself because of his loyalty to Jason."

"Damn." I look at Wells again. He's behind the bar now, a white towel slung casually over his shoulder, laughing at something Kasey says.

I look at Kasey too.

His mouth is turned up in a comfortable smile, the shape of his eyes tilted in humor. His lips are parted, jaw relaxed, shoulders confident as they stretch the chest of his half-buttoned Henley. It's nothing at all like the way he spent the day, wound so tight I thought he might snap. It was obvious he didn't want me to be on the ranch, and if I'm being honest, I'm not sure why I pressed it, like a thumb in a sore bruise.

Maybe I'm holding on to some shred of hope that if I stick it out, he'll pull off some of that armor and we can find each other again, at least in friendship. We're going to be spending the next few months together; we might as well find a way to enjoy it. But I saw the way he frowned when I kicked off my sandals in the barn, moving around the cement floor barefoot as I helped him tack up two of the horses. And I saw the way he threw a look toward Rhett, as if to say *Don't you dare fucking ask* when he thought I wasn't looking. Like he might be embarrassed by all of this, having to entertain his ex-girlfriend in an uncomfortable and very fake marriage just to keep the vultures away from his family.

He was quiet and broody, pinched with discomfort. And still, I wouldn't leave.

"Aren't you ever worried that he'll end things?" I ask Layla, eyes bouncing back to Wells. "That he'll break your heart?"

She looks mildly surprised by the question. "No. Not at all."

"How?" I ask, a smidge incredulous. "How can you be so sure?"

She considers. "If I've learned anything it's that nothing's guaranteed, so why spend life anticipating the worst things that *could* happen? Wells could wake up at any moment and realize he doesn't love me anymore, and it would break me, for sure. But waiting for it every day could very well be worse than it actually happening. I need to hold on to the joy and love and hope of it all, for my own sanity. You know?"

"I'm familiar with that kind of anticipation," I admit. Hell, it's why I left. I couldn't bear the thought of either of us wanting an out one day, so I got ahead of it. Ripped off the Band-Aid. There've been plenty of days that I regretted it, but also plenty where I've felt justified. The way we burned . . . it was too hot, too explosive to be healthy.

"Hey, girls!"

Layla and I turn our attention to the freckled girl heading right for us, her strawberry-blonde hair brushing against the tops of her shoulders. "Hey, Liv!" Layla says, pulling out a stool beside her.

The girl sinks down into it, her patchwork quilt purse sliding off her as she smiles at me. "You must be Ava," she says, tucking her hair behind her ear before holding her hand out to me. "I'm Olivia."

"I remember you," I say. I'd been at the bakery next to her mom's café enough growing up. "You're Rhett's girl, now?"

She beams. "Yeah. Still feels a little weird to say."

"More like he's *her* man," Layla says with a burst of laughter. "I'm not sure I've ever seen a guy so whipped."

Olivia grins. "He's still making up for . . . well, you know."

"Ah," Layla says, nodding. She turns to me. "So . . . tell us all about it. I want to know every detail."

"About what?"

She laughs, not unkindly. "You and Kasey! What was he like as a teenager? I was too young to know much of anything back then."

"Me too," Olivia says.

Wells materializes out of thin air, dropping three cold bottles of beer on the table. "You ladies need anything else?"

"Oh," I say, eyeing the beer. "Uh, I'm actually okay—gotta drive later."

"Okay," he says. "Sure." He picks up the bottle closest to me and takes a long swig before kissing Layla on the cheek and disappearing again.

"Damn, he's whipped too," I jest, watching him stride back to the narrow alley behind the bar. "Anyway, Kasey was . . . *good*," I say. "He had a real good heart and was very protective of me. I was a stick of dynamite, blowing up his life."

"What do you mean?" Olivia asks.

I sigh. "I just always felt like I was ruining him. I was never good at following rules and he'd end up in the middle of all my messes."

"It couldn't have been easy, you being the sheriff's daughter," Layla points out.

"Oh my gosh, that man has a stick so far up his ass when it comes to the Bennetts!" Olivia exclaims before shooting me an apologetic look. "No offense."

I laugh. "None taken. And you're right—he hated that we were dating, which only brought more heat on Kasey. His parents didn't love it either, knowing who my father is. We'd have to sneak around just to see each other."

"Why did you leave?" Layla asks. "Was it because of Kasey?"

Yes.

No.

"I was afraid, I think, of what my life would look like if I never made it out of here." It's vague enough that I don't feel so raw letting the words out, but it still feels heavy to admit out loud.

"I get that," Layla admits. "But you're back now. Maybe . . . maybe there are still feelings between you both?"

The insinuation has my heart catapulting. I frown, looking back and forth between the girls. "Our feelings are long dead and buried," I say bluntly. "Trust me."

Layla's mouth pinches.

"Sorry if this is overstepping," Olivia chimes in, her voice lowering as she leans in, "but Rhett told me you and Kasey were engaged for real once."

Layla's attention snaps to Olivia as the words hit me like a slap in the face. Rhett knows? I mean, why wouldn't he? There's no reason to think Kasey wouldn't confide in at least one of his brothers about it, even if the whole thing lasted all of five minutes.

"Does this arrangement have anything to do with . . . You know, *that*?" she continues. "Like maybe trying again?"

"Who's asking?" I throw back. It comes out harsher than I mean for it to, but it's hard not to feel affected by the weight of history I've been trying to keep from falling on top of me.

Olivia straightens, her eyes widening. "Me," she assures. "Rhett didn't ask me to, or anything—"

"Look," I say, glancing around at the tables full of other patrons and keeping my voice quiet. "Kasey and I have history, sure. But it's been ten years, and we're two completely different people. This wedding isn't about anything more than convincing the rest of town that we aren't committing any felonies with a fraudulent marriage so the Bennetts can keep the ranch, even though that's *exactly* what this is, okay? I knew Kasey wouldn't want to lie to his family about it, but outside of them and us three sitting here, no one else can know the truth or we risk all of this going up in flames. But just because we're pretending doesn't mean anything is there, either."

They nod. "Understood," Layla says.

"Got it," Olivia echoes.

Silence wraps around us before the sound of rowdy cheers comes from the bar, where two patrons are locked into a game of quarters.

"Still," Layla eventually says, "this *is* a wedding, and you *are* a bride, right?"

I stare at her. "Yeah . . . I guess so."

She smiles softly. "Let Olivia and me be a part of it. I'm sure there are things we can do to help plan? It'll be at the church, right?"

"That's the plan," I grumble. "We just have to pass Pastor Brown's tests first."

WEDNESDAY COMES IN A BLINK, AND SOON KASEY AND I are back in Pastor Brown's office. It's been raining all morning, and the air inside the church is musty and stale. I try my best to not let it affect me, but I have to breathe slowly so I don't start gagging.

"You plan on living here?" the pastor asks. "In Saddlebrook Falls."

"Of course," I say. "Kasey's family's ranch is here. We wouldn't dream of leaving."

He eyes me curiously. "You left once. You'd be content with a life on the ranch?"

"I left to go to school. To become a lawyer."

"A lawyer," he hums. "Just like your mother."

Kasey is quiet next to me, but I feel him go still.

"She was a lawyer too," I agree. "But I'm nothing like her."

Pastor Brown looks at me a moment longer before his eyes flick to Kasey. "What about you?"

"What about me?" Kasey asks, voice low and rich.

"How does your family feel about bringing Miss Jones back into the fold? Are they happy to know of your reunion, or are they just as in the dark as the sheriff is?"

It takes everything in me not to scoff.

Kasey seems unperturbed. "They know," he says. "They support it."

"Were they supportive of your relationship when you were younger?"

This has Kasey hesitating. "My parents were . . . concerned, at times."

"About what?"

He swallows. "Who her father is."

"Ah." Pastor Brown angles his head. "I see. And is that still something they still hold concern for?"

"No." The finality in his tone is obvious.

I can't help but wonder, if this were real, *would* his parents still worry? Kasey struggled with it back then, carrying the weight of their apprehension alongside his own feelings. It was why we kept our relationship private, even from all our friends. I'd convinced myself I was doing him a favor by asking to keep the depth of our feelings a secret from everyone else—I thought it might help keep him unshackled from any expectation or disappointment. I never wanted to stir up more drama where he was concerned. But the truth was a little more layered than that, and deep down I knew—even then—that all I was really looking to salvage was my own freedom.

My whole life I've found it easy to keep the power in my relationships. As long as I liked a guy less than he liked me, I'd come out on top when things ended—because they always ended. Most of them crashed and burned. I never even imagined the possibility of something lasting longer than a few months because I'd been a part of so many versions of the same damn story: the burst of an initial spark that would eventually ignite into passionate chemistry. And then, the first signs of trouble, usually jealousy or an attempt at control, would lead to the inevitable dismantling of the whole shebang.

I'd dated dozens of guys who followed that exact trajectory all throughout high school, as if the blueprint had been etched in stone. Something about the familiarity of it felt safe. There was no pain or loss in knowing love was temporary, like an itch that needed scratching, until the itch went away and the scratching became a nuisance.

But with Kasey . . . From the very first time he kissed me, I knew things were different. All the rules I'd grown accustomed to changed even before I understood what was happening. His smile was a warm and steady glow inside my heart, his eyes a free fall with no rope to save me, and it was a fool's chance in hell to think I'd ever hold the power over him. He was the first boy I liked far beyond the bounds of my control, and I knew that whatever impending doom was pointed our way, the fallout would wreck me.

"What about children?" Pastor Brown asks, eyes flitting back and forth between the two of us.

My stomach clenches painfully as a heavy wave of nausea rolls through me. I try my best not to let it affect me, but I have to breathe slowly so I don't start gagging. I press the back of my knuckles against my lips and inhale deep through my nose. "What about them?"

"Have you discussed it? If you plan on having any? How many?"

Kasey doesn't skip a beat. "As many as Ava wants to give me."

"So there's no goal in mind?"

"The goal, Pastor, is to support her as best as I know how. If she wants children, we'll have them. If she doesn't, well, then we'll have each other."

My eyes snap to his face, finding his expression calm. Steady.

Pastor Brown frowns. "Surely you're allowed an opinion on the matter?"

Kasey nods. "Of course." His expression is sharp, gleaming like the edge of a knife. "My opinion is I'd rather not create any expectations over what my wife chooses to do with her body."

The words hit me like a freight train.

"Bathroom?" I ask, standing abruptly from my chair. The legs whine against the hardwood floor.

Pastor Brown's brows bunch. "Down the hall, to the left."

I race across the room, pushing through the office door so hard it nearly slams against the wall. Covering a hand over my mouth, I will my stomach to hold it in, to give me just a few more seconds to get to the toilet.

"Ava?" Kasey's raised voice comes from somewhere behind me.

I find the sign for a bathroom hung on a wooden door with a brass knob and crash through it. Inside is a single toilet and sink, and I make it just in time.

"Ava!" Kasey shouts again over the sounds of my retching. I have a distant awareness of him coming through the door. "Shit," he says, voice laced with panic. Warm fingers skate gently around the curve of my neck, pulling my hair back and away from my face as the contents of my stomach begin to spill out of me.

It feels like it goes on forever, but hardly anything comes out. I haven't eaten since dinner last night—a mistake, I know—so it's just bile and acid working their way through me. My throat burns raw by the time things seem to settle down.

"Hang tight," Kasey says, and then his hands slip away, and I feel the loss of him like an old, festering wound. I close my eyes, letting the darkness take root as I heave into the toilet again, but nothing comes out. There's just the sound of the sink faucet turning on and off again, of shuffling boots against the linoleum floor.

And then he's back.

One hand wraps around my shoulder, coaxing me back to lean against the broad expanse of his chest. Kasey reaches to push the lever on the toilet and flush away my sick, and then he's pressing a cool, wet paper towel to my forehead, to my lips. "You all right?" he murmurs softly in my ear.

He's warm and solid and smells like wind, like pine and grass and Texas skies. I close my eyes again, basking in the feel of him, in the feel of this. "I think so," I say back. "Sorry . . . I must have eaten something—"

"Don't apologize," he counters, voice stern. But his hands . . . his hands are *so* gentle as they soothe over me, running up and down the length of my arms, dragging across my collarbone and the top of my shoulder. I sink deeper into him, letting him hold my weight.

"Thank you," I say. It comes out in a whisper.

His cheek presses lightly against the top of my head as he lets out a slow breath. It's only now I realize his heart is flying, pounding through the front of his chest against my spine. "What do you need?" he asks. I feel his rough swallow, the tension in his fingers.

"I need to eat something," I admit. "I'm starving."

His hand stills in the crook of my elbow. "Your stomach is upset, and you want to eat?"

I squeeze my eyes shut. "Yeah . . . sometimes this happens though. When I'm hungry." I pray he doesn't question it further.

"Okay." He shifts to get his feet under him. "Maybe some crackers and soup? Something gentle?"

"That's perfect." I smile. "But . . . I don't think we're done with our session."

"Fuck the session," he mutters. He helps me stand, keeping his arms around me for support. "That guy's pissing me off."

"At least go tell him I'm not feeling well. Maybe we can reschedule." I bite my lip. "We need this ceremony."

I turn to face him, finding his expression still tinged with worry. He's quick to shutter his emotions. "Yeah, okay," he agrees. His thumb swipes against the inside of my wrist before letting me go. He fishes his keys out of his pocket, handing them to me. "You okay to get to the truck on your own?"

I nod. "Yeah. Definitely"

"I'll go talk to Pastor Brown. Meet you there soon."

CHAPTER TEN

KASEY

My palms sweat as I hurry down the aisle through the heart of the church, aiming for the heavy double-doors that lead out to the parking lot where Ava waits. I've already taken too long. Pastor Brown was visibly frustrated with us having to end this appointment early, but he was reasonable enough to understand that we are *not* going to force Ava to continue a meeting when she's not feeling well. He said we'd gotten through enough, and anything we missed can be added to our second session.

When I get to the truck it's already running. The air conditioning is cranked high, and Ava's leaning forward so the cool air blows right in her face. "Sorry," I rush out as soon as I open the driver's side door. "You okay?"

She smiles, but it's weak. "Never better."

"You still nauseous?"

"Mhm."

"Do you need to go back in?"

"Fuck no," she protests. "Just drive and let me focus." She squeezes her eyes shut and scooches forward in her seat so that her face is an inch from the air vent. With the sun shining through the truck's windows, I can see she's a little green. My heart cartwheels as concern takes hold.

I jump into the seat and peel out of the lot.

When I tell her I'll take her to my cabin and then go back out for food, she whines and insists we stop for food on the way. "The ranch is outside of town and it'll take too long. Food is the only thing that's going to help. Trust me. I need to eat."

I don't understand how hunger can lead to . . . well, *this*. But I oblige, stopping at June's Café for a quart-sized container of potato soup and a handful of packaged crackers. When I ask if they have any cans of ginger ale, Olivia looks through the large front windows at Ava, still hunched over in the truck. "Is she okay?"

"I have no idea," I say honestly.

She must hear the worry in my voice, because she runs to the kitchen and reappears a minute later with a whole pack of the soda.

"Thanks for this."

Olivia waves a hand. "It's nothing. Let me know if she needs anything else—I'm happy to run something over."

I dip my chin in thanks, and then hurry back outside.

Ava nearly moans at the smell of the soup as I tuck the brown paper bag it's wrapped in on the bench seat between us on top of the case of ginger ale. "Holy shit," she whispers, eyes still closed. The air conditioning blows her dark air out around her face. Even queasy, she looks . . . radiant.

Blood rushes into my face as I force myself to drive.

When we finally pull up to the front of my cabin, I grab hold of the food and ginger ale and push out of the truck so I can go help her out. But when I round the hood and make it to the other side, she's already swinging the door closed and marching up the steps to the front porch.

"Damn," I mutter.

She shoots me a glare. "Less gawking, more moving."

I chuckle, some of the tension in my shoulders easing. "Yes, ma'am."

Inside, I pull a bowl out from the cupboard and fill it with half the container of soup. Ava waits at the small wooden table next to the bay window, strands of sunlight slicing through her hair. I set the bowl and a spoon in front of her with a package of crackers, and then fill an old mug from the cupboard with some ice and as much ginger ale that will fit.

"Thank you," she says between spoonfuls of soup.

"You need anything else?"

She shakes her head, mouth full.

I can't help but watch her eat. It's clear that she's really, truly hungry, but I'm still nervous that all of this food she's pouring into her stomach will just come right back up. She reaches for the mug—a chipped brown one that reads *COWBOY* on the side—and tilts it toward her lips, taking a drink. Her eyes flick to me, standing in the middle of the kitchen like an idiot.

"What?" she asks, setting the mug back down.

"Just making sure you're okay," I admit.

She picks up her spoon again. "Don't you have a ranch to run? You should be out with the horses."

"Not until I know you can keep all this down."

She stills, the spoon stopping halfway to her mouth, a dollop of soup spilling onto the table. "Kasey, I'm fine."

I cross my arms over my chest.

She sighs and goes back to eating.

To her credit, she eats the entire serving and two packages of crackers. She also drains the mug of ginger ale. There's a flush in her cheeks again—a good sign, for sure. "Want more?" I ask.

She shakes her head.

I'm about to ask her how her stomach's feeling, by my phone rings, the loud tune echoing through the small kitchen. I pull it out from my back pocket and see that it's my mother.

"Hey, Mom," I say when I answer. Ava shifts her eyes down to her empty bowl.

"Hi, honey. You in the barn?"

"I'm at home. I'm probably headed out there soon though. Is everything okay?" The dread is immediate. Anxiety claws at me, my mind flashing with images of a full army of sheriff deputies surrounding the main house.

"School called. Liam's gotten himself into some trouble, and I was hopin' you might be able to go get him. I'm home with James and . . ." She hesitates. "Well, Brooks isn't havin' a good day."

"What happened?" I ask. My tone must change, because Ava's gaze cuts back to me.

She sighs. "He got in a fight with another boy. Apparently made his nose bleed."

"Fuck," I mutter. "All right, I'll go get him." Mom had Brooks add all of us to the emergency pick-up list after Melody died in case something like this happened. "Want me to bring him to you?"

"Yes," she confirms. I know by the way she says it, Liam is in for some tough love. "I'll be here waiting for y'all."

"Yes, ma'am. Love you."

"Love you too, honey. And thank you."

"No problem," I say before hanging up. I look at Ava, who's still watching me from the table. "I have to go. Shouldn't be long."

"Where to?" she asks.

"My nephew got in a fight at school and needs to be picked up."

"Can I come?"

I look at her. "You want to?"

She shrugs. "Why not?"

"How do you feel?"

"Better, now that I've eaten." She stands to bring her bowl to the sink, turning on the faucet to give it a quick rinse. It's . . .

strange, to see her moving so comfortably around my kitchen. "Is he at Rattlesnake Ridge?"

"Yeah." It's the elementary school we all went to, Ava included.

Turning the water off, she looks around for a towel to dry her hands. When she doesn't find one, she wipes them along her jeans, leaving streaks of water around her thighs. "Let's go," she says, heading for the door.

THE SCHOOL'S ADMINISTRATION OFFICE IS STUFFY AND loud with children flowing in and out for various reasons: to call home, to get a bandage from the nurse, and one young boy even came in to declare he thinks he has lice, which led to more hustle and bustle as the receptionist and vice principal worked to get him into the latter's office for a thorough examination.

Ava and I wait for a whole twenty minutes before finally being called on by a woman with graying hair who looks to be about sixty. I was expecting to be met with haughty impatience over Liam's actions, but there's a warm and gentle smile spread across her face. "Kasey Bennett?" she asks.

I stand, nodding and reaching a hand out. "Yes, that's me."

She takes my hand. "I'm Principal Wuthers. I've got Liam in my office, if you'd like to follow me."

"I'll wait here," Ava says from her seat.

"You're more than welcome to come too," Principal Wuthers offers.

"Oh, it's okay. I'm not family," she concedes, and then must think better of it because she rushes out a hard and fast "*Yet!*"

"All right," the principal says, looking back at me. "Right this way."

I follow her through a door and down a narrow hallway. She

eventually turns to a closed door on the left, pushing it open to reveal a slumped and quiet Liam, sitting in a chair.

"Liam," she calls. "Your uncle is here."

Liam turns to look at me, his face red and eyes full of tears. "Hey, buddy," I say, taking the open seat beside him in front of the principal's desk.

"Would you like to tell him what happened, or would you like me to?" she asks him, taking her own seat.

He looks down into his lap. "You can," he mumbles.

"I'd like to hear it from you," I counter.

Liam groans dramatically, stretching his legs out in front of him like he can't bear to sit there any longer. "Max Greene called me an orphan."

I frown. "Does Max Greene understand what an orphan is?"

"He said I already don't have a mom, and soon I won't have a dad either 'cause his dad said mine doesn't want to be alive anymore."

I turn to look at the principal, brows raised.

She purses her lips. "While I certainly do *not* condone Max's words, they also do not give Liam the right to resort to violence."

"He pushed me first!" Liam yells loudly. "I told him to fuck off and he pushed me down into the sand, so I got up and punched him."

Again, I turn to the principal. "Sounds like he was defending himself."

"Three other student witnesses have confirmed it was Liam who physically harmed the other child first."

"Yeah, Max's *friends*," Liam spits out.

"All right, Liam," I say, reaching a hand out to wrap around his small shoulder. "It's okay. We'll figure it out."

"Unfortunately," Principal Wuthers announces, "school policy mandates a day of suspension for a first offense of physical violence. Liam will need to spend the day at home tomorrow, and hopefully, with some guidance and support from family, he can return to us on Friday in better spirits."

I clear my throat, leaning forward so my head floats over her desk. "His mom just passed away," I say, "and as you can imagine, things have been really hard at home. Don't you think you can extend a little grace, just this once."

Her face softens. "I'm sorry, but I'm afraid with something of this magnitude we need to follow the rules. Liam will, of course, be welcomed back with open arms on Friday, and our school counselor, Miss Savannah, is here to support him through his emotions."

"Fine," I mutter, standing. "Do I need to sign anything?"

"I'll send a report to Brooks via email. You can sign Liam out at the front desk."

I nod, nudging Liam on the shoulder. "Let's go, kid."

Liam gets up on his feet and follows me back down the hall to the front office. "You okay?" I whisper.

His shoulders hike up to his ears, but he doesn't say a word. The ride back to the ranch is quiet, apart from Liam shooting Ava a few curious glances from where he's wedged between us on the bench seat. We find Rhett waiting on the porch steps of the main house, sipping from a bottle of beer.

"Hey!" he shouts toward Liam as he jumps out of the truck. "What did I tell you about that anger?"

The question catches me off guard—I wasn't aware Rhett's already addressed the subject of anger with our nephew. "Let him explain," I call back, giving Rhett a sharp look. I don't care what school policy is, Liam didn't do anything wrong. Rhett and I would have done the same thing to defend ourselves in his situation.

Rhett's eyes narrow. "Fine. Explain."

So Liam does. This time, he shares that Max and his friends have been heckling him for weeks, calling him a "sissy boy" who misses his "mommy."

"Who the fuck's this kid's dad?" Rhett asks with an icy tone.

"I'm not sure," I answer. I tried to place who his parents might be the whole ride back.

"Greene?" Ava chimes in behind me. I almost forgot she was still here. "Might be Silas Greene."

"Oh shit," Rhett says. "The owner of the hardware store!" He points a finger at her, the rest of his hand still wrapped around his beer bottle. "You're good, Ava Jones."

She grins. "He's friends with my dad."

"And he doesn't like us," I add. "Not since *our* dad robbed his store."

"Makes sense that he'd be encouraging his kid to be a dick."

"Hey," I warn. "The kid's innocent. He's just mirroring his father."

"You're right," Rhett agrees. "His *dad* is a dick, and he's going to regret the day he decided to fuck with my nephew."

Liam laughs. I roll my eyes. "Rhett," I scold. "I'll talk to him. *You* need to stay out of trouble, for fuck's sake." I won't say more in front of Liam or Ava, but he knows exactly what I'm talking about.

"Maybe I can help," Ava suggests.

All three of us Bennetts turn to look at her. "How?" Rhett asks.

Ava smirks. "Just give me a few days. I'll come up with something."

It's honestly a little scary to see that look on her face again, the one she used to get while planning revenge against someone who'd wronged her. She always had a flair for the dramatics, and she was so good at creating elaborate schemes to ensure her target felt the weight of her vengeance. I remember swearing to myself I'd never give her a reason to aim that weapon my way.

I was always on her side of things, even when I didn't necessarily agree with what she was doing. Back then, Ava valued loyalty more than pretty much anything else. I think she had a lot of broken pieces of her heart that needed mending, and now as I look at her, I can't help but wonder if she still does.

It's a reminder, really. To protect myself in all of this.

"Look, Liam," I say in an attempt to get this conversation back on track. "You didn't do anything wrong. Sticking up for yourself might sometimes look dangerous to other people, and your principal is responsible for lots of kids in that school—she's doing the best she can to keep order. I get it. But I want you to hear me say that, in this family, we will always support your right to defend yourself."

Liam grins. "Thanks, Uncle Kasey."

"That said," I continue, and his smile drops. "If I ever hear that you're the one out there starting problems, you will absolutely be facing the consequences. We are *not* bullies, and we do *not* find joy or humor or fun in the pain of other people. Do you understand me?"

"Yes, sir," he confirms. "I hear you, I promise."

I grip his shoulder and pull him in for a hug. "I'm sorry that you had to deal with Max and his friends. You're going through a lot right now, and their words are nothing but a cruel attempt to make themselves feel bigger. I know it's hard, but you have to brush it off as best as you can, okay? You're a strong kid, Liam, and you're smart as hell. Don't let kids like that get the best of you, okay?"

Liam nods again. And then he asks, "Why do people hate our family?"

Ava snorts, crossing her arms over her chest. The question is a gut punch. Even Rhett blows out a long breath.

"What do you mean?" I ask.

"You know exactly what he means," Rhett chides.

I shoot him a glare. "I want to hear it from Liam."

Liam's eyes bounce between us, no doubt trying to decipher all the things we're not saying. "It's just that, it feels like people don't like us, or think something's wrong with us. When grownups hear my last name they look at me funny."

I sigh. "Well, I guess our family has sometimes found it difficult to get along with other families from town. Grandpa Bennett didn't always behave well—he acted like a bully, himself. And a lot of the grownups remember the way he treated them. Your dad and us brothers have tried to undo some of that bad reputation, but it hasn't exactly been easy." I look at Rhett again. "We're still working on it," I admit. "But we all want you and your brothers to have an easier time. And you can, I promise. But it starts now. The choices you make today will mold you into the man you're going to be in the future. Does that make sense?"

"Yes, sir," Liam confirms.

"And remember," Rhett adds, "when you make poor choices that hurt other people, it affects the rest of this family. *Especially* your brothers." There's a hard line set in his jaw, and I feel the weight of his own regret in the air around us.

I keep my eyes on Rhett when I say, "Everyone makes mistakes. It's a part of life. The goal is to be a better man tomorrow than you were today."

Rhett flashes a grin that doesn't quite reach his eyes.

The front door swings open, revealing my mom on the other side. She's wearing a yellow house dress, her hair pinned in a neat bun on the top of her head. "There you are," she says, looking at Liam.

"Go easy on him, Ma," I say. "Let him tell you his side."

She tuts. "Don't I always listen to you boys and your *sides*?"

This time, Rhett's smile is genuine. "She's got you there," he says.

I laugh, turning back to Ava. "How are you feeling?" I ask.

"Fine," she says. And I believe her.

"Wanna go for a ride?"

CHAPTER ELEVEN

AVA

On Friday, I pick up Layla from the ranch in my Range Rover and drive us to Luna's Bakery.

"Have you thought about what you might want?" she asks, looking at me from where she sits in the passenger seat. She's wearing white linen shorts and a black-and-white-striped shirt with a pair of black leather sandals. I'm intrigued by her simple-yet-sophisticated style, much more in line with my colleagues at the law firm than what I'd expect to see here at home. Although, I remember her mother, Lynette, always showing off the money she married into. Maybe Layla gets it from her.

"For cake?" I ask.

She nods.

"Something simple. Vanilla, maybe."

She looks offended. "Not even marble? Or red velvet?"

I shake my head. "I think it's best to keep all of this as easy as possible." I do *not* need to be out here caring about wedding details. "What?" I ask when Layla's brow furrows.

"You're allowed to still have *some* fun with this, you know."

I sigh. "I'm not sure Kasey would agree."

The last couple of days have been . . . confusing. I'm still frustrated with myself for letting my nausea get as bad as it did during our appointment with Pastor Brown, but Kasey handled it much more graciously than I expected. It made me feel like he still cares —at least more than he lets on. And then letting me tag along to pick up his nephew from school launched a riot of emotions in me, seeing the way he managed the situation and advocated for Liam.

It felt . . . *good* to be included in something like that. Like maybe, at the very least, we can keep a real friendship alive during this marriage. And who knows, I might actually let myself enjoy being integrated into moments with his family and not have to keep such a guard up.

But then he asked me to go riding with him, and things went downhill pretty damn quick.

"Even if he doesn't agree," Layla says, pulling me back to the present. "To hell with it."

I laugh. "You know, that's actually a motto I can get behind."

We pull into the lot in front of the bakery and make our way inside. There's a handful of people in line already, so Layla and I trudge to the back and wait our turn. When we make it to the counter, Luna is thrilled to see us, her hazel eyes rounding wide. "Ava! And Layla! What a power duo the two of you make. I love to see it."

I give her my best smile. "You know me, always looking for new ways to harness a little bad-bitch energy."

Luna chuckles. "What can I get you girls?"

"Actually," I say, hesitating a little, knowing things are about to become *really* real. "We were hoping you might have availability to book a wedding cake? For just over a week from now?"

It looks like Luna stops breathing altogether. Her gaze moves to Layla. "You and Wells?" she asks quietly.

Layla shakes her head and looks back at me. "No actually—"

Layla doesn't get the chance to finish her sentence because Luna's already screaming. "Oh my *god*, Ava, *areyoufreakingkid-*

dingme? You and Kasey?! You're lying! Is this some kind of joke!" She clutches at her chest, her breaths coming in short sputters. The near-dozen or so other people scattered throughout the bakery eye us with open fascination.

"Kasey and I are getting married," I declare, loud enough for the whole room to hear.

There's a collective gasp around the bakery, and then silence. Luna's eyes fill with tears. "My girl," she says, obviously dazed. "My precious girl! I *knew* you two would end up together. I just knew it!"

"Yeah." I force a wide smile. "I guess it was just written in the stars!"

Layla, to her credit, doesn't skip a beat. "They're so grossly enamored with each other that they're insisting on a ceremony the week after next, so we're hoping you can help?"

"Oh!" Luna exclaims. "Nothing would make me happier than to be a part of sweet Ava's big day."

The love in her eyes is so genuine it knocks the wind out of me. "Thank you, Luna," I say, and my heart squeezes. Of all the people in this town, she's the one I already deeply regret lying to.

"What kind of cake are you looking for? I can do two-tiered or three-tiered, maybe a chocolate mirror glaze?"

"Um," I say with a sweeping gaze along the pastry case, as if I might conveniently find a whole wedding cake to point to and claim. "I was thinking something easy—"

"What about something decadent," Layla chimes in, "like dark chocolate with raspberry filling?"

I glare at her. "Oh, that's too much—"

"I could do that," Luna puts in. "But you know, Ava's always been more of a vanilla-and-sugar girl. Maybe we do something with vanilla bean and cookie butter?"

Okay, *fine*, I'll admit it: my mouth waters.

"*Ohhhh*." Layla is a lost cause too, apparently. "That sounds really good. We'd definitely want two tiers of that."

"What about a cake-topper?" Luna asks, her attention fully on Layla now.

I open my mouth to speak, but Layla beats me to it. "Do you have any men in cowboy hats?"

She shoots Layla a cocky smile, her face flushed from all the commotion. "I've got just about any kind of man you need," she says, winking.

"What about women who look like . . . lawyers?"

Luna and Layla turn to eye me up and down. It's almost comical, the way they analyze my silk black shirt beneath a gray blazer, paired with a pair of dark jeans. I blow out a breath.

"I've got one that looks pretty corporate," Luna says.

"That could work," Layla adds.

"I was thinking of something *simpler*," I interject. "Maybe just a sheet cake?"

Luna physically recoils. "A *sheet* cake? For a wedding?"

"Isn't that more of a birthday party thing?" Layla asks.

"I made one recently for Maeve's granddaughter," Luna says, nodding. "It had sparkle sprinkles and rainbow icing."

"That would be perfect!" I say. "I want exactly what she had."

Luna stares at me for a long moment. "You want sparkles and rainbows? On your *wedding* cake?"

"Yep," I confirm, nodding.

"Are you sure?" Layla asks.

I throw her a hard look, one that begs her to be on my side. I understand how ridiculous this sounds, especially after declaring on the ride over here that Kasey wasn't likely to agree to anything overly frivolous. But the truth is, I woke up this morning anxious as hell. I knew what I was doing when I pitched the idea of this marriage, but I didn't realize what it might feel like to go through the actual motions of it.

There was a time when I wholeheartedly dreamed of what it might be like to marry Kasey Bennett. And now . . . Now it just hurts.

I try not to think of the expression on his face two days ago as he watched me climb into the saddle of an old Thoroughbred he'd pulled out from the barn. It'd been a slip into the past, when warm summer nights balmed over our frenzied love and left us filled to the brim with a contentment I'd never known before and haven't felt since.

He looked at me with a reverence I've often wondered was even real, like I might have somehow fabricated it all on my own, turned the memory of his looks into something else entirely. But there it was, plain as day, on a face that might be ten years older but somehow still none the wiser.

"What?" I'd asked him, crashing through the moment like a wrecking ball.

His face wiped clean, brow arching. "What do you mean *what*?"

When I didn't respond, he cut loose a long exhale before turning to stalk back into the barn. He'd returned with a beautiful paint horse, careful not to look at me as he adjusted her saddle before he took hold of the horn and lifted himself up into it. He steered her out toward the wide-open pasture without a word—it was a good thing my horse knew to follow.

We rode like that, in silence, for over an hour.

"Right, yeah," Layla says, seeming to understand that I need this win, even if it's shaped like a seven-year-old girl's birthday cake. "You know, I bet Kasey would love the sparkles." She shoots me a conspiratorial wink.

"Okay," Luna agrees with clear hesitance. "I can make that happen. When do you need it?"

"Still figuring out details for the reception," I tell her. "The ceremony is the Friday after next at Magnolia Community Church though, so I imagine the reception wouldn't be long after."

"In the church?" Luna asks. "I'm surprised."

"Why?" I ask, feigning ignorance.

Her next words come out quieter, but I have every confidence the people in this bakery can still hear. "I didn't think the Bennetts were . . . *spiritual* people."

Layla snorts.

"They're spiritual," I counter. "They just aren't particularly religious."

"Hard to be when the people in that church every Sunday want to crucify them for *breathing* wrong," Layla adds stoically.

I've gotta hand it to her—she has balls.

Luna waves a hand. "You just let me know when you need it, and I'll make sure it's done!"

"Thank you, Luna," I say, reaching to give her a hug. Her arms wrap around me and squeeze tight. "Means a lot."

"Oh, I wouldn't miss an opportunity like this for the world, sweetheart."

Emotion clutches my throat all the way back to the car, where I have to work not to look too close to the sun for fear of tears falling.

"That went well!" Layla quips as she leans against the hood of my SUV.

I hurry to put my sunglasses on, eyeing the florist next door with a frown. "What do you say we hit up Eleanor for flowers some other time?"

She tilts her head. "You okay?"

"Yeah," I answer breezily. "Just ready to get out of dodge. I haven't been to a *mall* in years." Part of today's excursions include looking for a dress for the wedding. I've convinced myself it's not that big of a deal—I'll just find something that loosely resembles a wedding dress while *not* actually being one.

Layla smiles, checking her watch. "Olivia is off in a half hour. Let's grab a soda at June's while we wait."

THE DRIVE OUT OF THE COUNTY IS A MUCH-NEEDED relief. With every mile I put between me and Saddlebrook Falls, I feel my shoulders loosen.

Layla takes control of the music, plugging her phone in for a playlist she insists was "specifically crafted" for today's bridal activities. After listening to King of Leon's "Use Somebody" and One Direction's "Temporary Fix," it doesn't take long to understand the joke.

"Very funny," I mutter, rolling my eyes.

Olivia cackles in the back seat.

Layla winks, turning the dial to raise the volume as they both sing along, the outside sun-warmed air blowing in through the open windows. It helps ease away a bit more of the gnawing stress I've been carrying around these past few months, but I still can't help the low hum of anxiety that vibrates through me. As pleasant as both of these girls are to be around, it nags at me that our makeshift friendship is just as forced and calculated as my sham of an engagement to Kasey.

I'm thankful for it, of course; it certainly helps sell our new family dynamic to anyone looking. But buried deep in my soul is a long-standing ache for *real* friends, for *real* connection with people I can trust with all the good and the bad in my life.

We eventually make it to the mall in Williamson County, forcing an intermission on the Layla and Olivia karaoke show. Inside, three stories of shops sprawl out from the elevator banks at the center. We make a quick stop in the food court on the first floor for fresh soft pretzels.

"God, I love these," Olivia mumbles around a large bite.

"Luna should really consider adding these to her menu," Layla agrees, studying the coarse salt scattered along hers.

"I'm sure she would," I muse, tossing a ripped piece into my mouth. Cinnamon sugar coats my tongue as I sigh out in pleasure from this unexpected snack.

We make quick work of finishing them off before dumping

the paper liners they were served to us in, and then head for the ritzy department store on the far east wing of the third floor. It's certainly no bridal shop, but I have no doubt it'll deliver.

It helps that I honestly couldn't care less what I wear to this wedding. Finding a dress today is just something to check off the ever-growing list of tasks to complete so Kasey and I can seal the deal on this whole thing. Still, I don't have the heart to tell the girls how little I care. Even knowing that it's a ruse to save the ranch, they're eager than ever to be a part of the bridal traditions.

Layla leads us into the store, cutting a direct line for the dress section that sits between activewear and intimates. She saunters right up to a blonde woman in a smart blue pantsuit and declares, "We're here for the best wedding dress options you have!"

The woman's gaze scans over us as she absently strokes at the French twist pulling her hair tight behind her head. "Oh," she says, a bit startled. "I'm afraid we don't offer any bridal lines here."

"Do you have anything white?" I ask.

"Um . . . yes, I believe so—"

"Perfect." Layla nods. "We'll try one of everything, please."

The saleswoman looks at her for a long moment, and then sweeps a glance around the store. Other than an older woman studying a pair of kitten heels with intense interest and two teenage girls giggling at the thongs, there doesn't seem to be anyone else here. The woman shrugs, eyes sparking. "I've always wanted to work with brides," she says.

Twenty minutes later, the woman—Elaine—bursts into the dressing room with a wide smile and a trio of glass flutes on a tray filled with bubbling golden liquid. "Normally we only break this out for really high-end customers who are here to spend some serious money," she reveals in a hushed whisper, "but it's been so long since we've opened a bottle and I just figured *to hell with it*!"

Layla beams, clapping her hands. "We love champagne!"

"It wouldn't be a bridal fitting without a proper toast," Elaine points out. She holds the tray out between us in offering. Layla and Olivia don't skip a beat as they each reach for a glass.

Dread curls tight inside of me. "Oh," I say, flustered. "I actually don't drink."

Three sets of eyes narrow on me. "You don't drink?" Olivia asks, brows pinched tight.

"Not really." I shake my head. "I mean, sometimes, I guess. But I've been trying to cut back, you know?"

Layla looks unconvinced. "Not even one teensy *bridal fitting* glass?"

"I'm good," I assure her.

"Okay! No big deal." Elaine waves a hand like it's nothing, though I can tell she's a bit perturbed with my resistance after going through the trouble of bending the rules. "One of you two can have this extra glass," she says, setting the tray with the single remaining flute on the side table next to Olivia. "I've grabbed every dress we have that's white, and a couple that are ivory. There's even one that's a *very* subtle light pink!"

"Thank you, Elaine," I say sincerely. "You've really gone above and beyond for us."

She smiles. "I did my best with sizing but can grab you something different if needed. I'll be a holler away if you need anything!" She disappears back around the corner to tend to her station.

"Well," Olivia says, holding up her drink. "Cheers to saying yes to a dress!"

Layla matches the motion and lifts her glass too. She looks right at me. "Cheers to the beautiful bride!"

I take that as my cue to stand and get this over with. "I'll go try on the first one."

"Make sure to show us," Olivia calls out as I shut the stall door.

I roll my eyes, grinning despite myself, and slip out of my clothes as I eye the dozen dresses hung up on a built-in rack. My fingers tremble as I work to unbutton my pants, and I frown. I'm more anxious than I thought I'd be.

Down to my bra and underwear, I avoid looking in the mirror as I pull the first dress off the hanger and shuffle into it. It's . . . pretty, with a sweetheart neckline and beaded crystals beneath the bust. It's loose around my torso and long enough to wear in heels, with the white satin pooling around my feet. Definitely not something I would ever pick for myself, but I'm relieved that it works.

I step out of the stall and hold my arms out for the girls to see. Olivia eyes it up and down as Layla tilts her head. "It's nice," she says.

"Kind of looks like a prom dress," Olivia notes.

I laugh. "I can name at least five girls from high school who bought their prom dresses *from* a bridal store."

Layla snickers, taking another sip of champagne. "It's not bad," she declares. "But let's see what else is in there."

The next dress is tight—too tight. My eyes slip down to where the cotton stretches tight around my middle, and then I'm scrambling to rip the whole thing off. By the time I get my head and arms through the top of the third dress, frustration bubbles in my blood. This is all so stupid, and I never should have let Layla or Olivia come with me—

I catch a glance at myself in the mirror, and . . .

Wow. It's a cream-colored dress of lace and tulle with a plunging neckline and sheer flutter sleeves. Below the bust, the dress flows out into a gorgeous skirt with ivory-embroidered flowers. The back of it dips halfway down my spine.

It fits like a dream.

Emotion pulls a quick breath into my lungs. I like it way more than I should.

Swallowing, I tamp down my feelings and open the stall door, stepping out for Layla and Olivia to see. Their expressions are proof enough.

"That's the dress," Olivia says, softly.

"No question," Layla agrees.

"Yeah?" I ask, suddenly swirling in a jumbled mess of feelings. I move to the single-step platform, rising to stand in front of three mirrors to see the dress from all angles. It's . . . gorgeous.

"That's definitely the dress," Olivia says again.

"I think so too." I smile wide as I turn back around to face them, but my foot slips off the edge of the step. My hand flies protectively to my stomach as I stumble to regain control, and Layla catches the movement. Her brow furrows as her gaze narrows in on my palm covering my navel. "Are you hurt?" she asks.

I drop my hand, turning away from her to look back at myself in the mirror. "No!" I exclaim, a little loudly. "Totally fine. Just . . . lost my balance."

I can't help but watch her reaction in the mirror as fear overcomes me. She tilts her head, looking down at the glass of champagne in her hand. And then her eyes rise back to mine.

I shake my head almost imperceptibly.

Her eyes widen.

"Do you have shoes yet?" Olivia asks, completely oblivious.

I force a smile. "No, but I'm thinking something si—"

"Simple," she finishes for me, a teasing smile playing on her lips. "I think I saw a pair here that would match perfectly. I'll go get them so we can try!" Olivia sets her glass down and practically skips out of the dressing room.

I keep my gaze trained on the dress in the mirror.

Layla shifts in her seat. "Ava—"

"Olivia doesn't know my shoe size!" I abruptly announce. "I'm going to go help her."

I practically run from the room.

CHAPTER TWELVE

KASEY

va didn't stick with rodeo for too long, but she sure stuck around me.

Falling for her was essentially the beginning of a years-long drawn-out chase, one that had us both shifting back and forth between roles of pursuer and target as time went on. There was a learned language to our flirting, an unspoken choreography to the dance between us. She'd give me that coy smile, the one that rounded her cheeks into apples and crinkled the skin around her sapphire eyes, and I'd be snared like a wild dog. Then I'd say or do something brazen to let her know I was on to her and it'd send her off running.

It took some effort, but I learned how to play hot and cold too. I once went months without so much as looking at her at school and was thrilled with how it sent her spiraling. She'd been so determined to rope me back in that she started a rumor about us just to give herself a flimsy excuse to chastise me in front of everyone at a party, including her boyfriend at the time. The little minx.

She always had a boyfriend, or at the very least there was always some guy set in her sights. It was never me, not directly. But it was also somehow always me.

The smell of the bonfire wafts in the salty air through my truck's open windows before I even turn into the lot for Scorpion Bay. My body's already buzzing in anticipation because I know Ava's going to be here tonight—she made it clear enough when she'd stopped to talk about it in the hallway at school yesterday, right in front of me.

I'm not real big on these parties, not when work comes early every morning at the ranch, but I still try to make it out now and then with some of the guys from the team. Tonight's bonfire—an end-of-summer tradition—is a perfect excuse to hang out with my friends, but the truth is I'm only here for the dark-haired beauty who's front and center in all my dreams.

The cicadas are screaming tonight. I look up through my dirty windshield at the dusty orange sky beyond the dark plumes of smoke and wonder if it might rain. Definitely wouldn't hurt after all this heat we've had. The humidity's been downright suffocating. If the sky finally decides to open up, it'll be a relief for us all. And it wouldn't hurt to put out the lingering embers of this fucking dangerous fire the boys have started.

I park my truck in one of the last open spots in the lot and lock it up. It's another warm night—I can already feel sweat starting to pool along my spine beneath my red Mustangs jersey. I paired it with an old pair of jeans and my boots, which maybe isn't ideal beach attire but no one will ever catch me wearing a pair of sandals, that's for fucking sure.

"Kasey!" Someone calls my name from the top of a sandy hill that separates the beach from the lot. I turn to find Tomlinson stumbling as he climbs higher, an amber bottle in his hand. "The fuck took you so long?"

Tonight's supposed to be fun, *I remind myself.* Our first football game of the new season is next weekend, so this is our last hurrah before everyone tries to behave more than usual.

"Work," I holler back. Most of these boys only know the work put on that football field—they'd never be able to keep up with me and my brothers on the ranch. Lucky for me, it keeps me in good

enough shape that I don't have nearly as hard a time with all the conditioning we've been subjected to since the season started a couple of weeks ago.

"Fuck work!" *Tomlinson shouts back.*

Yeah, *I think.* See where that gets you in life.

I guess it's not exactly Tomlinson's fault that he's a moron. His parents are even bigger morons who spend so much time worrying about what their neighbors are doing or what they're buying or where they're vacationing that life has pretty much turned into a weird competition for them.

Getting the most while doing the least is not my idea of a good life. But it's also not my business how any of these guys decide to live theirs—unless they fuck with me or my family.

Or Ava.

Yeah . . . I'd inflict some serious hurt if any of these fucks even looked at Ava wrong.

I sigh, shaking the thought away. Just more evidence of the anticipation I feel at seeing her tonight.

"Want a beer?" *Tomlinson asks as I step off the blacktop and into the sand.*

"Nah, I'm all right," *I say.* "Don't think I'll be here long."

"Aw, why not? Everyone's here."

My gaze flits through the crowd, eager and impatient. "I got an early morning."

He frowns. "Shit. Doing what?"

I cut a glance at him. "We're hauling a few horses out to Forth Worth."

"I always forget you're into all that horse stuff. A true country boy!"

I nearly scoff. "I'll catch you later," *I mutter, moving down the sandy slope toward the people crowding around the fire.*

I find more guys from the team circling around a keg that sits in the sand, all of them juniors like me. Most of them are just as sauced as Tomlinson, but I'm relieved that a couple of them have drawn short straws as designated drivers and are looking out for the group. Football in Texas is its own religion, and it's easy for the fame and attention to make players feel invincible. Too many tragedies have taken the lives of good kids too soon, most of them revolving around parties like this.

"Have you seen Molly yet?" Richards asks me, driving the back of his hand into my chest a little too hard.

I shake my head—I'm not even sure who Molly is. "No, don't think so."

He nods toward a group of girls gathered on the edge of the shoreline. "The blonde with the pink tank top," he says. "I think I'm going to ask her out."

"Nice," I say. She's pretty, sure. Honey-blonde hair curls around her face from the humidity, long tan legs dipping out of a stark white skirt. Not my type, but I can see why he likes her.

My eyes move to the girl next to her, and my heart stops.

Ava wears a pair of jeans that mold to her curves, the waistline cut low enough to steal my breath. She's got on an oversized black Mustangs tee cut just below her chest, baring the soft skin of her stomach. The neckline hangs off one shoulder, revealing the line of her collarbone, and I get lost in the way it disappears beneath the cotton.

"You should really do something about that," Richards teases.

I turn to look at him, thrown off-kilter. "About what?"

"Ava Jones."

I force a small laugh. "It's not like that. I just . . . I know her from a camp thing we were both at a couple years ago."

He arches a brow. It's clear he doesn't believe me. "Word on the street is she's single again."

"Oh yeah? Says who?" The question comes out sharper than I mean it to.

Richards's smile grows wider. "Look man, just talk to her. What's the worst that could happen?"

If he only knew.

Ava laughs at something Molly says, playfully shoving her away. She shakes her head, her long hair dragging along her shoulders as she brings a red plastic cup to her lips. She's got a damn lollipop dangling from her mouth.

I swear, she's only gotten more beautiful in the last couple of years. I thought it hurt to look at her before, when she was spitting mad on that ranch. But now . . . now she's lightning in a bottle, so bright and violent I can't help but to be drawn in.

Her eyes dart toward where we stand as she sips from her drink, and I swear there's magic in the way our gazes touch, something supernatural in the way her focus sends a shiver up my spine. Thunder sounds from somewhere over the water, far in the distance, a sure sign of an impending storm. But the electricity in the air is coming straight from her blue eyes.

"I'll be right back," I say to Richards.

He snorts. "Good luck, Bennett."

Shuffling across the sand, I make my way toward Ava and her friends. When she notices me coming, she trails away from the group to intercept me, her eyes dancing with a teasing edge. "Kasey," she says through a grin, the white stick of her lollipop sticking out the side of her mouth. "Surprised to see you out for once."

"Are you?" I ask, a smile pulling across my face. We both know damn well she baited me here. And that it worked.

She ignores the question. "Big game next week. You ready?"

"You really here to talk about football, Ava?" My eyes are fastened to her lips, the way they swell around the candy hidden inside her mouth. It sends a lick of heat through me.

"No," she admits, the corners of her mouth rising, revealing a bright red stain on her tongue.

Fuck. "What are you here for, then?"

"Had to get out of the house," she says. "My dad's been insufferable lately."

I can't help but laugh. Ava's father is certainly that. "I bet he hates not being able to control you."

She shrugs. "Driving him crazy is one of my many joys in life."

"I bet I know a few ways I could help with that."

She arches a brow. "Oh yeah?"

I nod. "Yeah." I step closer, anticipating that she'll move away or find a reason to run, like she always does. I brace for it, for the letdown.

She doesn't.

I watch in fascination as she licks her lips, tilting her head back to keep her eyes focused on mine. "I'm all ears," she whispers.

I don't even register the decision, only realizing that I've reached for her when I feel her soft hair cascade along the hand I've buried behind her neck. She still doesn't move away. Instead, she pulls the lollipop out just as I dip to capture her wicked little mouth with my own.

Lightning cracks through the sky, booming with thunder.

I've never felt more alive.

Four whole days without seeing Ava, and I feel like I'm crawling out of my fucking skin. I refuse to let myself think about all the ways I'm *right* back in that place, desperate to know what she's thinking, how she's spending her days. I can't help but wonder if she regrets any of this yet, if she's finally realized what a bad idea it all is.

It's not too late to stop it.

I look at her now, seated next to me in a matching armchair while Pastor Brown studies us from the other side of his obnoxiously large desk. Her face is a perfect mask of patience, beautiful but guarded. I know her well enough to know there's a fire deep inside that she's learned how to keep hidden.

"As I stated in our initial meeting," Pastor Brown remarks, "today's session is all about heart." His focus bounces back and forth between Ava and me. "This discussion will allow me to evaluate the stability of the more . . . *intangible* strengths of your relationship. A common issue I see in young couples seeking to be married is that they are in it for all the *wrong* reasons—like lust, money, or status—when really, love and God should exist at the center of any marriage."

It takes effort not to react. I'm not sure how much love or God I have in me these days, but the goal is to make the old man believe plenty of both exists. I sneak another look at Ava and find her still calm and relaxed.

The good pastor starts off with a bang. "How do you like to fight?" he asks, flitting his gaze toward Ava.

She smirks. "That's actually one of our specialties."

"Do you fight often?"

"Not as often as we used to," she says carefully. "But even when we do . . . I'd call it a love language we share."

"How so?"

She tucks her hair behind her ear, revealing two small gold hoops hugging her lobe. "With me and Kasey, fighting is basically foreplay."

"Ah." Pastor Brown clears his throat. "You're saying that fighting often leads to . . . physical intimacy?"

My face heats. Ava just smiles.

He taps his knuckles against the surface of the desk, considering his words. "Tell me, do you find that . . . *strategy* leads to healthy resolution?"

"Oh yes," Ava says emphatically. "Lots of them."

Fucking hell.

"What about general communication with each other? Would you say that's something you excel at?" He looks at me to answer this one.

"Yeah," I say. "Definitely."

"Give me an example."

"We tell each other hard truths. Even when it hurts."

He considers. "What's Ava's biggest fear?" he asks.

Dread spikes through me. "What does that matter?"

"It's not so much the 'what' of it as much as it is ensuring that you know."

My traitorous eyes slip sideways and look at her. Her gaze is already trained on me, but it gives nothing away. There's a cautious expression on her face, one that I can't read. I look back at Pastor Brown and straighten, shifting in my seat. "Not having the opportunity to realize her fullest potential," I answer. "It's important to her that she has her freedom."

I don't know if it's the right thing to say here, in this room, under an old man's judgement. But at least it's honest, and I can't see how a little honesty would hurt. The truth is I've always known Ava never wanted to be tamed, never wanted to feel shackled to any man or course of life. And I know I complicated that with both my love for her and my dedication to the ranch.

She'd asked me to go slow, to be patient with her. And god—I tried. I tried so fucking hard to wrangle the intensity of my feelings for her, terrified letting it loose might scare her away. I thought I could reveal the way I felt little by little, like pressure escaping out of a valve slow enough that nothing would burst. After a couple of years together, I guess I thought she could handle it. I thought she would trust my presence in her life enough that the strength of my feelings wouldn't send her fleeing.

Boy was I wrong.

"Ava, what's Kasey's biggest fear?"

"Failing his ranch," she says plainly.

"And what would 'failing his ranch' look like?"

She levels him with a flat look. "It's been in his family for generations. There's a pressure he and his brothers naturally feel to make sure it flourishes for generations to come, but it's not easy. It's expensive, and at times risky. They don't like to show it, especially not to people in this town. But they worry."

I wait for the internal bristling, for the irritation at being exposed like that. But it doesn't come. I'm actually surprised to feel a sense of . . . *relief*, at the truth of it. A reminder to this man, to this representation of others in this town, that my family is human. That, like everyone else, we're doing our best.

"Do you trust him?" Pastor Brown asks.

The question sinks into my gut like a heavy stone.

Ava shoots him a frustrated glance. "What kind of a question is that?"

Pastor Brown shrugs. "One would argue it's a rather important one." He steeples his fingers and rests his hands on the desk in front of him. "Do you trust him?"

"Of course I do," she snaps. "I trust him with my life."

"And with your heart?"

Ava doesn't hesitate. "Yes." She doesn't look at me, doesn't so much as flinch on the topic. Her attention is wholly focused on him. "If I didn't trust him, I wouldn't . . . I wouldn't *be here*."

He nods, then he turns to me. "And you?"

"And me what?"

"Do you trust Ava?"

I look at her again, my heart hammering in my chest. "Yes," I answer, but it doesn't sound nearly as confident.

She must hear it, because she whips her head my way. Hurt flashes across her face before it smooths over and that mask of patience returns. My hands start to sweat as the question flips over and over in my mind. Do I trust Ava? *Can* I trust her, after everything? I want to, I think. But . . .

"She left home once," the pastor's voice cuts in. And I wonder if he knows how deep those words ring true, if he realizes the bull's-eye he's managed to hit.

I swallow. "Yes," I repeat, lamely.

"Should we talk about it?"

"Do we need to?" Ava chimes in, defensive. I don't blame her. "I'm not sure how it's relevant to anything."

Pastor Brown keeps his eyes trained on me, sensing my vulnerability like a wolf would sense a newborn calf. "Kasey?" he presses.

I blow out a breath, avoiding the pull to look at Ava again. "Ava left home the summer after we graduated, and it broke my heart," I admit. "Obliterated it, actually." I feel her go still in the seat beside me. "But I would be a fool to sit here and tell you it wasn't worth it. I mean, shit, she's a *lawyer* now. She went and found something for herself that this town couldn't offer her, and I'm proud she made that choice."

"Even if it hurt you?"

"*Especially* because it hurt me," I counter. "She could have stayed. She could have taken the easy way out to spare my feelings and try to make things work. But what would that have accomplished in the end, besides leaving her trapped in a life that doesn't fulfill her? It might have hurt, but she was brave. She knew what she needed, despite the pain it would cause. And she chose it. I could never fault her for that."

I suck down a breath, and for the first time since Ava walked into Wild Coyote and back into my life, the air reaches deep into my lungs.

"I see," Pastor Brown says, eyes glinting. "Tell me, do you worry she might leave again?"

Yes, I think, heart clenching. "No," I say aloud, with all the steeliness needed to keep up this ruse, both with him and with her.

I can't let her see how deeply I still fear the loss of her.

I refuse to show her that still-gaping wound.

CHAPTER THIRTEEN

AVA

The walls of my carefully built facade are beginning to crack deep in their foundation.

I'd expected this session to be more difficult than the first. Readied for it, even. It's easy to lie about my future plans with Kasey—moving in together, supporting each other's goals, crafting dreams for a prettily painted life ahead—but matters of the heart, ambiguous as they are, can be a little more difficult to portray authentically. The need to prove the love between us is real is the riskiest part of this whole plan because it's the biggest lie we're telling.

Tell me, do you worry she might leave again?

I glare at the man on the opposite side of this decades-old desk, and can't help the immediate urge to let my tongue fly. I know this is the exact sort of question that *should* be asked in pre-marital counseling. Still, I wonder if he can smell all the blood in the water.

And Kasey . . .

My chest squeezes at the raw vulnerability written across his face. It took restraint not to bring up the dark circles under his eyes when he picked me up this morning—probably from pulling extra work at the ranch lately. He already looked exhausted before this stupid meeting, now he looks even more depleted.

He's either a damn good actor, or he meant it when he said he didn't blame me for leaving him ten years ago. I'm honestly not sure if that's better or worse than hating me for it. I'd been prepared for his anger . . . but I'm at a loss for how to handle this distant resignation.

Pastor Brown shifts in his chair. "What if it happens again?" he asks.

I scoff.

Both men turn my way.

"Really?" I chide, keeping my focus on the pastor. "We're getting married, for fuck's sake."

Kasey's eyes widen in surprise.

Pastor Brown's mouth grows tight. "I don't mean any offense, Ava, but I *am* curious to know what's occurred between the two of you since you've been back that would give Kasey some assurance that you won't just up and leave again."

A fire smolders in the crevices of my heart. "I came back because the real world chewed me up and spit me out. I couldn't hack it." The words feel bitter on my tongue. "I'm not going anywhere."

Kasey's eyes burn a hole in my cheek. "Ava," he says low, but I can't look at him.

"So you're choosing Kasey now because you failed to build a life elsewhere?" Pastor Brown asks.

"No," I snap, impatient. "I'm not marrying Kasey because I *failed*. I'm marrying him because he's the best man I know. Because he's honest and he's steady and he's careful with my heart, because he's respectful beyond measure. I'm *marrying* him, sir, because I *love* him."

My chest rises and falls with the force of the words escaping right out of my heart, grateful that the slip works in our favor.

Frustration coils tight against my ribs at the utter injustice of having to sit here and prove *anything* to this man.

"I see" is all he says in return. His expression gives nothing away.

I finally steal a glance at Kasey and find his eyes still rooted on me. They're alight with a violent mix of hurt and sorrow and confusion. I have a deep urge to reach for him, to press my finger into his skin and smooth it all away.

Steely resolve seems to settle in his brow. He turns to the pastor with tight lips. "Ava and I have worked through all of this." The lie comes out smooth. "We both realized that even if we don't have all the answers, facing life together is a much better option than missing out on what we have." He straightens his back, squaring his shoulders. "Neither of us wants to do that again. I won't pretend there aren't still fears, but if we're looking at hearts today you should know mine is with *her*, always."

Pastor Brown smiles lightly, leaning back in his chair so far that it creaks. "Very well then. Let's move on."

I throw Kasey my best syrupy-sweet smile. "That went well."

His eyes rise to the sprawling blue sky, as if begging for a bolt of lightning to strike him down. "Yeah, I could see the glaring approval written all over his face."

I laugh, and his gaze drops to me. "Seriously, how fucked do you think we are?"

The corner of his mouth twitches. "Royally, probably." He pulls open the passenger door of the truck and I climb in. "But at least you didn't puke this time."

I shoot him a glare, and he smirks. "*You* looked like you wanted to," I volley. Despite his teasing mood, the storm that brewed inside those doors is still swirling.

He shrugs. "I distinctly remember you saying it was going to be easy because we didn't care."

"I didn't say it would be *easy*, I said it would be *easier*. I stand by it. If we weren't pretending, we'd probably be feeling real shitty about ourselves after that mess of a meeting."

He gives me a long, curious look before shutting my door.

Kasey drives us back to the ranch so we can regroup. We spend the fifteen-minute ride in a silence that, though not as awkward as they have been, is still not quite comfortable. At least it's a step in the right direction for the bone-deep flame of hope still flickering that we can find a way to be friends.

His face lights up when we pull up the main drive, and I follow his line of sight through the windshield to see a medley of bikes and balls scattered around the lawn in front of the main house. Layla sits on the front porch with the youngest of Brooks's sons in her lap, and Mrs. Bennett stands hands-on-hip on the front walkway, watching the two other boys chase each other around on scooters. My heart catapults at the sheer warmth and love in Kasey's expression as he takes it all in, and then swiftly dive bombs as he slows the truck to a stop and rolls down the window.

"Good to see everyone out playing," he calls out to his mom.

She looks at him and smiles, shooting a backward thumb toward the house. "Brooks is inside. They came over for dinner if you want to join."

Kasey hesitates, turning back to me. He must see the panic on my face, because he faces her again, saying, "Ava and I have some stuff to sort out, but can we take a raincheck?"

"Kasey," I whisper. "Don't *not* go because of me. I can just . . . wait at the cabin."

He ignores me.

"Of course," his mom says. She shifts her focus to me, smile widening. "Can't wait to catch up with you both!"

I give her a polite wave back before pretending to dig into

my purse for Chapstick. I have a great deal of respect for the matriarch of the Bennett brothers; I know how hard it must have been to raise this family while constantly being thrust into the center of so much town lore. Still, I'm not ready to face her yet.

I'm not ready to explain myself—not when there's still so much Kasey doesn't know.

"How's he doing today?" Kasey asks, his voice considerably lower.

"He's all right," she answers. "It's been a good day."

He nods. "Good. I'll call you in the morning, okay?"

"Okay, honey. Love you."

"Love you too," he says before rolling up the window. I take a deep breath when we hit the small side road that leads directly to his cabin, and he throws me a smirk. "Scaredy cat."

"Am not."

"Not usually," he agrees. "But I like that it's my *mother* of all people who gets you flustered."

I roll my eyes. "Just drive, Kasey."

He laughs as I turn to look out the window, spotting a golden horse alone in a corral. It's the same one who nuzzled me in the barn when I came to talk to Kasey after he agreed to our plan. "What's her deal?" I ask, my gaze skimming down her long mane.

Kasey sighs. "She was rescued from a ranch after the owners were reported for animal mistreatment."

I whip my head to face him. "She was abused?"

"Not physically hurt, not that we can tell. But there wasn't enough food to go around for all the animals, and she was severely dehydrated when a vet got to her. We've had her for about a month and we're still working to get her saddled, but we're hoping she'll let us ride her soon."

I've always known the Bennetts' work here isn't just about training horses and selling them for profit. It's a long, tiring fight to protect the ones who need help, to rescue and keep the most vulnerable safe. I've regretted that I never got to see Kasey in action, knowing how much the work means to him.

I've seen him earn belts in rodeos and I've seen him train at camp. But I've never watched him rehabilitate a horse here on the ranch. Between my father's strict rules and my fierce independence, I didn't let myself integrate with Kasey's family and therefore never visited the ranch during daylight hours. He snuck me in on countless nights, but *not* for anything horse-related.

Deep down, I feel a rippling desire to see it all now, to understand this part of him that I shied away from back then. "I hope she lets you too," I finally say.

When we make it inside the cabin, I immediately unbuckle the straps of my heels and throw them aside before sinking into the plush couch.

"You really should wear better shoes," Kasey grumbles on his way to the kitchen, still making his disapproval of my fashion choices as obvious as ever. "Want coffee?"

"Sure," I say, kicking my feet up. A sigh of relief flows through me knowing our counseling sessions are over, but I can't help the worry that pinches tight in my brow. "What do you think Pastor Brown is going to do?"

Kasey snorts, pulling two mugs from a cabinet and setting them in front of the coffeemaker. One of them is pink, and I eye it curiously as he adds coffee to the filter before setting it to brew. "Your guess is as good as mine."

"What do we do if he rejects us?"

He shrugs. "You're the brains of this whole operation, sugar. I'm sure you'll think of something."

My chest flares with indignant annoyance. "It wouldn't kill you to be more helpful," I say. "I mean, you have this whole wide-open ranch—"

"I already said no, Ava." He throws me a stern look. "No ranch."

"Fine." I huff out a breath, sinking further into the couch.

"Plus, I'd think sitting through two of those fucking awful meetings is plenty proof of my help."

I wince. "I feel like he hates us."

"Does that bother you?"

"No," I say. "I don't care what anyone thinks."

"Liar," he mumbles under his breath. He turns his back toward me to watch the coffee trickle into the pot.

I glare at the back collar of his shirt. "Excuse me?"

"You heard me."

I scowl. "I do *not* care what people think of me, Kasey. I never have."

He turns to look at me over his shoulder. "Have you told your dad yet?"

"No."

His mouth kicks up. "Hm."

"Not because I care what he thinks!" I argue. "You know that man is going to make our lives hell when he finds out. The closer it is to an actual ceremony, the sooner I can get out of his house. I'm being strategic."

Kasey turns to face me again. He leans against the counter, crossing his arms over his chest. "How is it?" he asks. "Being home?"

I sigh. "Same as it used to be."

"Gloria?"

"Would very much rather I *not* be there." She hasn't spoken more than five words to me in the last few days—I think her patience over my presence is wearing thin.

He frowns. "You can stay here if you need to. You don't have to wait until the wedding."

I hold back a snort. "Shacking up out of wedlock? This town would riot." He smiles, but I can tell he's serious. "Come on, Kasey . . . you want me here less than Gloria wants me at home."

"That's not true," he argues, and I arch a brow. "Okay, maybe

I was a little . . . *reluctant*, at first. But that doesn't mean I don't want you here, Ava."

I blink at the sincerity in his tone. After all the vulnerability he let loose today, I've been ready for him to disappear behind his mask, but he seems more willing to show his cards.

"Did you mean it?" I dare to ask.

"Mean what?"

"You don't blame me for leaving?"

There it is again, the proof of his hurt. It's in the hard set of his brow, the downward slope of his mouth. "Of course I don't." His voice comes out so soft I almost can't bear it.

"How?" I manage through a knot forming at the base of my throat.

His expression turns indecipherable. "Like I said earlier, you made a brave choice. Can't fault you for it."

We stand, staring at each other, as the energy in the room dips low.

"I'm sorry," I murmur. "For what it's worth . . . I'm really sorry for leaving."

He turns around, abruptly giving me his back again. "All good." He pours fresh coffee into the mugs before pulling creamer out of the fridge and dousing each drink. After stirring, he carries them over. "Here," he says, holding out the pink mug.

The side of it reads *COWGIRL*, and I can't help but think that it might have been a woman to bring such a thing in here. Not that I have any right to worry about the comings and goings of women in Kasey's life—I gave up that right a long time ago. "I drink it black," I protest.

"I know you well enough to know your sweet tooth is a mile wide, sugar. Just enjoy the damn coffee."

Holding back a retort, I take a tentative sip knowing it's still hot. I wince at the burn on the tip of my tongue, but the coffee is *good*. Kasey's right: try as I might, I've always loved things on the sweeter side. But Tobias was a health nut, and I guess it just became easier to absorb his habits. "How do you know my tastes haven't changed?"

He gives me a small smirk. "Call it a hunch."

A dimple ghosts his cheek, and I can't help but look at it. "Okay," I say, forcing my thoughts—and gaze—away from him. "I have a couple minor updates. I reached out to an old college friend who specializes in estate planning and trust law. She reviewed the inheritance trust and confirmed a marriage is all we need. I asked her how soon the land ownership could be transferred after one of you got married, and she said there's really no waiting period. I personally think we should give it a few weeks so we don't encourage any thoughts about fraud. Maybe a month. But technically, the marriage itself will be all we need to stop your uncle from trying to make a claim to the land."

"What would happen if he tried before we transferred ownership?"

"The case would be reviewed, and the court would see the land is supposed to go to you and your brothers. We'd be able to present our marriage as proof of the stipulation being met. Technically, we wouldn't even have to proceed with transferring ownership anytime soon, because Huck wouldn't be able to win any rights to the land. He's banking on none of you being married as a means to weasel himself in. But since our little deal isn't going to last forever, we'll want to get the land in your name sooner rather than later."

"Makes sense," he says, nodding. He turns to look at the dark television screen as he thinks it all through. "What will you do? After?"

"After this is all done?"

His eyes turn downcast. "Yeah."

"I'm not sure," I say honestly. I take another small sip of the coffee, enjoying the comfort it brings.

"Are you really going to stick around?" he asks, voice quiet.

Apprehension claws at my lungs, making it harder to breathe.

The truth is I have no idea what to do from here—planning ahead has become rather complicated. But I know I can't go back to Miami, and there's really nothing else left. "I think so," I answer carefully. "I have a lot of things to figure out."

He lifts his gaze to me, his eyes full of a hundred questions. I ache to answer them all, to lay myself bare. He used to make me feel so confident about myself, so *capable*. I wonder what he'll say when he knows the truth.

When he finally speaks, his tone is wistful. "For what it's worth, you *are* brave, Ava. And this world is still yours for the taking. You didn't fail out there, and that Tobias guy is just a loser who didn't know how to let you shine."

My eyes sting with emotion, and I have to take another drink of coffee to stop the tears in their tracks. "I don't know," I admit. I drop my gaze to my lap, and my hair falls like a curtain to hide my face from him. "I'm not sure I have what it takes."

He reaches out a hand and gently pushes my hair back behind my shoulder. When I look at him, his eyes are simmering. "You do," he says.

And it sounds like he means it.

CHAPTER FOURTEEN

KASEY

I'm in *way* over my head.

Rhett carries two handfuls of beers over from the bar, followed by Colt Rustler balancing a tray of shots. I eye the clear liquid sloshing around each one with a healthy level of skepticism. "That better not be tequila," I mutter.

Wells grins. "It's definitely tequila. I can smell it from here."

I grimace. "That's *definitely* not a good sign."

"Drinks for the husband-to-be!" Rhett shouts loud enough for the whole damn bar to hear. A raucous cheer erupts from the tables around us, which only eggs him on. "Body shots coming soon!" he hollers. "Also, looking for volunteer bodies!"

"Jesus," I groan, hiding my face behind my hand.

Spurs is crowded tonight with a mix of tired cowboys, beautiful women, college-aged troublemakers, and even a rogue table of bikers in the far corner who stare down anyone who gets too close. It's busy as hell—the vibe so much different than the lower, grumpier energy we get at Wild Coyote. I usually try to avoid places like this, but tonight I'm soaking in the pulsing vitality, hoping it's enough to distract me from the torment a certain wild-mouthed brunette is wreaking on my mind.

I'm marrying him because he's the best man I know.

Because he's honest and he's steady and he's careful with my heart.

I'm marrying him, sir, because I love him.

It was real. I could tell from the look on her face that Ava wasn't lying when she said the words that nearly buckled me in that office. It was like shooting out of a fucking chute in a championship rodeo. I've replayed them over and over again, wrestling with myself over the urge to try to talk to her about it.

I've been working so hard to keep myself safe from the feelings I still hold, but I'll be damned—I think Ava might have let 'em all loose at that moment.

The guys drop a shot and a beer in front of me. I immediately throw back the shot.

Rhett frowns. "Dude, couldn't even wait for the cheers?"

Wells laughs across the table.

I shrug. "Sorry. Needed it."

Rhett's eyes narrow.

"That's okay," Colt says, "we have plenty more." He unceremoniously drops another shot in front of me.

"To the groom!" Rhett cheers.

"To the groom!" Wells and Colt echo.

I lift the drink, chest still squeezed tight. "To Ava," I say before tipping it back.

Colt slaps a hand over my shoulder, grinning from ear to ear. "Heard you have it bad for this one, Kase."

My eyes snap to Rhett, who snickers as he sits down next to Wells.

"Well, I mean, we *are* getting married."

Colt doesn't know that my upcoming nuptials are anything but real. I don't trust anyone other than my family with truths that could hurt us or Ava. "Never thought I'd see the day you got wifed up." He turns his gaze to Rhett. "Also never thought I'd see him with a girl at all. Must be something in the water y'all are drinking." He shudders. "Keep it the hell away from me."

"You should try it," Rhett says over the music.

"Fuck no." Colt frowns.

"Olivia told me Ava's got a dress," Rhett says, looking at me.

My throat constricts. "Yeah?"

"You didn't know?"

"I don't really keep tabs on what she's doing," I say defensively.

"I'm with Colt—I can't believe you're getting married," Wells says, tipping beer into his mouth.

Rhett snorts. "Me either."

"It's not that big of a deal," I say.

They both look at me with growing amusement.

"Marriage is like, a *huge* fucking deal," Colt chimes in.

I shoot him a glare, like I don't already know.

"What do you like about her?" he asks, genuinely curious.

Rhett and Wells lean in.

It takes effort not to roll my eyes. "She's . . . beautiful." *So fucking beautiful.* "And she keeps me on my toes, you know?"

"How is she in bed?" Colt asks, wagging his eyebrows.

I shove him so hard he falls out of his chair.

"Fuck!" he yells, hurrying to get back up. "Geez, it was just a question. No reason to get fucking testy."

"That's my future wife you're talking about," I growl. "Show some respect."

He throws his hands up in surrender before setting his chair upright and sitting back down beside me.

I turn to look at my brothers, who are both hiding knowing smiles. I point a finger at them. "Don't."

Rhett raises a hand to his forehead in salute.

"I'm surprised Sheriff Joe hasn't paid us a visit yet," Wells says, looking from Rhett to me. "Does he know?"

I shrug. "Ava's avoiding it. But if he hasn't heard from someone else yet, it's only a matter of time."

"How do you think he's going to take it?" Rhett asks, voice low.

Anxiety pummels through my gut as I look sidelong at Colt. I might not blame him for what happened at his family's ranch, but I'm still fucking pissed his older brother Ellis put us all in such reckless danger. "Honestly, I'm more worried about him hearing about something else."

Colt's eyes skip around the bar as he sips from his sweating bottle. He must feel the weight of my attention though, because he drops the bottle and scratches the back of his neck. "Look, I'm furious with Ellis too. But he swears it's on him if shit goes south."

"And you trust him?" I ask. "Ellis only ever looks out for himself."

Colt looks at me with a level of hurt so profound it nearly steals the breath from my lungs. "Well the fuck aware," he grumbles. "Still, I've never seen him like this. He stopped drinking, stopped fucking around with his loser friends. He's helping Wylie Jo with the baby and taking on more work at the ranch. I think he's hoping if he keeps his nose clean, it'll keep anyone from sniffing around." He looks me in the eye. "But if they do, he *promised* me he'll take the fall. For all of us."

I blow out a breath, letting the words sink in. "I hope so," I manage.

WELLS DRIVES US HOME WELL AFTER MIDNIGHT. WE ALL have early as fuck mornings to show up for, but it was damn near impossible to get Rhett and Colt out of those barstools. It honestly loosened some of the strain in my chest to see them both happy and laughing, especially after everything that went down at

Rustler's Ranch, so I didn't push our exit too hard until I realized they were starting to tip into too-drunk territory.

Both of those boys have been involved in things I'd never wish for them to experience, between our lawless fathers and the illegal shit we've *all* run at one point or another. It all needs to stop, for both families, but I can only really control my own. I never realized how much Rhett carries on his shoulders—I thought he was just born to be a hellion, full of our father's genes. Had I known all the things he was going through and all the ways he was trying to save our family, I would have set him straight a long time ago.

I don't blame Colt for that card game going sideways, but that boy *is* a fucking hellion, and as much as I love him it's hard not to worry about his influence on Rhett.

Rhett asks us to take him to Wild Coyote. He's been calling the apartment upstairs home more and more these days, and I have a hunch he's not the only one—a point proven when we pull into the lot and see lights turned on through the windows of the second story. "Olivia's in there," he explains sheepishly from the back seat.

Wells chuckles. He turns around to smack him on the knee. "Enjoy your night."

"See you bright and fucking early."

"Don't be late!" I shout as he gets out. "I better find you in that barn at sunrise, or your ass is grass."

Rhett swings the door shut and scampers off to the bar's front doors.

"Good to see him happy," Wells says as he pulls back onto the road that takes us home.

"Yeah," I agree. "And you too, kid. You and Layla—it feels right."

He flashes a bright, unfiltered smile.

When we eventually pull up to my cabin, I'm surprised to see lights shining out of my windows too. "What the hell?" I mutter, squinting through the truck's window.

"You expecting someone?" Wells asks.

"No."

"Want me to come in with you?" Wells asks, sensing my apprehension.

I think about Mean-Eyed Maverick and his gang of outlaws who are probably looking for vengeance. I'm not sure it'd be cops at this hour . . . "No," I tell him. "Just wait here a sec, yeah?"

Wells nods, and I get out of the truck, acting as normal as possible. There's no use trying to hide the fact that I'm home—anyone inside would've heard us pulling up. I make my way toward the front porch, craning my neck to try to get a glimpse through the front window. It's not until I'm climbing up the first couple of steps that I see a mess of long brown hair pulled up in a loose bun and an old red Mustangs sweatshirt.

Ava.

I exhale out a sigh of relief. But then a different kind of panic slices through me.

I turn to wave Wells off before opening the door. Ava tucked herself cross-legged into the far corner of my couch, hugging herself around her middle. When she looks up at me with a small smile, I notice the skin around her eyes is red and puffy.

Like she's been crying.

Any remnants of the buzz I still had outside is gone in an instant. "What's wrong?" I ask, eyeing her up and down.

"I'm so sorry for just showing up like this. I just . . . I needed to get out of my house."

"Don't be sorry." I take a few steps toward her. "Are you okay?"

"Were you on a date?" she asks, before squeezing her eyes shut. "Actually, never mind, you don't have to answer that. It's none of my business."

"No, it isn't," I agree. "But no, I wasn't on a date. How would that look if someone saw me?"

There's no mistaking the relief in her eyes, or the swoop I feel in my chest because of it. "Oh," she says. "Right."

I study her face, looking for any clues that might help me understand why she's here or how to help her. Kicking out of my dirty boots, I make my way over to the couch and sit down beside her, keeping a respectful distance between us. I'm worried that if I press too hard, she might bolt. She's here, which means something's wrong. But I know from experience I need to let her come around to opening up. "You hungry?" I ask. "I have some leftover pizza in the fridge."

She shakes her head. "No, thank you."

My eyes drop to the sweater she's wearing. A small grin pulls at my lips. Reaching out, I hook my pointer finger inside the hem at her neck and gently tug. My knuckle brushes along her collarbone, and I feel her lean into it. "If I remember correctly, you stole this from me junior year."

She smiles too, but it doesn't quite reach her eyes. "It's my favorite."

"Still looks good on you."

She flushes, her fingers toying in her lap.

"Want a drink?" I ask. "I think I have some beer."

"Maybe just some water?"

"Okay," I say, getting up.

I make it halfway through the kitchen before she says, "Kasey, I have to tell you something."

It's the fear in her voice that stops me. I turn back around to face her, my worry spiking. The flush in her cheeks has disappeared and the rest of her face has gone pale.

And then she says two words I wouldn't have ever expected to come out of her beautiful mouth.

"I'm pregnant."

CHAPTER FIFTEEN

AVA

Kasey looks at me, utterly dumbfounded.

I wait patiently for the words to settle, for the secret I've been keeping to finally make its crash landing. I wait for those brown eyes to squeeze shut in anger, for his jaw to tic and his neck to roll. I wait for him to start yelling about how I'm trying to trap him in a marriage without giving him the full truth. About how I'm still the reckless and irresponsible and *selfish* girl I've always been.

But none of that happens.

Kasey just looks at me, frozen in shock. He looks and looks and looks. I don't even think he's blinking, but his face is shadowed in the dim kitchen light, and my eyes are too watery to know for sure.

"Kasey?" I ask, voice trembling.

His eyes flare wide. "I'm sorry," he says, shaking his head. Like this might be some kind of hallucination his mind is serving up to fuck with him. He looks at me again, squinting. I can see the way he's internally working to piece this all together. "What did you say?"

I let out a quick breath, standing to face him as fear rattles through me. "I'm pregnant, Kasey. I'm so sorry I didn't tell you before now."

His gaze drops to my stomach before rising again to meet mine. "How . . ." he starts, but stops, stumbling over his words. "But we . . . I don't—"

My heart breaks at his confusion. Shatters that his first reaction would be to think he might have something to do with it, even though we haven't slept together in ten years. The proof of his shock is another deep layer of my own guilt and regret. "It's not yours," I say carefully, feeling something long dormant inside my soul wither and curl in on itself. "When I left Miami to come back home, I was already pregnant. I found out two weeks before I left."

Kasey's expression shutters, his face slackening. "Tobias?" he asks. It's barely a whisper.

I nod.

He looks down at his feet, taking in a deep breath. "Does he know?"

I can't help but cringe. "Yeah," I answer softly. "He knows."

Kasey looks back up at me, the question clear in his eyes.

"It's what he used against me," I explain. "With the partners. He told them I was 'knocked up.' That I was planning on keeping the baby and would be too distracted to commit to the firm in the ways it needed me to. It's why they rescinded my partnership agreement."

His eyes flash with a fierce intensity that siphons all the air from the room, the sharp edge of his jaw pulsing. "Isn't that illegal?"

I shrug. "I could try to sue them for discrimination, but they'd bury me. They're lawyers with way more resources than I have. It's not worth the fight."

"So, what? You just . . . *lose* the opportunity? You're forced to walk away from everything you worked so hard for all these years?"

"They didn't fire me," I say. "They've actually sent over a dozen emails asking when I'm coming back. But I won't ever be made partner—that's no longer on the table."

Fury flashes over Kasey's face, there and gone in the span of a breath. He eyes my stomach again with scrutiny. "It's why you were sick," he says, almost to himself. He scrubs a hand over his jaw before stuffing his hands into his pockets, rocking back on the heels of his feet. "Wait, you said you're planning to keep the baby?"

I nod. "Yes."

And then I see it: his smile. It's gone before I truly have a chance to catch it, but my heart knows it was there because it pounds furiously.

"How far along are you?"

I swallow. "Thirteen weeks. I just started my second trimester. The doctor in Miami said I'm due at the end of November."

"How do you feel?" he asks, and there's genuine curiosity behind his words.

"I'm okay," I say. "The nausea has been a little rough, as you saw, but otherwise I don't really feel any different."

He nods, eyes falling to the ground again. After a long moment he asks, "What does this mean, Ava?"

"What do you mean?"

He clears his throat. "What does this mean for me? For us?"

"It doesn't mean anything." I walk into the kitchen until he's a mere foot away, reaching a hand out and pressing it to his chest. His heart is galloping, and I imagine he's thinking of all the ways I'm trying to take advantage of him and his family.

I desperately need him to understand I was never trying to trap him, that I don't expect him to bear any responsibility for my mistakes. "I know I've been keeping this truth from you, but I've been trying to figure out how to justify it alongside asking for this marriage. This baby *isn't* your responsibility," I promise. "I'm going to do whatever I can to make sure it doesn't disrupt your life. I'm prepared to do this all on my own."

"What about Tobias?"

I exhale slowly. "He's made it clear he doesn't want to be involved. He has no interest in being a father, trust me."

"What if *I* want it to mean something?" he asks. There's a softness to his expression, a spark of hope that draws me nearer as the question sends me into a freefall. "What if I want to take responsibility?"

"Kasey," I breathe out. "You don't mean that."

He presses a tentative palm to my cheek, and I lean into the warmth of it. "You shouldn't have to raise a baby alone, Ava. You'll need support. You're going to need help with things. What about a crib? I mean, christ—what about labor?"

"I'll manage just fine on my own," I assure him. "I've been reading books and making lists. I've got enough money saved that I can take a decent break from work when she's born—"

"She?" he asks, eyes widening and dropping once more to my stomach. His free hand reaches for my waist, gently gripping and pulling me closer.

Emotion stings my eyes and claws at my throat. "I mean, I don't know for sure yet. I won't know the gender for another few weeks. I still need to find a new doctor here and make an appointment, but I just have this feeling." I smile. "In my dreams, she's always a girl."

Our bodies are flush now, and it's . . . dizzying. Intoxicating and unexpected. And against my better judgement, I keep finding new ways to lean deeper into him. Kasey's so warm and steady, and he's always felt like home. Still, even after all this time. "Ava," he whispers, his breath fanning along my cheek. Emotion glistens his eyes as his mouth tips up in a lopsided, happy grin. "You're having a *baby*. I'm not going to let you face this alone." His thumb swipes tenderly against my jaw. He's careful, every movement slow and tentative, like he doesn't want to scare me away.

Tell me, do you worry she might leave again?

"It's too much," I quietly protest, as a lone tear slips down my cheek. "I can't keep letting you fix my mistakes, Kasey, I've already put you through so much—"

"Ava," he says gently. "Everything we've been through . . . we both contributed to it, *all* of it. The good and the bad. God, we were so young. We've both made mistakes, both took things for granted—it was never just you. I . . . I thought—" He swallows. "I thought we were ready to spend our lives together, but really, I was just so desperate to keep you. I shouldn't have pushed you. I shouldn't have proposed."

My heart pounds as I feel the weight of what he might be about to say, what he might be trying to ask me for. What I already know I don't have to give. "Kasey—"

"Please just let me finish," he pleads. "I felt it, in Pastor Brown's office. The things you were saying—it felt real, Ava. And I've been trying to keep my distance from you, but the truth is I have to fight my feelings every step of the way because when you're near me, it all just goes to shit. Even when we were kids, I used to try to fight the way I felt about you, but it never worked. It never fucking works, and . . . I don't know, maybe . . . maybe we can try this again."

His eyes are bright with so much hope that I have to look away. Despair ratchets through me, twisting through my insides until everything clamps into uncomfortable knots. All the old fears and anxiety I used to wear like a second skin press into me all over again, smothering me like tar.

Kasey was always so good at communicating his feelings. It's something I've envied, but I don't know how to tell him how I feel when I don't even *understand* my own feelings. I don't know how to articulate all the ways his love and support drive me deeper into my own self-loathing, because I don't know how to give him back what he gives so freely, so easily.

I make myself look at him before I say the words that burn

like acid all the way up my throat. "I think you misunderstood," I explain. "I don't—I don't know if us being together was ever a good idea."

Hurt darts across his eyes, and I know my words have landed with precision. The hands that cradle me so lovingly drop to his sides as he takes a firm step back. "Liar," he whispers.

"Kasey, please."

"No, Ava. Ten years later and you're *still* doing it."

My sorrow gives way to frustration as my blood heats. "Doing *what*?"

"Acting like this isn't what we've both always known it is!" he barks. "Acting like my feelings for you are one-sided. Like the way I feel about you isn't more than some school-age crush."

"I am *not* eighteen years old anymore, Kasey," I snap. "I'm not the same girl I used to be, regardless of what you may think. We had something real when we were kids, but it was young and naive. We're older now, and I know myself better. I've lived through so much beyond what we had—this baby is proof."

He scowls, his face twisted in bitter resentment. I watch as he walks to the small kitchen table and drops into a chair, looking downright miserable.

I hate myself for hurting him all over again.

"Ever since I came back you've been making your opinions about me loud and clear: you don't like my shoes, my clothes, or how I take my damn coffee. You want to strip me of all the things that make me different from who I was when I left so I can get back to being the girl who was *yours*. But I'm not her, Kasey. I can't be her—not anymore. Not when I have to focus on being *this*," I say, holding my palm against my stomach. "I have to be *hers*." A quiet sob bubbles up and out of me as tears stream down my face.

Kasey studies me for a long time. Eventually, he asks, "Why did you leave, Ava?"

I stifle a scoff. This is the last place I want this conversation to go. "I didn't have a choice," I admit.

His gaze narrows. "Then why did you say yes? Why did you let me put that ring on your finger?"

"Because *I wanted you.*" My voice breaks. "But I didn't trust myself." The words spill out of my mouth, revealing a fractured part of myself I never intended for him to see.

"Didn't trust yourself to do what?" he asks.

I let my gaze trail along the hard set of his jaw, deciding how far I'm willing to go. "Stay," I answer honestly. I move to sit down in a chair on the other side of the table as I work to gather my thoughts. "I didn't trust myself to stay here. I wanted to say yes to you, Kasey. When you asked me to marry you, I felt so *unbelievably* happy. Like every dream I ever had was coming true. But then I remembered who I am, and . . . I didn't trust myself to stay."

"Why?"

"I'm not sure I even know how to. It's like this . . . this curse. Sometimes I think I was built to run from everything good in my life. The last thing I ever wanted to do was hurt you." I let out a bitter laugh. "And it's exactly what I did anyway. I convinced myself that if I left, I'd find some relief from the pressure of this place, and maybe I'd learn to be still. I even thought maybe I could come back to you someday, but . . ." I let the words die off. "I mean, it's not like I could've asked you to go with me—"

"*Why?*" he demands, color rising in his cheeks.

"You would have said no," I say plainly. "You wouldn't have come."

"*Yes I fucking would have!*" he snaps, rising to his feet with a strong push that sends his chair flying behind him. "You didn't even give me a chance."

"You have the ranch, Kasey!" I yell. "I know what it meant to you, what it still means to you. I would *never* put you in a position where you have to choose between it or me. I already know what you'd pick!"

"I would have chosen you," he insists, and the sincerity in his eyes crack me wide open. "I would have *always* chosen you."

He shakes his head, turning away from me. "I'm going to bed," he says, sounding defeated, before disappearing down the hallway.

I hear the soft click of his bedroom door as he pulls it shut behind him.

CHAPTER SIXTEEN

KASEY

"Well, look who it is," Rhett grumbles from inside a barn stall, a shaving fork gripped in his hand, looking a little green around the gills. "All this '*I better find you in that barn at sunrise, or your ass is grass*' bullshit and you don't even show up 'til fucking ten."

He's right, I'm late. But I don't have the patience to deal with him this morning. "Sorry," I mumble.

"Yeah." He nods. "You better fucking be."

Wells strides in, leading a retired racehorse we've been working with back into his stall. He raises an eyebrow as he looks from Rhett to me. "Fair warning. He's a little cranky," he tells me, nodding to Rhett.

"Seven shots and half a dozen beers will do that to you."

Rhett suddenly hunches over to gag in the corner. When nothing comes up but a mouthful of spit he aims in my direction, he takes a moment to collect himself before straightening and looking back at me. "I still showed up this morning." He glowers. "I think I'm still *drunk*, actually, and yet I almost have this whole barn clean."

I sigh, working to press down my own irritation. "Look, I'm

sorry. It was a late night." Not a lie—I didn't get into bed until almost two in the morning after that disaster of a conversation with Ava, and then I tossed and turned all night with more fucking nightmares. "I must have slept through my alarm."

"Late-night visits from pretty brunettes can have that effect," Wells quips with a sly grin. "I mean, hell, I know all about it."

"That's not what happened. She was just here to talk."

"Yeah, yeah, whatever you say." He laughs. But his smile slips as he really looks at me. "You okay?"

"Fine," I say, turning to reach for a saddle pad so I can get the golden mare Ava pointed out the other day ready for a ride.

Rhett grumbles something under his breath to Wells, but I don't hear it and I don't want to. I ignore them both as I focus on my task of getting the horse ready for a ride before leading her out of the barn. She puts up a bit of a fight at first, none too happy with being saddled, but after a few affectionate strokes along her nose and some murmured praise, she allows me to do what's needed.

There are two corrals that sit relatively close to the big barn, just outside of the wide doors, as well as a third tucked around the corner that we haven't been using as much lately without Brooks in rotation on this training schedule. It's further away from any prying eyes and, not trusting myself to keep my cool with my brothers today, I decide it's where we'll go.

Leading the mare takes effort because she's not very trusting. She might've let me get a saddle and bridle on, but she doesn't like it when I encourage her to keep moving with light tugs and lets out loud snorts in obvious protest. It takes controlled patience— something far easier to extend to her than to Rhett—but we eventually make it into the open pen.

"Good girl, Goldie," I murmur, dragging my hand down her long neck. She huffs out a frustrated breath before leaning into my hand, and I laugh. "You're torn, aren't you, girl? You want to trust me but aren't sure how."

Sounds a lot like another fiery girl in my life.

I test her willingness to cooperate by lifting my foot and setting it the stirrup, pushing a little weight in through my leg. Goldie takes a step back, shifting on her feet, but then holds still for me. I smile at her, telling her what a beauty she is, hoping she can feel my respect and care.

But then I shift my weight onto my leg and fully stand in the stirrup, and she rears back with a loud whinny, forcing me to bail.

I repeat the exercise, continuing to push weight into the stirrup while rewarding her with affectionate strokes and praise. Eventually, she lets me stand in the stirrup while I rub along her shoulders, and I think I'm close to earning my way into the saddle.

But then my phone chimes from my back pocket, and I let out a muffled curse as the sound sends Goldie rearing back again, tearing down all this trust we've just built. "Just what I need," I mutter, pulling my phone out to silence the notifications—something I should have done before I pulled this horse out. It's a rookie mistake I shouldn't be making.

I notice Ava's name across the screen where a new text message has come in. *Just got a call from Pastor Brown*, it reads.

A second text buzzes in a moment later. *We're on for Saturday's ceremony, if you're still in this.*

I stare at the words, unblinking, as my heart jumps into my throat.

If I'm still in this?

If *I'm* still in this?

If this woman only fucking knew how much I was still in this, even after last night's conversation went to absolute shit. I should have never walked away from her, should have never left her alone in my kitchen with tears streaming down her face. But even with the panic swelling inside me, the truth of my feelings for her still bleeds out like a rotting wound and I'd bet damn good money they're a perfect match to hers.

Last night wasn't the first time I've let myself be vulnerable with Ava Jones only for her to try to throw it back in my face and make me feel crazy, and I have a strong suspicion it won't be the last. But as pissed as I am at the cruelty of this cycle we seem to be in, I woke up this morning knowing one thing for damn sure: we might be ten years older, but she and I have unfinished business.

We might *always* have unfinished business. Until a miracle strikes down from the heavens and Ava finally opens her heart to me in all the ways that matter, I'm going to be bucking on this fucking ride, holding on to all the shreds of hope I can find. The worst part is, knowing how stubborn she is, I might go to my *grave* still pining for her.

I can pretend all I fucking what, but it's not going to change the truth.

I look down at my phone again and scoff. If I'm still in this *my ass.*

I fire off a nice and short *Yep* before tucking my phone back in my pocket, huffing out a long breath that matches the one Goldie lets out. "Sorry, girl," I murmur, stepping toward her with a tentative arm out, knowing I need to regain ground. "If it helps, you're not the only girl currently scared of me."

Her dark brown eye catches hold of mine, curious and observant.

"What do you say we take a break? And later, when I pull you out again, you let me ride you around this corral?"

She lifts her head high, as if seeking out the sunshine. I take it as a good sign and give her a loving pat on her rump before leading her back to the barn.

A LIGHT KNOCK SOUNDS FROM THE FRONT DOOR JUST as I'm about to get into the shower. Pulling my robe off the hook in the bathroom, I wrap it around myself then trudge warily toward the door. I briefly look down at myself to make sure I'm decent before pulling the door open, finding my mother on the other side.

"Mom?" I look her up and down. "You okay?"

"Of course! Are you?"

I can't help it—I laugh. "Yeah," I answer, smiling. "What are you doing all the way out here? I would have come to the house."

She waves a hand. "I wanted to come to you." Her gaze moves to the space above my shoulder, sneaking a peek inside the cabin.

And then it dawns on me. "She's not here, you nosy woman."

"What are you talking about?" she asks, feigning innocence as she steps closer, forcing me to take a step back so she can come inside. "I'm here to see you."

"Uh-huh," I say, still smiling. My mother puts up with a lot from all of us, and she's never failed to provide my brothers and me with whatever we might need. I'd consider her my biggest supporter in life, without any hesitation. But she's also not usually one to get super involved in our personal lives. "Let me go turn off the shower," I say. "Give me a sec."

"No problem!" she chirps, heading for the kitchen. I notice the way she scans my living room, like she's looking for anything that might be different.

Shaking my head, I go back into the bathroom and turn off the faucet. I pick up my dirty clothes and dump them in the hamper in my room, and then make my way back to the kitchen where I find her seated at the table. "You want anything? Water? Beer?"

"A beer sounds wonderful," she says. A rare choice for Mom —she pretty much stopped drinking when Dad did, I think in an effort to show support . . . . *and* to keep alcohol out of the house.

I pull two bottles out of the fridge, popping them open before setting them down on the table. "To what do I owe this visit?" I ask, curious.

She takes a big sip of her beer, her eyes closing as she swallows it down. "Damn, I almost forgot how good that is."

I chuckle. "Especially after a long day," I admit.

She looks at me blankly. "Sweetheart, it's been a long fucking decade."

Her blunt honesty catches me by surprise. "You okay, Mom?"

She nods. "Fine. Tired, but fine. Brooks went to the grocery store today—it's the first time he's left the ranch since . . ." Her voice trails off.

My chest squeezes. "How'd he do?"

She shrugs. "Okay, I think. I didn't press too hard, but he got plenty of groceries and seemed in good spirits when he got back."

Relief overcomes me. "That's so good."

She nods. "Layla's really been a huge help with the boys. That girl will be an incredible mother someday, if she chooses to be."

My pulse spikes as my thoughts careen to Ava. "I went and saw Brooks and the boys the other day," I say, pushing the thought away. "They seem happy, considering. I know Liam just got in trouble, but—"

"Wasn't his fault," she finishes for me. "I know, I know. I used to get calls from the school constantly with you boys, and more than half the time you lot were being blamed for shit that had nothing to do with you."

I take a sip of my beer, letting the cold carbonation burn against my tongue. "This town isn't always fair," I say.

"Nope," she agrees. "You know, your father has been up and moving around a lot more these last few weeks. He still hasn't gone outside the house, but he's been doing what he can to help with things so I can be there for Brooks and the boys." She pauses, considering her words. "I know he's been worried about all this inheritance stuff, but I think you and Rhett talking to him about it and asking him to step up might have made him realize he could be doing more."

Her gaze slices to me, gauging my reaction. My brothers and I have always had a complicated relationship with our father—especially Rhett. But Brooks and I were old enough to see plenty of his good days before his accident, before his wild and reckless lifestyle turned against him and cost him his leg. It's been over twenty years, and I still miss that man dearly.

"Anyway," she continues, "I told him what you and that girl of yours have cooking to stop this ranch from going to Huck."

"Really?" I ask, tentative. "What does he think?"

"He thinks you're making too big a sacrifice," she says, her voice stern enough to tell me she feels the same way. But then her eyes soften. "But he's really damn proud of you, Kasey."

I take in the words, letting them permeate. "And you?"

"I think it's noble, honey. The Bennetts have always protected family above all else. But I have to admit, I worry about you. I worry about where this leads."

I sigh. "You don't have to worry about me, Mom. I know what I'm doing."

"Do you?" she asks, really looking at me.

No, I want to say. Instead, I go with, "I'll be fine."

She nods, taking another pull from her beer. And then she says, "You know, I saw how bad it wrecked you when Ava left. And I've seen you with a new girl here and there over the years, but I don't think you've really given your heart away to anyone else, have you?"

"No," I admit. "I haven't."

"Why not?"

"Honestly? I think Ava still has it," I say, forcing out a dark chuckle. "I think she always will whether she wants it or not."

Her eyes narrow. "Does she know that?"

"I don't know," I answer. "I think at her core she might, but it scares her. I'm not sure she knows how to let someone really love her."

"Your father was like that," she says. "Rhett too. Vulnerability is incredibly hard for some people, especially when they've had to live through hard things. But don't be afraid to show her that love isn't *just* scary, Kasey, if that's what you want."

I blow out a breath. "Thanks, Mom," I say, giving her a small smile. I can't help but wonder what she'd say if she knew Ava is pregnant, how that might change her mind about what we're doing.

Either way, it wouldn't matter.

Because I'm going to marry her, come hell or high water.

CHAPTER SEVENTEEN

AVA

"Let me curl your hair," Layla insists, her expression hopeful as she stands in the middle of Kasey's kitchen. "You've got such gorgeous long hair. We don't even have to put it up!"

Olivia nods, looking from Layla to me. "I'm a disaster with makeup or really anything useful in this situation, but I can make us some lunch! Or can I open the bottle of champagne? I brought orange juice for mimosas."

"Champagne?" I ask, my gaze bouncing back to Layla.

"I think I'll just stick to orange juice for now, if that's okay?" Layla asks.

Olivia nods, heading for the fridge. "You got it."

Layla shoots me a knowing smile and I try not to scowl, wondering if she's calling my bluff, baiting me to see if I ask for orange juice too. When I don't say anything, she pulls out a chair tucked beneath the kitchen table and pats the back of it, as if to beckon me to sit. "It'll take fifteen minutes. Twenty tops."

"Fine," I manage to let out, still trying to extricate myself from the self-induced pity party I've been stuck inside all morning. Nausea reared its ugly and vindictive head the moment I

169

opened my eyes, and that discomfort paired with the emotional recoil of knowing I'm marrying Kasey today, even after everything we both said to each other the other night in this very kitchen, has been a lot to manage.

He gave up his cabin this morning so I'd have a place to get ready while he prepares for the day's festivities at the main house with his brothers. I haven't physically seen him since the night I told him I'm pregnant, though not for a lack of trying. I've texted him a few times to try to meet and continue our conversation with calmer heads, but he refused to answer, putting me on a communication timeout. I had half a mind to show up here unannounced again, but something told me not to push.

I move to sit in the same chair Kasey knocked over last time I was here, doing my best to block the memory firmly out of my mind.

"Thank you," Layla says, giving my shoulder a soft squeeze before plugging in a curling iron she pulled out of her tote bag.

Olivia moseys over with two glasses, setting both down on the table in front of me. "The one on the left is just juice," she chirps happily before heading back to the counter.

"Thanks!" Layla and I say in unison.

I stare at the cup on the right with dread, but then Layla reaches for it, using it to nudge the left one closer to me before pulling it up to take a drink.

She took the cup with champagne in it and left me the one with orange juice.

She helped me keep my secret.

I turn to look over my shoulder at where she stands behind me, wondering if she made a mistake. But she sips from her drink and winks.

A burst of emotion swells inside of me at her kindness. I've been wondering for days if she'd really put it all together in that dressing room, and it's a relief to know that not only did she realize the truth, but she's also decided to keep it under wraps.

Thank you, I mouth.

She nods, then turns my head back around to part my hair into sections. "So, how are you feeling about today?"

"Honestly? Starting to regret that we didn't just elope in the courthouse."

"Why didn't you?" Olivia asks.

"It's important people think it's real . . . I convinced Kasey that we needed to make a show of it."

Layla curls a piece of hair around the iron. "Who's all going to be there?"

I lift a shoulder. "It was posted to the church's bulletin board as an open ceremony."

I hear Layla suck in a breath behind me. "Yikes."

True to her word, it takes her less than twenty minutes to have it all curled. She even pulls a beautiful hair comb from her bag with pearls and rhinestones that she sets in above my temple.

When she asks if she can do my makeup too, I give in and let her do her thing, feeling a serene sense of comfort at the feel of her soft brushes gliding against my skin. It's a foreign sensation to have anyone do something like this for me—my mother was already gone by the time I cared about things like makeup—and I have to fight the emotion that threatens to take hold.

"There," Layla finally says, tucking her things back in her bag.

"Wow," Olivia breathes out, staring at me from across the table like I'm some kind of alien.

"I know, right?" Layla says back, smug as hell.

"What?" I ask.

"You look . . ."

"Fucking hot," Layla finishes, and Olivia laughs.

I stand, wanting to see for myself. What I find in the bathroom mirror catches me completely off guard. Since leaving Saddlebrook Falls, I shed most traces of the wild southern girl who used to raise hell and layered on new pieces of the woman I was so focused on becoming. But the woman I see in front of me now looks like who I might have become had I never left, a version of me who really might have been Kasey Bennett's wife.

My hair is curled around my face and shoulders, brushing along the length of my arms and back. The comb sparkles in the bright bathroom light, casting small, glittering rainbows on the walls and ceiling. Layla used soft brown eyeliner along my lashes paired with a dark mascara that brings out the blue in my eyes. My cheeks are flushed with the barest hint of a peachy-pink blush, and my lips are glossed with a simple, nude tint.

For the first time since I left, I'm realizing I've been hiding myself behind the mask of the woman I've tried so hard to mold myself into. One who's sharp and savvy, if a little distant. A woman who can't possibly be too hurt by anything because her heart is locked up tight and shielded behind a wall of thorns. But in my reflection now, I see the clear traces of my softer edges, of the warmth and spirit I know I still carry.

Layla and Olivia peek in from the hallway, eager to know what I think.

"Do you think he'll like it?" I ask them, suddenly more nervous than I've ever felt in my life.

I realize too late everything the question reveals. But neither of them calls me out on it. "He's going to love it," Layla says confidently.

"He's going to lose his mind," Olivia adds.

"Ready for your dress?" Layla asks.

I take a deep breath.

Ready or not—here we go.

"Ava, listen to me—"

"*No*, Dad! I'm sorry, but no," I seethe, squaring my shoulders as I stare my father down. I honestly thought I'd be able to skirt through this ceremony without him knowing what I was doing, but as I prepared to walk down the aisle, he was waiting for me outside the closed doors. "You shouldn't be here. I have to go!"

His face grows red with the force of his anger. "*I* shouldn't be here? At my own daughter's wedding? I should be a part of this, Ava! I should have heard this was even happening from *you* and not from Eleanor pointing out a damn bulletin board—"

"Yeah, and what would you have said?" I interject. "The only reason you're here right now is to save face because you know the whole town will be expecting you to walk me down that aisle and give me away. Don't pretend like you believe in this marriage, Dad. You've made your feelings about Kasey and his family *really* fucking clear, haven't you? You don't believe in Kasey. I'm not sure you even believe in me."

His eyes widen. "That is *not* true, Ava. I've *always* believed in you."

The emotion in his voice is enough to give me pause. I don't think I've ever heard him say anything like that.

"Look," he continues, "you won't talk to me, honey! I have no idea why you came home or how the hell we're standing in this church right now so you can marry that damn Bennett boy. I hated the way you left this town in the dust, but it settled something in me to think you might finally be *happy* out there in the world." He rubs his face. "I need to know why you're doing this . . . Is Kasey pressuring you? Did something happen? He doesn't deserve you, Ava. He never did."

"You've never given him an actual chance!" I bite back. "You never cared to *try*. Kasey is a good man, Dad. He's treated me with more respect and support than anyone else *ever* has." I let out a deep sigh. "This is exactly why I didn't tell you. I'm making this walk alone . . . You're more than welcome to join us for the reception."

"Ava!" he snaps, but I ignore him. I give Darla Brown—the pastor's wife—a small smile and a nod, and she looks back and forth between the two of us before relenting, pushing the double doors open.

Inside the nave, the air is warm and smells of flowers, and I have to hold my breath as I take the first slow steps inside. A hush falls over the room as dozens of eyes turn toward me. Rows and rows of pews are full of people from town and the sight of them all sets me on edge—they're only here to bear witness to this mess, eager to be a part of this moment so they can chew it between their teeth and spit it later amongst each other.

I hear my father's frustrated exhale behind me, but I don't look back. Instead, I trace my eyes down the worn, carpeted path to the altar where my almost-husband waits. I don't look at him yet—I'm not ready to see what might be written on his face. I'm not ready for the proof of his resistance to this, for the disapproval in his eyes or the tightness in his mouth.

I know how he looks when I've riled him up—in all the good *and* bad ways. I'm not sure I have the strength to see his displeasure right now, not when we're supposed to be convincing all these people that this is real. That we're still so crazy about each other all these years later, we couldn't possibly wait another second to make our forever official in the eyes of God. So I look at all the pink and white roses, at the silver-striped tie Pastor Brown has tucked into his navy suit jacket.

The journey to the steps in front of the altar takes an eternity and yet ends in a blink. I eye the four steps, the only thing remaining between me and the man I know stands waiting. Looking down at my dress, I pinch a bit of fabric, pulling the skirt away from my feet so I don't trip.

But then he's there—not at the top of the steps, but next to me with his hand stretched out between us. His tanned wrist is exposed from beneath the light gray jacket he wears, the smell of pine and leather swirls around us. I finally look up to face him, finding his brown eyes warm, his mouth at ease. His unruly waves are combed back away from his face, a simple black tie knotted against his neck.

He looks at me with a calm and steady patience that catches in my throat. It takes me three full breaths before I can rein in my own emotion and take his hand, letting him lead me up the stairs. When we reach the top, his hand stays firm around mine, squeezing gently as we turn to face each other.

"Dearly beloved," Pastor Brown's voice booms across the room, startling me. "We are gathered here today in the eyes of God and in the presence of family and friends to witness and bless the joining of Kasey Bennett and Ava Jones in holy matrimony. Marriage is a covenant not to be entered lightly, but with reverence, honesty, and love. We are all here today to celebrate not just this union, but the weaving together of families, of friends, and of a shared future."

The words spill out into the space between us as my eyes stay locked on Kasey's. My heart beats so hard in my chest I think if he looked down he might be able to see it through my dress, but he just looks at me. Watches me.

"Let us bow our heads and pray." There's a beat of silence as everyone does as instructed. I know from experience the whole congregation is closing their eyes, but Kasey and I just keep looking at each other. "Heavenly Father, we thank you for the gift of love and for the blessing of this sacred moment. We ask for you to surround Kasey and Ava with joy and to strengthen them in their journey together, from now and forevermore. Amen."

The room fills with an echo of "Amen" before it goes silent again.

"Now," Pastor Brown says, "I would be remiss to move on to vows before asking if any of you in this room can show just cause as to why these two should not be lawfully married? Speak now, or be forever bound to hold your peace."

My heart hammers as I wait for my father to shout his disapproval, to call this all a sham. I wait for anyone else seated below to call out a protest, to inflict their judgment on us here in front of everyone.

But the room stays silent, and so Pastor Brown goes on.

"It is tradition during a marriage ceremony for the couple to exchange vows, to make promises together in the eyes of God that will help carry them through the future. Kasey," he says, turning to face the man in front of me. Kasey finally rips his gaze from mine, looking at the pastor and nodding. "Do you take Ava to be your wedded wife, to live together in the covenant of marriage? Will you love, comfort, honor, and keep her, in sickness and in health, in joy and in sorrow, as long as you both shall live?"

Kasey looks back at me, and there's something in his expression I haven't seen since we were teenagers. "I do," he replies, steady and sure. His hand squeezes mine again.

My eyes burn hot, vision blurring.

"And do you, Ava, take Kasey to be your wedded husband, to live together in the covenant of marriage? Will you love, comfort, honor, and keep him, in sickness and in health, in joy and in sorrow, as long as you both shall live?"

"I do," I say, the words a near whisper. My fingers tremble in Kasey's grip, and his brows bunch above his nose.

"May I have the rings, please?" Pastor Brown asks. Kasey hesitates, eyes fastened to mine, before dipping his free hand in his pocket and fishing out two gold bands. He drops them in Pastor Brown's waiting palm, clearing his throat and looking down at his feet.

Pastor Brown holds up both rings, pinched between the thumb and pointer finger of each hand, presenting them to the whole congregation. "The union of marriage is a circle, a symbol of eternity and unending love. As you place these rings on each other's hands, remember that your love, too, is without end."

My hand trembles again, my shoulders shaking with a shiver. I focus my gaze on Kasey's face, silently begging him to look up at me again, to assure me that this is okay.

"Kasey, please take this ring and repeat after me." Kasey's eyes flash to the pastor's outstretched hand as he takes the smaller of the two rings. "With this ring, I thee wed. With all that I am, and all that I have, I honor you."

Kasey's eyes land on me again and the relief I feel is immediate. He lets go of my right, quickly reaching for my left and lifting it between our bodies. "With this ring," he repeats, his voice rumbling through me as his eyes lower to where he holds the gold band at the top of my finger. "I thee wed. With all that I am, and all that I have, I honor you." He gently slides the band down over my knuckle until it rests in place. When his eyes lift back to me, I nearly topple over from the force of it.

"Ava." Pastor Brown turns to me. "Please take this ring and repeat after me: with this ring, I thee wed. With all that I am, and all that I have, I honor you."

I take the band that glints beneath the overhead lights and position it over Kasey's ring finger, taking a deep breath as I look right into his gold-flecked eyes. "With this ring, I thee wed. With all that I am, and all that I have, I honor you." My skin grows hot and tight around my body as I push the band down. When it reaches the bottom of his finger, Kasey's hand flexes, and his fingers wrap around mine.

"May the Lord bless you and keep you both. May His face shine upon you and be gracious unto you. May He lift His countenance upon you and give you peace this day, and all days." Pastor Brown straightens his back, lifting his chin high. "By the authority vested in me by God and the state of Texas, I now pronounce you husband and wife. What God has joined together, let no one put asunder. Kasey, you may now kiss your bride!"

The room bursts into a cacophony of sound as the townspeople applaud. Kasey tugs me to him, eyes careful on mine as the space between us disappears. And then he's leaning his face down toward mine, the smell of spearmint and aftershave beckoning me in like a long-lost friend.

With just an inch between us he hesitates, holding still. Our breaths come together as we both seem to wait for the other to make the next move. His eyes drop to my mouth, anchoring there, and I slip into so many echoes of this very moment—of him, hovering above me, looking at me just like this.

"Ava," he breathes, bringing me back to this place. To this new version of him so different from my memories, and yet the very same.

"Kiss me, Kasey," I whisper back.

And then he does.

His mouth sinks into mine, lips warm and pressure light. The shape of them is still so familiar, I'd know him even in the dark, even with my eyes closed. He cradles my neck and jaw in one hand, wrapping the other high around my waist before it skitters down to the small of my back, pressing me into him. It feels like coming home, like the sweetest solace.

Everything around us disappears until it's just me and him and the memory of our love, of what once was so enthralling and all-consuming I thought I'd never be alone again. I'm dizzy from holding my breath, but I can't let go of him, can't get my lungs to cooperate. A sound escapes my throat as I wrap my arms around his neck and pull him tighter to me. He groans low and opens his mouth in sweet reward, sliding his tongue against the seam of my lips until I part for him too.

It's transformative, the way we're no longer on the altar of this church, newly married and fumbling with the past. Now, we're right back in it, hands clinging and breaths catching, molten need pooling white-hot between us. I want to go back in time to the night he held me over uneven mounds of sand and whispered his love for me over and over again, his breath fanning across my face and palm pressed to my heart. I want to look that girl in the eye and scream at her for the thoughts running through her head, for the pressure that she let build and build and didn't trust him to help carry.

The pressure of his grip on my hips grows as he struggles to pull himself away. The sound of the room around us floods back in, a low murmuring of voices and disgruntled gasps. When his lips leave mine, it's a loss that pierces sharp into my heart. Pastor Brown chuckles next to us, albeit stiffly. "I think that's enough," he warns.

But I'm not sorry.

And based on the heat in Kasey's eyes, I don't think he is either.

CHAPTER EIGHTEEN

KASEY

I feel like I've just been electrocuted, like my entire body was set ablaze with the heat and force of Ava, before it disappeared and the dark settled back in, leaving me twitchy and reeling. I grip the bottle of beer in my hand so tight my knuckles turn ghostly white. The knot of this stupid tie at my neck suffocates me, and I reach to pull it loose so I can breathe.

"I've never seen so many people in here," Wells observes, seemingly unaware of my struggle to merely exist beside him, his eyes scanning along the swell of people stuffed inside Wild Coyote. Every seat inside the bar is taken, and at least a hundred more people are somehow still packed in, standing in any open space they can find. It's an untraditional reception for sure—we aren't feeding anyone some fancy dinner, and we sure as shit don't have a DJ or live music or even a dance floor, but Wells has been slotting quarters into the juke box, and Olivia arranged for some of her coworkers at the café to work the bar so my family could enjoy the night.

"They're going to clean us out of booze," Rhett adds. "I've already changed more than half the kegs, and I don't think we have many bottles left in inventory."

"Well, that's something," I say. "At least we get to make some money off this train wreck." We've been running a tight ship lately when it comes to finances. The ranch only brings in a modest profit during our best years, so our main priority is keeping things in the black. The bar does a decent job at funding anything our family might need above and beyond what the ranch can provide, but with Melody's medical bills and funeral, things are tighter than they've ever been.

If this reception is any indication of a changing of the tides, of the *good* this marriage to Ava will lead to in keeping my family afloat, there's no doubt that I owe her a serious debt for talking me into this.

"Train wreck?" Rhett balks, as if he can read my mind. "Dude, I saw the way you two kissed up there on the altar. Something tells me you're having a *great* night."

"It didn't mean anything," I grumble.

"I'm calling bullshit," he counters, grinning like a fool. His black cowboy hat is pressed low against his brows, his pale gray eyes sizing me up like he can plainly see all the things I'm wrestling with.

I roll my eyes and turn away.

"Hard to think of any of this as a train wreck when we get to enjoy a cake like *that*." Wells points his chin to the center of the bar, where a monstrosity of a rainbow cake is on display. He and Rhett both start laughing.

It looks nothing like any wedding cake I've ever seen, but Ava seemed pleased when Luna brought it in, her relief when she thanked her genuine.

The mere thought of Ava fires off an instinctual urge to lay eyes on her. It takes a moment to sort through the sheer amount of bodies but I eventually find her across the room, standing with Layla and her mother, Lynette. It's obvious Layla's making a strong effort to buffer against her mother's curiosity, but Ava's face still looks pinched with discomfort.

"Do me a favor," I ask Wells, keeping my gaze trained on her. "Play something slow?"

Wells nods. "It'll take a few minutes. There are already a few other songs queued up."

"That works." I start pushing through the crowd toward her, but then change course. I head behind the bar and find the bottle I tucked in the fridge earlier this morning, pulling it out and unwrapping the foil along the top. After dismantling the wire cage, I pop the cork and pour a hefty amount in a lowball glass since we don't have anything fancier.

"Kasey," someone calls over the murmur of conversation just as I walk back out onto the floor. I turn to see Ellis standing near the door, smiling, flanked by Colt and Wylie Jo.

I frown.

His face falls, and I almost feel bad. But then I remember all the reasons why I'm mad at him, and a familiar irritation takes root. I'm tempted to ignore him and continue on to Ava, but Ellis starts gliding through the crowd toward me, and I know I'm not going to get out of a conversation with him.

"Hey," he says when he reaches me, his smile reignited. "Congratulations, man," he says, pulling me into a hug. I go stiff as his body curls around mine, but if he notices he doesn't let on.

"Thanks," I mutter, pulling back. I nod a hello to Colt and Wylie Jo. "Glad you all could be here."

"Sorry we didn't make it to the ceremony," Ellis cuts back in. "We had a fence go down this afternoon, and a few cows got loose. Most of them stayed close, but it took a few hours to find the last two. You know how it goes."

I nod, giving him a polite smile. "Definitely. It's no problem at all," I assure.

"So, which one is she?" Colt asks, looking around the room. Our fathers have been friends since they were our age, but they grew up outside of Saddlebrook Falls, and Ava and I were pretty secretive about our relationship in high school. Wiley Jo is scanning the bar too, but when her eyes settle on someone, I follow her line of sight to where Rhett's still standing.

"I'm actually on my way to her," I say, turning back to Colt. "Give me a few minutes and I'll bring her around to say hi."

I don't wait for any of them to respond, turning on my heels in the direction of Ava.

My eyes skim along the length of her dark hair as I walk up behind her. "I have something for you," I murmur into her ear, giving both Layla and Lynette an apologetic look as I pull Ava away. I don't miss the goosebumps that rise at the back of her neck as she turns to face me, her smile pulling into something more genuine. "You do?" she asks, letting me tug her with me.

When I'm confident that we're alone enough to avoid anyone overhearing, I hold out the glass for her. "I was hoping I could make a toast," I say.

She blinks slowly at the drink. "Kasey—"

"It's safe," I promise.

Her eyes rise back to mine, her right cheek pulling with the curve of a new smile. "Okay," she says, taking it from my hands.

I hold up my beer between us, and give her every ounce of my attention. "I want you to know that no matter what happens between us, I will always be here. I will always stand up for you and support you in whatever ways you allow me to." My eyes drop to her waist, to her stomach hidden beneath all the lace of her dress. "For both of you."

She inhales a sharp breath, her hand lifting to cover the place where I've narrowed my focus. I lift my gaze to hers and smile. "I mean it, Ava. All my feelings aside, whether we like it or not, we're family now, and that means something to me."

Her eyes flutter closed for the briefest of moments, and when she opens them again there's no mistaking the way they shine. "Thank you," she whispers.

I hold my beer higher, clinking it softly against her glass. "To us," I murmur.

She lets out a watery laugh that I feel deep in my bones. "To us," she agrees. We both take a drink to seal the deal. "Mm," she hums, peering into her glass. "Is this—"

"Sparkling apple cider." I wink.

Her eyes soften. "That was very thoughtful."

A song ends, and the low thrum of an acoustic guitar plays through the speakers before Keith Whitley starts crooning "When You Say Nothing At All." Holding a hand out between us, I ask, "May I have this dance?"

The way her eyes flare wide has me by the throat. She glances at my hand as her cheeks tinge the sweetest shade of pink. I love how soft she is when she hangs up that armored attitude and gives me her trust.

She tucks her free hand in mine, and I set both our drinks down on a nearby table.

"Kasey, look," she breathes out, and I force my eyes away from her to look around the room. The whole bar has gone quiet. Everyone has circled around us, their focus trained on the new bride and groom with rapt fascination. I catch my mother's gaze in the corner, where she sits at a table with June and Olivia. She eyes us curiously, something deep and knowing in her expression.

I press Ava closer, tucking her further into my body, wondering if the baby growing inside of her can feel me too. If it's possible for her to hear me as I float my mouth to her mother's ear and quietly ask, "Do you think they believe us?"

Ava slides her cheek against mine as she pulls her face back to look at me. "Maybe we should give them one more kiss?" she whispers, already watching my mouth. "Just to be sure?"

And then she's pressing up onto her toes, hesitant and a little unsure. I answer with the slow dip of my head until I feel her mouth on mine, and just like in the church I'm jolted by the sheer fucking force of it.

I reach a gentle hand around her throat, tipping her chin up with my thumb so I can gain better access to her mouth. A low and quiet whimper escapes her as she melts into me, her hands dragging roughly up my back. It's vibrant and daring, and my stomach curls like smoke.

WE DON'T STAY AT THE RECEPTION FOR LONG.

It's obvious Ava's exhausted, whether from her pregnancy or the day's long-winded performance. After the dance we shared in the middle of the bar, our guests became even fiercer in their pursuit of learning our story, hell-bent on pelting us with every question under the sun about where Ava's been and the progression of our relationship and how we decided to get married so fast. They circled us like vultures, and after seeing Ava flinch when Mayor Moore sidled up beside her, looking like a wolf in sheep's clothing, I decided to get her the hell out of there.

We stumble through the front door of my cabin in the dark, the relief of the silence settling over us. I reach to turn on the lamp in the corner and watch the way it bathes Ava in a warm, golden light. She turns to me, a tired smile on her face. "I can't believe it's done."

I huff out a breath. "Kind of feels like it should have been harder?"

Her smile grows as she leans against the back of the couch, reaching down to unclasp her shoes. "I don't know. I think Pastor Brown is really onto something with those counseling sessions. It takes a *strong* couple to make it through that shit."

I hum out my agreement, watching as her fingers pull a thin strap from a silver buckle around her ankle. Before I know it I'm moving, sinking down to a knee in front of her, my gaze rooted on the red lines of irritation that mar her skin. "Why didn't you say anything?" I ask, my voice rougher than I mean for it to be. When I raise my eyes to meet hers, dark curls curtain around her face, and I'm reminded for the hundredth time tonight that she's without a doubt the most beautiful thing I've ever seen.

"Say anything about what?" she asks, surprised.

I drop my gaze back to her ankle, lightly grazing a finger along the indentation from the strap. "You were uncomfortable in these shoes, Ava." Shit, I remember how Melody's feet used to swell when she was pregnant with the boys, how Brooks would prop her feet up in his lap so he could rub the ache out of them.

Why wouldn't Ava say something? Why wouldn't she trade these godforsaken shoes for something more comfortable? I glare at the steep slope of the heel, hating that she'd wear anything that would hurt her. Making a mental note to buy her some slippers, I let my finger trail down her ankle and hear her suck in a small breath.

"It's fine, Kasey. It's not even that bad."

I don't believe her for a second.

Gingerly pulling the shoe away from her heel and off her toes, I let it fall to the floor before turning my focus to her other foot. I loosen the strap around her ankle and find more welts and the start of a blister on the top of her foot that makes me see red. "Fuck these goddamn shoes, Ava," I grumble, pulling the second shoe off and dropping it next to the first.

When I grip the arch of her foot between my hands, I feel her resist, wanting to pull away from me. But I sink my thumbs into the fleshy curve anyway, and the moan that comes out of her mouth nearly makes me see stars. "Oh my *god* that feels so good," she whispers, dropping her head back. I circle my thumbs deep into her skin as my eyes trail down the column of her throat, skimming the low neckline of her dress.

"I really like that dress, you know," I murmur as I keep working through a massage, letting the weight of her leg rest on my thigh.

"You do?" she asks, dropping her gaze back on me.

"Yeah." I nod. "I do."

She catalogs the jacket stretched over my shoulders and the loose tie at my neck. "I've never seen you in a suit," she says, a smile playing on her lips. "It's . . . weird."

I bark out a laugh. "I tell you how much I like your dress and you tell me my suit is weird?"

Her smile widens. "The *suit* isn't weird. It's actually a very handsome suit," she clarifies. "It's weird seeing *you* wear it."

"It's the first time I've worn one," I admit. "Even for Brooks's wedding, we all wore pearl-snaps and jeans."

Ava giggles, nodding. "I think that's what I expected to see," she says. "But I guess that wouldn't match the whole southern-church-vibe we had going."

I gently set her foot down on the floor before picking up the other again, searching out her pressure points. She doesn't moan this time, but her eyes roll back in her head, and it makes me instantly hard. "Can I ask you something?"

"Of course," she says around a contented sigh.

"What the hell was with that cake?"

A loud laugh booms out of her, and it makes my heart pound.

"I don't know." She throws a hand over her face, as if to hide from me. "Layla and I went to the bakery and she and Luna were so excited to build this dream wedding cake and I just couldn't do it. I think I got spooked. So I told Luna to replicate the sheet cake she made for Maeve's granddaughter's birthday."

I rumble out a laugh as I set her foot down, rising to stand in front of her. I gently tug her hand away from her face, forcing her to look up at me. "Why'd you get spooked?" I ask.

She sighs. "They were talking about tiers and cake toppers, and I just couldn't say yes to any of it. I couldn't even picture what I might want if this were real. I don't know . . . I just needed to make an order and get out of there."

I nod, understanding. And then I decide to test a theory. "It's hard to make arrangements for something when you know it's just pretend," I say. "When you don't actually want any of it." I pinch the fabric of her dress between my fingers before slowly sliding my hand up her waist.

"Kasey," she whispers, her eyes falling closed. "What are you doing?" But she makes no effort to pull away.

"Touching you," I answer simply, letting my fingers drag along the top of her shoulder.

"Why?" she pleads.

I lean closer, eyes locked on the diamond and pearl pin in her hair.

"Tell me you don't want this." The air crackles around us, the hair on my neck standing as shivers crawl down my spine.

"Kasey," she whines.

"Go ahead, sugar," I breathe, baiting her. "Lie to me. Tell me this doesn't mean anything, that *today* didn't mean anything to you. Tell me you still think you're better off without me."

"No," she objects, her eyes opening to sink into mine. "*God*, is that what you think? That's not what I meant at all." My pulse thrums so wildly I feel it reverberate through my throat. "I don't think I'm better off without you," she continues, squirming against me, those stunning sapphire eyes sparking in the dark. She smells like apples from the cider I gave her, and I want to take a bite. "It's *you* who's better off without *me*."

The words wrap around me and squeeze tight. Everything goes still, and I have to rein in a dark, bitter laugh. "You don't see it, do you?" I ask, voice rough. "You really don't see how much I've always loved you."

A tear slips out of her eye, sliding down her cheek. I brush it away with a swipe of my thumb. "I do," she admits.

I shake my head. "No, you don't, because if you did, you'd know I could *never* be better off without you, Ava. Ever." I reach out and clutch a piece of her hair, wrapping it around my fist. "You know what I think?"

Her eyes shutter closed again as I tug her head back, her mouth going slack. "What?"

"I don't think you would have left," I say. "If you'd stayed back then, if you'd married me, you'd never have left, Ava. We'd still be together. We'd probably fight every goddamn day and you'd drive me out of my mind, but you would have stayed." I let my open mouth trail lightly along her jaw. "You know how I know that?"

She keeps her eyes closed, but I see the way her skin pinches between her brows, the way her lips press tight. "How?" she whispers.

"Because you're not your mother."

Her eyes fly open, the surprise in them obvious enough to know I've hit the bull's-eye.

I let my gaze roam her face, soaking in the soft skin of her cheeks, the curve of her nose. The slope of her lips and the way she keeps them parted. "You looked beautiful today," I say, leaning in to press a soft kiss to her forehead, lingering against her skin for far too long before finally pulling back.

And then just like I did the last time she was here, I disappear inside my room and leave my new wife alone in the dark.

CHAPTER NINETEEN

AVA

A muffled groan pulls me from sleep.

It takes me a handful of seconds to remember where I am, recognizing the bedroom only when I pull the blankets higher and catch a whiff of the familiar woodsy smell of *Kasey*. Then I remember I'm in his guest bedroom—*my* new bedroom— the unfamiliar weight of the ring on my finger a perfect match to the stone in my gut.

I strain my eyes and look around the dark room, trying to figure out what stole me from sleep, but I literally can't see a thing —it's *so* dark out here on the ranch without streetlights or porch lights from neighboring houses. I'd been exhausted when I peeled my dress off and fell into bed, and I don't even remember what kinds of furniture decorate this room. There's a window on the far wall I'm pretty sure looks out the back of the cabin, but the curtains are closed and out of reach. Maybe it was an animal outside? One of the horses in the pasture?

"Run!" a male voice shouts from somewhere in the house, tone urgent and full of intense, bloodcurdling fear. I scramble to sit up, tossing the blankets off my body and twisting to plant my feet on the cold hardwood floor. A shiver runs through me as I

push off the bed to do just as the voice directed and *run*, but my big toe makes contact with the biting edge of something hard, sending a jolt of pain that radiates through my foot.

"Ow!" I squeak, the urge to cry out muffled only by the fear of a possible intruder. It would be just my luck to stub a toe and lead them right to me. I bend over to rub at the skin, giving myself to the count of ten to wallow in my suffering before moving again.

There's an unmistakable sound of shuffling coming from across the hall: a thud of something smacking against the wall, the low groan of a bed. *Kasey*, I realize, and a new bolt of fear slices through me. And then I'm running again, because if there *is* an intruder, it sounds like they've already found him.

This time I make it across the room, brushing a hand along the wall to guide me toward the door. I search for the doorknob, cursing when I can't find it, but then I try the other side and my hand closes around the cool metal, twisting and pushing until I'm in the hallway.

There's a little more light here, bleeding out from an open window in the living room, but it's still not much. I can just distinguish the outline of Kasey's bedroom door on the other side of the hall right as I hear a muffled "*Fuck you*" from inside.

I don't hesitate.

Bursting into the room, my eyes fly to the broad male form in the center of the bed, the light of the moon through the window like a spotlight in the heavy darkness. His sweat-soaked face is crumpled in anguish, the sheets around him twisted into knots and clutched tight in his fists. His dark comforter lies in a heap on the floor at the foot of the bed, a rogue pillow teetering on the edge behind his back.

It's Kasey—*just* Kasey, I realize with striking relief. No intruder to be found. He's in the throes of a nightmare, his body thrashing as he grunts and mumbles his protests against whatever's happening to him behind closed eyelids. He barks out a strangled curse, his brows pulling together and etched in fear.

I hurry over to him. "Kasey," I say, shaking his damp shoulders. He flings out an arm but I block it from hitting my knee. "Kasey, wake up!"

His eyes fly open as his chest heaves. "Ava?" he asks, voice hoarse, his terror far from abandoned.

"It's me," I say calmly. "You were having a nightmare."

"A nightmare," he repeats, squeezing his eyes shut as both frustration and relief war across his face.

"Just a nightmare."

He groans, leaning forward to bury his face into my lap, a heavy arm wrapping firmly around my hips to draw me in closer. I soothe my hands across his back, rubbing my fingers into the taut muscles still clenched tight. "You're okay," I tell him, tracing the divots of his long spine. "It was just a dream."

He curses softly, his face pressed against the fleshy meat of my thigh. "I'm so sorry," he mumbles.

"Don't be," I insist, dragging a hand up to his neck so I can knead my fingers into his shoulders. "I'm just glad you're okay. I thought someone had broken in. It sounded like you were fighting someone off . . . I thought you might be hurt—"

He abruptly sits up to look at me, his eyes wild. "You thought I was being attacked and you still came in here?" he demands.

I nod, swallowing.

"Ava, don't ever put yourself in danger like that. You could have been hurt—"

"I wasn't," I say back. "No one's here, Kasey. You're safe— we're both safe."

He blows out a long breath, and I feel his hand tremble where it still grips my waist. "I'm sorry," he says again.

"You don't need to apologize. I just want to make sure you're okay."

He looks at me, face pained, but stays quiet.

"What were you dreaming about?" I ask. "It sounded awful."

"Nothing," he says quickly. "Just . . . stupid shit."

"Kasey," I press. "That wasn't nothing. Maybe if you tell me about it, it'll help your body settle down. It'll help your brain process that none of it is real."

A shadow passes over his expression, and I realize he doesn't *want* to tell me. "I'm okay, sugar. We don't need to talk about it."

I frown. "Is it about me?"

"No," he assures me. "Nothing like that."

"Then tell me," I try again. "Let me help."

He groans again, pulling my left hand into his lap and running a thick finger over my new gold band. Even in the dark, I see the ways his muscles bunch at his shoulders, the strong curve of his biceps as he shifts on the bed. It suddenly becomes clear to me: he's hiding something.

"Kasey?"

"Something happened a few weeks before you got back into town," he says, his voice tight. "I can't tell you much or it'll make you an accomplice."

Dread sinks through me. "You can tell me, I'm a lawyer. I'm bound to confidentiality."

"But I haven't hired you—"

"Consider it a consultation," I interject firmly. "Plus, as your wife, you're protected by marital privileges. What you say stays between us, I promise. Tell me what happened."

He just looks at me, pressing his lips into a firm line.

"Does it have to do with the ranch? With Huck?"

"No." He shakes his head. "Something else."

"Something with your family?"

"Rhett's a part of it," he concedes. "And Wells too, I guess— he was there. But it's something *I* did, not them."

"Something you did?" I repeat. "Like . . . a crime?"

Again, he doesn't answer.

"Kasey, I just committed fraud by marrying you to help your

family keep the ranch. I'm already complicit in things that have to do with you. Whatever it is you've done . . . let me help."

"It's a lot worse than fraud, sugar," he says.

My stomach flips. "I need to know," I tell him. "I'm married to you—if there's something you're worried about . . ." I decide to take a different approach. "If something happens to you, it affects me now. And it affects *her* too," I say, hoping he understands what I mean.

"Fuck," he says, looking utterly miserable, and lets out a resigned sigh. "You have to promise you won't freak out."

I narrow my eyes. "It would take a lot to freak me out."

"You swear?"

"I won't freak out, Kasey." I swat at him. "Just tell me."

He raises his brows like he might want to bet me on it.

And then he says something that decidedly freaks me out.

"I killed someone."

I gasp, eyes widening, as I cover my mouth with both hands.

"Oh good," he mutters. "Love that you're totally not freaking out."

"You *killed* someone?"

"Shhh," he shushes me, looking out his window for any potential midnight onlookers. "Quiet, Ava," he demands.

I wince. "Sorry," I say through my fingers.

"It was self-defense," he's quick to say. "Rhett got caught up in some illegal card games and someone pulled a gun, shot two undercover cops—"

"*Cops*?"

"—and then turned the gun on Rhett. I swear he was going to shoot him, Ava, I didn't have a choice."

"Holy fucking *shit*."

"The guy who hosted the game promised he'd take the fall if anyone starts sniffing around, but . . ." He trails off, looking blatantly scared.

I don't even know where to start. "Who knows?"

"Ellis, Colt, and Wylie Jo Rustler—we were on their property, and it was Ellis's game. The other two were at the table along with Rhett. Wells and I got there later, and Olivia stayed in the truck, but she knows." He frowns. "Layla probably knows too."

"Who else was there?"

"Two undercover cops who were there to investigate Ellis were both killed by a man named Maverick. None of us knew they were cops until things went to shit and they pulled their badges. Maverick had two guys with him. One was killed, one ran away."

Shit, I think. "Do you know the man's name? The one who ran away?"

Kasey shakes his head. "Maverick ran with a rough crowd. None of them were saints. But I don't know any names."

"Would you recognize him if you saw him again?"

He considers that. "Maybe? I'm honestly not sure, it's all kind of a blur."

"What about . . . ." I try to find the right words. "What happened to the bodies? The guns?"

"Ellis dealt with all of it. I didn't ask, and I don't want me or my brothers knowing; I think it's better to remain ignorant in case anyone starts sniffing around." A shadow passes over his face again, the weight of this secret pressing down around him. "You must think I'm a monster," he whispers, his voice breaking.

"No," I say quickly, reaching out a hand to cup his face. "I'm . . . *processing*. I guess I'm in a bit of disbelief. But I know you, Kasey—you're not a monster. You were protecting your brother. Anyone else would have done the same thing."

He scoffs. "I wish it had been anyone else," he admits. "The anxiety is eating me alive."

My heart breaks at the vulnerability written in the lines of his mouth, the exhaustion I now recognize in his eyes. "Hey," I say, tilting his face up to look at me. I scooch closer to him until my legs are pressing into his, my hand gliding along his jaw. "You're all right. We're going to figure this out together."

He looks at me with a reverence that steals my breath. "How are you not running from me?"

Emotion pinches behind my eyes as I give him a small grin. "Tried that already, remember?"

He huffs out a laugh, but he keeps his eyes trained on me.

The air between us charges as I feel his pulse thrum beneath my pinky.

"You're going to be okay, Kasey," I say again. "I promise."

His eyes squeeze shut as his shoulders slump.

I reach for the comforter and pull it back up on the bed, spreading it out around our legs. His eyes open and his gaze catches mine as I slide up beside him, dragging the blanket with me as I go. "Come on," I say gently. "You need sleep."

"Ava." It's only a half-hearted protest.

"Come on," I say again. "Come lie with me."

Kasey relents, settling his weight back down on the bed. He sinks into the mattress, holding an arm out in silent invitation.

I take it, curling my body against his and resting my head on the strong expanse of his chest. He rumbles out a pleased sigh, not quite content, but still edged in relief. "Thank you," he murmurs, the low timbre of his voice vibrating through my cheek.

I trail light circles across his skin with my fingers until his breathing evens out, and he falls back asleep.

We stay like that, clutched in each other's arms, for the rest of the night.

CHAPTER TWENTY

KASEY

I wake the next morning bleary-eyed, squinting at the bright stream of sunlight spilling through the window, and curse the fact that I'm late for barn chores again. And then I realize there's an unfamiliar ball of heat pressed up against my ribs.

Looking down, I find a chaotic nest of dark curls fanning my chest as a wickedly bony and still-sleeping Ava snores softly on my right pec. Her mouth is parted open so wide I wouldn't be surprised if she caught a fly or two in there. There's even a steady stream of drool flowing out of the corner of her lips, right onto my nipple.

Christ, she's gorgeous.

It takes a sincere level of effort not to dive my fingers into her hair, to rub against her scalp in hopes she makes that soft, satisfied grunt I used to try very hard to coax out of her but haven't heard since before she left. The realization slams into me that, even after years of dating, this is the first time I've woken up in the morning with her in my bed. That she's *staying* here, that I could theoretically be waking up like this *every* morning.

My eyes zero in on the ring finger of her left hand, the metal band shining in the morning light. I hold my own in front of my face to study it as the reality of what we've done prickles up my arm.

We're married.

Ava Jones is my *wife*.

She shifts against me—lifting a bare leg out of the covers to slide over the tops of my thighs—and I freeze, sucking in a slow, tortured breath. It seems my body is *highly* aware of the fact that Ava is in this bed with me. And Ava's not wearing any pants. I dare the briefest look down the length of both our bodies to catch the tiniest glimpse of the white cotton underwear she has on. It's enough to send all the air rushing out of my lungs and all my blood rushing straight for my dick.

I have to get out of this fucking bed.

Closing my eyes, I remember that—wife or not—Ava is *not* supposed to be in bed with me. I'd made it perfectly clear when we discussed this arrangement that she would be sleeping in her room, and I would be sleeping in mine. We may have had a little hiccup thanks to my stupid fucking nightmare, but *now* look. I'm trying to maintain a semblance of control as my feelings for her keep slamming into me like a battering ram, but waking up with her half naked and draped over me like this, wearing my ring on her goddamn finger, is *not* helping.

I reach for my phone on my nightstand, finding a handful of texts from Rhett, telling me not to worry about work today and to enjoy my *honeymoon*.

"Fuck," I whisper softly, looking back down at Ava.

She's sleeping hard. The poor woman is exhausted.

I spend the next seven minutes carefully disentangling from her, replacing the form of my body with the softest pillow I have so that by the time I'm standing at the side of the bed, she's clutching it with an affectionate death grip. I gently pull the comforter up around her, tucking her in, and allow myself the reward of a quick kiss to her temple before tiptoeing out of the room.

I pull on my robe from the en suite and head for the kitchen, deciding the least I can do after dumping my most dangerous secret on her last night is cook her some breakfast. Making a mental note to go to the grocery store and stock up on more food since there's two of us now—*two and a half?* I think with a sudden pang of joy—I reach into the pantry for the pancake mix I haven't touched since the boys spent the night camping out in my living room.

That was a handful of months ago, so I check the expiration date and give the box of batter mix a good whiff before deciding it's fine enough. I grab what I need around the kitchen and get started. By the time a crumpled and sleepy Ava comes padding out of my bedroom, there's a warm stack of pancakes on the table with all the fixings. I even found a container of strawberries I took from the main house a few days ago and then swiftly forgot about.

"Wow," she says, eyeing the table with the intensity of an apex predator as she pads out of my bedroom, a pair of my sweatpants rolled at the waistband and hanging loosely from her hips.

I pull a chair out. "Hungry?"

Her gaze swirls across my bare chest peeking out through my robe, that same hunger fastened tight. "Starving," she says.

My mouth goes dry as I wait for her to sit. When she does, I can't help my fingers from brushing a section of her hair back over her shoulder, watching as her skin erupts in goosebumps. "Milk?"

"Just water, please."

I move to grab a cup from the cabinet near the sink. "I really should get out to the barn," I say, hoping she can't hear the *want* in my voice.

"Okay," she responds lightly. "I think I'm going to go home— to my dad's house, I mean—and grab all my things."

"Surprised he didn't show up yesterday."

"Oh, he did." Her tone is gruff.

I turn to look at her, arching a brow.

"He tried to walk me down the aisle," she explains. "I basically told him to fuck off."

"Yikes. Who told him?"

Her eyes go stormy. "Eleanor, that traitor."

"Do you want me to go with you?"

"No, no that's okay. I'll be fine."

"What do you need to grab?" I frown. "Anything heavy?"

She smiles, staking four pancakes on the plate I laid out for her. "Nothing heavy. Just some clothes and my laptop. Some files for work. A few bags. I promise it's not a big deal. I'll probably only be an hour or two."

"Okay." I nod. "You up for dinner at my parents' tonight?"

She accidentally squeezes out a huge glob of syrup, worry creasing between her brows. "Oh—um, yeah! Definitely. That sounds great."

Liar, I think, amused. "No one's gonna bite, I promise."

She pushes her tongue into her cheek. "Right. Of course." Turning her gaze to me, she asks, "Anything I can bring?"

I shake my head. "Why don't you rest when you get back? Take the day to . . . settle in. There's a tub in my bathroom I've never used. Plenty of movies to stream. Whatever you want."

Ava gives me a long look before she tilts her head and smirks. "Are you trying to take care of me?"

"No." I bristle. "But you've had a lot thrown at you the last few weeks. I'm sure all that stress isn't good for . . ." I'm not sure how to finish the sentence. Stress isn't good for her? For *the baby*? Who am I to say what's good for either of them?

I need to get the fuck out of here.

"Look, just rest. The cabin is yours—take whatever you need."

I don't give her a chance to respond before I march back into my bedroom to shower and change. By the time I come back out, the table is cleared, the dishes rinsed and drying by the sink, and her Range Rover is already gone.

"DIDN'T EXPECT TO SEE YOU THIS MORNING," RHETT teases as soon as he sees me. "Surprised you're not handcuffed to your headboard, or rubbing oil over your wife's ti—"

"Knock it off, Rhett." I shoot him a dark glare.

"I'm just saying, Liv and I are still in that *have to spend every waking moment together* phase and we aren't even married."

"Layla and I are still in that too," Wells agrees. "Not sure it ever goes away."

"Yeah." I nod, smiling my sincerest *I'm going to fuck you up* smile. "Ava and I know what that's like. Except in our version, it's more of a legal requirement than a desire thing."

Wells barks out a laugh. "Sure didn't look like a *legal requirement* last night."

"Should have seen it coming," Rhett adds, shaking his head.

"Seen *what* coming?"

"You falling for your crazy-ex-girlfriend-turned-fraudulent-wife all over again."

"She's *not* crazy," I argue, downright irritated at their continued use of that word. Rhett and Wells look at me with growing amusement, which does nothing to help. "And I'm not falling for her."

Can't fall for someone you never stopped being in love with, my sore ego unhelpfully adds.

"You start in the second barn yet?" I ask, grumbling.

"No," Wells responds.

"Perfect." I grab a rake, shovel, and wheelbarrow and take it all with me. "You know where I'll be."

My irritation only grows as the day goes on. I shouldn't have told her about Maverick, shouldn't have let her in so far with something that could easily destroy us both. I told myself I was going to keep a firm distance for my own sanity, and then I go and fuck it up her first night she's here.

It becomes near impossible not to think about the way she dragged her hands across my back to soothe my terror, how she held my face and looked at me with those startling blue eyes. I think about the curve of her bare knee, the waterfall of hair cascading across flushed skin.

I spend hours mucking and raking and feeding and brushing and still don't chase a single thought of her away. Her face burns behind my retinas, and every time I blink against the bright rays, she's there, smiling at me like I mean something to her.

By the time I get back to the cabin, the late afternoon sun is leaning heavy toward the west, throwing the first traces of golden light across the porch. Ava's pulled out a kitchen chair and propped it against the house, where she now sits cross-legged in one of my old high school hoodies—one she *didn't* steal from me ten years ago, which means she found it in the back of my closet.

Her hair is damp from a recent shower, her face clean of makeup. I don't even make it to the stairs before the past snares me and I see her the way I once did. As the girl she once was.

So full of sunlight, of beauty that still knocks the wind out of me.

She used to bring me to my knees with nothing but a look. If she realizes the power she has over me, if she learns how easy it'd be to give her every part of me all over again, would she take it?

She clears her throat, observing me with a guarded curiosity. "What?" she asks.

I shake my head, focusing on the ground between us. "How was your day?" I ask.

"Fine," she says, her expression neutral, giving nothing away. "How was yours?"

"Fine," I echo. "Did you get what you needed from your dad's?"

"Nice and easy, just like I said."

I notice the open beer she's holding in her hand, and frown. "What's that?" I ask, nodding to it.

Ava smirks. "A beer."

I bite the inside of my cheek to keep from grinning—the fucking brat.

She must notice because she starts fighting her own smile. Holding the bottle up, she says, "It's for you."

"For me? Why?"

She shrugs. "Figured you could use it."

My eyes trace along her face, pleased to see she indeed looks rested. I amble up the porch steps and reach for the beer, taking a long sip as I lean against the railing in front of her. I note traces of her fucking soap in the air and fight the urge to lean in. "You look good," I tell her. "Very . . . clean."

She laughs. "Well, that's a relief. Though I can't say the same for you." Her eyes dip down to my stained shirt and dirty jeans, and she grimaces. "You stink," she says evenly.

"Now I remember why I never wanted a wife," I mutter, pushing off the railing toward the front door. "Still good with dinner?"

"Yep," she calls out behind me.

I let the front door swing shut behind me and release a long, long breath.

CHAPTER TWENTY-ONE

AVA

I keep things simple for tonight's dinner, opting for my favorite pair of jeans and a comfortable white V-neck that's just oversized enough to not make me feel insecure. I've noticed a definite rounding of my stomach in the last week, bringing forth feelings of immeasurable joy and debilitating fear. If I'd have pictured what my life would be like even just a year ago, the last thing I would've ever imagined would be sitting in the guest bedroom of Kasey's cabin, a wedding ring on my finger and a baby in my belly. Especially considering it's not *his* baby.

I won't be able to hide this pregnancy for too much longer—I have maybe a month, six weeks at most. A part of me feels like I should rip the Band-Aid and tell everyone about my pregnancy now, but another part of me—an achingly tired and more desperate part—wants to hide it forever. To get through this marriage and find a way to run away again before I have to face the judgement I know is coming.

The longer I wait, the more I risk someone discovering it and wrongfully assuming the baby is Kasey's. I'd never be able to forgive myself if word got around that we might happily be expecting our first child together, knowing what that might do to him, to his family.

Especially after he already offered to help me, to take responsibility.

My heart clenches at the sheer selflessness.

Kasey is the kind of man Tobias could never, ever hope to be. Not when his first instinct was to give me all the reasons I should end the pregnancy, and then take it to the partners to use against me when I refused. I haven't heard from him in weeks, and it makes me anxious. It could be that he's finally given up on trying to control me, but he's not exactly the type to give up when someone around him doesn't submit.

I sigh, leaning over to pull on the old boots I brought over from my dad's house, figuring it's time to get over my general boycott of a practical wardrobe. I've held on to my tailored suits and pencil skirts for as long as I could, to every scrap of power I was able to create for myself outside of the walls of this town, but that's over now. Plus, Kasey's right—the heels were starting to hurt.

The boots still fit like a dream, and I can't deny how much more comfortable they are. At least it'll make Kasey happy to see I've finally made the switch. *Not* that I'm particularly interested in making him happy.

Standing to go meet Kasey out in the living room, I'm surprised to find him hovering in the open doorway, watching me with an unreadable expression on his face. "You ready?" he asks, shifting his weight from one foot to the other.

"How long have you been standing there?"

He shrugs. "Not long." But I can tell from how he quickly looks away, trying to hide a dark expression, that he's been watching me for a while.

"Liar," I tease.

He rolls his eyes, muttering, "You still think *very* highly of yourself."

The insult lands roughly, though I'm not surprised—he's said much worse. Still, after the last few days of seemingly *getting along* with him, the words hurt. But when I really look at him, I realize he's . . . anxious. Maybe a little bothered. "You okay?"

"Fine." But his hands clench into fists at his sides as he seems to be getting more and more worked up about something. "Let's go."

I frown, deciding it best to listen as I head toward the bedroom door. But instead of turning to walk down the hallway in front of me, Kasey flattens himself against the wall to let me pass. As I brush past him, I hear the unmistakable sound of his deep inhale, feel the faintest flutter of his nose against the top of my head.

Oh. *Oh.*

Heat pools low in my belly as I realize Kasey's not irritated—at least not in the way I thought. He's . . . turned on. And he's trying to fight it.

The ego of a half feral cat blooms inside of me, stretching out and scratching at the door to be let loose. Suddenly, this feels like a challenge. And I'm nothing if not a petty girl who *loves* a good challenge.

When Kasey reaches for his keys on the counter, I tell him it's a good night for walking, pointing to the boots on my feet as assurance that I can handle the trek. The truth is a walk along the pasture sounds divine, and it gives me plenty of opportunity to have a little fun with my handsome new groom.

I've had these jeans long enough to know they're *just* at that level of worn to be forgiving of some of my new curves, since it's not just my stomach that's been rounding out. I walk with the swagger of a jungle cat, swinging my hips side to side as we make our way toward the main house. Kasey stays quiet behind me, but I feel the weight of his attention like a caress against the back of my neck.

"What are you doing?" he asks gruffly when we're a little over halfway there.

I turn and bat my eyes through a mask of innocence. "What do you mean?"

His stare turns near-lethal.

I grin, turning back around to continue on.

By the time we make it to the house I figure I've won our little game, since Kasey hasn't uttered another word, but just as I'm about to round the corner to the front of the house, a thick arm curls around my ribs and yanks me backward.

I'm pulled off my feet by the sheer force of it, hurling into a wall of stone that turns out to be Kasey's chest. I forgot what it was like to be *handled* by him. How he used to lift me like it was nothing, used to overpower me in the best of ways—a wildly underrated benefit of dating a cowboy who regularly works ranch chores.

Kasey spins me around so I'm facing him, then backs me into the side of the house. My heart hammers as he wraps a palm around my waist, squeezing, pulling my hips against him. "Have I told you lately how crazy you make me, sugar?" His eyes glow with fierce desire and wicked challenge.

I grin, arching into him. "You know, I think you may have mentioned it once or twice, but I honestly don't remember. Care to remind me?"

"*Really* fucking crazy," he murmurs, eyes dipping to my cheek before falling to my mouth.

"Well, that's too bad." I hold up the back of my hand to show him the ring on my finger. "I think you're kinda stuck with me now."

He doesn't look at it, keeping his gaze trained on my lips, his eyes growing distant and murky. "Yeah? You think?"

"Yeah. Well . . . at least until—"

I'm interrupted by a kiss so fierce it buckles my knees.

Kasey devours me.

Calloused fingers drag against the skin beneath the hem of my shirt as his tongue strokes deep into my mouth. His hips press harshly into mine, trapping me against the wall with a low grunt. I'm consumed by the heat of him, *everywhere*, all over me, as his other hand angles my face to better fit against his, like two long-separated pieces of the same puzzle, finally slotting together.

There's no mistaking it: *this* kiss isn't to prove anything to anyone else.

This one is just for us.

"Be good, Ava," he says roughly into the curve of my ear as he tries to pull away from me.

"You're the one pinning me against the house like the world is ending," I rasp, clutching him tighter, not ready to let go.

He groans as he reaches for my wrist and tears himself loose, like it's the last thing he wants to do.

"Behave," he begs.

"Or *what?*"

I'm pushing too hard—I know it. I see it in the way he's obviously fighting a losing battle. And yet, I can't stop.

His eyes are so dark they match the night sky.

"Fuck," he growls, turning away from me, reaching to adjust himself through his pants. "Let's go."

He leaves me panting and breathless and much colder than I was mere moments ago.

But as I push off the wall to catch up to him, I can't help the wide smile that pulls at my cheeks. I feel more alive than I have in *years*.

DINNER GOES WELL, ALL THINGS CONSIDERED.

I feel like a fish out of water sitting at the table with Kasey (who won't look at me), both of his parents, Layla, and all three nephews. Rhett and Wells are tending the bar—they've picked up shifts for the next few nights to give Kasey and me a chance to "get comfortable" with our new living arrangement—and Brooks opts out of dinner altogether. Without any of his brothers around, the spotlight of everyone's attention falls on Kasey and, therefore, *me*.

But I expected it. How could I not? Kasey just committed fraud for this family, to protect their home and their assets. Everyone at this table knows our marriage isn't real—except maybe the boys who probably don't even know the ranch was under threat to begin with—and it's honestly kind of freeing not to have to lie or put up any pretenses about it.

"So, Ava," Mrs. Bennett asks over her plate of barbecue chicken and collard greens, "what brought you back to Saddlebrook Falls?"

I swallow down a mouthful of food. "My job sort of went . . . sideways," I explain.

Kasey snorts, jaw ticking.

"Aw, that's too bad," his mom says, scrunching her nose. "But there's no place like home to figure out what's next!"

"You're a lawyer?" Mr. Bennett asks.

"Yes, sir."

He grunts, slicing a gaze to his wife. She picks up a bottle of white wine and points at me.

"Would you like a glass?"

"Oh, no thank you—I'm trying to cut back."

"Good on you!" Mr. Bennett gruffly declares.

"What about you, honey?" she asks Kasey.

"I'll stick to my beer, thanks."

"I'd love some," Layla chimes in.

"That's my girl." Mrs. Bennett beams.

I try not to let it sting.

I'm not sure why it even would.

Honestly, my nerves aside, this feels . . . *good*. To be in the mix like this, to be only one of many instead of one of so few, it's new for me—but I like it. As teenagers Kasey and I made a lot of effort to avoid our parents, so I never really saw the possibility of what things could have been like on the ranch if I'd stuck around. I was always so worried about what Kasey's parents would think of me that it never occurred to me that I might enjoy it. I've been at this table for less than an hour and I already can't wait to come back. Like maybe we could make this a weekly thing, something to look forward to.

And then the sting of the truth pierces in, that we can't do this forever. That someday I'm going to have to give it up.

My mind spins back to earlier in the day, when my father came home for lunch to find me packing up my things. He'd tried to make conversation, pestering me with questions, and it'd felt so *wholly* different than this.

"Have you heard any of those Bennetts talk about their ranch?" he'd asked, watching me unplug my laptop cord from the outlet next to my bed.

Those Bennetts. I scoffed. "Of course they talk about the ranch, Dad. They live on it."

"What about an inheritance trust?" he continued to probe. "Have you heard anything about that?"

I turned to look at him, feigning confusion. "What inheritance trust?"

"The one that says one of those boys has to be married to gain ownership of the ranch."

"I'm not sure what you're getting at. Brooks was already married."

"Well, he's not anymore. And they never transferred the land into his name when he was."

There'd been undisguised curiosity shining across his features as he watched closely for my reaction. He looked almost . . . gleeful. "How the hell would you even know anything about their inheritance, Dad? Isn't that kind of personal? I mean, shit, I know people around here have a reputation for being nosy but this feels like another level."

His eyes narrowed into thin slits, a look I'd seen so often growing up under his roof. "Did you marry that boy so his family could keep their ranch?" he asked flat out.

I scoffed. "How *dare you* even insinuate we would be a part of something like that!"

But my outrage had done nothing to sway him. "I'll figure out the truth, Ava. I always do."

I decided not to tell Kasey about any of it. He's got enough on his plate of things to worry about. My father doesn't scare me; he never has, despite his best efforts. If anything, knowing the Bennetts are in his line of sight only makes me want to rub this marriage in his face harder.

Kasey and I stay for dessert at the insistence of Mrs. Bennett, but halfway through my slice of peach cobbler he catches me yawning and quickly announces our departure, citing the early morning he has with the horses to make up for Rhett and Wells being at the bar tonight.

"Has Brooks been out there?" Mr. Bennett asks.

Kasey shakes his head. "Not yet, Dad."

"He's doing so well though," Mrs. Bennett adds, eyes on the three young boys who are clearly listening.

"We're fine," Kasey insists. "He can take all the time he needs."

"Maybe I could help with some things," Mr. Bennett says aloud, studying the corner of his napkin.

"No need." Kasey slaps a hand on his shoulder. "Promise."

Our walk home is less eventful, although Kasey does seem a lot less bothered. "Did you enjoy yourself?" he asks quietly, eyes fixed on the path ahead as he stuffs his hands in his pockets. He'd had three or four beers during dinner, and I can see the way the alcohol turns the tips of his ears pink like it used to.

"Yeah, I actually did," I say. "Your mother is really nice."

He smiles. "She's a good woman."

"It must take a big heart to support such a big family."

"She's got it. We've all put her through hell over the years and she's never failed to support us."

I think about my own mother and how she couldn't find a single quality reason to stick around, back when I was still trying to impress her with my good behavior. "You're really lucky," I say.

I feel him look at me. Eventually, he looks away.

"Was last night the first that you've had nightmares like that?"

"No," he says. "I've had them most nights since it happened."

I try to choose my words carefully. "I was thinking . . . I might be able to get into my dad's online records to see if anything about that night is on his radar. If any law enforcement office is going to come after you, I'm fairly certain he'll know about it." My gut tells me Dad doesn't know or he would have tried to use that against me too. But it doesn't mean it won't still come.

"I can't ask you to do that, Ava."

"You're not."

"If he found out you accessed his data, you'd be directly implicating yourself."

"I don't care."

"You *should*," he snaps.

"Well, I don't." I smile. "I used to do it all the time."

The fight loosens in his expression as a smile threatens to break through. "You used to access the sheriff's database?" I nod. "For what?"

I shrug. "I used to background check guys who asked me out. Sometimes I'd try to dig up dirt on someone's family if they wronged me."

"Shit." He laughs, shaking his head. "Did you ever look me up?"

"No," I say quickly. "Never." And it's the truth. My father

always had a strong dislike for the Bennett family, starting back well before I was born. It was one thing to hack into his files for my own personal gain and enjoyment, but it'd felt slimy to use that kind of stolen access against people *he* despised. Also, I was a little scared of what I might find—I didn't want Kasey to be a bad guy.

For the first time in my life, I'd chosen to trust someone.

"I don't want you getting mixed up in any of my shit, Ava. Not now that . . ."

"Now that I'm pregnant?" I throw him a half-hearted grin.

He nods.

"I can take care of myself," I promise as we approach the cabin, the porch light Kasey left on illuminating the front steps.

"You've always made that clear." His face is void of emotion, but I can hear the dejection in his voice.

I sigh. "Hey, about earlier—"

"Yeah," he agrees, "about that. Look, I'm sorry, Ava. I shouldn't have kissed you. You told me you aren't interested and I never should have touched you."

"I never said I wasn't interested," I throw back, frowning. "Maybe I don't want you mixed up in my shit, either. Maybe I'm trying to protect you too. I meant it when I said that we aren't the same kids we were back then, but that doesn't mean I don't still *feel* for you, Kasey. Especially after . . ."

He eyes me carefully, something alight in the edges of his face. "Especially after what, Ava?"

"Especially after the last few days." I throw my hands out in supplication. "After the wedding, and *kissing* you, and sleeping in your bed. After that fucking dinner we just had with your family, Kasey." My heart pounds hard in my chest, but it feels *good* to let this out. To be honest with him—and with myself. "I tried really hard to forget about you after I left. I knew I'd hurt you and I *hated* myself for it—I still do. But it felt like the only choice. I was going to hurt you either way so I figured getting it over with would at least let you move on with your life.

"I never planned on coming back. I never planned on seeing you again, because I knew if I did these feelings for you would come back too. And maybe . . . maybe it wouldn't be so bad to give in to this thing that clearly still exists between us. At least this time you *know*."

His eyes narrow. "Know what?"

"That I'm not good for you! That I can't promise you a future. That I'll probably hurt you again at some point, because even though I care about you, I care about myself more. I'm selfish, remember? It's who I am, who I've always been."

His face softens as he moves to stand in front of me, pressing his palm against my jaw. He smells like soap and leather, like everything good and safe. "You're not selfish, Ava. You're just scared." He tilts my face up so he can look me in the eye. "But you don't need to be. We can figure this out together." The pads of his fingers drag across my skin, rough and tender, full of hope.

I close my eyes and unspool a breath, conflicted by his words. The *want* in me is waging a brutal battle against the *run*. It would feel so good to give in. To let him make me forget how unworthy I am.

To this day, he's the only person who's ever known how . . .

Just like that, the battle is won.

"Make me forget, Kasey," I whisper urgently, clutching at his shirt.

And he does.

CHAPTER TWENTY-TWO

KASEY

There's something about *touching* Ava that rocks me to my core. Changes me on a deeply cellular level.

It's a hopeless, joyful torment.

A pure, unfiltered eruption.

Without her I am nothing. *With* her, I am the entire goddamn world. She is the answer to every question, the light in every dark room. She's the air in my lungs and the blood in my veins and when she smiles at me like she is right now, I come *alive*.

Goosebumps erupt on every inch of my skin as I pull her mouth to mine. There's nothing careful about the way I kiss her —it's a claim, a promise made between two hearts, written in permanent marker, sealed with a blade across a palm. It's a pouring out of hurt and secrets to make room for things better held, like *adoration* and *protection*. Like *love* in its rawest form.

From the moment she walked through the doors of Wild Coyote—no, since the day she walked onto that fucking football field—I've been caught in the excruciating crux of trying to guard myself against the terror of what it is to love Ava and succumbing to every hair-trigger whim to tear my heart out of my chest and shove it into her hands, praying she'll just put me out of my misery and *take it*.

She's everything I want so badly wrapped up in a bow of temptation set out to destroy me—because that's exactly what happened before. Ava *destroyed* me, and here I am like a fucking fool, asking her for *more, please.*

I have her shirt off in less than a second. My blood is rushing inside my body, crashing through my limbs and blaring through my ears. My skin feels too tight, like I'm swollen with my need for her, threatening to break.

"*Kasey,*" she gasps. Her nails dig into my shoulder as her head rolls back, eyes fluttering closed as my mouth drops to her neck.

"Ava," I murmur against her skin. Confident. Crazed.

My hands sink down the length of her body, palm her ass, grip her thighs, and lift. She wraps both hands around my face, her dark hair a curtain around us as she bends her neck to kiss me again. I nearly trip carrying her up the stairs, clumsy and aching. By the time we get through the front door, I've unfastened her bra and she's pulling it down her arms.

"It doesn't bother you?" she rasps. Her blue eyes beckon me like the sea in Scorpion Bay, where we waded through the water without a stitch of clothing. Before I was unmade and reborn in the back of my truck on that midnight beach.

"What?" I don't remember the question, mind held hostage by the memory of the first time I got to see her come.

"My . . . pregnancy."

"*Yes,*" I hiss, leaning forward to lick up her neck as I settle her hips against the back of my couch. *God*, yes.

She stiffens. "Wait," she breathes. "It does?"

"What does, Ava?" I don't think I'm keeping up, but it's hard to stay focused when her perfect fucking tits are bare and her nipples are hard against my shirt.

"Does my pregnancy bother you?" she asks, frowning, and I realize where I've gone wrong.

"Fuck no," I grit out. If she only knew how *hard* it makes me to think of Ava as a mother. The baby growing inside of her might not share my blood, but I'm desperate to claim her too, to make them both *mine*. The list of things I wouldn't give for it is miserably blank.

I watch the worry on her face transform to something softer, something much sweeter. I hate that I made her doubt herself, even for a second. Doesn't she know what she is to me? "Sugar, I don't think I've ever been more unbothered about something in my entire fucking life."

She laughs, and I love it. That I'm earning those again.

I lean in to catch it with my mouth, but the couch slides against the hardwood and sends me stumbling forward. I curse, lifting her back into my arms. "My room or yours?" I ask, gaze snagging on a clump of hair that falls forward off her shoulder, dangling against her breast.

"Yours." She bucks her hips against my stomach, seeking friction as I walk with her.

"Almost there, baby," I promise, feeling her need unfurl and pull taut. Her lips wrap around my earlobe, teeth scraping and sinking into skin. I grunt as pleasure rushes through me—I always loved that fucking spot, and she knows it.

My bed is still unmade from when she left it this morning. When I'd come in to get ready for dinner, I studied the place her body had been, wondering if I imagined the whole thing. Her tan leg hooking over my waist, the flimsy white panties she'd had on. I wonder what she's wearing tonight, what I might find beneath these jeans. I drop her in the middle of the bed, and as if she can read my mind, she starts unbuttoning her pants.

"No." I catch her wrist, stopping her. Her eyes hook into mine, a divot forming between her brows. "I want to," I say with a shaky exhale.

But first, I just want to fucking look at her. Her deep, rich skin. The heavy curve of her breasts. The swell of her stomach, proof of her magic. Of her magnificence.

"Kasey," she pleads, squirming. "Please."

Closing my eyes, I let this all sink it. Let it soak into my heart. "Okay, sugar." I nod, looking back down at her. "Let's get you out of these." I carefully, *slowly*, reverently unbutton her jeans. Pull the zipper down. Catch a glimpse of lavender lace.

My breath hitches. Heart stops.

"Fuck."

Ava shimmies beneath me. Impatient. Whining.

I pull the denim down her legs and reveal more lavender. *More* lace. More soft, perfect skin. I let the pants drop unceremoniously to the floor at my feet and straighten.

And look.

"Your turn." The words scrape from her throat. "Let me see you."

I reach over my head to grip the back of my shirt, pulling it up and off me. My fingers hook into the leather of my belt buckle and start yanking, but Ava props herself up, rising up to her knees. Lays a warm hand over mine. "I want to," she echoes.

I grin down at her. On her knees, her face reaches my chest, and as she fumbles to work the buckle, she presses an open-mouthed kiss over my heart. Another against my ribs. I close my eyes as she blazes a trail across my skin, licking and sucking and kissing. It's a slow and tortuous pursuit. Everything I need.

A metallic thud sounds, and I realize my belt has joined my shirt and her jeans on the floor. I open my eyes to find hers fastened to my fly, where I'm straining uncomfortably. She licks her lips. Looks up at me. "Can I?"

"Ava," I groan. "You can do anything you goddamn please."

Her pupils swell, those beautiful sapphire blues chased away by a startling black.

She works my jeans much faster than I did hers, fingers frantic and fumbling with a desperation that matches my own.

The tension in the air around us is so thick it crackles, and I wonder if there could possibly be anything better in the entire universe. Or any other universe. *No,* I quickly think. Surely not.

She gets my pants loose, shoves them down my thighs. I hear her deep inhale as she takes in the sight, reaching to wrap her hand around me. She gives me one, lazy pump. "I forgot how—" She swallows. "Remember our first time?" she asks, eyes lifting to mine.

I nod. I'd been so scared of hurting her, but she promised she could take it. Said we wouldn't be made not to fit together. "You made it so good for me, Ava. You always did."

She snorts. "You did all the work."

I reach to grip her chin, lifting her face. "You're going to make it good for me again, aren't you?" Her cheeks grow crimson as she attempts to nod, the flesh of her face swelling around the tips of my fingers. I hum with approval, anticipation zipping up the back of my neck. "Show me."

She pulls her face out of my grip and turns her attention back to my dick, flattening her tongue against the head. The feel is . . . exquisite. Mind blowing. So good. Her hand wraps around the base, giving me another languid pump while her tongue dips lower, pausing, rising back up.

"Yeah," I grit out. "Perfect."

She hums, and it vibrates through me. I nearly lose it, but force myself to breathe in deep. Try to slow my racing heart down a little.

But then she wraps her lips around me, sucking me into her mouth, and it's too much, too fast. Her cheeks hollow as I disappear further inside of her. My stomach clenches, molars grind, until I feel the back of her throat. "Fuck," I mutter, gripping her hair at the base of her neck, tugging her loose. "Don't make me come yet, Ava."

"Already?" She grins, her lips slick. Filthy.

"It's been a long time," I concede, taking a step back. "Get on your knees."

And she does. I praise her with soft murmurs as I kiss up the length of her spine, gripping her hips tightly between both hands as I pull off her underwear. I dig my fingers deep into her flesh, anchoring, holding her still. My mouth reaches the back of her neck, and she tilts her head to the side to give me better access. I suck at her throat, scraping my teeth against her skin, relishing the whine it draws out of her.

I stand again, straightening. Lifting her ass higher so I can see her better. She's more than wet—dripping, actually, down the inside of her thigh—glistening in the moonlight. I'd wondered if pregnancy would make it harder for her to be turned on, to want something like this, but she seems more than ready. Like perhaps she wants it even more now.

"Look at you," I whisper. I want to taste her, but I'm not sure I have the patience. It's been *ten years*, and I'm worried if I don't get inside her, soon, I might actually die.

"I missed this," she mumbles into the mattress. "Missed *you*."

My heart stutters.

I graze my fingers through her slick skin—just enough to tease. She perks her ass higher. Begging. Nudging herself against my dick. "We don't have to do this, sugar." I need to say it, to tell her, but the thought of stopping kills me.

Her head tilts on the mattress. Blue eyes catch mine beneath the beautiful drape of her hair. "In case I haven't made it perfectly clear, Kasey, I want you to fuck me. Immediately. *Roughly*."

Fuuuuuck. "Hold on," I rumble. "Let me—" I reach for the drawer of my nightstand.

"No need." She laughs. Face warm and affectionate. Like maybe I forgot that any form of birth control is a silly idea at this point.

As if I could possibly fucking forget.

"But what about the baby?"

Her eyes soften. She lowers her hips, turning to face me again on her knees. "When I saw the doctor in Miami, he told me I still —that I *should*—" She pauses. "I was thoroughly tested, for me and the baby. When was the last time you were tested?"

Shit. Oh well, no getting around it now. I blow out a breath. "I haven't."

She frowns. "Ever?"

"Well, not since . . ." I swallow. Look at the wall behind her. "Not since you."

Her gaze turns sharp. I can practically feel her mind spinning. "You haven't been *tested* since me, or you haven't . . ."

My expression must give me away, because her eyes burst open. "Both," I say anyway. Just to be clear.

"Kasey," she breathes. Her shock unfurls, and so does her regret. It floods into her eyes like a tsunami.

I shake my head, reaching to swipe a thumb across her cheek. "None of that."

"How? *Why*?"

I shrug. "I tried, a few times. But . . ."

A tear spills out of her eye and gathers in the space where my thumb meets her skin. "Stage fright?" she teases with a watery laugh.

"Nah." I trace a line over her lips. "They just weren't you."

"Kasey," she says again, eyes closing. When she reopens them, there's a hunger there, an unmistakable want. It's intention made physical, and it makes me shudder. "Come here." She grabs hold of my hand, pulling me onto the bed until I'm over her, cradled by her legs.

"Are you sure?" I ask, still hesitant.

"You won't hurt her," Ava promises, knowing. "You could never." She lifts her head to kiss me, licking into my mouth.

I grunt. Splay a hand across her heart. Feel it beat beneath my palm. And slowly, leisurely, *divinely*, sink into her.

We both exhale out sounds of relief.

There's a distant instinct to pause, to give us both a second to adjust. But my body has other ideas, gently rocking into her, needing to move, to reach deeper. I press a kiss against her cheek, her jaw. My hand slides up her neck and around her throat, gently squeezing. "You feel—"

"*Good*," she mumbles, gasping.

"Yeah?" I sit up on my knees. Look down at where we're joined. "How good, sugar?"

She lifts her hips to better meet mine, the rhythmic slapping of skin on skin filling the room around us. It's entirely too much. Nowhere near *enough*.

Her hand covers her breast, squeezing. Pinching.

I watch. Spellbound.

"Really good," she finally says. Her mouth widens with every thrust, fingers pulling at the skin around her nipple. Her cheeks are such a beautiful shade of pink. And her eyes—they're on me as feverishly as mine are on her, taking in the tensing muscles in my chest as I move, to the roll of my shoulder as I lift her hips higher.

And then our gazes snag. Hook together. And I'm lost.

I snap my eyes closed. "Stop," I beg. "Please."

We both go still. Panting. Aching.

"Kasey?"

"I *cannot* come." I curse. "Not yet. Not until you do."

A soft exhale sounds before a light giggle. "Do you want me to look away?"

"No." I scrub a hand down my face. "Maybe."

She hums. "I've got an idea. Why don't *you* stay still, and just watch me?" She arches a little, shifts her ass down against the blankets. "I'm so *full* with you, Kasey," she whispers, "I don't even need you to move."

Her hand leaves her chest, skimming down the length of her stomach, until her fingers splay over herself, between us. She swirls them, coats them in her arousal, and lets out a long, tortuous breath.

And boy, do I fucking watch.

I watch her work, building herself up. Watch her fingers start to tremble and slip as she clenches around me, moaning softly.

Her cheeks flush brighter.

Her breaths grow shallow.

And I can't help myself.

I sink my thumb into my mouth before pressing it against her, replacing her pressure with my own.

I want to do this.

I want to make her come.

I start moving again, thrusting into her, using my free hand to push her left leg higher until her knee floats above her ear. Her legs are open so wide I can see every inch of her, every inch of *me*, as we move together.

It's indecent. Obscene.

It pays off, because soon Ava's tensing, arching like a crossbow off the bed. Her body clamps around mine, fluttering, teetering. And then she's falling, screaming into a pillow, and I come so hard inside of her I nearly black out from the force of it.

It takes several minutes before either of us can move.

Several minutes to piece my mind back together.

Eventually, Ava calms down enough to let out a mumbled *"Damn."*

Yeah, I agree. Damn.

I watch closely as I pull out of her, as my cum drips out with me.

I frown. That won't do.

Using the same thumb I used on her, I sweep it all up to push it back inside, careful not to miss anything. When I'm done, my eyes lift to her stomach. To her watchful gaze.

Biology be damned, they're both going to be mine.

CHAPTER TWENTY-THREE

AVA

I wake to the sound of a distant hum, a whirring that sweeps against my mind and pulls me from dreams of saltwater kisses and sun-warmed sand. I know before I even open my eyes that Kasey's not here, not in this bed or anywhere in the cabin. My heart can sense it: his absence. An emptiness I'd gotten so used to I almost forgot what it was to be full.

Until he made me remember.

Stretching lazily in a cocoon of blankets, I turn to the window where sunlight streams in across the room, wondering how long he's been gone, if it'd been hard for him to leave. Did he kiss me on his way out? Does he have any regrets about what happened last night?

You're going to make it good for me again, aren't you?

My face instantly heats with a warmth that sinks all the way to my belly. I didn't think I'd ever have Kasey again like that, and now that I have, I can't imagine anything else. I dated other people after leaving Saddlebrook Falls—it took a while to open up to the idea, but eventually I did and life started to move on. A couple of boyfriends even made it past the six-month mark, and then there was Tobias, of course, but even he only lasted a couple of years.

Still, no one ever compared to Kasey. Not even close.

At some point I started telling myself that no one *could*, that my relationship with Kasey existed in the perilously beautiful vacuum that is young love, full of naivete and the intensity that only two kids with varying degrees of formed frontal lobes could possibly accomplish. So I'd stopped comparing anyone to him altogether. Figured, what was the point, if I'd never have something like it again anyway?

I didn't anticipate Kasey asking himself the same question, but coming to a wildly different result.

I tried, a few times. But . . .

I swallow down a painful pang of regret. I can't imagine Kasey was somehow waiting for me—he had no idea I'd ever come back. I shamefully left without so much as a note. No explanation. And yet . . .

I can't help thinking about the *almosts*, the girls who were turned away. How far did things get before veering off track? Did he try to bring girls home? Did they make it into this bed? Did he stop, mid-kiss, and change his mind? Did he politely drive any of them home, walk them to their front door with a quiet, sullen apology?

I groan, pulling a pillow over my face as the humming around the cabin grows louder. A motor of some sort. Machine, I think— not a car. Curiosity gets the best of me as I scramble out of bed, pulling an old rodeo T-shirt from Kasey's dresser and shoving my head and arms through it. The hem reaches halfway down my thighs and it's baggy enough to hide my stomach, so I don't bother with pants.

There's a mug of coffee waiting for me on the kitchen table and, by the looks of it, Kasey's dumped all the creamer in Texas into it. A single white flower sits through the handle, one that matches a wild cluster growling along the bottom of the front porch steps.

The smile that grows on my face is easily a mile wide.

Suddenly the sound outside is blaring. I move to the front door and swing it open, finding a shirtless man wearing a black cowboy hat and jeans, straddling a riding lawn mower as it moves along the fence line of the pasture. I squint, trying to see his face, and quickly realize it's Rhett.

He must feel me watching him, because he turns to look at me, throwing a hand up in a friendly wave.

I wave back.

"Sorry!" he shouts. A shit-eating grin blooms across his face, and I make a show of rolling my eyes. I don't know if he's pleased that he woke me at this late morning hour or if he thinks he caught me red-handed wearing his brother's shirt, but either way I'm not going to overthink it. Probably.

Disappearing back inside, I decide to leave the screen door open to let in some fresh air. It smells like cut grass and horses—all things earthy and so *very* Kasey. It's comforting. Soothing, even. I go back for the coffee, tucking the flower in my ear, and grab my laptop from the guest bedroom before falling into the plush corner of the couch, throwing my feet up on the coffee table.

My conversation with my father has been gnawing at me since yesterday, enough to make me want to look and see if there's anything I might be able to scrounge up regarding Bennett Rescue Ranch or Huck Bennett himself. But once the internet browser opens on my screen, my mind turns to something else entirely and I find myself typing Ellis Rustler and Colt Rustler's names into the county search for public records.

A handful of arrests and criminal charges comes up for each of them, but nothing on a major scale. Definitely nothing recent. All of it reflects the typical kind of trouble that bored young men with impulse control issues might find themselves in. Ellis was caught stealing a pack of cigarettes from a convenience store three years ago, and before that there are documented instances of drunken fights and illegal gambling. Colt has fewer marks, mostly around underage drinking.

I'm thrilled to find no active warrants for either of them. It doesn't mean charges can't still come regarding the night of the shooting . . . but if cops had anything substantial on a case like that, they'd be quick to make arrests, and my gut tells me they'd go over the Rustlers' before coming after Kasey.

It's a bone-deep relief.

The search for Huck Bennett yields a much longer list of results. In his near-sixty years of life, there's a lot to sift through: an early criminal history around bootleg moonshine and illegal gambling, property deeds for various residential homes in the Houston area, a handful of marriage licenses to various women and *just* as many petitions for divorce. This guy clearly hasn't learned the concept of happy wife, happy life. There's an old record of foreclosure on a commercial property in Galveston for some sort of business in tourism and—

I blink. Lean forward toward the screen.

In the section for civil suits, a new petition was filed only three days ago. One day before our wedding.

I click to open the file.

"Knock knock," someone calls from out front.

I slam my laptop shut, turning to the screen door. "Who's there?" I call back.

A sigh. "Less kid jokes and more grown-up gossip!" It's Layla. I've been wondering when she might try to corner me.

"Less-kid-jokes-and-more-grown-up-gossip, who!" I counter, stuffing my laptop into the couch cushions. When she doesn't respond, I follow up with a curt "Coming!" as I work to wiggle off the couch and hurry to the door, where I find her peeking in from the other side of the screen.

I pull it open, giving her my best smile, and watch her eyes glide down my body. "Okay, so you guys are *definitely* at least sleeping in the same bed."

I look down at the rodeo championship shirt I'm still sporting. "It's not what it looks like," I say quickly.

She throws me a *I couldn't possibly believe you less* look.

"Okay," I relent, rolling my eyes. "It's exactly what it looks like. Just . . . come in."

"I brought snacks." Layla holds up a canvas tote as she passes. "Kasey mentioned you had a pretty fierce sweet tooth."

I frown. "Kasey explained my *eating habits* to you?"

"God no. That would be weird." She laughs, moving to the kitchen to set the bag down. "But he made sure his mom knew to have dessert on hand during dinner. You know, in case you sprouted an extra head and needed to be tamed by something quick."

I groan. "Wow, that's not embarrassing at all."

She turns around. Leans against the counter. "I have a feeling it has something to do with you being pregnant." She says it as plainly as if she were presenting the weather, but I can see the excitement dancing around the edges of her face.

"Okay," I relent. "Let's just get this over with. What do you want to know?"

She smiles, and it's . . . *genuinely* happy. "When did you find out? Do you know the gender? Oh my god, I bet Kasey is over the moon—"

I laugh. "Slow down, killer. I found out a few weeks before I left Miami. I don't know the gender yet, but I should know in a month, maybe? I still have to set an appointment . . ." I trail off, realizing that Layla's *frowning*.

"Did Kasey go visit you or something?"

"No."

Her eyes drop to my stomach.

And I realize what's happening. "It's not Kasey's," I hurry to say. "It's, uh—I was already pregnant. Big reason why I came home."

Shock slips over her face. "Wait. Does he *know*?"

"Of *course* he knows, Layla."

She seems relieved, though her frown deepens.

"I told him before the wedding. I wouldn't have . . ." I pause. "I made sure he knew."

She nods. Pushes her hair behind her ear, like she's trying to choose her words. "I know it's none of my business, but it seems like you two are . . . close, again."

"Yeah," I draw out. "Guess so."

"And you just admitted to sleeping in his bed."

"Yep." I nod, forcing a smile.

"What does he think about—" Her eyes dip to my stomach again.

Sugar, I don't think I've ever been more unbothered about something in my entire fucking life.

"He's . . . supportive."

"Huh," Layla hums, studying my face. Geez, the girl's good—I've got to remember to be careful with this one. "Well, great!" She claps her hands together, like now that we've gotten *that* out of the way, we can get back to our regularly scheduled programming. "Do you like honey buns?" She turns back to the bag on the counter. "I've also got cinnamon rolls or these chocolate waffles shaped like dinosaurs that the boys really like."

My mouth waters as she pulls out various packages of food. "Layla," I say sincerely, "you might be my *favorite* person today."

She laughs brightly. "Yeah, until Kasey comes home and bends you over this—"

"*Layla!*" I squeal, and we both burst into more laughter. "I admitted to sleeping in his bed, not sleeping *with him*."

She throws me a deadpan look. "You have a hickey the size of the Gulf Coast on your neck that you didn't have at dinner last night."

Well, *fuck.*

Layla and I spend the next hour gorging ourselves on everything she brought over—well, *I* gorge myself while she mostly watches with captivated interest—and she leaves with a tight hug that surprisingly makes me *very* teary-eyed.

"Pregnancy hormones," I insist.

"Sure." She pats me on the head, grinning. "See you soon, I'm sure!"

I watch her shuffle down the stairs and back toward the main house thinking, in another life, we would have made *great* sisters.

In the hours after she leaves, the reality of everything crashes back down around me: our fake marriage, this baby, the things I let myself tell Kasey last night while he held me in his bed. By the time he gets home I have a whole speech prepared to let us both off the hook, but as I watch him walk in through the door, it dies on my tongue.

Kasey is so . . . *handsome.* And filthy. His hands look like they were dipped in motor oil and his face is creased with dirt. He reaches to pull his hat off, revealing sweat-dried hair curling along his neck that I want to comb through with my fingers. His gaze finds me on the couch in seconds, his expression neutral, if not a little tired. "Hey."

"Hi," I say. "Are you hungry? We've made a serious come up on commercial baked goods, if you're interested."

His mouth twitches. "You must have been busy with hunter-gatherer duties."

I shrug. "I provide just as well as any man."

"Don't doubt it." His eyes skim down my body, taking in my shirt. He seems to linger on it, shoulders going stiff.

"Hope it's okay I helped myself," I say, embarrassment creeping in. How mortifying of me to just assume.

He nods once. "Of course." He doesn't move from where he stands. Instead, he just watches me. I fight the urge to try to covertly disappear beneath a blanket.

Is he angry? Maybe he should be. I wouldn't blame him, not when I told him I couldn't promise him anything and then turned around and begged him to take me to bed. The last thing I want to do—that I've *ever* wanted to do—is hurt him.

His face betrays no emotion as he continues his perusal, but when his eyes land on mine again, I can see it. The smile he's fighting.

And then he lets it bloom, lets it take over his whole face, and it fists the air out of my lungs.

Eventually he seems to shake off the weight of . . . whatever *that* was, and bends to remove his boots. "How was your day?" he asks.

"Hm, let's see." I hold out a hand to count with my fingers. "I slept in *gloriously* late in the world's most comfortable bed, had the pleasure of being awakened by a half-naked cowboy with a John Deere fetish, was rightfully spoiled with the aforementioned sugary baked goods, and had a nap on this couch—"

He straightens so fast I'm surprised it doesn't send him falling backward. "Half-naked cowboy?" he asks, face grim.

I nod, solemn. "Rhett was riding that lawn mower like they share a *very* intimate relationship."

He hangs his head. "I'm gonna fucking kill him."

I laugh, and it tugs at the corner of his mouth.

"Layla came by. She knows I'm pregnant."

"She does?"

"Yeah. She figured it out. You know, for a girl who didn't know her ex-boyfriend's best friend was in love with her for years, she's actually pretty perceptive."

"What did she say?" he asks, ignoring my quip.

"She had . . . questions. And lucky for us both, I had answers." He gives me a dry look, so I say, "After realizing the timeline, she mostly wanted to know what you thought about it."

"Ah."

"And I said you were *unbothered*."

His eyes flash as he walks toward me, a dark hunger there and gone before I can even really process it. He leans down to press a quick kiss to the top of my head before loping into the kitchen. "Good," he says, opening the fridge.

"I asked her not to say anything," I add, scrambling off the couch to join him. "I mean, people will know eventually, obviously, but it'll be on our terms. Oh, and I do have some news about your uncle."

This gets his attention. He swings the fridge door shut and looks at me, cold beer in hand. "What news?"

I frown. "He filed a motion to the probate court, a demand to compel distribution of the ranch. He listed the inheritance trust stipulations in support of his claim as well as the fact that your father hasn't been seen working in years and therefore likely isn't currently fit to keep things running, and . . . he also disclosed 'based on a source close to the family' that he believes his nephew has entered into a fraudulent marriage in an attempt to maintain ownership."

"Shit," Kasey snaps.

"Don't worry," I say. "I bet he made up the source. Or it could have been my father . . . At worst, it just means we have to fight the case. Prove this isn't fraudulent."

His eyes narrow. "And at best?"

I give him my best *already on it* smile as I propel myself up onto the counter. "At best, we file a temporary restraining order against him. Lay the groundwork to support the argument that he's delusional and grasping at straws. That he thinks he can lie his way into a multi-million-dollar land deed."

Kasey moves toward me, setting his beer down on the table, and without even thinking I open my legs to invite him closer, the denim of his jeans dragging along my inner thighs as his eyes reverently dance around my face. "World's most comfortable bed, huh?" He plucks the flower from my hair. I'd forgotten it was even there.

"I thought you were mad at me," I admit.

"For what?"

"I don't know. Taking advantage?"

He expels a breath. Shakes his head. And then leans further, resting his hands on either side of my hips. He's not touching me, not really, but he's . . . *everywhere*. And he's eyeing my neck like it's the long-lost Holy Grail.

"When I got home and saw you, saw *this*—" He presses his lips to where I know a hickey blemishes my skin. It's the faintest touch. Featherlight. And then his mouth moves to my ear. "Do you know how unbelievably *satisfying* it is to come home to you in my house, wearing *my* clothes, pregnant and safe?" The sharp edge of his nose grazes my hair as he inhales a deep, steadying breath. "I must be reverting back to Neanderthal-level instincts because seeing you like this makes me fucking crazy, sugar. If anyone's taking liberties with this situation, it's me."

Heat expands through every inch of my body. And yet—

"What about . . . *you*?"

"What about me?"

I sigh. "This could get messy, fast."

He snorts. "Ava, I think we sprinted past messy two and a half weeks ago when you barreled into this cabin and begged me to be your husband."

"I didn't *barrel* in here!" I swat him. "And I certainly didn't beg."

He laughs, a web of wrinkles creasing the contours of his eyes. And it fills me with so much contentment I might burst. "Whatever you say, sugar." His voice *rumbles* through me. And then he's backing away, picking up his beer. "I've got a shift tonight. I'm gonna shower and head back out."

I frown, watching him turn the corner into his room. "Wait!" I shout. "Can I come?"

CHAPTER TWENTY-FOUR

KASEY

The breeze kicks up with a violent gust just as I shut the truck door, nearly taking my hat with it. I press it further down along my brow and turn to find Ava—my north star —back turned to me, already making her way across the sand. For a moment, I just watch her. Use the time to try to shove some air into my too-small lungs.

The small wooden box in my pocket has somehow found a way to lodge itself in my throat, and I feel a little delirious. I don't think I've ever been so nervous about anything in my life, but I've also never felt so sure. It's a small ring—the smallest ring they had at the pawn shop—but it was all I could afford with my spring rodeo winnings and the money Brooks let me borrow last week when I told him I needed a new fuel system in my truck. I'll have to figure out a way to pay him back, but . . . that's a problem for another day.

Still, small as it is, I looked at it and immediately knew it was the one. Kind of like the way I felt about Ava the first time I looked at her. That has to count for something, right?

Ava stands at the shoreline looking out into the water. Her hair whips wildly at her back, dancing along the dark-tanned skin of her arms. We've been spending most Saturday afternoons so far this summer here at Scorpion Bay, where no one is around to bother us and we're free to be ourselves. Where we can be us.

Ava's never admitted it outright, but I notice the way her body loosens every time we leave Saddlebrook Falls. I think she's spent so much time performing for people that she's lost a piece of herself along the way—and I don't fault her for it. I know how much it hurt her when her mom left, how she felt like she wasn't good enough to make her stay. How it changed her father, hardened him, made him look at her with an edge of regret.

She's never admitted to any of that either. But if there's one foreign language I've learned to speak, as muddy as it can get sometimes, it's Ava and all her insecurities. So when she spins around to smile at me as I close the distance between us, when I see the way her hard edges have melted away, leaving the soft and vulnerable traces of the girl I've grown to love so deeply, I make a promise to myself that I'll spend the rest of my life finding ways to give her more peace like that.

Her eyes drop to my feet as the saltwater air curls around us. "One of these days I'll convince you to take your damn boots off at the beach," she chides.

I grin, sure she's probably right. She has a way of convincing me to do a lot of things. "Yeah, yeah." A strand of hair catches on her lips, and I reach to tug it loose. "But today is not that day."

She smiles, eyeing the small duffle I'm carrying. "What sorts of treasures did you bring me this time?" she asks.

My nerves spike as I turn to walk away from the water. "Candy, mostly." She laughs, trailing behind me as I aim for flatter ground. I find a decent patch of clean-looking sand and drop the duffle, unzipping the top flap to pull out the flannel blanket we like to sit on. It's still sandy from last weekend, so when I flick my wrists to snap it open, it sends sand flying at Ava. "Shit," I mutter, dropping the blanket to move in front of her. "I'm so sorry."

She wipes her face with her hands, laughing. "Don't worry," she croons. "Payback's a bitch." Before I know it, she's shoving me to the ground, tackling me in the world's most uncoordinated flop of a takedown that somehow ends with her pinned beneath me. She huffs, cheeks pink, and thrusts her hips to knock me loose and flip us around, letting out a satisfied hum when she sits up to straddle me. But I think I'm the one who's won.

A burst of hunger takes over as I sit up to cup the back of her neck, pulling her mouth to mine for a deep kiss. She lets out a surprised grunt before wrapping her arms around my neck. Her chest melts into mine as her lips part, letting my tongue in to stroke against hers. I'm instantly hard and she knows it—her hips move in light, teasing circles, creating just enough friction to drive me insane.

"I love you," I murmur against her mouth before diving in again. Her responding whine sends me to the moon, and I realize—this is it. Fuck the blanket, fuck the wine, I don't need any of it. I just need her.

Slowly working the ring box out of my pocket while she's distracted with kissing me, I flick it open with my thumb and bring it between us, pulling my mouth away from hers. She looks down at it, sapphire eyes flaring with shock, and every ounce of nerves I've felt all morning disappear.

"Marry me, Ava," I say between uneven breaths. "I can't imagine a more perfect life than one spent with you."

"Kasey," she breathes, and my name sounds so absolutely perfect from her lips. Her eyes well with emotion as she digs her fingers into the back of my neck.

"Be my wife, sugar."

She smiles, and it rivals the sun's warmth. "Yes," she says, laughing. "Yes, Kasey!"

I pull the ring from its satin nest and she lets me slip it on her finger. And then she's pushing me down into the sand, kissing me with so much urgency it feels like our last day on earth.

I won't realize until far too late—that's exactly what it is.

I should have known Ava would make friends with every fucking person in here. Even Sunny and Boone, the bar's two meanest dipshit regulars, are eating out of the palm of her pretty little hand. She works the crowd like she was made for the attention, for the glory of having every set of eyes in the building on her.

And boy, are they on her.

It used to bother me, when we were younger. She'd pull shit like this at parties full of people we didn't know, and it would scare me. I'd worry someone might want to take advantage of her, might want to *take* from her, and it fucking made me crazy. But Ava required her own agency, and eventually I came to learn that she could fend for herself. That she thrived in the performance and was much more comfortable with *that* version of herself, who had the power to pull you in and leave you wanting more. I think, for her, it felt safer than being honest.

It took a while for me to understand the deep-rooted fears Ava carried that stemmed from issues with her parents—her mom's abandonment and her dad's detachment left her struggling with things like vulnerability and self-worth. But once I understood those pieces of her, it made it easy to love them all.

Her eyes find mine across the room. I've been watching her flirt with two cowboys for about five minutes; they're from a ranch about ten miles north of here and don't come in often, but when they do they're always respectful and keep to themselves while spending a decent amount of money on drinks. Tonight they brought a couple of women with them, though at the moment, I don't see them.

I throw her a *Should I be worried?* look. Humor dances in her eyes as she shoots me a wink back. She leans closer to the man on her left, murmuring something that has him slapping the table and shaking with laughter. And then she pats him on the shoulder and leaves them, heading right for me.

"Jealous?" she asks as she takes an empty seat at the bar. Her smile could power the lights in this place for weeks. Fucking brat.

Yes, I think. But I don't give her the satisfaction. Instead, I pull a tall glass from the stack and fill it with ice water, setting it in front of her. "You having fun?"

"Oh yeah." She nods, taking a long drink. "I'm curious—do you think a cocktail server in a bar like this would make as much money as a lawyer?"

I know it's a joke, but a lick of pleasure rushes through me so hard and fast I have to close my eyes to steady myself, that she's even *thinking* about what it would be like to work here. With me. I should have paid more attention in biology class, because I don't have the words to explain the things she does to me. "More, actually," I tell her, hoping she doesn't notice the stumble. "Especially with a face like yours."

I woke up this morning with Ava's heart beating against my ribs, and as I stared up at the ceiling thinking about everything we'd done, I felt the urgency of this second chance slam into me. I know this little marriage deal was only supposed to be a convenient way for us both to solve some problems—but after last night, shit's changed, and I'm not a kid anymore. I'm smarter now. I can see through the bullshit lies she tells herself because she thinks it's better that way.

And I'm not gonna let her keep getting away with it.

"I hope it's okay with you, but I'm going to try to liven the place up." She scooches off the barstool and lands on her feet, angling away from me.

"What does that mean?"

She looks back at me over her shoulder, throwing me a wry grin. "You'll see."

Within minutes, Ava's rallied to get at least eighty percent of our patrons onto their feet after feeding quarters into the jukebox.

The sound of bagpipes fills the space as "Copperhead Road" starts playing, and Ava squeals, quickly working to show the group the steps before the lyrics start. At first, no one gets it, but they're enamored by her dazzling insistence and do their best to follow along as she shoots her feet out on the ground in front of her, the heel of her boots clacking against the hardwood floor. Eventually people start catching on, and soon they're all stomping in unison to the beat of the song, eyes stuck on her feet to follow her lead.

I watch from behind the bar, in disbelief and a little awe.

"The fuck is she doing?" Rhett says, coming up behind me, eyes glued to the girl of my dreams as she punches a hole through my heart.

"Dancing," I say simply.

He looks at me. Looks back at her. "Shit."

"What?"

"You really are fucked."

I roll my eyes, turning to face him. He's been upstairs *checking on Olivia* for the last forty-five minutes, and now his collar's obviously crumpled and his hair's a mess. "You'd know all about it, wouldn't you?"

He frowns and turns away, shouting, "Not sure what you're talking about!" over the music.

"You have lipstick on your neck, idiot!" I shout back.

"Excuse me," someone asks from behind me. I turn to find one of the middle-aged women who came in earlier with the cowboys. A quick glance tells me the other woman—her friend, I'm assuming—is back at the table with them.

"Yes, ma'am," I say politely as I approach her. "Can I get you something?"

"I'd love a lemon drop martini, please," she says as her eyes trail down my bare arms. She's wearing a tight black dress that reveals more than I care to see, but I respect her confidence.

It's not the first time someone from out of town has come in and ordered something you'd probably find on any other menu, but not ours. We actually don't even have menus. We have a couple of cheap beers on tap and whatever bottles are currently on the shelf, which are mostly whiskeys.

I give her my best customer-service smile as I lean forward on the bar between us to spare myself from having to yell over all the stomping going on behind her. It pains me a little, actually, that I can't watch Ava. "This isn't really a fancy bar and we don't have a lot of fancy tricks. Don't even own a single martini glass, I'm afraid. But I *can* give you some vodka with some lemon juice squeezed in, if that's something you think you might like."

She clutches at her chest, face flushing as she laughs. "Oh my, you cowboys are all the same, aren't you?"

I narrow my gaze, not understanding.

Her eyes now rake over my face in a way that feels . . . weird. Uncomfortable. "You might not be able to give a woman everything she's asking for, but you still find a way to give her what she needs." Her tongue makes a sweep along her bottom lip as she watches for my reaction.

I frown, impatient. "Lady, do you want lemon juice vodka or not?"

Now she's leaning forward too, running her claw-like red nails up the skin of my forearm. "What're you doing tonight?" she asks in what she must think is a sultry voice.

I pull my arm back and straighten. "Working."

Her brown eyes pinch in challenge. "What about after?"

"Kasey!" Ava shouts over the Red Clay Strays song that's now blaring through the bar's speakers. I lift my eyes over the woman's tired blonde hair to see Ava marching back toward me. She looks adorably windblown and there's a sheen of sweat along her forehead. My heart snags as I take it all in, distracted enough not to notice the dangerous edge in her gaze. "I've been looking for you," she says, eyes trained on the woman between us.

The woman rears back. "Me?" she asks.

Ava scoffs. "No, not you. *Him*."

Her tone is sharp enough to let me know what's coming. "Ava," I say—a gentle warning, even though there's a strong part of me that would love to see her show her teeth. Especially over me.

"Actually," Ava continues, her focus still centered on the woman. "I'd appreciate it if you kept your fucking hands off of my husband."

And *there* it is. I beam.

The woman's eyes grow wide as she looks back and forth between us. "I had no idea—I'm so sorry!"

Ava shrugs. "I imagine you wouldn't. You seemed too busy cataloging all the things you'd like to use him for to notice the ring on his finger." Her eyes finally rise to mine, and there's something playful in her expression now. Her own gentle warning. "But to be fair, he likes to flirt with other women when he knows I'm looking for him—tries to get a rise out of me. It's a little game we play because the sex it leads to is always *so* damn good."

The woman gasps, snatching her purse off the bar. "Pig!" she yells at me before turning back to the table her friends are sitting at.

"What is the matter with you?" I ask Ava, though I can't help the grin that slices across my face.

She giggles, rolling her eyes. "*You* were the one putting the foundation of our marriage in jeopardy, flirting with someone in front of all these people. And so quickly after saying your vows to me?" She tsks. "You make it too easy."

"Says the woman flirting with *two* guys." She laughs again, playful. "Plus, you know what my flirting looks like, sugar, and that was *not* it. Though I have to say, jealousy looks real good on you."

Her eyes flash, and suddenly I'm back in my room, watching her put her mouth around me. Watching her touch herself as I start to move inside of her.

She must sense it, because her expression changes. Morphs into something on the cusp of feral. Wild.

I swallow. "Be good, Ava. I've still got a few more hours here."

"So do I." She grins, letting her gaze linger on my mouth.

And then she's off again.

CHAPTER TWENTY-FIVE

AVA

I doze off in Kasey's truck on the way home from the bar. It's past midnight, and I'm exhausted. The next fleeting sense of awareness tells me I'm in a soft bed that smells like Kasey and a strong arm is hooking me closer to a warm, broad chest. It's so comfortable, so *right*, that I immediately fall back to sleep.

The next morning, he's gone. Again.

I pull on one of his old shirts. Again.

I find a coffee waiting for me in the kitchen. Again.

This time, the flower is purple.

I make good use of my morning by looking for OB-GYN practices within a fifteen-mile radius. It's something I've admittedly been avoiding, but now that Kasey—and Layla—know, it's time to do the responsible thing and get back on track with appointments. Turns out, there are half a dozen doctors open to new patients. I research each of them and land on the one that feels like a perfect balance between sterile modern medicine and crunchy intuitiveness.

I call and set an appointment for two days from now.

After sifting through some work emails and responding to a

handful of new inquiries from current clients, I decide to open the chain with the partners and reread their last email. Braden, the youngest of them—and the most reasonable—penned a detailed list of accolades and assurances that my place with the firm is as secure as ever, and that just because I'm no longer in consideration for partner, my role with them is still deemed very valuable. They understand my leave but hope it is only temporary and would love to welcome me back to the office as soon as I'm able to return.

I know he's trying to be nice and soften the blow, but the words rip into me all over again, made worse by the fact that Tobias's name seems to sneer at me from the carbon copy line. *He's* a partner now, so *he's* included on communications such as this. *He* gets to virtually witness the fallout of a disaster that *he* helped create.

It's a slap in the face. And I'm still *so* angry.

I ignored the last text he sent me on the morning of the wedding, begging me to talk. Quite frankly, I'm sort of hoping his chase will die off and I can go on with the rest of my life without ever having to speak to him again. I know it's *technically* his baby growing inside of me right now, but he made it very clear that he wanted no part of being a part of her life.

Wiping at my tired eyes, I decide to shift gears again. For the next hour, I learn everything there is to know about Texas estate laws, temporary restraining orders, and their state precedent in land disputes. Drafting the paperwork is easier than I anticipated, but I send it to a colleague for a second set of eyes, just in case.

I'm starting to feel a little restless alone in the cabin, so after helping myself to a long bath in Kasey's bathroom, I pull his shirt back on along with a pair of jeans and my boots before braiding my hair out of my face and swiping on some mascara. I noticed a couple worn hats hanging on the wall in Kasey's closet—probably older ones he doesn't wear anymore—and try them both on in front of a mirror before choosing the brown one. It's decorated with a plain leather band and *feels* so much like him.

The walk down toward the barns is *nice*. We're deep into spring now, and the sun heats the land enough to ease it back into its purpose: plants grow, flowers bloom, and the horses out in the pasture graze, tails swishing lazily behind them. It's such a stark contrast to the metropolitan bustle of Miami where natural vegetation is hard to come by. The truth is, deep down, I've always loved Texas—I just love my autonomy more.

Soon, the barns are in sight, and I spot Kasey in the biggest corral just outside, riding the golden mare he recently told me wasn't allowing anyone on her. I guess I shouldn't be surprised that it'd be him she learned to trust. One of my favorite things about horses is that they don't take more than what they need, and they don't give in to anything that's not real. There's no posturing, no trickery. They come to you when you're in your truth so they can show you theirs.

"Ava?" I turn to find Kasey's youngest brother, Wells, gripping a stack of boxes.

"Morning!" I give him my cheeriest smile. "Can I help with that?"

"Oh. No, it's okay, thanks. Are you looking for Kasey? I can get him if—"

"Nope. I was actually hoping I could . . . help. With the horses, maybe? Or I could organize the barn?"

He grins. "Uh, I'm about to distribute some meds if you want to tag along? Nothing major—it's mostly just vitamins."

I nod. "I'd love to!"

Inside the barn, Wells shows me the binder with all the paperwork outlining who needs what. He shows me how to fill the oral syringes with the vitamin paste, and how to sweettalk (and gaslight) the horses with a little pre-dose shot of apple sauce. After the third horse guzzles his once-a-day like the rodeo champ he probably is, I feel like I've got the hang of it. Wells must agree, because he lets me handle the rest—it's a level of trust I don't take lightly, one that I intend to keep earning with Kasey's family however I can.

I get through all of the stalls in the big barn in about an hour and then fill more syringes before heading into the second. I'm delighted to spot the golden mare tucked in the back corner, her beady, knowing little eye keeping tabs on me as I work. Kasey must be out with a different horse now. "You finally let him ride you, huh?" I ask her across the barn.

If she answers, I'm not sure of it. But I hope she feels a sense of accomplishment. She's not on the list for getting vitamins—not every horse is. But I can't resist giving her a custom shot of straight applesauce anyway, because good girls of *any* species should get a treat.

She's eager for it, like she knows I wouldn't steer her wrong. When the syringe is empty, she chuffs out a satisfied burst of air. I edge closer to her, reaching out to weave light fingers through her long yellow mane. "Such a pretty girl," I murmur softly, keeping my eyes trained on hers. Her head dips before she winds her neck toward me, nuzzling her nose into my shoulder.

"She likes you," Kasey says.

I nearly startle. "She's a sweetheart," I say back, looking over my shoulder to where he stands at the entrance of the barn, leaning against a beam like he's been there a while. "I imagine we're not supposed to have favorites but . . . she's mine."

"Of course."

I narrow my gaze. "What do you mean '*of course*'?"

His eyes flit to the mare still nudging into my shoulder. "She bucks so fucking hard," he says. And then looks at me again.

I shrug. "Smart girl."

He snorts. And then his eyes rise. "You're wearing my hat."

"It seems we're beginning to uncover a new and potentially toxic trait of mine."

"Which is?"

"Pilfering. Kleptomania. Sticky fingers."

Humor dances in his eyes. "What do you think we should do about that?"

I shrug. "Hell if I know. I'm the one with the problem."

"Keep it."

"I'm not sure that actually solves my impulse to loot treasure from your bedroom, but—"

"Always so fucking stubborn," he mutters under his breath. "I'll leave you two divas to it. Headed to the office if you need anything. Should be wrapping up soon."

My heart clenches as he turns away. I'm not sure where the feeling comes from. "I won't," I call out. "But thanks!"

The crown of his hat twists as he shakes his head, marching back out into the warm afternoon sun.

I FIND WELLS AGAIN AFTER CLEANING OUT THE REST OF the syringes and putting everything back where it came from, and ask him what I can do next. If he's bothered to have become responsible for showing me the ropes, he doesn't show it. He actually seems to enjoy it. Like maybe spending time with his older brother's new mail-order bride seems like it might just be worth his time.

Wells explains that they feed most of the horses twice a day, and that it's about time to prep for the second feeding. There's a whole separate binder for this, outlining which horses eat pellets and which eat Bermuda hay and how much. Like before, Wells oversees for the first few stalls, watching me measure out portions into a wheelbarrow before taking them to each horse. And then he leaves me to it.

I have to admit, the work is rewarding. There's something about getting face time with each one of them, of giving them what they need to thrive, that feels purposeful. By the time I'm done there's sweat beading down my temple and I'm hungry enough to be a little nauseous, but I feel content in a way I haven't felt in weeks. *Months*, even.

Outside, Wells is at the fence of the closest corral, watching Rhett lead the golden mare on a long lead inside.

"I saw Kasey out with her earlier," I say leaning against the fence.

Wells nods. "Normally we'd only pull her once a day, but since she let Kasey in the saddle, Rhett wants to see if he can push that good behavior further."

"He wants to see if she'll let him on her too?"

He nods again.

"Does she have a name yet?"

"Kasey started calling her Sugar a couple days ago. It's not on any paperwork yet, but it seems to be sticking."

My heart rockets up to my throat.

We both watch as Rhett leads her around the outer perimeter of the fence line, working her into a light trot. I pay close attention to the way he keeps focus on her eyes and body, looking for any signals she might give him. He talks to her too, a low murmuring that I can't make out. It hums on the breeze.

"I can see why you guys do this," I say.

Wells grins. "It's not easy. Some days can be pretty bleak. But . . . yeah. Today's a good one."

Rhett stops the mare in the center of the corral and gives her a small, affectionate neck rub. I feel a warm hand press into the small of my back, and look up to find Kasey next to me, eyes on his brother. "Think she'll let him on?" I ask him quietly.

His lips curve into the barest hint of a smile, but he keeps his gaze forward. I turn to watch just as Rhett tucks the toe of his boot into a stirrup. And then he's rising, swinging a leg over the mare's back before he drops his weight into the saddle.

I feel myself holding my breath.

The mare takes a step backward, head rising. And then

another step back. Rhett clicks his tongue and gives her a light tap of his heels against her belly, and she takes off in a beautiful trot.

"She's so strong," I say, pride bursting through me as I watch her transition into a gallop with her head held high.

"She is," Kasey agrees. "And so fucking beautiful."

I turn to look at him, finding his gaze already on me.

Everything around us disappears. "Stop," I say.

"Stop what?"

"Looking at me like that," I whisper. It's too much, and I'm not sure what it is about this moment that's making me emotional but emotion clutches at me all the same. I feel exposed. Raw.

He blows out a breath. But doesn't say anything.

We watch Rhett ease the mare back to a careful stop. Her mane is a curtain of golden light in the dipping sun. I realize Wells is no longer here, that Kasey and I are alone. "I made a doctor appointment," I say over the silence. "It's in a couple of days."

Kasey looks at me. Straightens. Clutches the fence a little tighter. "Do you want me to take you?"

When I look up at him, his expression is so confident, so *earnest*. If he's disappointed in me shutting the earlier moment down, he doesn't show it. But still . . . "Kasey, I really need you to know there is *no* pressure here. It's my responsibility to take care of myself, and—"

"Ava."

"I just don't want you to lean into something now that you might regret later, and—"

"Ava."

"—as scary as it all is, I *think* that I can do this—"

"Of course you can do this," he says, nudging into me with enough force to get me to close my damn mouth. "You're a cowgirl, sugar. You've always been a cowgirl. And cowgirls don't back down when the world starts bucking. You're stronger than you give yourself credit for." He blows out another long breath before looking out toward the setting sun. "It's okay though, because now you have me around again to remind you."

My blood becomes effervescent. "I'm not sure I'm really a cowgirl."

He smiles. Leans in close enough that I can smell the soap he used in the shower this morning. And says, hot against my ear, "That hat would beg to differ."

CHAPTER TWENTY-SIX

KASEY

The scent of lavender is so strong in this lobby that I have to fight the urge to cough. Tendrils of cool steam plume from a diffuser in the corner, tucked beneath a bushy houseplant with small string lights woven throughout. The soft sounds of crashing waves permeate the dimly lit room, and I wonder if it's all intended to evoke a sense of calm and tranquility.

If so, it's not working for Ava. She sits next to me, leg bouncing, fingers thrumming incessantly against the muscle of her thigh. I can *feel* the anxiety radiating off her. She's been wound up all morning, from the second she opened her eyes. "What if she has a goose head?" she'd asked, staring up at me from her pillow, hair fanned out around her.

I ran my fingers up and down her arm in soothing rotations. "You're going to love that little goose head with all of your might," I told her.

"What if she has claws for hands? Not like werewolf-shifter claws, but like . . . like *talons*. What if she has the feet of an eagle—"

"Then you'll love her little eagle feet, and we'll make sure to keep her off the furniture."

She frowned. "I haven't felt her move yet. What if something's wrong?"

"Ava," I said gently, reaching for her face. "She's going to be perfect. No matter what kind of head she comes out with."

When we first walked into the office, we were greeted by a hand-painted wooden sign that read *At Your Cervix* in bold red letters, and Ava seemed to relax a touch. The stout woman behind the large front desk smiled softly, asking for Ava to fill out a few intake forms, and now that she's done with them I can see her mind at work. The longer we sit here, the more she's spiraling all over again.

"Distract me," she whines, slumping in her seat. "I feel like I'm going to have a heart attack." Her words catch the attention of another woman who also must be waiting for an appointment, but she quickly looks away.

I tug her into my side. Press a kiss to the top of her head. And whisper, "Please don't *ovary* act."

She swats at me. "*Kasey*!"

"Shhh." I laugh. And then she does too.

"How long have you been sitting on that?" she asks.

"About five minutes," I say smugly.

"Ava Jones?" a petite nurse calls from an open door, clipboard in hand. She's wearing a dark green set of scrubs with—

Fuck.

Ava deflates beside me. "It's a sign," she mutters, eyes glued to the pattern of geese covering the woman from shoulders to ankles. She stands, looking down at me, a little unsure.

I stand too and give her a hard kiss. "I'll be right here if you need me, okay?"

"Okay," she mumbles, a little dazed. "But if I come back with a sonogram picture of an ancient sea creature please don't laugh."

"I would never," I promise.

I watch her disappear into the fluorescent-bright hallway with the nurse. And then the door shuts.

And I wait.

The truth is, I'm just as fucking scared as Ava is.

Fifteen minutes later, the same nurse reappears. Her eyes find mine immediately. "Kasey Bennett?" she asks.

I rise to my feet. "Yes, ma'am."

"Would you mind coming back with me?"

Nerves shoot through my limbs. "Everything okay?"

"Ava is asking for you." Her face is stoic and gives me nothing to work with.

I nod, following her back to an exam room with a closed door, emotion fisting my throat the entire way. The nurse knocks twice before pushing the door open a few inches and peeking her head in. "Ava? I have Kasey here with me."

"Thank you," I hear her say. Her voice is small. Watery. I can't see her yet, but I can tell she's crying, and my fear ratchets up another ten levels.

The door opens wider and . . . there she is, lying on the exam table. The Bennett Rescue Ranch shirt she grabbed out of my drawer is pulled up and tucked into her bra, exposing the soft skin of her torso, her small bump on full display. A blanket made of what looks like paper is draped over her lap, and her feet are cradled by a set of stirrups that are braced from beneath the table. Her legs are closed, though, and a woman with a blonde ponytail moves some sort of wand over Ava's stomach.

There's no doubt Ava's been crying, but her smile is so wide it immediately balms over every ounce of worry. She's . . . happy. Beaming. "Talon feet?" I ask. Breathless. Unmoored.

She shakes her head. "Even better. Look." It's only now I notice a small screen attached to the big machine that Ponytail's wand is plugged into. The black-and-white image is grainy, but there's an unmistakable flutter. Butterfly wings, soaring into the sky.

And then the image goes dark as Ponytail shifts the wand, pressing up from the bottom of Ava's stomach now. I keep my focus trained on the screen, waiting, until some sort of bean-shaped white blob appears, five small circles cresting over it.

A foot, I realize. An *indescribably* small foot.

The wind knocks clean out of me as I look at Ava. Tears are streaming down her face, eyes glued to the monitor.

"You can get closer," Nurse Geese says, pressing a gentle hand between my shoulder blades. Encouraging me forward.

My gaze slips back to Ava. She's studying the monitor as Ponytail moves to another new angle, soaking in everything she sees on that screen like her life depends on it. But her arm is extended out, hand reaching for me. In a blink, I hold it in mine.

"Do you see how pretty she is?" Ava whispers, salty tears coating her rosy lips.

"Of course she is," I murmur back.

"She?" Ponytail says with a small smile.

Ava looks at her, abruptly pulled from what's happening on the monitor. "Can you tell yet?"

The woman nods. "But it seems you already know. It's a girl, honey."

Ava's eyes squeeze tight as a joyful sob rattles through her.

I move closer, hunching over her, pressing hard kisses all over her face. "So damn incredible," I mouth into her cheek. "So fucking perfect, Ava. Look at what you're doing. Look at what you're capable of."

She clutches me tighter. Holds on to me with so much weight it forces me down to a knee. And even though I know she doesn't *need* to hold on to me, because she's got this on her own, I hope she never *ever* fucking stops.

"It really is cute." Ava swirls the last piece of warm bread into the even warmer dip between us. She pops it into her mouth and assesses me with a playful smirk.

"What's cute?" I say, even though I already know what's coming.

"You are such a gentle crier," she says. "Quiet but *weepy*, you know?"

"You were sobbing before I even got into the room," I point out.

She arches a finger toward herself. "I am a sausage-casing stuffed too full of raging hormones. *You* are—"

"How are you kids doing over here?" June asks, coming over from another table, eyeing the already nearly polished-off spinach and artichoke dip that she dropped off less than five minutes ago. She frowns. "I'll go grab you some more of this," she says a little quieter, as though not to embarrass Ava in front of the other patrons.

Ava simply shrugs, totally unbothered, and peers at the wedge of lemon on the brim of my water glass like it's a butter-seared steak as June walks away.

"Easy tiger."

Her eyes flick up to mine, ravenous. "What?"

"Food's coming. Just give the kitchen a few more minutes to make sure your hamburger isn't still bleeding."

"I know the food's coming, Kasey, I was here when we ordered it." She rolls her eyes dramatically. But they land back on my lemon wedge.

I laugh. "Besides your insatiable appetite, how are you feeling?"

Her eyes soften. "Really, really happy."

The door to the café jangles open behind me, courtesy of the bell hanging from the top of the door, and Ava's gaze moves over my shoulder. And then her face hardens. Before I know it, she's rising out of her seat. "Ava?" I ask, frowning. I twist in my seat and watch her march toward the man who just walked in—it's the owner of the local hardware store.

"Excuse me," she says. "Silas, right? Silas Greene?"

The man tilts his head, bushy brows pulled down. "Yeah?" he grunts beneath an ungroomed beard.

"You have a kid named Max, right?"

And then I remember—Liam's fight. *Shit.*

"Yeah," Silas grunts again. "So?"

"Thought it might be important for you to know your kid is a *menace.*"

Silas frowns. "Who the hell are you, lady?"

"I'm a good friend of Liam Bennett, and I'm really disappointed to hear some of the shit Max is telling him at school about the recent *death* of his *mother.*"

Silas's face goes ruddy. "That kid nearly broke my kid's nose," he barks. "He had no right—"

"Do you recognize me, Silas?" Ava interrupts.

His mouth tightens before letting out a firm "No."

"Well, you probably should. I saw you at enough parties growing up. You were the too-old creep who always found a way to hang around a bunch of underage girls. You know my friend Molly *pretty* well, if memory serves. From back when we were *sixteen.*"

This has Silas blanching. "I don't know what you're talking about."

Ava nods and gives a dry laugh. "I imagine it's all a little hazy, but trust me when I say I have the means to make you remember. I'm a lawyer now. And my father is the sheriff. You know Sheriff Joe, don't you?"

Silas looks uncomfortable. "What do you want from me?"

Ava grins. "Listen. Liam's a good kid. He's been through a lot, but he's still just a kid. He doesn't deserve to have to go to school and be *bullied* about things in life he can't control. Making fun of his grief is below the belt, Silas, and you need to teach your son some fucking manners."

She takes another step forward, and the instinct to rush over and pull her away becomes almost intolerable, knowing the risk she's taking by standing up to this brute of a man. Nearly the entire café is watching their heated discussion unfold, and I'm worried Silas might lash out. But I force myself to stay seated, to let her lead, because this is also one of the things I *love* about her: her fierce determination to stand up for what's right. Her total lack of fear.

"Your son had that punch coming, Silas," Ava continues, "and you and I both know it. This is your chance to raise a young man who treats the people around him better than you did. If I hear that Liam has any further issues with Max, you'll pay for the things *you've* done and I'll make sure he learns the lesson anyway. Got it?"

Silas takes a step back, nodding.

"Good." Ava sighs. And then smiles politely like nothing happened. "Hope you enjoy your lunch!"

Silas, it turns out, doesn't enjoy anything, because he leaves as soon as Ava turns to stride back to the table. She sinks down into her seat looking quite pleased with herself. I can't help but grin. "You good?"

She nods. "Always love getting to knock something off the to-do list."

June comes back around with a tray of plates, looking at Ava with obvious amusement. "I've got more dip," she says, setting the dish in the middle of the table with a fresh basket of warm bread. "And two burgers. Anything else you two need?"

Ava's already staring down her burger, licking her lips.

I chuckle. "No thank you, June. This looks amazing."

She smiles, and then saunters off again.

Ava doesn't hesitate to pick up her hamburger, taking a giant bite. Her eyes roll back in her head as she chews and . . . dammit.

She's going to make me hard in the middle of this fucking café. "Good?" I husk out, mouth dry as my eyes trace the line of her lips.

"So good," she moans, and . . . *fuck.*

I try to discreetly adjust myself under the table. Ava's been sleeping in my bed since that first night she came in—but it's been just that: sleeping. My want for her is a constant, physical ache, but I'm trying so hard to navigate this new chance with her in a way that doesn't spook her. So I let myself drink her in and hang on to every burst of emotion her face conveys with each bite of her food.

"Quit leering, Bennett," she gripes, eyes squeezed closed with pleasure.

I laugh, picking up my own burger. "I'm honestly a little jealous."

"Of my burger?" she asks around the large bite she just took.

"Yeah. The things I would do to be that bur—"

A chair scrapes loudly against the linoleum floor from a table next to us. We both look over to find Nosey Maeve collecting her things as she glares at us. It's clear she was eavesdropping, but we hardly said anything sinister.

"Hi, Maeve," Ava says lightly with a small wave. "So nice to see you."

But the old crone wants no part of Ava's pleasantries. "That was quite the show you put on for everyone, Ava," Maeve says, looking utterly unimpressed. "You ran Silas clean out of the building."

Ava gives her a thousand-watt smile. "So happy to hear you enjoyed it."

"You're a married woman now. I'd have thought some of these childish antics would calm down. And you," she says, pointing her hard stare my way. "You would let your wife fight your battles for you?"

She looks downright scandalized. It takes effort not to laugh in her face. "I mean no disrespect in saying this, ma'am, but my wife likes to fight. It actually turns her on. Who am I to deny her such opportunities?"

Maeve scoffs, and Ava laughs.

"You two might be married, but there's no hiding your sins under the eyes of God."

"Jeez, Maeve," Ava grumbles. "A little dark, even for you."

Maeve gives Ava a long-suffering look. And then she says, "You really shouldn't eat red meat that's not cooked all the way through while you're pregnant, Ava. Lord help that poor baby of yours."

CHAPTER TWENTY-SEVEN

AVA

"There's no way she could have known, Kasey," I whine.

Kasey holds a careful expression as he watches me from across the kitchen table. It's just after midnight, the only source of light in the room coming from the dim overhead bulb of the stove, and I'm doing a number on a plate full of scrambled eggs and toast. I woke up a half hour ago to a particularly violent bout of nausea and made fast friends with the toilet in Kasey's bathroom.

He'd held my hair and rubbed soothing circles across my spine, just like he'd done before in the church. Once the retching calmed down, he pressed a kiss to the top of my shoulder and beelined it for the kitchen to make me food, knowing it was what I needed. I'd expected a bowl of cereal or maybe a piece of fruit, but I eventually emerged (after rigorously brushing my teeth) to find him shirtless at the stove, spatula in hand.

"Ava, it's okay," he says gently. Calmly.

"No, it's not! If Maeve knows, we can safely assume *everyone* knows. That woman is the literal nucleus of gossip in this godforsaken town."

"Maybe she doesn't know for sure," he tries. "Maybe it was just a guess."

I roll my eyes. "I'm wearing your shirts, which are baggy enough not to show anything. And she knows better than to stir up something *that* big if it's possible there isn't truth to it. I don't understand the *'you might be married but there's no hiding your sins'* comment, like, what was that shit?"

His lips twitch. "Well, I think she probably assumes the baby is mine. That we . . . conceived before we were married. Which—to be fair, Ava—is a fair assumption considering we've only been married for five minutes."

"Oh my god, a baby out of wedlock, fucking cry me a river. And I'm sorry," I say, closing my eyes as hormone-raged bursts of light shoot inside my brain. "Are you asking me to be *fair* to the damn woman who just verbally accosted us during a perfectly decent lunch? She ruined my burger—*ruined my whole appetite!* —and now I'm gagging over a porcelain throne in the middle of the night like a frat boy."

Kasey tries hard to fight his smile, but it's a losing battle. I, on the other hand, *cannot* seem to do away with this intense anger. "What did you think was gonna happen, sugar?" he asks. "You're my wife, and you're pregnant. Of course people are going to think she's mine."

My mind snags on his use of the word *she* as a bright solar flare of joy crashes through me, briefly soothing over all the anger. And yet: "I didn't expect the fucking doctor to violate one of the most important laws of his whole practice and tell Maeve about my pregnancy. Do you think she pays him for intel? Fucking crooked witch." I cover my face in my hands and groan. "I didn't expect to have to answer questions about this until well after . . ." I trail off. Oops.

Kasey's eyes blaze. "Until after what, Ava?"

I sigh. Pick up my fork and stuff egg into my mouth. Look up at the ceiling.

"Ava." He sits back in his chair. A picture of patience. "Until after *what*?"

"Until after we annul this marriage."

There's no mistaking the hurt that sweeps over his expression. But he doesn't let it deter him from stating the obvious. "That may be so, but you're right. If Maeve knows, I'm sure a lot of other people probably know now too. And I'm sorry for that. I'm sorry that this is going against your plans, I *really* am. But let's look at it from another angle. You're going to be a mother. There is a baby inside of you with the most beautiful, non-taloned feet I've ever fucking seen. *Fuck* Maeve. The only way her bullshit works is if she actually gets under your skin. Don't let her get under your skin, Ava."

My eyes burn with a well of tears, and I worry that if I let myself start crying, it's going to take a good long while before I'll be able to stop. Kasey doesn't *get* it . . . He doesn't see why people assuming the baby is his is *reckless*. I know he means well—god, his heart is so good. Sometimes I can't stand how good he is.

I force down a deep breath and try to make him understand. "I'm already taking so much from you, Kasey," I eventually get out. "It's not that I want to keep the baby a secret forever—I know there's a ticking clock with this. And I think it's beautiful that you want to help with her, I really do. But I wanted time to figure things out. I wanted time to establish what the next year of my life is going to look like before saying anything to anyone else. If the whole town thinks the baby is yours . . . it just makes things harder."

He looks at me for a long, long while.

"Your doctor didn't violate HIPAA," he eventually says, tone devoid of all its usual warmth. He sounds downright dejected. It twists inside my heart. "That was Maeve's great-niece in the lobby. She must have recognized us."

I deflate. "I didn't even notice anyone else in there."

"Understandable." He looks down. Like he can't bear to look

at me, to face my words head-on. "You were pretty focused on generating power through all that fidgeting."

I hurt him, and he's still trying to make me smile.

God, I don't deserve him. Which is exactly why I need to stop him from hurling himself at my problems.

"Kasey, I'm not . . ." I start, fumbling. Nervous. "I'm not saying I don't want this. I'm not saying I don't want you."

"Okay." He nods once. "What are you saying?"

"I just . . . I don't want you to have to keep cleaning up my messes. I don't want the town to look at you and judge you for burdens that aren't yours to bear. To just let you take responsibility for this, so quickly, feels like a bad idea. Like someday you might hate me for it."

"Ava, I'm not trying to rope you into saying something that's out of touch with reality. I know I didn't put that baby in your belly. I'm not asking you to lie about that, or to give me something you're not willing to give me. I know you can do this on your own." He takes a steadying breath, and looks at me like there's nothing else he'd ever want to look at again. "Since I met you, I've been *desperate* to take care of you. Borderline out of my mind with a need to honor you and protect you and— and even when you're terrorizing me with your stubborn fucking brattiness, you're all I want. You make my world spin, sugar. And I want you to know what it is to be truly, deeply, madly loved. You *and* all your messes. Without conditions."

There's no stopping the tears now. They flow down my skin with the force of a torrential downpour. Because I *do* know what it is to be truly, deeply, madly loved. And it's all because of him.

It's the exact thing that terrifies me most.

Picking up my fork again, I stab a piece of egg with all the might of a deflated balloon. "For what it's worth," I whisper, "I *really* like these."

A smile spreads across his face, eyes sparking with amusement.

He shakes his head in disbelief. "Jesus. You are going to put me in an early grave, woman."

When I'm done—when I've licked the plate clean—Kasey scoops me into his arms and brings me back to bed.

THE NEXT COUPLE OF WEEKS GO ON WITH A comfortable routine. Kasey heads out to work before the sun rises every morning, leaving behind a warm mug and a different colored flower. I ease into the day, spend lazy hours bundled in his bed soaking in the smell of him or laid out on the couch with my laptop. I hear back from my colleague on the restraining order paperwork and, now confident that I've got it all right, I get it ready for Kasey's signature.

Most afternoons I venture down to the barn, enjoying the quiet walk along the way and the horses once I get there. I admire Kasey and his brothers and everything they do as they all take turns teaching me something new. I let the warmth of a downcast Texas sun sink into my skin and fill me with hope for a future that might be *just* like this.

I still get emotional. A little shaky with anxiety. Sometimes I want to jump in my Range Rover and drive away and never look back. But I know there's no place to drive to, and even if there were—I don't *really* want to go. It's just something I wrestle with. Something that cages me in at times, makes me feel small and incapable.

On those days, I stay in. I curl up with a blanket and turn on a movie, or text Layla to come over with sweet treats. I never tell her about all the ways in which I worry, but I think she picks up on it. Sometimes she brings Olivia, or the boys. Sometimes it's just us, and we lie on opposite ends of the couch, staring up at the ceiling beneath a shared blanket. Silent, but together. It's . . . nice.

One Wednesday morning I wake up with a jolt. The sun is up

and Kasey's long gone, but something feels . . . different. My awareness spins around the room, searching for the source of my rapidly increasing heartbeat.

And then I feel it.

Well, feel *her*.

I clasp my hands to my stomach, gasping. It's the most beautiful, wonderful, breathtaking feeling I've ever experienced in my entire life. There, deep in my belly, is the faintest flutter, like someone is tickling me with the pad of their pinky finger from the inside out, teasing with happy little strokes.

"Oh my god," I breathe, eyes filling rapidly with tears.

I sink back into the pillows, into the sheets and blankets that smell like Kasey and sunny days and *home*, and simply close my eyes and *feel* her. For the first time since taking a pregnancy test in my sterile, cold Miami apartment and watching it far-too-quickly turn positive, I truly let myself be excited. For the first time, I don't worry about all the things that could happen to make this harder than it already is. I don't think about all the ways I feel like I'm failing or how I don't measure up. How, maybe through some existential karma from mistakes made in a previous life, I'm just not wired to be worthy of the things I so desperately want.

I just let myself exist in it.

This baby, I realize, is everything I never knew I needed. She is hope manifested, a calling to something greater than myself. She is and will be my reason for getting up every day, for fighting against the pain of the world to carve out a little slice of something calmer, something safer. And the truth is, when I let myself dream about that slice, of all the glimpses of what it might look like, it's not just me and her.

I lie in bed and feel her kick and promise her that I will make sure we are happy. I promise her I will never leave her, that I'll never run from her, and it's the surest I've ever been about something in my *entire* life.

Eventually the fluttering stops, and my mind relaxes, and I feel

. . . calm. But also really, really happy. And desperate to tell Kasey about it, to watch the skin crinkle outside his eyes while he looks at me the way he does, like he already knows the slice I want and all the ways to help me get it.

Bounding out of bed, I throw on the shirt he wore last night to bed and a pair of sweatpants I find in his drawer. My jeans are starting to get too tight, and I know I need to go shopping, but I'd probably still wear his clothes anyway so, also, what's the point? I brush my teeth and run a comb through my hair and scour through the house trying to find a pair of socks to put on under my sneakers.

Outside the air is warmer than it has been, and I'm sweating before I even make it ten feet from the house. The sun is shining so bright, I'm not sure anything could wreck this mood I'm in.

It probably should've been the first clue, but I'm too blissfully ignorant to realize it.

I make it more than halfway down to the barns before instinct kicks in, a sudden intuition that something's wrong. A curling plume of dread I've long grown accustomed to. *Watch out*, it says lovingly. *Trust no one.* I used to be fond of it, of the ways it helped me move through life. But now . . . now I just feel exhausted.

Suddenly Layla is in the distance, running toward me. I scan her up and down for any clues, but her face is set with determination the moment she sees me. "Ava!" she shouts, the smallest lilt of worry in her voice.

I stop moving. But she keeps running until she's right in front of me. Panting.

"Ava, they need you at the main house."

"What is it?" I ask.

"Something bad, I think. Let's go."

She turns on her heels and kicks off, so I do too. The back of the house is already in view, but so far, I don't see anything. Is Kasey hurt? Did something happen to him? Maybe that's why

Layla came to get me, and not him. "Is Kasey—" I start to ask through uneven breaths.

But the question dies on my tongue, because now I see.

Kasey looks unhurt, standing tall beneath the sunlight, his dark hat firmly on his head. He's turned away from us so I can't see his face, but written in the lines of his posture is all the evidence I need that he's not happy. On either side of him are Rhett and Wells, both with arms crossed in front of them. They, too, are stiff and unyielding forces.

Farther in the distance, sitting a few yards away, is a silver BMW I don't recognize, a rental, I think. But it looks like a car I've been inside hundreds of times, whisked off to romantic dates and dinner parties and charity events for the firm. And standing next to the car, in a dark-blue suit that looks a little crumpled, is a man with cold eyes and an even colder heart. A man I've been ignoring for weeks as I hoped my silence would be enough to make him go away forever.

Guess I was wrong.

CHAPTER TWENTY-EIGHT

KASEY

"Want me to kill him?" Rhett asks, keeping his voice low.

I wince.

"Shit," he says regretfully. "Sorry. I meant 'Want me to hurt him?'"

"No," I grit out, staring at the shitstain of a man glaring at us from the middle of the driveway. His dark-blond hair is combed back, glossy from too much product, and he's wearing a suit that looks expensive enough to pay for all the repairs needed in the barn. Nothing about him looks like it belongs anywhere around here.

At least he has the good sense not to come any closer.

"Know who he is?" Wells asks.

I exhale through my nose. "I think it's Ava's ex from Miami."

"Why would he be here?"

I don't answer, because the likely answer is he's probably here for Ava. *Or* the baby. And despite the fact I have no right to decide so, he's not going anywhere near them.

"Where the hell is she?" Tobias shouts again.

For the *third* fucking time.

"I don't know what you're after," I finally call out, "but this is private property and we've already asked you to leave the polite way—"

"I think I've made what I'm after pretty clear, but since you rednecks clearly lack the intelligence to keep up, I'll say it again: I'm looking for Ava Jones, and I'm not going anywhere until I see her."

"Yeah," Rhett mutters, tone full of violence. "This guy's fucking dead."

"What makes you think she's here?" I ask, ignoring my brother.

"Lady at the bakery said she'd be at 'Bennett Rescue Ranch' so I plugged it into my map app and here I am." His gaze flicks from the house to the roof of the barn just visible behind it. To the corral where a black stallion nudges a ball around with his nose, happily unaware of the tension growing over here. "Is she back into horses or something? Is this some kind of wilderness spa camp?"

Wells snorts.

"Unless Ava extends an invitation for you to come here and see her," I say, "I'm not allowing you past the driveway."

Tobias rolls his eyes, annoyed. "Of course she wants to see me, I'm her goddamn boyfriend. Who are you to police who gets to see her, anyway? This is ridiculous."

"Boyfriend?" Rhett smarts, pointing a thumb at me. "That's weird, 'cause last I fucking checked she's married to my brother. Pretty sure husband trumps"—he waves a hand in Tobias's direction—"whatever the hell you are. Time to get lost, dickhole."

Tobias goes still, eyeing me with new regard. "*Married*?" he snorts. "You've got to be fucking kidding me."

"Tobias!" We all turn around to see Ava and Layla running down the dirt pathway. Ava's flushed with anger, glaring at him. "You have no right to be here!"

"You fucking *married* this hillbilly piece of shit?"

Rhett lurches forward but I thrust a hand out to push against his chest and stop him.

Ava stops herself about ten feet behind us. "You have *no right* to be anywhere near me, Tobias. I told you I wasn't coming back."

He marches forward, sneering at Ava. Wells and Rhett join together in creating a wall to block him, and Rhett shoves him hard in the chest. "Hear that? She asked you to *leave*, motherfucker."

But Tobias doesn't hear him, because he's zeroed in on Ava. "I will *not* allow the mother of my child to shack up in some podunk town with a backwoods loser like a bitch in heat!"

I hit him so hard in the jaw it audibly cracks. "Don't *ever* fucking talk to my wife like that," I shout as he falls to the ground.

"Damn," Rhett grumbles. "I would've had him."

I flex my hand, testing for pain. "It's my fucking fight."

"You're gonna pay for that, you cocksucker!" Tobias screeches from the ground, clutching his face. "I'm going to sue you for everything you're worth! This fucking property will be mine by the end of the year!"

"Yeah, yeah, get in line."

Ava stomps forward, pushing between me and Wells. Instinct has me reaching to pull her back, to tuck her close and keep her safe, but I know I can't stop her. That she needs to face him. She leans down, pointing a finger inches away from his nose. "You were asked to leave multiple times by the owners of this ranch and you didn't listen. You knowingly trespassed and made a scene big enough to establish yourself as a threat. My *husband* acted in self-defense. If anyone's going to be paying for this, Tobias, it's *you*!"

"Fucking bitch!" he yells.

This time, it's Ava who punches him, and I'm hurling forward to grab her around the waist, pulling her back so she's not in striking distance in case he decides to do something stupid enough for me to end his miserable life. Ava's a ball of tension, muscles so rigid I have to grip her tight. "Don't you fucking pretend to care about me or *my baby*. Go back to Miami and stay gone, Tobias, or I'll make sure the partners at the firm hear from every single one of these witnesses!"

Tobias rises to his feet, still clutching his jaw. I wonder if it's broken. Hope it fucking is. His gaze bounces from Ava to me, eyes empty of anything good, and it's enough to momentarily pull me into a panicked flashback of another man with depthless eyes who died from a shot from my gun. "Leave," I growl at him, chest heaving.

He keeps his eyes on me as he spits a mouthful of blood on the ground. Doesn't turn his back until he's around the hood of his stupid fancy car. And then he's sinking into the driver's seat, starting the ignition, and roaring back down the driveway.

"Well. Shit." Rhett turns to face Ava and me, his gaze narrowing in on her. "Did that fuck-for-brains call you the mother of his baby?" My heart sinks. So does Ava's body in my arms. I shoot Rhett a sharp glare that tells him to back off, but he doesn't. He gives me a sharp glare right back. "What did he mean by that?"

"Knock it off, Rhett."

"Do you think he'll come back?" Layla asks, her expression worry-stricken. "Maybe Ava and I can go somewhere, get a hotel room or . . ."

"Olivia's house," Rhett offers, though he's clearly upset. "I'm sure she'd love to put you two up."

"Ava's not going anywhere," I snap. "She's safest here on the ranch. With me."

Wells looks at Ava with a careful expression. "You know him best," he says, not unkindly. "Do you think he'll come back?"

Ava hesitates, her chest rising and falling with the force of her adrenaline. "I thought it possible that he'd come looking for me." She turns to look at me, her eyes full of shame. I reach for her hand and give it a light squeeze—she has nothing to feel guilty about. She'd told me this might happen, and it's not her fault that it did. "He's never really been one to accept defeat in *anything* in life. It's what makes him a good lawyer."

Wells's gaze jumps up to meet mine. "Our workload on the ranch is already overcapacity. Without Brooks—" He sighs. Resets. "Unless Ava comes down here with you every morning, she's alone up at your cabin. We have fences around the perimeter but they're to keep horses in, not people out. He could come back and go looking for her."

"Then we'll move into the main house," I counter, frustrated. "I'll keep her close and—"

"Kasey," Ava says softly.

"*No!*" I look at her and swallow roughly. "You have nothing to be afraid of. We'll make sure of it. *I* will make fucking sure of it."

Now she's the one reaching for my hand. "Will you walk with me?" she asks, voice featherlight. "Please?"

My heart beats so hard I feel like it might burst from my body. Every ounce of my focus narrows in on her face, on the worry creasing between her brows and the tight press of her mouth. I just got her back. I just fucking got her back and I will *not* let some dumbass piece of shit in a suit come here and support her thinking that she's too goddamn messy, that *his* mess is *hers*.

I squeeze my eyes shut. "Fuck that motherfucker," I mutter quietly, trying to catch hold of the reins on my fear.

"Please, Kasey," she says again, her blue eyes watery.

I sigh. Give her a small nod. And follow her into the field, out toward the fence line of the mustang pasture. Once we're well out of earshot from everyone else, Ava turns around and hugs me, hard.

"I'm so sorry," she murmurs into my shirt.

I dig my fingers into her hair, rubbing gently against her scalp. "Ava, you have nothing to be sorry for. Absolutely nothing. You haven't done anything wrong."

"Maybe not directly, but . . . I don't know what I ever saw in him. I mean, he was nice in the beginning. Fun, you know? But there were red flags that I just willingly ignored because I thought, who cares? What's the point?"

I want to tell her he never deserved a second of her time, but I'm not sure it would be helpful. She already knows it. So I don't say anything, combing my fingers through her hair to help her relax.

"It's always been easier with guys like him. When I don't care as much, you know? It feels so much safer. But this baby feels like —like a wake-up call, you know? Like life is so much bigger than my fears, and I want to figure out how to let the *right* people in so I can feel safe with them too. I know . . . I know my history with Tobias changes the way you look at me—"

"No. I'm going to stop you right there," I rumble, pulling her face up to look at me. My eyes trace the slope of her nose, the curve of her mouth. As if it's the first time. As if I haven't already seen every piece of her. "There is nothing you could ever do that would change the way I look at you, sugar. *Nothing.*" I stretch my thumb across her chin. Press it into her bottom lip. "It drives me fucking crazy to think of someone else touching this mouth. Warming your bed. And when I think of all the ways you've been hurt. . ." His voice drops to a dangerous whisper. "I can't stand it."

Tears gather in her eyes as she leans into me.

"But none of it could ever change the way I look at you. Ever."

"I felt her this morning," she whispers, looking utterly heartbroken. "I felt her move when I woke up. I was on my way to come tell you."

My heart fists in my throat. "Come here." I pull her into my chest. Wrap my arms around her and rest my chin against the top of her head. "What can I do, Ava? Tell me what to do, and I'll do it."

She lets out a long, tired breath. "I don't think it's the worst idea in the world to stay at Olivia's for a night or two."

"Ava."

"I'm not running," she says quickly. "I promise I'm not running from you. I just . . . I feel too raw and exposed. Like I'm cracked wide open, and all these people know things about me that I wasn't ready for them to know, and I've never been good with vulnerability, and it feels like . . . like a *lot*. And my heart wants to ask you to whisk me back to the cabin and hold me tight until morning, but—"

I close my eyes and brace for it.

"I just think we need to take a beat. Between Maeve and Tobias, I'm feeling unsteady." She pulls back to look at me, pressing her lips together before her mouth lifts into a small smile that doesn't quite reach her eyes. "I'm trying to do things differently, Kasey, and part of that means taking the time to process through my feelings before acting out impulsively. Just give me a little time to focus on myself."

I groan. Pull her back into me. And let her words sink in. "I'll give you all the time you need," I concede. "Just know I'm right here when you need me. Always. You hear me?"

Her arms wrap tight around my middle as she presses her face into my chest. "I hear you, Kasey."

CHAPTER TWENTY-NINE

AVA

"I can't believe I missed it," Olivia grumbles after Layla and I spill the beans on everything that happened earlier, tossing a piece of popcorn into her mouth before looking at me with wide eyes. "Not that I think your ex-boyfriend stomping up your husband's driveway to demand you like a piece of property is entertainment fodder, or anything."

It's almost enough to make me laugh. "I get it," I tell her. "I'd probably feel the same way if roles were reversed. I love a good messy outburst."

"You should have seen Rhett," Layla said. "I've never seen him so mad, and I've seen him get angry plenty."

Olivia nods. "He can go from zero to death metal pretty fast, but we've been working on it, you know? He just gets really protective of his family."

I can't help but wonder if I'm part of that designation for him.

"I don't mean to sound like *that* girl or anything," Layla continues, "but it was kind of hot seeing our men get all peacocky like that. We did good, girls."

Olivia sputters out a laugh.

"I just feel so bad," I admit. "I can't believe Tobias actually came here."

"Don't feel bad," Layla says, reaching to wrap a slender hand around my forearm. "Trust me, the Bennett brothers *live* to come together and fight against a good threat."

"How long were you with him?" Olivia asks. "Tobias, I mean."

"About a year and a half," I say. "We worked together at a law firm in Miami and eventually started seeing each other."

"Workplace romance, how scandalous."

I snort. "The only person I scandalized was my damn self." I came clean to her about my pregnancy during our earlier story-telling.

"Was he always such a turd?" Layla asks, scrunching her nose. "No offense, but he was a *raging* asshole today. I can't imagine he'd have the capacity to be a delight."

"Oh, he has range, trust me." I sigh. "He knows how to turn it on. How to charm the people around him. And he can be really fun when he wants to be. But I realized somewhere along the way that so much of that side of him is performative—a means to get what he wants. I think his base-level self is the dick version."

"Sounds like a lot of men," Layla grumbles.

Olivia looks at her. "Kind of reminds me of Jason."

The energy in the room shifts, and I'm not exactly sure why. But then Layla says quietly, "I don't think he was a base-level dick. But I *do* think he was lost and took it out on the people around him." She looks at me and helpfully clarifies, "Jason was my ex. Who I was with before Wells."

"Ah." I nod. "Wells's best friend."

"Yeah. I think Jason could have become what you're describing, the way Tobias is, if he wasn't careful. But the way I knew him . . . I don't know, he was so young, you know? And there was so much pressure on him to succeed from literally everyone around him besides me and Wells. I like to think that he could have been a good man, that somewhere deep down he wanted to be."

"Makes sense," Olivia says. "The way this town treats football players is . . . weird." She laughs.

I snort. "I dated a handful in high school. Every one of them was so full of themselves . . . well, except Kasey. He was the only one who actually gave a shit about me. I guess it was sort of my MO to date assholes."

Olivia smiles. "Sometimes dating an asshole works out, but I don't think it's an ideal strategy."

Layla throws a popcorn kernel at her, giggling.

I shrug. "They're fun. There's a thrill to it, you know."

"Oh, *I* know." Olivia smiles.

"Sounds like Kasey had nice guy syndrome. Is that why things didn't work out?"

"Nice guy syndrome?"

"Yeah, you know—when you get the ick from a guy because he's too safe—"

"There was *nothing* safe about Kasey."

Silence wraps around us as confusion paints Layla's face. "But you said he actually cared."

"Yeah, but . . . For me, that was the *most* scary."

"Not gonna lie, girlfriend," Olivia says. "I don't get it."

I laugh, stretching out on her couch. "I guess . . . well, my mom left when I was young, and my dad wasn't the easiest parent. I always felt very alone as a kid, but I also learned how to be okay on my own. How to control the chaos around me, you know?" Both girls nod. I swallow. "And then Kasey just *showed up* and changed everything. He made me feel like my feet weren't on the ground anymore, like I could fly if I wanted to. He was so confident . . . He looked at the sun like it was his to wrangle, and I found myself *needing* to be his sun. It knocked me off-balance. I didn't know what to do with it or how to trust it. People in my life kept leaving me behind, so I learned how to leave first to keep myself safe. But with Kasey . . . I tried to shove all my fears away, but they just kept clawing back. There was nothing safe about Kasey because of the way *I* felt about him. And then he proposed, and all the fears I'd been trying to hold at bay just came crashing down on me. I couldn't handle it, so I left."

"What were you scared of?" Layla asks. "If he proposed, if he wanted to marry you, you weren't going to lose him, right? So what was there to be scared of?"

I frown. "My mom left," I say simply. "She thought she wanted her life to look one way, and then it turned out she didn't actually want that anymore, so she left. And she hurt people when she did."

Understanding sinks in. Layla's eyes soften. "You didn't want to become her."

I take a deep breath. "The way she hurt me . . . I don't want to do that to anyone else. And I was scared that I'd eventually do it to Kasey."

"What about now?" Layla asks. "I know getting married to him wasn't about love, but it doesn't take a rocket scientist to see that you guys *are* in love. Are you still scared of hurting him?"

"Oh, god, yes," I admit. "Terrified. And it doesn't help that I have deranged exes showing up or that . . ." I look down at my stomach. "Or that I still have plenty of baggage. Maeve knows—that I'm pregnant."

"*Fuck*, that woman is truly plugged in. How does she do it?"

I laugh, and it comes out watery. "She assumes it's Kasey's baby, which doesn't exactly help my worry about all the doom and gloom I'm bringing him."

Layla turns to look at me head-on, right in the eye. "Ava—and trust me that I say this as lovingly as possible—I don't think you know anything, girl!"

My brows sink over my eyes. "Um . . . what?"

"You said you wanted to be Kasey's sun?" Here gaze lifts to the ceiling. "You *are*. Don't you see it? He literally looks at you like you are the entire world wrapped in one lady body. You could bring that man all the doom and gloom you have and he'd still be on his knees for you. Stop stressing so much about hurting him. You're just . . . all you're doing is hurting yourself."

A new veil of silence settles over us as I let her words sink in. I think about the way he hugged me this morning, the grip of his fingers against my ribs as if to not let me go. I think about the baby moving and the slice of life I promised her I'd find for us. Closing my eyes and sinking my head back against the armrest of the couch, I let out a quiet groan. "I really am fucking things up, aren't I?"

"No," Layla says gently. "You've been through a lot, and you're figuring it out. You're human. I guess I just hoped it might help to hear from an outside perspective that you're both over the moon about each other. So maybe just . . . enjoy it?"

I smile. "I'll try."

"I still can't believe you've been hiding a whole-ass *pregnancy*," Olivia cuts in.

Layla and I lock eyes. She hasn't revealed that she's known since before the wedding, and I'm getting the sense she's not going to. I'm grateful for it, because I'm not sure whether Olivia would feel slighted, even if Layla finding out was purely accidental.

"Rhett was so unhappy about it," I eventually say.

Olivia waves a hand. "He'll be fine."

I groan. "I don't know. He looked at Kasey like he was really disappointed."

"Give him a minute to process," Layla suggests. "He was pretty worked up about Tobias, so the timing of finding out his sister-in-law is carrying *not* his brother's baby wasn't exactly ideal, you know?"

Okay. Fair point.

"He'll be *fine*," Olivia says again. "I promise."

I nod. "Thank you for letting me crash here."

"Oh! Of course! It's actually really fun—I've never had a girls' night in this house before."

"Have you ever thought about moving onto the ranch?" Layla asks.

Olivia shakes her head. "Not really. I'm not opposed to it, but Rhett doesn't even really sleep there much. When he's not staying the night here, he's usually at the apartment above the bar."

"Does your mom like him?"

Olivia beams. "She *loves* him."

"What about your mom?" I ask Layla. "Does she like Wells?"

Layla's nose scrunches. "It's getting better."

"Yikes. Sorry."

"No, no. It's okay. She was just really banking on me being a rich NFL wife and not living in sin with a cowboy."

I snort. "Your mom and my dad sound pretty damn similar."

"Pretty sure my mom and her husband have been on double dates with your dad and his wife."

"Oh," I mutter. "Goodie."

I HAVEN'T BEEN TO THE SHERIFF'S STATION SINCE I WAS a little girl. Even before leaving Saddlebrook Falls, it was a place I firmly avoided.

Inside the unassuming two-story building, my father was a legend. He was strength and order, a beacon of safety for the people in this town. And I understood it. Even if I firmly disagree with a lot of the ways in which he yields his power, there's no denying he's always been successful at keeping our town safe.

I used to feel jealous of the way other people looked up to him, that to someone else he was even worthy of being looked up to, because the truth is, despite what he is inside *this* building with *these* people, to me he'll forever be the cold and irrationally controlling father who barely looked at me inside our home.

Staring up at the building, at the tinted windows that run along the length of the dark brick walls, I try to smother my dread. This is the absolute last thing in the world I want to do today, but as I lay awake last night listening to Olivia and Layla's even breathing from their makeshift beds in the living room, sound asleep, a thought ripped through me so viciously I couldn't ignore it.

All these fears I hold about running from the people I love . . . I suddenly wondered if that's something he might be able to relate to. If my father didn't care about me, he wouldn't have tried to control me so hard. His parenting strategies were fucked, no doubt about it—but what if he was doing his best in the fallout of our family being torn apart, just like I was? What if we were both running from each other?

I never so much as gave him an inch. Between my stubborn defiance and his crushing force, there wasn't an opportunity for us to genuinely connect or communicate about the things we were going through. And then I thought about the baby growing inside of me, and if—god forbid—something ever happened to make her feel like I wasn't enough for her . . . wouldn't I give anything for a chance to prove her wrong?

It's completely possible that this goes nowhere, that I'm opening myself to the risk of being hurt by this man all over again. But I know, without a shadow of a doubt, that I'd deeply regret not trying. This, at the very least, is something I can offer to him *and* to myself: it's a chance.

I take a deep breath, and then pull open the door.

The first thing I see when I walk inside is a long desk. A pretty woman with dark hair smiles at me from where she sits behind it, leaning forward to get a better look at me. "Good afternoon, can I help you?"

I give her a polite smile. "Hello. I'm here to see Sheriff Joe Jones. Is he available?"

Her brows pinch. "Is he expecting you?"

I shake my head. "No, but . . . I'm his daughter, and I was just hoping I could drop by and steal some of his time."

"Oh!" Her face lights up. "Well, isn't that just peachy keen! Let me phone his desk line and see if he's in his office—just one moment." I watch her pick up a corded phone and tuck it between her ear and shoulder, dialing the extension to my father's office. And then she pauses, looking some place out the window while she waits.

I hold my breath.

"Good afternoon, Sheriff—I have a visitor here for you. It's your daughter! Isn't that nice? Anyway, I just wanted to check that you were in before I send her up." A pause. Her eyes flash to mine, and my stomach sinks with lead. "Of course. Absolutely. Yes, sir. Okay." She hangs up the phone, and I can barely contain my nerves.

"Is he available?" I ask, hands sweating.

"He's in the middle of an evidence review but is just wrapping up." She waves a hand toward a collection of half a dozen chairs against the wall of the lobby. "Why don't you have a seat? He'll be down in just a minute."

I nod, and my heart does a somersault. "Sure, thanks."

"Can I get you something to drink? Bottle of water? Cup of coffee?"

"Oh, that's okay," I say. "I appreciate it, though."

She smiles. I sit down.

And I wait.

I distract myself with my phone, opening my text thread with Kasey. *Checking in*, I write. *Missed you last night.*

His response comes in immediately. *Come home, sugar.*

I smile. Home . . . what a concept.

"Ava?"

I look up, finding my father in the mouth of the long corridor behind the reception desk. Stuffing my phone back into my purse,

I stand. "Hello. Sorry for dropping by unannounced. I hope this is okay?"

His eyes flick to the woman at the desk before moving back to me. "No problem at all. Why don't you come with me?

I nod, following him up to his corner office on the second floor. I spend a good few minutes looking at the view from the huge window that takes up half the wall, eyes catching on the trees in the distance, knowing that just a few miles farther, my cowboy waits for me.

"Everything okay, Ava?" my father asks, pulling me back into his office, where he stands just behind me.

I turn to face him, forcing a wide smile. "Yes," I say.

He frowns. "Look, if something's happened, you can tell me, sweetheart. I'll make sure you're not wrapped up in any of it—"

"Dad," I cut him off. "It's nothing like that. This is . . ." I waver, fidgeting with my fingers. "This is about us. You and me."

His brows arch high. "Oh." He nods once. "Okay. Come have a seat." He pulls out a chair in front of his desk and waits for me to sit before pulling out the second for himself. I'm surprised he doesn't take his seat on the other side of the desk. Our knees are mere inches apart as he looks at me carefully.

"Thank you," I say, "for seeing me. I, uh—I wanted to tell you that I'm sorry, for not coming to you before the wedding. I realize that I probably should have made a real attempt to let you know what was happening. I can't imagine finding out about something like that from someone else, and it wasn't fair to you."

His eyes widen in surprise as he leans back into his chair. For a while, he just looks at me. But eventually he says, "Thank you, Ava. It means a lot to hear that from you."

I nod. "I know we haven't had an . . . easy relationship. But I'm home now. And I like to think I'm a bit more mature than I was when I left. So, I guess what I'm saying is, I would be open. To trying."

"Trying?"

"To mend things," I clarify. "Or . . . at least to start fresh."

His eyes go distant as he raises his gaze to look out the window behind me. When he looks at me again, there's soft openness, a glimmer of something that feels like hope. "I would like that very much, Ava," he says. "More than you know."

This time, my smile is not so forced. "Good. Okay, yeah." I know there's more I need to tell him, but I just want to bask in the feeling for a second, still not quite certain it won't be ripped away from me.

He must sense my hesitation, because he offers something else instead.

"Ava, in the spirit of transparency, I'm going to tell you something that I think you should know. And I want to hear your honest response, okay?"

"Okay." I nod.

He regards me for a moment before saying, "Huck Bennett is determined to take over the Bennetts' ranch, and I've gotta admit, I'm in support of it. Bud Bennett has been a thorn in my side since we were kids. He was a bully in school and a bully in every bar he stepped foot in. He's a drunk who always thought he was above the law. The Bennetts mostly keep to themselves these days, but I've had plenty of run-ins with his boys to know the apples don't fall far."

"Dad," I scoff, immediately defensive. "That's hardly fa—"

He holds a hand up. "Let me finish, Ava."

I press my lips together tightly, and wait for him to continue.

"It is my personal belief that Huck's vision for the land could be really good for this town. He wants to build a rustic resort to bring in tourists. He wants to offer excursions like hiking and horseback riding. He wants to build a whiskey distillery right alongside it. All of that would be incredible for our economy, and I know Mayor Moore is highly supportive of Huck's efforts. That said, I've reviewed the trust details extensively, and Huck does not have rights to any of it, what with your marriage to Kasey—if your marriage is real.

"Now, before you say anything, let me tell you this: no matter what, I will protect you. I love you, Ava," he says roughly, and I notice the sheen of emotion in his eyes. "I want to keep you safe. I've failed you in so many ways, and I know that. But I've always wanted you to be safe. If you've gotten wrapped up in something to help Kasey and his family with this problem of theirs, I'll make sure you stay clear of it. But if you tell me that it's all real—if you tell me that you love that boy and you want to be his wife—well, honey, I'm going to choose to believe you. If that's what gets us back on some better footing, I'm going to believe you."

"I love him, Dad," I say in a rush. My heart pounds in my throat as I look him in the eye and beg him to hear me. "I love him and I want to be his wife. And . . . I'm going to be a mother, Dad."

His mouth falls open as his eyes drop to my stomach.

"Yeah," I say, a watery laugh escaping up my throat. "And you deserve to know that this baby isn't Kasey's. I came home pregnant. But Kasey is so happy, I don't even have the words to explain it. He's *so* happy and wants to raise her with me."

"Her?" The word slips out of his mouth, gaze still fastened to my belly.

"Her," I confirm, tears falling down my cheeks. "We're having a baby girl, Dad."

CHAPTER THIRTY

KASEY

I don't sleep.

For two nights, I lie awake in the dark and watch as moonlight shifts against the ceiling, thinking about Ava and all the things I want to tell her. There's so much I wish she knew, so much I don't even know how to express with words, about how deep and unyielding my love for her is. As scared as I am that she left, I'm choosing to trust that she's not running. I know she's been through so much and she has every right to process things in a way that feels best for her.

But goddammit, I miss my wife.

A roll of light shines through the house. Approaching headlights. A quick glance at my phone tells me it's just after midnight. I jump out of bed and pull on a pair of sweatpants, heart bursting with the hope that Ava's back.

But when I get to the front of the house and look through the window, it's Rhett's motorcycle sitting just beyond the porch steps. Rhett stands beside it in clothes that also look recently thrown on. He's pulling off his helmet. And then he's looking up at me.

Fuck. Something's wrong.

I move to open the door and step out onto the porch. "What is it?" I ask? My pulse is uneven, breath hitching. "Is it Ava?"

He shakes his head. "No."

"Brooks?"

"No. It's all right, Kasey."

"Tell me why the fuck you're here then," I grunt.

He sighs. "Colt called."

And just like that, the world stops spinning. I lean against a wooden beam and brace myself for the worst. "What did he say?"

"Cops showed up at Rustlers Ranch about an hour ago. Ellis told them everything."

Shit. Shit shit shit. "Everything?"

Rhett tosses his helmet on the seat of his bike and comes up the steps to stand next to me. Wrapping a hand around my shoulder, he says, "He told them he was hosting a game night. That he'd invited Maverick's crew and a couple new friends he made too. He said Maverick was losing the game, and then losing his cool, and the two new friends turned out to be cops who tried to shut Maverick down. That Maverick pulled a gun, shot the cops, and then pointed it at him. So Ellis shot him first."

Relief slices through me like a whip. I let out a long, slow breath. "He said he did it."

Rhett nods. "Yep. Didn't even say we were there. Didn't say Colt and Wylie Jo were there either. He took the fall for all of it, told them where to find the bodies, and they arrested him and took him in."

"Fuck." Ellis promised me he'd take the fall if it came to it, but Ellis himself is a selfish career criminal and I didn't exactly trust him. "What about ballistics? I still have the shotgun—"

"Colt said Ellis told them he ditched the gun over a bluff, hours out of town, scared about getting caught. He said he doesn't remember exactly where. They obviously aren't going to find it, but he did his best to explain it away. I'm sure they'll try to look but . . ."

"So it's over?"

"Well, there's obviously still a bit of a process. With Ellis admitting to everything, there's not a whole lot of reason for those badges to investigate anyone else. And without placing any of us at the game, the cops don't have anyone else to talk to."

"There was that one guy, who came with Maverick. The one who ran."

"I doubt he's going to come forward. His boss is dead, he doesn't owe him anything anymore. And coming forward means putting himself right in the middle of it all. There's nothing to gain from it." Rhett shakes his head. "He would be stupid to say something."

"How's Colt?"

"A little shaken up. But . . . he said the way the cops were talking to Ellis, it sounds like they're more interested in Maverick being dead than in Ellis's gambling. Ellis's story means he acted in self-defense. *And* he's cooperating. Colt thinks his time away won't be too long, and that Ellis will be a better man for it."

"Damn." I look out into the distance, where the dark sky meets moonlit trees. "That could have been you, Rhett. It could have been me. It could have been every one of us, at some point or another."

For a while, Rhett doesn't say anything. And then he takes a deep breath and mutters, "I know."

I look at him. "We have a second chance too. With this ranch. With each other. I know you aren't exactly happy that I got married for it, and I want you to know that I understand. Regardless of my feelings for Ava, it was a little reckless. But it should get Huck off our backs and . . ." I scrub a hand over my face. "This family has struggled in every fucking way that counts and, *fuck*, I don't want to suffer anymore. I don't want to have to scrape together good days. We deserved so much more than we were given from Dad and his brothers, and I want to make sure we give the boys something better than we have now."

Rhett squints at me. "What are you saying?"

"I'm saying . . . no more fucking around. Let's look at the books on the ranch, find ways to be financially stronger so we aren't killing ourselves to stay ahead. Let's look at the bar and do the same. No more fucking illegal bullshit. No more fighting or reckless behavior. We need to stop giving the people in this town more reasons to hate us. Let's find ways to mend our relationship with the community. Find ways to bring in some fucking peace."

"Shit," Rhett grumbles. "I expected you to be kissing the ground, not waxing poetic."

I shove him on the shoulder, and he laughs. And then his face grows serious.

"Look," he says. "I'm sorry. For being there that night, for not letting you in. I thought I was doing the right thing, but it's no excuse. I knew I was putting myself in danger. And if you hadn't come, I . . . Fuck, man, I might be six feet below ground. You're talking about second chances, and I get it. I'm living out mine, and I want to be worthy of it. I want my family to be proud of me, and a long life with Olivia, and maybe some of our own kids one day, you know? I refuse to be like Dad and raise them with an iron fist that's wrapped around a fucking bottle."

I grin. "Change, Rhett," I agree. "It starts with us."

He looks at me with a knowing smirk. "Speaking of kids, jackass. When did you find out Ava's pregnant?"

"Before the wedding," I admit. "She didn't want to get married without me knowing."

"Well, that's a relief," he mutters. "How do you feel about it?"

I can't help the smile that spreads across my face. "I don't know how to explain it, but I don't think I've been happier about anything in my entire life."

Rhett chokes out a sound of surprise. "Oh fuck, man. I knew you were in deep with this shit, but I didn't realize it was like that."

"Yeah." I shrug. "I'm fucked."

"What about her? What does she think?"

"I don't know," I say honestly. "She's spooked."

"She'll come around."

"I hope so."

He looks at me, swatting me on the chest with the back of his hand. "Did you see the hit she got in on that fancy fucker?"

I nod, grinning. "Yeah. I saw."

"Kinda hot."

"Kinda like when Olivia hit *you*."

Rhett frowns. And then smirks. "Guess we like 'em feisty."

AVA'S WAITING FOR ME ON THE PORCH STEPS WHEN I get home from work at the barn. It's been a long day, and the sun is just about to set. The light from the sconce by the door illuminates her with a golden halo that makes her look like a goddess, like an angel sent just for me. She's got the comforter from my bed wrapped around her shoulders and a six-pack resting on the step below her. Two bare feet peek out from the blanket, two sets of toes pressed into the grainy wood. "Hey cowboy," she says, eyes sparking in the twilight surrounding us.

I stand still in front of the house. Look up at her. Drink her in. I'd readied myself for another night without her here, but . . . damn, the relief is almost indescribable. "Hey, sugar."

"How was your day?" she asks.

"Long. But good."

She nods. Stays quiet.

"That for me?" I ask, jutting my chin toward the beer.

She shrugs. "Depends." Her eyes are darker tonight, more ocean than sky. They regard me deeply. Knowingly.

The corner of my mouth lifts, just a little bit. She's baiting me, looking for me to chase her. So achingly familiar my heart kicks to life inside my chest. "On?"

She pats the porch next to her. "Come sit."

I take off my hat and hang it from the end of the porch railing before slowly climbing the steps, careful not to knock over the beers before settling down beside her. There's an inch of space between us—far too much for my liking, but she's in control tonight.

"Thank you," she says quietly, turning to look up at me. "For knowing what I needed, and supporting it. And I'm not just talking about the last couple of nights—I mean all of it. From the beginning, it feels like you've known what I need even before I do. You see me in ways most people don't, and I'm not sure how to explain how much that means to me."

I tap a knee against hers. "I'll always see you, Ava. Sometimes you're all I see."

Rosy lips curve into a soft smile. And then she looks down at the ground. "Why do you want to be a part of it?" she asks.

"A part of what?"

"The baby. Her life."

"Oh." I nod. And all at once I understand. I lean forward to rest my arms against my knees and look out into the setting sun, tracing the golden rays that stretch deep into the dark blue of impending night. "When I first saw you, I knew I wanted you. And not just physically, you know? I hung on every single smile you ever gave, even if it wasn't for me. And . . . I thought about what it would be like to have you. To have a future with you.

"I think I was always careful about sharing my feelings with you, because I didn't want to scare you. But, sugar, I was literally planning it all inside my mind. I love the ranch, but I'm not sure I'll stay forever. And I found myself imagining the house I would build for you. The kids we might have. What you'd wear on a beach vacation."

Ava sputters out a laugh. "Not much, probably."

I smile. "Trust me, that's how I imagined it too."

She leans her head against my shoulder. "It sounds beautiful."

"Yeah." I suck in a breath. "I guess what I'm saying is, when I closed my eyes to dream up a future of everything I might ever want, it was *always* with you. Even after you left, even when my heart was broken, it was like any visions of the future just sort of dried up. I've probably created a thousand different versions of it in my head, but it always included you. And, Ava . . . this baby is a part of you. Over the course of these past few weeks, I've been able to dream again. Except now, she's in all of them too."

Ava's eyes well with tears. "Dammit."

I frown. "What, sugar?"

She sniffles. Wipes at her eyes. "That was a really good answer."

I laugh, and so does she. Deciding the space between us can get fucked, I wrap an arm around her shoulders and pull her into me, pressing a kiss on the top of her head. She smells like sugar and vanilla, like everything good and right.

Ava slips an arm out of the blanket to reach for a beer from the cardboard package and twists off the top. "I told my dad about her," she says, handing me the bottle.

I take it and look at her carefully. "You saw him?" I ask. "Did he find you at Olivia's?"

She shakes her head. "I went to his office and asked to meet." Leaning back into my side, she presses a kiss to my shoulder. "I've been running from a lot of things for a long time, Kasey. And I think it's time I started facing them instead."

"What did you tell him?" I ask, taking a long sip from the bottle.

"That I wanted to try to make things better. He spoke honestly about this ranch dispute with your uncle, and in return I told him the truth about you."

I take a second to think through what she's saying. "You told him about our deal?"

"I told him that I love you," she counters. "That my choice to be married to you is one I would make over and over again if given the opportunity. That I'm having a baby, and you're going to help me raise her."

My heart stops. I pull away to look down at her, catching her eyes. "I am?"

She nods, smiling. "Yeah." Her eyes are full of tears again, and this time they spill over onto her cheeks. "I think what I'm saying is . . ." She stops.

"Say it, Ava," I gently coax.

"I want to stay," she finally says. "For good. I want to be with you. I don't want to pretend anymore." She opens the comforter that hangs from her shoulders, revealing her bare body as she stands, lifting one foot over my legs so she can settle herself down in my lap.

Firecrackers blast through my chest as I groan, setting my beer down to grip her ass in my hands and look her in the eyes. "This was never pretend to me, sugar. Not a single fucking minute of it. 'Bout time you finally caught up."

CHAPTER THIRTY-ONE

AVA

I knew as soon as I walked into my father's office yesterday that I would end up back here, wrapped in Kasey's arms while he looked at me like I was indeed his sun. I think I knew it all along, but it hit me hardest when I realized that I wasn't there to defend my choices or defiance.

I was there to give him my truth.

And the truth is, plain and simple, that I've loved Kasey for just about as long as he's loved me. Even when I played games with his heart. Even when I ran from him and made him chase me into the depths of my own fears. Even as I sit here and wonder if I'm even worthy of everything he gives me. I *love* him, and it's about damn time I sat still with something good in my life.

"Why are you crying?" Kasey asks, voice deep and shaky, like the rumble of an old tractor over the pasture. His thumbs swipe at my tears as he looks at me with so much reverence that my heart kicks against my ribs like a wild stallion.

I'm so tired of all the ghosts of *us* haunting my every waking hour. I'm ready to start again, ready for something new with him. "I'm crying," I say, squeezing my eyes shut, "because you smell *so* bad. It's making my eyes water."

Kasey's mouth falls open, the corners of his mouth lifting. "You're a fucking brat, you know that?" He shakes his head and sighs. And then he's launching me up into the air, those bulky arms carrying my weight as my legs wrap around his waist. The blanket from his bed falls to the ground. "This is the smell of a real man, sugar," he says, eyes devouring every inch of me.

"Take a shower, you dirty cowboy," I say, watching the way his mouth changes. The way his cheeks pull. "And take me with you."

He kisses me so hard everything around us disappears. I feel him moving, carrying me into the house, but I'm dizzy by the intoxicating way his tongue parts me open and strokes deep into my mouth. This man, this perfect man, who loves me enough to heal parts of me that he had nothing to do with. Who has the patience to wait for me, to hold me through it, even at the risk of his own heart.

His nose scrapes along the underside of my jaw, grip tightening around my waist. He grunts. Nips into the flesh below my ear. Roughly pushes his hips into mine, pinning me tightly against a wall. "Never again," he says, pulling back to catch my eyes, his full of so much need. We're in the darkened hallway, mere feet from the bathroom. "I mean it, Ava. I won't lose you ever again."

It feels like a cannon blasts inside my chest, everything all at once becoming too vast and shapeless and heavy with a pressure that both terrifies and grounds me. "You never lost me," I tell him. "I'm the one who lost myself, Kasey. I've always been yours. There's no version of life I could ever live that would keep me from wanting you." I fist the front of his shirt to pull him back to my mouth, desperate for him.

And then we're moving again. He smacks the switch on the wall to turn on the light, and I catch a glimpse of us in the mirror: him, utterly breathtaking in dark jeans and a black tee, his hair a rumpled mess from being stuffed into his hat all day; and me, naked and wrapped around him. He must sense that my attention has been pulled elsewhere, because he leans away from me again, eyes trailing across my face. When he follows the line of my gaze to the mirror, his eyes turn black as midnight, pupils blown wide. "Ava," he grunts again, fastening his mouth to my neck.

It takes three tries to get the shower faucet turned on, mostly because he's not looking. The water comes out freezing cold at first, so we pass the time dragging our fingers and mouths over each other with a shared hunger that burns bigger and brighter with every moment that passes. Once the room is filled with steam and the ends of Kasey's hair begin to curl, he sets me gently on the ground so he can get undressed.

I step into the shower as he pulls off his shirt, letting the warm water glide over my skin while he watches in rapt fascination. "Fuck," he groans, fumbling at the button of his jeans.

I let my fingers trail down the center of my breasts, dipping below my navel and further still. His eyes are anchored on me as he roughly shoves the denim of his jeans down his broad thighs, struggling to get them past the swell of rock-hard muscle, growling in frustration. And then they give, and he kicks them off, and within seconds he's in the shower with me, pushing me against the wall with a fever that floods my bones.

"Easy, cowboy," I murmur, rising to my tiptoes to lick into the hollow of his throat. And then I playfully push him into the running stream of water, grabbing the bar of soap from the small shelf and lifting it to his skin. Mint green streaks across his tanned skin, washing away the day's sweat and grime. "I want to take care of you too."

He closes his eyes, beads of water collecting on his lips, his chin.

I drag the soap across his chest, lifting my other hand to rub the suds against him, feeling the ripple of his chiseled chest.

Kasey's hands reach for me, gripping tight against my waist and pulling me against him. He's hard, hungry, pressing into my stomach with unmitigated want. "Ava," he whispers, bending down until his forehead rests against the top of my head. "I love you so much."

"I love you too," I tell him. And for the first time, it feels like a glimpse of everything we might get to have instead of everything I might not be able to give him. "I love you more than—*oh!*" My eyes widen and I look up at him as a huge smile grows. "Kasey!"

His eyes bounce back and forth between mine, a deep groove forming between his brows. "What is it?"

"The baby—she's moving!" I drop the soap, letting it fall to the bottom of the tub with a loud smack. Peeling his hands off my waist, I press them to my stomach instead, just as another burst of fluttering movement bounds through me. "Do you feel that?"

"I—" Kasey closes his eyes in concentration. Both of us go silent and utterly still. When it happens again, Kasey's eyes shoot wide open. "Fucking *hell*," he says, his wet smile rippling. "That's her?"

I nod, matching his smile with my own. "That's our girl, Kasey."

He looks down at the place his hands cup the swell of my belly with so much reverence it knocks the wind out of me. "Hi, my little love," he murmurs softly. "You have no idea how happy I am to know you." He drops to his knees, pressing a warm kiss to my belly, just below my navel. Water from the faucet hits the back of his head and ricochets around him, droplets of water spraying against the wall of the shower. If it's uncomfortable, he doesn't seem to care. "I saw your foot," he says proudly. "And your perfect beating heart. You're already so beautiful. I'm going to spoil the heck out of you, sweetheart. And I'm going to protect you and your mommy with everything I have, I promise. I'm going to take such good care of you."

"Kasey," I say, breath hitching with the force of my tears.

He looks up at me, so, *so* happy. "I mean it, Ava. I'm going to love and protect you both forever. I fucking promise."

"Come here," I say, tugging him up. He rises back to his feet and crowds into me, kissing me with a new wave of hunger that has me curling my toes. I pull away and bend over for the soap. "Behave, Kasey. I haven't finished cleaning you up yet."

He pouts, and I laugh. But he tries to hold still while I wash the rest of him. He eventually loses patience again, and this time when he presses me into the wall, I don't stop him. He keeps me there, pinned and at his mercy, for long, languid kisses that burn low in my belly. I slide my fingers through his hair, pulling at his nape. Blaze a trail down his spine so I can get a good squeeze of his ass.

When I reach between his legs to wrap my hand around his hard length, he sputters out a low groan that rumbles straight through me. "Turn around and put your hands on the wall," he says roughly.

Anticipation curls tight as I do, turning my back to him and lifting my hands high on the wall above my head. He takes hold of my waist to keep me steady as he nudges his knee between my legs, pushing side to side until my feet are spread wide. And then he's pulling my long hair back behind my shoulders, collecting it in a pile against my spine. "I don't think you understand how fucking turned on your swollen belly makes me, sugar." He grips the end of my hair, wrapping it around his fist. His other hand slides between my legs, fingers swirling in my need for him. His voice is low and dark against my ear. "You want me too, don't you?" I nod and he hums, teasing featherlight brushes against my clit. "I know, I know. Let me give you what you need."

He pulls my waist back until my ass is hovering in front of him and uses my hair to angle my face up to the ceiling. And then he presses deep into me with a single, hard thrust.

We both groan loudly over the sound of the running water.

"Fuck," he mutters. "*Fuck*, sugar."

"Yes," I gasp. "Fuck me, Kasey."

He's not gentle about the way he moves inside me, the way he drives his hips into mine, hurling me higher and higher as pleasure blooms through me. His free hand lifts to my breast, squeezing and kneading and pinching. When he pulls my head back further, licking up the side of my neck, I come so hard my vision blanks.

"That's my girl," he murmurs, breath curling around the shell of my ear. "I'm greedy tonight, sugar. Give me one more."

He frees his fist from my hair and turns us until I'm facing the back of the shower, his body blocking most of the water from hitting me. Pressing his palm against my spine, he bends me over until I'm hinged at the waist, facing my own shins. The speed of his thrusts increase as the rhythm becomes erratic. Wild. "Give me one more," he says again, voice straining.

I'm *so* close, feeling him move this deep inside of me. My skin begins to tingle as he drills harder and faster. I reach up between our legs to feel where we're joined together, to feel the way we fit so perfectly like this, and it sends us both straight over the edge.

Later, after cleaning ourselves again and finally getting out of the shower with pruned fingers and toes, we lie naked in his bed. His comforter is still out on the porch, but he pulled the one from the guest bedroom and brought it in here. I listen to the sound of his breathing while he trails a light touch up and down the length of my arm.

"My dad asked me if you treat me well," I whisper.

His eyes seem to hang from mine, the weight of his heart right there for me to take. "Oh yeah?" he says with a low rumble. "What'd you tell him, sugar?"

I press my palm to his cheek. Trace the slope of his jaw with my thumb. "I told him that, twice now, you've found me at my darkest, at my loneliest. And you've shown me how to breathe again."

His eyes squeeze shut as his face leans into my touch. "Marry me," he says, an open mouth pressed to my collarbone. "Marry me for real, Ava. On this ranch. The way we wanted." When he looks up again, there's a tenderness in his expression that soars through me. "Please?"

"Yes," I whisper, clutching his face. I pull him to me for a hard, watery kiss. "Absolutely *yes*."

EPILOGUE

KASEY

Out here, in the wild and unruly plains of Texas, there are no structured ceremonies to uphold, no vows to repeat or promises to make. There is only us—Ava and me—and the love that burns through us like a fever, melting our bones until we become one.

When I proposed to her all those years ago, I pictured exactly this: our closest loved ones gathered together on the ranch, where the horses whinny and flick their tails as they watch us with curious eyes. I pictured my mother's smile and my father's stern gaze, and my brothers at my side in support.

My bride walks toward me now, dark hair unbound and flowing down her back, the swell of her belly growing with every day that passes. My heart and my home. My beautiful *wife*, who I will cherish every single day that I draw breath. I should have known it would always come back to this, that in any universe we'd find our way to each other, no matter the cost. Every second of the pain and torment of losing her is nothing compared to the soaring joy that consumes me now. It was all worth it.

"Are you crying?" Rhett whispers loudly beside me in his best pearl-snap and jeans.

I shrug, keeping my eyes on my girl. "Probably."

"She's beautiful," Wells says from Rhett's other side.

"Yeah," I hum. "She is."

"We should have laid down some pavers or something," Brooks grumbles from the end of our line. "She's going to fall."

I squint my eyes against the bleeding light of the setting sun to look at my older brother, grinning. "She's not going to fall. She's wearing her boots." She hasn't put on a pair of heels in months.

Brooks doesn't look convinced. "If my niece gets hurt, there's going to be hell to pay."

My grin widens. Ava and I both worried this wedding might send Brooks right back down into a fit of dark depression—but he's surprised us with his resilience, spending multiple afternoons helping to clean up the pasture and ready it for the small cere- mony. He's also shown a lot of excitement for the baby, teaching the boys it's going to be their job to look out for her and keep her safe.

Only my family knows the baby isn't mine by blood—and the sheriff, I suppose. We never made a plan for what to tell everyone else, but when word got out and spread that I'd already knocked up my new wife, we decided we didn't care. What was the point?

Truthfully, I like it better this way, anyway. I'd rather everyone know that baby is a Bennett, regardless of the blood that flows through her veins. Tobias already sent a signed document releasing all parental rights, and Ava didn't put up an ounce of a fight.

"She's not going to get hurt," I promise, looking back at Ava who shoots me a sly smile that damn near makes my legs wobble.

"Would you five pipe down over there?!" Layla screeches from my left. She glares down the line of my brothers, her raven curls bouncing around her face with the force of her admonishment. "This isn't the time for discussion."

"Sorry, sunshine," Wells mumbles.

"I didn't even say anything!" Sawyer protests, earning him a hard shoulder-nudge from Wells. He winces. "Sorry."

Layla shakes her head, turning back toward Ava.

Though she walks alone down the makeshift aisle lined with terracotta pots overflowing with wildflowers, Ava pauses when she reaches where her father sits in a wicker chair, holding her hand out to squeeze his shoulder. They've been making strides with a new open door between them, and I know him being here for this means the world to her, even if his wife wouldn't make it.

I study the sheriff now, recognizing the emotion that fills his harsh eyes. I can't imagine it's easy for him to be on this ranch, seated mere feet from my father—but he's here. And it's enough to spark a kernel of respect for the man who's brought us such misery over the years. I hope for Ava's sake he continues to put his daughter's happiness first.

Besides her father and my parents, the only other people seated in front of us are Olivia's mom, June, and her boyfriend who works with her in the café, Luna from the bakery, and Colt and Wylie Jo Rustler. Ava invited Luna under the guise of wanting another, smaller celebration just for family that included her father, Brooks, and Sawyer who all couldn't make the church wedding, and I invited Colt and his sister in hopes it would show their family that the Bennetts are here to support them, even when things get hard.

Ellis may have orchestrated the card game that went to hell, but he didn't pull any triggers that night. Cops linked the bullets in the dead cops to Maverick's gun, but they never found the gun that killed Maverick. Ellis told them he drove it hundreds of miles north and chucked it off the side of a deep ravine. After agreeing to a plea deal that convicted him of organizing an illegal gambling ring and obstruction of justice, charges for the death of Maverick were dropped. Apparently, Ellis's public defender made a decent enough case that Maverick was shot purely out of self-defense, and that he would have never been killed in the first place had he not flipped that table and started shooting. Without a charge for his death, the cops didn't care too much about finding that gun—which is currently locked in a safe under my bed and registered to my father, who has no idea my brothers and I were there that night.

I'm determined to make sure no one else ever finds out the truth. Ellis will be sentenced early next year, and he's looking at a maximum of fifteen years. I'll be in that courtroom to show him support when he learns his fate, and I'll make damn sure his brother and sister know they have five other brothers right here should they need anything.

Ava finally reaches me, her warm hands slipping into mine as the sun casts a golden glow around her, and I know with soul-deep surety that I'm the luckiest man in the whole damn world.

"Hey, sugar," I murmur as I lean down to kiss her rosy cheek. She smells like frosting and cinnamon, tastes like a drop of honey on my tongue.

"Hey, cowboy." She smiles up at me. "Crying already?" She reaches to wipe my face with her thumb, and we both laugh. "Ready to do this for real?" she asks.

I lift my eyes to the dimming evening sky. "Fucking *finally*."

ACKNOWLEDGMENTS

I'll forever be thankful to every single reader who reads, shares, talks about, posts about, or even LOOKS AT my books. Because of you, I get to keep doing this. Because of you, this world exists. I don't know what I did to deserve such amazing people in my life, but I don't take a single second of it for granted, ever. Thank you, thank you, thank you

To my team:

Logan: I would not be able to keep myself sane (or organized!) (or on schedule!) without your beautiful force in my life. Thank you for supporting me, protecting me, advocating for me, traveling with me, and for being the sassiest (cutest) cheerleader. ILYSM!

Britt: You continue to push me to be great and I know I wouldn't be here without your support. Obsessed with you, your humor, and your knack for making me look damn good—I look up to you in so many ways and am so proud to get to work with you.

Lauren: You make me a better writer with every project! I have so much fun sending you projects because I know you'll shoot me straight and love on my characters just as hard as I do. Thanks for being in this with me since the beginning!

To my family, who drives me forward every single day: I love you.

ABOUT THE AUTHOR

Michaela is a hopeless romantic from the western desert who writes grippingly tender romance novels featuring diverse characters and messy, beautifully relatable storylines.

Stay tuned for exciting announcements at michaelajeantaylor.com

BOOKS BY MICHAELA JEAN TAYLOR

Love In The Rockies

Only You

This Love

End Game

Saddlebrook Falls

Sunshine

Peaches

Sugar